BORN
OF
HATRED

By Steve McHugh

<u>Hellequin Chronicles</u>

Crimes Against Magic

Born of Hatred

BORN
OF
HATRED

STEVE McHUGH

47NORTH

Text copyright © 2013 by Steve McHugh
First published in 2012 by Hidden Realms Publishing

Published by 47North, Seattle
www.apub.com

ISBN-13: 978-1-4778-4809-8
ISBN-10: 1-4778-4809-6
Library of Congress Control Number: 2013941257

Cover design by Eamon O'Donoghue
http://www.eamonart.com/

For Keira.

You have always been, and shall always be, my Mim.

PROLOGUE

Montana Territory, America. 1878.

The bear was huge. Even compared to other grizzlies, it would have been considered a monster. I'd seen several of her kind since arriving in Montana. And so long as I kept my distance and avoided them, they tended to do the same with me. Something told me I wasn't going to be as lucky this time; there was a cub.

I leaned forward and brushed the neck of the young palomino mustang I rode. She had been an expensive purchase and well worth the money. She was even-tempered, but kept some of the fire of her breed. Above all, she was hard to spook. She stood her ground when there were predators or hunters nearby. She seemed almost fearless—hence her name, Valor.

The bear stalked forward, putting herself between her cub and the perceived threat. She was maybe thirty feet away and a low growl sounded in her throat, the moonlight only serving to enhance its resonating power. I couldn't see this ending well.

"Not here to hurt you, girl," I said softly. I knew talking to the bear was useless, but damned if I had any better ideas. I wanted to get down from Valor to prepare for any confrontation, but I knew that any movement could trigger the very fight I was trying to avoid.

Outrunning the beast was impossible. With me on her back, Valor was no match for the grizzly over short distances, and we wouldn't get enough of a head start to make a difference in the long run, not to mention that the surroundings hardly afforded a good escape. I pulled the reins, moving Valor further back into the stream, leaving a few dozen yards between us and the bear. I'd only stopped for a drink, and to catch a few fish, thinking we'd be gone before any local wildlife would notice us.

The bank on the far side was home to several huge trees and bordered by a fifty-foot-high cliff. There was a slope that led up toward the top of the cliff, but it was a hundred feet up the bank and there was no other way to get to higher ground.

The bear took a few more steps forward and splashed at the water, her eyes never leaving Valor and me.

"Don't make me kill you, girl," I said. "I don't want to make an orphan of your cub there." If she charged, I knew I could kill her, but killing an animal for wanting to protect herself and her cub hardly seemed fair. Unfortunately, a warning wasn't going to deter the grizzly if her mind was set on a fight.

She rose on her hind legs, eight feet of solid muscle, razor-sharp claws and teeth glistening in the moonlight. She roared.

In the dead of night, and so close to the cliff wall, the sound was more ferocious than it might have been. It reverberated around me, and Valor shied back a few steps, her head raised high, until I calmed her once more.

The bear moved forward and roared again. Violence was coming, I was certain of it. I'd have to orphan the cub—a death sentence. More humane just to put it out of its misery.

The bear tensed to charge and a massive explosion of noise sounded above us, then a second one moments later. Gunshots.

The bear turned and ran back into the woods, the cub following in its mother's wake, the need to fight overridden by the need to get as far away from the noise as possible.

I led Valor onto the bank with the high cliff and dismounted as a third shot rang out. A fourth was right above where I stood. In my experience, hunters don't usually run after their prey, shooting the whole time.

I guided Valor into the nearby tree line, hoping to avoid a confrontation if the gun wielders ran down the slope from the top of the cliff toward the stream. I heard a crash high above me.

I stepped back and craned my neck to get a better look as something tumbled through the top of the nearest tree, breaking through the branches as it fell. It wasn't until he was halfway down that I saw it was a human boy.

White glyphs immediately flared across the back of my hands, moving up my wrists before vanishing from view under my coat sleeves. I raised my hands, palms out toward the boy, blasting a torrent of air to cushion his fall. There was little I could do about the larger branches without hurting him too, but he hit the ground with only a small bump and was immediately covered by hundreds of falling leaves and twigs.

I dashed over and found him lying on his back. Blood soaked one side of his face, covering his shoulder and half of his chest. There was a nasty cut just above his temple. It wasn't life threatening—cuts to the head always look worse than they are—but it needed to be cleaned and closed.

The bigger problem was the damage the large branches had done on the way down. While his arms and legs weren't broken, when I touched his ribs he stirred slightly and winced before quickly slipping back into unconsciousness. The ribs were either broken or badly bruised, and I hoped he hadn't punctured a lung—a wound I'd seen happen before with broken ribs, and in many circumstances lethal this far from anything resembling a doctor.

"Hey, you," a man shouted.

I turned to watch two men on horses trot toward me. One had a revolver out and ready to use, I recognized it as an army Colt.

"Step away from the boy," he said, his voice rough and deep.

The second man sat in the saddle of his brown horse and watched. A sparkle of metal shone on his lapel when the moonlight touched it. A sheriff's badge.

"He's hurt," I said, and stepped between the armed men and the unconscious boy.

"He's a thief and a murderer," the first man said, moving his horse closer. "And you will hand him over to us."

"To shoot while he's unconscious?"

The man's eyes narrowed and he pulled his jacket aside. "You see this badge? It says I'm a deputy sheriff. My friend over there is a deputy, too. The boy is a criminal, and we'll kill him any way we can. Now move aside."

"I don't care about your badge," I said.

The first deputy pointed the Colt at me. "You're not from around here, now are you?"

"No, I'm from England. But that doesn't really matter—I'm not about to hand over a badly hurt boy to be executed. I'll take him to town. If he is what you say, he'll see justice."

"You won't find many friends around these parts, Englishman, especially if you don't obey the law. Now, you'll move aside and allow us to take him, or we'll go through you."

The second deputy's hand had dropped to his gun, which was still holstered. My Winchester rifle was still in its own holster, attached to the side of Valor, along with my *jian*, a Chinese sword.

I stepped aside, seemingly to allow the deputy access to the boy, but it put me next to Valor. The man nodded curtly as he turned his attention to his prey, giving me time to grab the still-sheathed *jian* and slam the hilt into his throat as he rode past. I spun, dragging one of the two silver daggers out of the blade holster on the small of my back, and threw it at the second man. The blade missed his head by a hair's width, but it had the desired effect of making him lose his concentration. And the next thing he knew, the end of my Winchester rifle's barrel was pressed firmly against his nose.

"Make a move and you'll find a big hole where your face used to be," I said, dragging another, identical Colt from the deputy's holster and flinging it into the woods behind him.

His partner's horse trotted past, the unconscious deputy slumped forward. "I'd leave now and go help your friend," I said.

"This isn't over," he said.

"It is for today. Now leave. If this boy did as you say, I'll bring him in myself."

"You have the authority to do that?" he asked incredulously.

I removed the barrel from his nose. "You have no idea of my authority. Get out of my damn sight."

I watched the deputy guide his partner's horse back into the woods away from us. I doubted they were the type of people who kept their promises, and I wanted to be far away before they decided on a repeat performance. I walked over to the boy and looked down at him. A murderer and thief. He opened one eye—the other was already swelling closed.

"Who are you?" he asked, his words broken as he spoke through the pain.

"Nathan Garrett," I said. "You're safe now."

"I'm Sam," he said softly before passing out once more and leaving me with one burning question.

What the hell have I gotten myself into?

CHAPTER 1

Basingstoke, England. Now.

She lay on the floor, panting. Her chest rose and fell quickly in an effort to get as much oxygen into her body as possible. Her bare midriff, the muscles taut and inviting, the skin tanned and beautiful, glistened with sweat—only one thought entered my mind. *Oh crap.*

"You want a drink?" I asked, picking up a bottle of water from the floor.

Sara sat up and caught the cold bottle in one hand when I threw it to her. As she drank, water dripped down her chin, landing just above her sports bra and trickling down between her breasts. I stared at my bottle of water and considered tipping it down my pants. I settled for drinking it, while ensuring that my gaze fell on nothing that could be considered sexy. A stack of blue mats sat at the end of the huge gym hall. There is nothing sexy about a blue gym mat. That did the trick.

"So, you want to go for another round?" she asked.

I turned back to her just in time to catch the half empty bottle of water she'd thrown at my head. "That's not nice," I said with a smile. "You're going to have to be taught a lesson."

Sara got back to her feet and put herself in a fighting stance. "Come on, old man, let's see if you've still got what it takes."

I tossed both bottles aside and deflected the punch I knew was coming. I pushed her arm aside and stepped around her, keeping my distance, making her do the work. Sara might have only been human, and only been fighting for a few months, but what she lacked in experience, she more than made up for in tenacity and quickness.

Her foot spun around, trying to catch me in my ribs, but I blocked it with ease. Unfortunately, she knew what I was going to do and quickly switched tactics, throwing a punch, which I wasn't positioned to block effectively. I took a glancing blow off my cheek as I dodged aside. "Good shot."

Sara smiled. She'd remembered not to get dragged into a conversation with the person you're fighting. Concentrate on the person trying to knock you out, not on having a chat.

She threw another punch, this one to distract from her attempt to knee me in the stomach. I wasn't distracted. I grabbed her thigh, falling back and using my momentum to drag her over and dump her on her back.

I hadn't expected Sara to grab my arm as she went over, pulling me with her. So, I was the one who ended up on my back, with Sara straddling my chest. Her smile beamed as she undid her ponytail, letting her long blonde hair fall loose over her shoulders.

"Old man," she said

"You're a fast learner." I tried to sit up and she pushed me back.

"Not yet. You must learn patience." She laughed, mocking a familiar speech I'd given to her when she'd wanted to learn quicker than she was capable of.

I pushed her hand away, which caused her to lose her balance. She fell forward, her face coming close to mine. She inhaled sharply as our mouths almost touched. Her pupils dilated as she licked her lips invitingly. I looked into her green eyes and wanted to take her, wanted to feel her naked skin against mine, to feel her moving around me as I entered her. The moment lasted longer than it should have.

"Would Nathan Garrett report to employee parking? That's Nathan Garrett to employee parking." The loudspeaker announcement brought us both back to our senses.

"We should go," Sara said, and rolled off me, going over to grab her bottle of water.

I lay on the ground a moment longer and tried to think of something calming. The gym mats weren't going to be enough. When finally ready to move, I got back to my feet and made my way to the intercom by the main entrance, pushing the button and informing whoever was on the other end that I would be half an hour. Tommy could come find me himself if it was that important. I didn't work for him.

"You okay?" I asked Sara, who hadn't spoken in a few minutes.

"I have a boyfriend," she said softly. "I love him. I love being with him; he's fun and sweet and treats me well. Something I've not had much experience with."

"I know."

"So why do you make me forget all about him? How is it that you have this effect on me? That I want to do incredibly bad things to you every time I see you?"

I shrugged. "I'm sorry, Sara. If you want me to stop training—"

"No," she snapped. "Tommy and you both told me that if I'm going to be his assistant, I need training. And more than one person has said you're the best to do that. I just want to be able to train. Without the desire to rip all your clothes off and fuck you on the floor."

"I don't know what to say. Maybe we both need a cold shower, and to try to keep it professional in the future. No matter how difficult that might be. I don't want you to do anything to jeopardize the happiness you have at home."

"I won't," she said, sounding certain. "I can control this. I just need to avoid draping myself over you in future." She picked up her bag and slung the strap over one shoulder. "I'll go shower and tell Tommy you'll be up soon."

"Thanks," I said, and then she was gone, leaving me with a great desire to bathe myself in ice-cold water for the foreseeable future.

As it turned out, once I'd showered and dressed, any longing I felt was buried deep inside me as I walked through the busy office building owned by my friend Thomas Carpenter.

Technically, it's two buildings; one was three stories and the other twenty-five, joined together by a walkway above the staff parking area outside. I looked out of a nearby window, down at the smaller of the two buildings. It's the only entrance to the larger building and includes enough security to make getting into the White House seem like a walk in the park. Six lifts, all glass except for the floor and ceiling, each containing a thermal imaging unit and metal detector. Runes, carved into the very structure of the building, ensured that no one could use their abilities unless authorized. I looked down at the small bracelet on my wrist; the runes carved into the wooden beads allowed me to access my magic. Each staff member wore one, even the humans, so that no one could be identified from appearance alone. Each bracelet was designed for that person only, and not all bracelets were created equal.

The larger building had similar runes carved into the steel and concrete. It wasn't overkill. My friend Thomas—or Tommy, as he liked to be known—was once a private investigator. Now he runs his own investigations firm, and he's managed to piss off a lot of powerful people in the process.

But none of the measures were there to protect *him*. As a six-hundred-plus-year-old werewolf, he's quite capable of taking care of himself. But he'd never have forgiven himself if his people got hurt because of a lack of care and protection.

I made my way through to the lifts, saying hello to the various people who knew me, and gaining a few odd glances from those who didn't. When everyone else is suited and booted, the man wearing jeans and a hooded top, and carrying a leather biker jacket, sort of stands out.

As the lift doors opened, revealing the mirrored walls inside, another loudspeaker announcement sounded. "Can Mr. Garrett please go to the employee parking lot?"

I stepped into the lift and pressed the button for the ground floor. I had no idea what Tommy wanted, but I was already certain it wasn't going to be good.

By the time I'd reached the smaller building, I'd already devised a dozen scenarios in which Tommy asked me to do something either ridiculous or dangerous. Probably a combination of the two.

I walked along a curved corridor of the smaller building, passing armed guards. I occasionally glanced down through the glass sides at the reception below until I reached another set of lifts. The green button lit up when I pressed it, flashing slowly as the lift made its way up the three floors toward me. The reception lifts had glass walls and moved slower than the normal ones so that the occupants could be easily monitored.

I took the lift down to reception and said hi to a few more people as I left through one of the two revolving doors and into the parking lot outside. I found Tommy and Sara standing beside a large black Toyota Hilux truck. They were deep in conversation, which stopped when Tommy saw me.

Sara had changed into a blue blouse, her hair pulled back into a ponytail. She glanced up as Tommy threw something at me, which I caught one handed. A set of car keys.

"Are we going somewhere nice?" I asked.

"Sara, can you give us a moment?" Tommy asked.

Sara walked away to a respectable distance before playing with her phone and pretending that she wasn't trying to listen in.

"I need your help."

I raised an eyebrow. "Since when do you need my help?" I gestured to the building behind me. "There are a dozen people in there who would die for the chance to help you."

"I need someone I can trust, no matter what happens."

"Why? What's going to happen, Tommy?"

He at least had the decency to look outraged. "Nothing," he sighed. "It's recon work I agreed to do to help a client. And I want you to be my backup."

"Keep talking."

"Fifteen years ago a nasty little bastard by the name of Neil Hatchell attacked and raped seven women. He got out of prison two weeks ago."

"There's more to this, I assume."

"He's a werewolf, and after he was done beating each of his victims half to death, he bit them. Three women died from the change, and another killed herself when she couldn't cope with what she'd become. He was charged by Avalon with seven counts of rape, three of murder, one destruction of a mind, and seven of gene manipulation without consent."

"So why isn't he dead?" I asked. Avalon doesn't look fondly on crimes like his. In fact, it was a surprise that Neil had been arrested at all. Normally, the Law of Avalon isn't shy about ending problems on a more permanent basis.

"No idea. Instead they stuck him in the Hole. Third floor."

The Hole was a prison on an isolated island in the North Atlantic. It's not on any maps, and it has a permanent no-fly zone around it for anyone not associated with Avalon. It's also one of only three prisons with enough capabilities to handle even the most powerful of creatures. It consists of ten floors, all underground; the more dangerous you are, the higher the number—and the further down you're kept. The upper seven are guarded night and day, while the lower three are left un-guarded and it's up to the prisoners to rule themselves. No one in their right mind wants to be placed down there. I've been down twice. Once I almost didn't make it back, and the second time was even less fun.

"Bet that wasn't a picnic. How the hell did he get out after only fifteen years? He should have served over two hundred years for the deaths alone."

"Again, no idea. But he's out and officially can't be touched; he's served his time and is a free man. Unofficially…well, that's where we come in. My client wants him checked out. So I want to bring you and Sara with me."

"You want us to go pay him a visit and make sure he's behaving himself? So why is Sara coming?"

"She's my assistant. She's been here two months, and she hasn't accompanied anyone on assignment. She needs to know the type of work we do. I figure with me and you there, there's nowhere safer for her to be."

"Except in the office here," I pointed out. "She's not ready."

"Is that Nate the fully trained professional problem solver talking, or Nate's penis?"

I couldn't help but chuckle. "My penis hasn't done a lot of talking lately."

"She has a boyfriend."

"Thank you for the relationship advice," I said. "I know this already. Nothing has happened between us, nor will it. She's had no weapons training."

"You'll keep her safe, you know it." He turned and walked back toward his truck, waving Sara to come and join him. He opened the door for her to get in and I sighed and followed. Tommy was right, although I'd never have told him that. Sara did need the experience.

As I opened the driver's door, I saw a big beaming smile on Tommy's stupid, smug face, and I already knew I was going to regret saying yes.

CHAPTER 2

We pulled up outside a pair of twelve-story-high, red-bricked buildings. I parked the car and stepped out into the cold air, surveying the large parking area with its expensive cars sitting idle beside an expanse of immaculate green lawn.

I closed the door and walked across the grass until I reached a small bench beside an expansive koi pond. The large fish came to the surface, clearly used to being fed by passersby, vanishing away back into the deep darkness when they realized no food was forthcoming.

"I don't even know how you got us through the gates," I said to Tommy, as he and Sara sat beside me. Unlike the other, smaller houses that dotted the area, all with drives and garages, these two taller buildings had a pair of huge iron security gates for cars to get through before reaching the outside parking area. I'd been more than a little surprised when Tommy had handed me the key card, which had gained us access.

"Friends in high places," he said with a smirk, "Same person who gave me this."

He passed me a folded sheet of paper, on which was written two sets of numbers—one four digits in length and the other six. "What are they?"

"The four-digit is the key code to the building on the left; the six-digit is the code to Neil's alarm in his penthouse."

"How the hell did they get that?" Sara asked.

"The code for the front door is on file at the security company. Only they can change it. The same company keeps the details for every resident's alarm. Anyone who lives here is required to keep the code on file in case of emergencies."

I memorized the two numbers and passed the paper back. "I assume you have a plan."

"You get in, look around, and get out."

"Actually, I'm a bit more concerned about why you need me here if you have the damn codes, Tommy."

"You're better at this stuff than me."

I stared at him for a good twenty seconds before allowing myself to say anything, just in case it was derogatory. "Fuck off." Apparently I hadn't waited long enough. "You're a powerful werewolf who could easily get in and out without problems. One quick change to your wolf form and you're basically the animal version of a damn ninja. So what's the real reason?"

"Neil's a wolf," he reminded me. "If you're caught in there, you can get away with little fuss. If I get caught by a werewolf, one of us is going to die."

"Why?" Sara asked.

"It's a territory thing. If I get caught on his ground, he'll protect it with his life, and there's no way the beast inside me will let a challenge pass when he attacks me. Best-case scenario, I get away without tearing him in half. Besides, even if I don't get caught, he's going to know a werewolf was in his home. Nate smells like a human, at least until he uses magic."

"What does he smell like after that?" Sara asked.

"Power," Tommy said. "And death."

"Well, that wasn't utterly depressing," I said, trying to lighten the rapidly darkening mood.

"She did ask," Tommy pointed out before removing something from his pocket and passing it to me.

I turned the small radio and microphone over in my hands. "I'm not going on a mob bust."

"It's that or you wear one of those ridiculous Bluetooth headsets, which are about as secure as yelling really loud. I need to stay in contact with you, just in case he comes home early."

I placed the radio in my pocket, clipped the microphone to my shirt, and pressed the earpiece home. "I assume you've done some recon work to know where he might be at ten in the morning?"

"Of course. Neil leaves his building a little after 9 a.m. and comes back at 3 p.m. He then leaves again at 6 p.m. and comes back sometime in the morning between 1 and 3 a.m. Twice he's arrived back with young women, who then leave a few hours before Neil surfaces. According to the notes, the young women were of...questionable virtue."

"They're hookers, is what you're getting at, yes?" Sara asked, which made me laugh.

"I'm surrounded by uncouth ruffians."

"And apparently you live in the nineteenth century," I said. "I'm going to break into his house before you call me a ragamuffin or something equally hurtful."

Even Tommy had to laugh, but it was cut short by a serious expression. "Nate, be careful. This guy is a nutcase. If he sees you in there, he'll attack you."

I forced a grin. "Isn't that why you brought me along in the first place?"

I walked off before Tommy could argue. We both knew that I was going into the house not only because he was concerned about killing Neil before we'd had the chance to talk to him, but because he knew that I could take care of myself better than anyone who worked for him. Over the centuries, Tommy and I had been caught in enough life-and-death situations to know that we could rely on one another to perform under pressure.

I entered the four-digit code and pushed open the front door. Warm air from the foyer beyond washed over me like a summer breeze. A single guard sat behind a desk opposite the building's staircase. He couldn't have appeared less interested in being there if he'd been sleeping. That changed the second he saw me, though. He straightened up and pushed the newspaper he'd been reading to one side.

"Can I help you, sir?" he asked.

"You're a bloody idiot," I whispered into the mic. "There's a damn guard."

"Sir?" the guard repeated.

"Oh sorry, jet lag tends to make me a little all over the place," I said with a smile and reached out my hand. "Nathan Garrett, I work for Neil Hatchell."

"*Mister Hatchell* is not here at the moment."

The distaste in his voice when he uttered Neil's name was clear; maybe he didn't approve of prostitutes being brought back to the upmarket building where he worked. Or maybe Neil was just a dick. I figured it was a little of both, and it meant that I could change tactics. "Okay, you seem like a nice guy…"

"Roger."

"Well, Roger, I don't actually work for Mister Hatchell, and I know he's not in."

"Then you should leave."

"Probably, but you see, Mister Hatchell was recently let out of jail. Did you know that? He served time for rape?"

The fact that Roger had turned the color of magnolia told me he didn't.

"I work for certain people who want to make sure he's behaving himself, sticking to the straight and narrow, if you will."

"You're his probation officer?"

"Exactly," I said. "My job is to keep tabs on him. He appears to have come into a lot of money when he was released, and we're not entirely convinced that he got it via legal means. I'm here to check that out."

"I still don't think I should let you—"

"Roger," I interrupted. "Do you know what your employers would say if they found out that the penthouse suite was occupied by a rapist, a former prison inmate, and someone who could be committing crimes as we speak? What do you think will happen to the equity of the other occupants? I don't think they'll be very happy. Now, if we do it my way and he's done something wrong, it all gets sorted quietly. But if not, then the press will get involved and the police will want to interview everyone in the building. It'll be a mess. Is that something you want to deal with?"

Roger shook his head.

"Good man. So here's what we're going to do. I'm going upstairs to look around and check that things are okay, and you're going to go back to reading your paper." I slipped a fifty-pound note onto the desk. "Something to say thank you. There's some more in it for you when I come back down, *if* you forget I ever existed."

"Deal," Roger said instantly.

I pushed the button for the lift and waited a few seconds for the number above it to drop down to GF and the doors to open. "Good man," I said to Roger again and pressed the button for the penthouse.

"Apparently, they didn't go inside the building to look around," Tommy said inside my ear.

"Well maybe next time you should send people who will do a better job."

"It was their first assignment—sit in the car and watch. I'm sorry, I'll speak to them when we get back to the office."

Anger drained out of me. "Okay, don't go overboard though. My first-ever assignment didn't exactly go to plan, either."

"Weren't you about thirteen?"

"Twelve," I corrected, "Even so, it wasn't the sparkling success that Merlin had been after. Anyway, we have another issue."

"Which is?"

"The lock on this door is a bastard of a thing. You sure I can't just kick the damn door in half?"

"Not exactly a stealthy option, is it?"

I mumbled something under my breath and placed my palm against the door's lock. White glyphs cascaded from my fingers, across the back of my hands, and down over my wrists and forearms, vanishing beneath the sleeve of my hoodie, where they would continue up my arms and across my chest and back.

Magic is a complicated beast. For the most part, you think about what you want to do, and, if you're powerful and experienced enough, the magic will form on those thoughts. Magic wants to be used, to flow freely from the sorcerer, no matter how dangerous that might be. In contrast, the actual control of magic is very difficult. Even the smaller uses of magic, like lighting a candle, require precise movements and power, so that you're not left with a big puddle of wax and a lot of fires to put out.

That's why young sorcerers are so dangerous—they don't have the control needed to temper their magic and have, on occasion, caused devastation when their power has exceeded their ability.

Using air magic to fill the inside of a lock in the exact same way as a key was both time consuming and tiring. When the magic touched the inside of the mechanism, I felt it as if I were using my own finger. It's a matter of remembering where each part was so that I could construct the key and turn it. One wrong move and I'd have to start from scratch, and it's not something that I could do in a hurry. The more complex the lock, the more of a pain in the arse it is to use magic to open it.

The lock on the penthouse was one of the more secure locks that I'd ever had to pick. The main problem was that you had to turn the key once to make it click, move the key back to its original position and then do it again, but this time the click came further away. It took me ten minutes to get the lock open. I certainly would have been happier kicking the door in.

The second the door closed behind me, a continuous beep sounded from an alarm panel on the wall next to me. I punched in the six digits and the beeping ended. That had been my major worry: What if Neil had changed the code and not told anyone? Turns out, I needn't have been concerned.

"I'm in," I said, and started looking around the spacious flat.

"You see anything suspicious?"

"Who in their right mind would have weird shit sitting around the second you stepped into the house, Tommy?" I asked. "He might be nuts, but I'm guessing he's not the 'hang the dead corpses of your victims from the ceiling of your home' kind of nuts."

I started searching the flat, but found nothing more than an incredibly tidy place and some questionable movies next to the huge TV in his front room. Off the large main room was a kitchen at one end and hallway at the other. The kitchen, like everything else, was so clean that I could make out my reflection in the marble worktops, and although there was a lot of raw meat in the fridge, none of it looked out of place in a werewolf's kitchen.

The hallway led to two bedrooms and a bathroom, all of which mimicked the rest of the place. "Tommy, there's nothing here. I've found some porn in the bedroom, which wasn't exactly a pleasant sight, but nothing illegal about it."

"What do you mean?"

"Extreme domination stuff," I said candidly. "Women being tied up, gagged, beaten, that kind of thing. Not exactly my cup of tea, but also not an indication that he's butchering women in his bathtub. Which, by the way, is also spotless." I walked to the large window at the end of the hallway and looked down on the parking lot below me. "People like this don't just give up and stop trying."

"I know," Tommy said. "They get worse, not better. All that pent-up rage and aggression he would have had in prison, he wouldn't have just forgotten about it."

"He's either letting it out somewhere else, or he's castrated himself and he can't do a damn thing anymore."

"Something isn't right here," Tommy said.

I rested my forehead against the glass pane and thought about where I would stash something I didn't want people to find. I'd want it nearby—I'd *need* it close so that I could go and look at it, to relive how I'd felt whilst I was doing whatever it was that had made me happy. "Did Neil take souvenirs?" I asked.

There was a rustle of paper before Tommy spoke. "He took their purses. Left them the money, but took everything else. The purses were recovered when he was arrested."

"Does it say where they were found?"

More rustling. "Attic."

"This place doesn't have an attic," I said.

I walked back to the master bedroom and glanced around. It was barely decorated, with a bed, TV, and chest of drawers. A wooden chair sat next to the window and a door led to a small but well-maintained bathroom.

The only other item in the bedroom was the large built-in wardrobe. I opened the double doors and revealed a long row of clothes. I hadn't given it much thought the first time around, but it wasn't cluttered or full. I cursed myself and pushed all the clothes aside, revealing two leather handles at the top of the cupboard, which, pulled aside, revealed a hidden room.

Once I'd removed the false panel of the wardrobe and tossed it onto the bed, I noticed a light switch just inside and above where the panel had been. I flicked it on, bathing the small room in light.

Once fully inside the room, I started my search. It took about three seconds before I found something wrong. Really wrong.

A desk had been placed under one of two lights, with a large pin-up board behind it, leaning up against the wall. It was covered with pictures of women. "Tommy, do you have pictures of Neil's previous victims down there?"

"Yeah," he said. "You need copies?"

"Text them to me."

Sure enough, after a few minutes, several texts appeared on my phone, and my fears were confirmed. "He has pictures of every victim up here."

"Anyone new?"

I scanned the photos, dozens in all, each overlapping the one closest to it until it formed some sort of hideous collage of stalking. "Four new girls, their photos are the same."

"The same how?" Tommy asked.

"He stalked them from a distance like with his previous victims. If he's hurt any of them, I can't see any evidence to say he did it in here." I opened the drawers on the desk and found a large map, part of which was circled in red pen with the word "farm" written beside it. I used my phone to take several close-up photos before continuing my search of the room.

"I might be wrong," I said after finding some thick iron chains, which were secured to both the floor and ceiling. "He's more than equipped to hurt people here."

"You sure?"

"There's a map with the word "farm" and a circled area; that mean anything to you?"

"A farm, you're sure?" Tommy asked.

"Ask me again if I'm sure about something, Tommy. Yes, I'm fucking sure."

"My client was informed that the police got a tip-off—some sort of suspicious activity taking place at an abandoned farm about thirty miles outside of the city. Apparently no one has had time to check it out yet; they've been getting crackpot calls about that serial killer in the news. Could the serial killer be Neil?"

"It's possible," I said. "It's worth looking into in any case." I stood and brushed my hands on my trousers before switching the light off and leaving the room. The LOA—the Law of Avalon—would want to look into Neil's activities. Hopefully, this time they'd make sure he couldn't get out again, preferably with a more permanent residency somewhere a little hotter.

I replaced the panel, ensuring nothing appeared too out of place, but as I stepped out of the wardrobe, I caught my foot on something and slipped back, landing with a bang. I got up to close the doors and paused when I heard the unmistakable sound of a shotgun being loaded. "Tommy, we have a much bigger problem."

CHAPTER 3

The blast missed me, and I hit the floor, rolling until my back was against the wall next to where the now-ruined door sat.

A second later, when my ears stopped ringing, I heard the sound of smashing glass from the direction of the living room. I edged along the wall and peered through the hole in the wooden bedroom door into the hallway beyond, finding it empty except for a discarded shotgun on the floor.

I sprinted into the living room to find one of the dozen windows was shattered. Although acutely aware of how exposed I was standing in the middle of a large open room, I made my way to the window and stared out, looking down the hundred and fifty feet to the ground below.

Neil was hanging from a rope about fifty feet off the ground, moving very slowly down toward his escape. The rope was attached to some climbing gear, which had been built into the curtain frame. It extended along the entire length of the room. A small box behind the frame contained the rope, obviously strong enough to hold a fully grown man, but small enough that it was easily concealable. It was quite a clever idea; smash the window, grab the rope and rappel down the side of the building.

"We've got ourselves a rabbit," I said. "Right now he's hanging from a rope at the opposite side of the building to you."

"On the way," Tommy said.

"From the speed he's going, I could probably get to him before he hits the ground. I don't think he's tried this before." I grabbed the rope with both hands, and created a cushion of air between my skin and the black rope. When I felt secure, I pulled myself up and through the broken window and began my descent.

I used the air magic to allow the rope to slide quickly through my hands without discomfort, while keeping enough friction there to stop me from falling without control. It took all of five seconds for an almighty bang to sound from beneath me. I looked down as Neil cursed loudly; dislodging himself from the roof of the soft-top car he'd fallen on. Unfortunately, by the time I'd reached the ground he was already off across the road and heading toward a large park, although a limp made it impossible for him to sprint anywhere at meaningful speed.

Tommy and Sara came around the corner as I jogged across the road to catch up with my prey. I waited until they caught up—there was no way Neil was going to escape us, not with Tommy tracking him. "He's in the park," I told them.

"Take Sara with you," Tommy said. "I'll head through the wooded area and cut him off."

Tommy didn't wait to hear any objections and ran off toward the dense trees.

"Be careful, stay close, and do everything I say," I told Sara. "You going to be okay with this?"

Sara nodded. "After what he did to those women, I'm not sitting it out."

We both set off at a run, following the direction that Neil had taken into the park. He wasn't exactly difficult to spot as he had stopped and was talking to a large group of young, well-built men a few hundred yards in front.

"Has he stopped for a chat?" Sara asked as we both slowed to a jog.

"Apparently there's no urgent need to escape—either that or he's an idiot."

"What's more likely?"

"Well, he let himself fall forty feet onto a car; I'm thinking he's not much of a genius. Be careful, I get the feeling we're about to have a new problem to deal with."

As we got closer, Neil turned to glance our way, and I could have sworn that he grinned before sprinting off at speed toward the distant tree line, his werewolf healing ability already having taken care of his leg injury.

Sara and I increased our speed, but the group of men whom Neil had been talking to stepped into our path forcing us to stop. "Can I help you?" one of them asked.

I ignored him and kept walking as the other six men slowly created a semicircle wall of muscle to bar us from following Neil. The one who had asked the question was a few inches taller than me, and much bulkier.

"Do you shave your head because you're going bald, or because you think it makes you look like a badass?" I asked. "Because if it's the second, then you might want to lose the diamond stud earring—it sort of destroys the image."

The bald thug laughed.

"Fucking twat him one, Danny," another of the group said.

"Ah, so you're the leader are you, Danny?" I asked. "You want to tell me why you're standing in our way?"

Sara moved so that she was next to me, but turned to face the men that stood behind us.

"That bloke paid us five grand to make sure you don't follow him. We plan on doing that."

"Don't do this," I said to Danny.

"Five grand is more than enough for us to fuck you both up."

"I think the little lady might like to spend some time with us afterwards," the thug closest to Sara said.

He reached out to stroke her face, but she slapped his hand away and pushed him back, which made him laugh, "You're a spirited little one aren't you?"

"Sara, the two on your left," I whispered without turning to look at her.

"No problem," she said.

"Well, I'm not getting any younger," I told Danny.

Danny cracked his knuckles. "Nice to see you're not going to run and hide."

The man on my right was the first to move, a hard right hand, which would have taken my head off if not for the fact that I saw it coming a mile away and was moving before it came even close to connecting. I ducked under his arm and slammed my forearm into his ribs. The air rushed out of him and I grabbed him by his t-shirt, spinning him around and releasing him at the exact moment so that he collided with Danny and Thug Four. The three of them fell to the ground in a tangled mess.

Thug Two darted toward me and, like his friend, tried to catch me off guard with a fast punch to the head. I grabbed his forearm with one hand and twisted his wrist with the other, stepping toward him and using his own momentum to take him off his feet and dump him on his head behind me. The third thug tried a different tactic and ran at me full tilt. I ducked at exactly the right moment and shoved my shoulder into his stomach, lifting him up and over me. He landed on the ground with a loud grunt, and a swift kick to the head made sure he wasn't going to be getting up again.

Thug One was back on his feet and had assumed a boxer's stance, along with Thug Three, who'd thrown the first punch. A quick sidestep and push from me brought Three's head directly into contact with an ill-timed punch from his friend, and after a second punch from me, Three was down for the count.

Thug One soon followed after I kicked him in the solar plexus with enough force to bend steel. He dropped to the floor and stayed there, just as Thug Four grabbed me around the chest in a bear hug, pinning my arms to my sides.

He had some strength in him as he easily swung me to face Danny, squeezing all the time. Danny came forward and threw a mean punch at my face. I slammed my heel down on Thug Four's kneecap, which popped. He began screaming in pain, letting me go as he fell to the ground. Danny threw another punch, which I deflected, catching him in the nose with a punch of my own. A savage blow to his solar plexus lifted him from the ground and dumped him on all fours, sucking in whatever oxygen he could manage.

All five assailants dealt with, I turned my attention to Sara who had one man writhing on the floor holding his crotch, and a second whose chest Sara was straddling whilst she rained punches down onto his face. I tapped her shoulder and she spun on me, a rage in her eyes until she realized I was no threat.

"You done?" I asked.

She glanced down at the messy-faced asshole who was moaning softly on the ground. She stood and kicked him in the crotch.

I assumed she needed a moment and walked back over to Danny, who was on his feet, a switchblade in his hand.

"Gonna gut you, fucker," he bellowed and came at me.

I caught his wrist in one hand and smashed my free forearm into his face again, and again, until he went limp and could no longer stand. When I was certain he'd taken all he could, I broke his wrist and left him to his whimpering. I joined Sara a moment later. She was rubbing her hand, which had turned red from the multitude of punches she'd caught the thug with.

"When we get back to the car, we'll get you a cold compress," I said.

We continued jogging toward where we'd seen Neil vanish. Before we'd made it halfway, Tommy left the trees and came toward us. He looked annoyed, more so than I'd seen in a very long time.

"What happened?" I asked.

"He disappeared," Tommy said.

"What? How?"

Tommy shrugged. "I have no idea; I followed him into the damn woods, had his trail the whole way, and then whoosh, he's gone."

"His trail ended?" I asked with more than a little curiosity.

"He jumped into a car and I lost it."

"Was someone helping him, or did he use his own car?"

Tommy shrugged. "Don't know. What happened to you two?"

"Neil paid off a few local thugs to try and stop us. Sara here took down two by herself, but she's hurt her hand."

"Let's get back to the car; we'll get something for it." Tommy must have noticed the change in Sara's demeanor. "That your first fight?" he asked as we made our way back through the park.

"Yeah," she said. "I've never hurt someone before. Apparently I had some anger that needed expressing."

We reached the still-prone men, one of whom jumped to his feet and fled when he saw us. The two Sara had taken down were still out, and I took a moment to check on them and put them both into the recovery position, just in case. I might not give a shit if any of them died, but I knew that Sara would. "Broken nose, ribs, maybe a jaw, and they'll have some nasty bruises, but other than that they'll both live."

Sara appeared noticeably relieved.

"So, what now?" she asked a few moments later.

"We get you something cold for your hand, then we go to the farm on that map and figure out what's going on," Tommy responded.

"Something odd is what's going on," I said to Tommy. "It feels off. More so than usual."

"What is it?" Tommy asked.

"Not sure, but something feels *wrong*. Neil is a dumb bastard who has enough power to kill and hurt people, and somehow instead of being executed, he's released early from prison and given a posh place to live."

When we reached the car, Tommy handed Sara a first-aid cold pack that he'd wrapped in a bandage so that it wasn't too cold against her skin. She winced as it first touched her red hand, and I considered the possibility that she'd broken a bone. But hopefully it was just bruising and would go down before too long.

"I want to come with you to the farm," Sara said to me. "I want to help."

"So long as you're sure. I don't think it's going to hold any real dangers, but that's what Tommy said about this place. If you like, we can drop you back at the office. Tommy has some trained medical staff; they can take a look at your hand and you'd be safe there. You have nothing to prove to either Tommy or me."

Sara shook her head. "I have to prove it to myself. If I work for Tommy, it's only fair that I know the kind of jobs his people will go through."

Tommy was busy spreading plastic covering all over the rear seats of the truck. "Fine with me," he called from inside the vehicle. "But this time we go in ready. No pissing about. If we need to, we level the damn place. Deal?"

"Let's go then."

Once we were all in the car, Sara swiveled around to look at Tommy, who had sat in the rear again. A puzzled expression crossed her face. "Why is the back of the car covered in plastic?"

I adjusted the rear view mirror, catching a glimpse of Tommy removing his top. "You trust me?"

Sara nodded immediately.

"Then don't look back, no matter what you hear back there."

Her concern was easy to spot. "Why?"

I started the engine. "Because once you see the change that he's about to go through, you never get to unsee it."

CHAPTER 4

Thomas's grunts and groans of pain only lasted for a short time, a minute at most. Silence soon descended and remained for a few seconds before the muzzle of a large wolf popped between the two front seats. Sara screeched in surprise, and Tommy rumbled a sound that was suspiciously close to laughter.

"Evil bastard," she chastised, tapping him on the nose with her hand.

"Have you seen your boss in his wolf form before?" I asked as Tommy's head vanished from sight.

"But never in a moving vehicle." She turned back to her boss and tutted, before going a little green. "There's blood all over back there."

"The change from man to wolf is a hard one; there's always a bit of body fluids left over."

A short while later, the sat nav indicated we'd reached the end of our journey. I stopped the car and switched off the engine before getting out into the cold. The bare ground outside was rock solid.

I opened the rear truck door, allowing Tommy to jump out. The big grey wolf sniffed the ground in a few places and wandered off.

"Why did Tommy go full wolf, instead of turning into his wolf-man form?" Sara asked as she joined me, hugging herself as tightly as possible with one busted-up hand. The winds whipped around the exposed farm, and although there were trees in the distance, the amount of open ground allowed the wind free rein, rattling around the dilapidated farmhouse and barn.

"The wolf-man form is better for fighting, but the beast inside still tries to get out. The beast is less of a concern in full wolf form, and it's also better for tracking."

"So why not change when we were trying to find Neil?"

"Too many humans around. They tend to notice giant wolves roaming the place."

Tommy stalked past, moving methodically and occasionally raising his muzzle to sniff the air. He turned his head to one side and darted off toward a small pile of old, rusty metal.

I moved to the still-open rear door, pulling out a briefcase. I inputted the code—one-four-one-four, the year Tommy had been turned into a werewolf—and popped the locks. I opened the case, and a gasp from Sara reminded me that not everyone was as used to seeing guns as I was.

I picked up one and showed it to Sara. "This is a Glock 22," I said. "It's a Smith and Wesson version of the Glock 17." I ejected the magazine and showed it to Sara. Tommy changed the ammo every evening, a habit he'd gotten into after he'd left a magazine full for too long and it misfired.

"This gun has fifteen bullets, all silver tipped." I grabbed a spare bandage and strapped the ice pack to her injured hand, then placed the gun in the working one and showed her how to hold it. She was lucky that her injured hand wasn't her dominant one. Although Sara was nervous, and her hands sweaty, she complied without complaint.

"Does this have a safety?" she asked, aiming the gun off into the empty distance.

"It's part of the trigger. You pull the trigger, the safety disengages."

Tommy made an appearance before I could explain more. "Anyone here?" I asked.

Tommy barked twice.

Sara raised an eyebrow in question.

"One bark means yes, two means no," I pointed out. "You find anything else?"

Tommy barked.

"Something bad?"

Tommy made a whining noise that meant he wasn't sure.

I turned to Sara. "Keep the gun pointed at the floor unless your life is in danger. You do what I say at all times, clear?"

Sara nodded. She was clearly scared and trying not to show it.

I stopped her as she walked off to follow Tommy, who had made his way to the farmhouse. "Don't worry about being scared," I said. "That's good. Be scared, use that fear. You'll be okay, I promise you. There's no one here. Tommy is probably just getting a scent of some dead rats or something. But if there is anything here, they're not getting past Tommy and me. I promise you that."

Sara nodded, seemingly ready for whatever was about to come. Or as ready as anyone can be. I reached under the truck seat and grabbed a bulletproof vest Tommy kept for emergencies. "Put this on," I said, passing it to Sara.

She did as she was told, handing me the pistol as I helped her strap on the vest. "Don't you need one?" she asked, taking her gun back.

I shook my head and we started off to follow Tommy.

The roof of the farmhouse was all but destroyed, and vines had grown high enough to obscure most of the windows on the ground floor. Part of the brickwork was crumbling, leaving a large hole in one side of the farmhouse, just big enough to stick your head inside. If anyone was living inside, it could only have been due to a lack of other choices. Tommy sat outside the main entrance to the building. He saw Sara and me approaching and pawed at the door. "Is Timmy in there, boy?" I asked. "Did he fall down a well?"

Tommy growled.

"What does that mean?" Sara asked.

"Fuck off," I said, gaining a chuckle from Sara and momentarily breaking the tension.

Tommy regained my attention by pawing at the door once more. I sighed and tried the handle, surprised to find it didn't open.

"Why would an abandoned home have a locked door?" I placed my hand against the door lock, and white glyphs lit up across the back of my hand. A fierce blast of air hit the lock and ripped it from the doorframe, the metal bouncing around inside as the door swung open by itself. "Not at all creepy," I said to Tommy, who nudged the door further open with his nose and padded inside.

"You ready?" I asked Sara.

She nodded, and we followed Tommy into the house.

However decrepit the outside had appeared, the interior was even worse. The staircase was rotten and falling apart, and wooden boards jutted dangerously from the wall. Anyone who actually managed to get upstairs would have found only empty air where the floor above used to be. I stared up through the massive hole in the ceiling, where sunlight streamed through the ruined roof.

"Who could stay here?" Sara asked.

There were no doors, and the plaster had fallen from most of the walls, leaving bare brick or wood in its place. "Someone desperate," I said. "Or someone who doesn't want to be found."

Tommy's bark could be heard from the rear of the house, so Sara and I walked toward it, carefully watching where we placed our feet for fear of falling through the floor. Surprisingly, the floor held—in fact, it was of good quality. Someone had done recent work on it.

We found Tommy sitting in front of a door in what used to be the kitchen. Rat droppings littered the floor where once-white tiles now lay broken and stained.

Tommy's bark turned me away from the apocalyptic scene before me. He was staring up at the shiny new lock that had been fitted onto the basement door in front of him. It was a heavy-duty job, and using magic to knock the lock out of position as I had with the front door would probably just rip the door apart, causing more noise than just kicking it in.

"So we have a falling-down house with a locked front door and a basement door with a brand new lock. Anyone else got a really bad feeling about this?"

Tommy barked.

I motioned for everyone to stand back and then kicked the lock as hard as possible. The door didn't budge. It didn't even sway as the shock traveled up my leg. "Steel posts inside the door," I said, rubbing my knee.

"So how do we get in?" Sara asked.

"With noise," I said, as orange glyphs flared to life over my hands. A blade of fire extended down from one hand, stopping after a few feet. I sank the blade into the door, just under the lock, and dragged it up in one smooth motion. The sound of steel sizzling made more noise than I'd have expected, but after a few seconds I removed the blade and booted the door once again. This time it slammed open into the plasterboard behind it. The residual heat from the metal started a small fire, which I quickly put out with my hands before removing the glyphs altogether.

"How'd you do that?" Sara asked, her mouth agape.

"Fire magic," I said with a smile, which was broken by a deep growl from Tommy as he descended the steps into the blackness beyond.

"You want to stay here?" I asked Sara, who shook her head.

I closed my eyes as the orange glyphs came back to life. When I reopened them, the world was a mixture of red and orange, allowing me to see in the dark. It wasn't as good as Tommy's night vision, but it was better than falling down a flight of stairs.

I led Sara down the stairs, making sure she didn't trip. Once we reached the floor, I found Tommy, crouched in the corner. His hackles were up and a low growl was emanating from his throat. A girl sat in front of him. Her hands were above her head, tied behind a pipe, or pole, of some sort. Long hair covered her face, but it was easy to tell that she was dead.

"Take Sara out of here," I told Tommy.

But before he could say or do anything, Sara had knocked a light switch, bathing the entire room in a low, white light. It took her two seconds to spot the body, and she screamed, probably more from shock than anything else. But then she spotted the large mass of blood on the walls and floor and realized what had happened here, and for a moment I thought she was going to faint.

"Oh my God, oh my God," she said over and over.

"Tommy," I said. He dashed over to Sara and began to nudge her toward the stairs. Getting pushed by a normal dog can move a fully gown person, getting pushed by a thirteen-stone pack of muscle like a wolf will move *anyone*. Sara had little choice but to comply and she soon vanished back into the house. After changing back to his human form, Tommy would call whomever he needed to, and hopefully give me enough time to figure out what had happened.

I looked around the room. Someone had covered all the windows with cement, and it looked old. This place had been prepared in advance. I turned back to the dead girl and noticed the marks and bruises on her arms. Moving closer, I got a good look at the deep cut that had severed her throat, but even from a distance I could tell it was deeper than it needed to be to kill someone. It had been done with a lot of anger.

I got a closer look at her face, a mass of bruises and cuts. Her entire front was drenched in blood, cumulating in a large pool that spread out from under her bare legs, which were covered in smaller cuts and bruises. Whatever had happened here had been premeditated and prolonged. If there's one thing I know when I see it, it's torture. And the poor girl in front of me had gone through hell.

CHAPTER 5

I took my time searching the prison that someone had created for his victims. At first I'd thought Neil had to have been responsible, but he was the kind of person who wanted instant gratification. Whoever had built the prison wanted their victims to suffer for a very long time.

Loft insulation covered parts on two different walls, where thick, black welding tape held it in place. I pulled some of the tape off and found that the insulation had been added over what appeared to be concrete-covered windows. The room had been made pretty much soundproof.

The pole the woman had been handcuffed to was fixed to the floor and ceiling with steel rivets. Four huge steel rings sat in the opposite wall, where blood smeared the white plaster. The wear on the steel suggested that they'd once been used to hold thick chains, but I couldn't find any remains of them in the room.

The sound of cars pulling up outside flooded through the open door at the top of the stairs. Tommy had probably called the police, and I needed to finish before they cut off my access to the basement.

I made my way to where the four holes in the wall were and placed my hand in the dry blood. I couldn't see them, but I knew that black glyphs were spreading out over the palm of my hand, crisscrossing over my wrist and up my arm. Blood magic is addictive and dangerous. Most sorcerers use it to aid with healing, or to make their magic more powerful. But some use it for horrific ends—curses, controlling people, torture.

A few seconds later, when I'd finished gathering information from the blood, two things surprised me. First, the blood was from four different people. And second, they were all male.

When finished, I walked over to the dead woman and placed my hand on the pool of blood under her legs, using the same magic as before. Information about her flashed through my head. I was about to remove my hand, when all of a sudden a wave of power jolted through me and it took all I had to not collapse to my knees. Some form of magic had been used on her, and it had been incredibly powerful.

When I'd caught my breath, I thought about wiping my bloodied hand on my jeans, but decided against it and instead made my way out of the basement and back through the house to the outside where a gun was pointed directly at me.

"Stay where you are," shouted a well-dressed man with shoulder-length black hair.

I did as was told whilst a young, red-headed woman walked toward me. She was both confident and beautiful, and her eyes sparkled with an assured power. "I'm Director Olivia Green, with the LOA. You must be Nathan."

She held out her hand, which I stared at for a second, before showing her the blood on mine.

The black-haired man took a step forward, his gun still trained on me.

"Step back, Agent Greaves," Director Green said.

Agent Greaves stared at me for a heartbeat before lowering his gun, but he didn't step back.

Director Green clearly wasn't in the mood to argue and just ignored Agent Greaves. "Where did the blood come from?" she asked me.

As she got closer, I saw that her irises were a pale blue. She was an air elemental, and she was readying her power. I decided honesty was the best policy. "Body of a woman in the basement. She's handcuffed to a metal pole, and she's human. Also there were four others killed down there. All human, all male."

"How the hell can you possibly know that?" Agent Greaves said, with a dismissive tone.

I raised my palm to show the agent and allowed the Blood magic glyphs to come back to life.

"Blood magic," he hissed, but held his ground for a few seconds to make a point that he wasn't scared before walking off without another word.

I turned to Director Green. "None of the men were killed by magic, although there's no telling what was done to them after they were killed. The woman though, that's different. A lot of power has been used on her. Can't tell you more than that, though."

"Thank you for the information. I'll have people look into it."

I walked past her before she could say anything else and kept moving until I reached Tommy and Sara, who both stood next to Tommy's truck.

"We need to talk," I said to Tommy. "Now." The anger in my voice was easy to decipher.

We stopped out of earshot from anyone trying to listen in, a few hundred yards from those now searching the house. "I should knock you the fuck out," I said.

"Nate...."

I raised my hand to interrupt him. "Ten years ago, Mordred tried to kill me, but only succeeded in wiping my memory. Three months ago, I get my memory back, go find and kill the son of a bitch, and then come to find you. I told you all of this. I told you that Avalon was almost certainly involved in what happened, and that they might try to find me to finish the job they'd started. And how do you deal with this? By inviting them to meet me as I walk out of a crime scene with *fucking blood* on my hands! Jesus, Tommy. Avalon wants me dead, and you basically deliver me to their police force. Good fucking job."

"You done?" Tommy asked, with a touch of anger himself.

I grunted something noncommittal.

"I'm sorry I didn't tell you that the person who asked for my help was Olivia."

"The fucking director? This just gets better."

"Hey, you had your turn. Now you get to shut the fuck up and listen."

There was a silence between us that lasted only a few seconds, but it felt like a lifetime. There were probably only six people in the world who could speak to me like that and not get a punch in the mouth. And Tommy knew he was one of them. I shut my mouth and listened.

"Olivia needed my help, and I agreed," Tommy said. "I didn't want to argue with you, so I didn't tell you. She's not a cop, she's LOA, and I *needed* your help. I thought it was going to be a nice easy job, snooping around Neil's house. I had no idea what we'd find, but I swear to you I thought at most we'd just find enough to let the LOA look into him further. I'd have never brought Sara with us if I thought for one second there might be any real danger.

"Besides, you shouldn't be too concerned about me telling Olivia that you were helping me. Your past is so deeply hidden in Avalon that no member of the LOA, agent or director, will ever be able to gain access. You know this."

"Damn you," I said softly.

"I really *am* sorry for not telling you. But I'm also sorry that I had to lie to Olivia."

"What did you do, Tommy?"

"She wanted to know who you were, your past, that sort of thing. I told her that you were a member of the Faceless."

The Faceless are bodyguards, assassins, thieves, or whatever else their master needs them to be. Each high-ranking member of Avalon has their own personal Faceless, and each of them wears a mask so that no one knows what they really look like. There are no files on members, and only their masters know their true identities as all of them are bound to do their masters' will, no matter how disturbed or unpleasant it may be. While they worked for Avalon in an official capacity, they were utterly loyal to their masters' whims.

"Are you serious?"

"I needed to explain why any checks would come up negative. And preferably something that would make her not *want* to check in the first place. I wasn't left with a whole lot of good options. The Faceless were the obvious choice."

I shrugged my agreement; he had a point. "Okay, there's only one problem."

"And that would be?"

"You ever met an ex-member of the Faceless? It's a 'till-death-do-you-part' sort of group. And even that doesn't always mean their work is done."

"You'll think of something." Tommy gestured behind me. "She looks angry, think fast."

I turned as director Green strode toward me, determined and clearly having decided that she'd given Tommy and me enough time to chat. "I don't believe we were finished talking, Mister Garrett."

"Evidently not," I said as Tommy wandered off to check on Sara.

"You brought the girl here," Director Green said, meaning Sara. "That was stupid."

"Well, you asked Tommy to look into Neil, and that led us here. It wasn't my idea, and I know Tommy well enough to know that he was hardly expecting to find a torture chamber out here. And, like I said, *you're* the one who asked for his help."

"And I didn't expect him to include a member of the Faceless in this mess."

"Your disdain is easy to hear, Director Green," I said with a smile. "You know nothing about me. Before you judge, maybe you should change that."

"Every Faceless I've ever met has served only his or her master, like a good little lapdog. What makes you so different, Mister Garrett? What makes you so goddamn impressive that I should decide to trust you?"

"First, I'm ex-Faceless. Emphasis on the *ex*. Second, whoever built that basement did it for one reason, to kill people in it. And whoever he is, he's very skilled at killing. This isn't the work of some amateur, like Neil, who doesn't know what he's doing. Neil may be a powerful predator, but he's nowhere near a professional. Professionals don't make the mistakes that he's made, and they're not caught easily."

"Anything else?"

"You got a wipe?"

Director Green pulled a small pack of baby wipes from her pocket and passed them to me. "Keep the pack."

I thanked her and cleaned the blood from my hands, stuffing the remaining pack in my pocket before explaining about the photos I'd found in Neil's house.

"Shit," she whispered. "This just gets worse and worse."

"One more thing." I gestured at the open country surrounding us. "Tommy mentioned that you were called with a tip that someone saw something weird at the farm. You see any way someone could just happen to spot something suspicious out here? You can't see the farmhouse from the road, unless you're stopped at the gate and looking in. I'd bet a million quid that whoever made that call is the same person who slit the girl's throat. And that's not Neil. My guess, Neil's doing the legwork and the killer called to cast suspicion on him. To give himself some breathing room while you chased your tail. I'm guessing someone called to tell you that Neil was out. Maybe he's no longer useful to whoever he's working for."

"Fuck. Look, I'm needed here to sort all this out, but I'll contact you and Tommy tomorrow morning." She turned and walked away, rejoining the agents buzzing around the crime scene.

I put the card in my pocket and moved to stand next to Tommy and Sara. "Can we leave now?" Sara asked.

"I assume so," I said.

"Drop me back at the office," Tommy said. "Then take Sara home."

I waited until Sara had gone back to the car before speaking to Tommy. "There's more to this than some dead girl in a basement and a bunch of photos in some asshole's hidden room, isn't there?"

Tommy looked around, a nervous habit he had tried to get rid of. "That's putting it mildly. If I'm right, this is going to turn into a huge fucking mess by tomorrow morning."

CHAPTER 6

I dropped Tommy off at his office, but he'd been silent the whole way back and it was beginning to concern me.

"They tortured that woman," he said before I could ask him anything. "I could smell the blood. Can you come pick me up before you go home? I think there are a few things we need to talk about."

I said I would and told him that I'd return in a few hours to give him his car back.

"How's your hand?" I asked a still-quiet Sara.

She flexed her fingers and wrist. "It feels sore, but no more throbbing pain. Why, where are we going?"

"We need to talk," I said. "About what you saw."

"I saw a dead woman." Her words were spoken softly, just above a whisper.

I didn't really know what to say to that. "I'm sorry" felt too small a phrase to use for the horror that Sara had witnessed. Instead, I drove in silence for a few more miles, leaving the motorway and driving down some quiet country roads until we reached a dirt road. We bumped and jolted down the road for half a mile, the width just big enough for two cars, but there was no one else around at one in the afternoon on a weekday. At the end of the road sat a large grassy clearing.

I stopped the car and got out. Sara joined me a moment later.

"I've never been here before," she said as she followed my gaze.

The clearing ended fifty feet in front of where we stood, replaced by a drop of a few hundred feet into the New Forest below. From our vantage point, we could see for miles, all of it green and peaceful. Very few people knew of the spot, so thankfully there was no fence to protect idiots from falling down the slope spoiling what was a spectacular view.

"It's so quiet," she said as she walked toward the edge, stopping a few feet back and peering down the slope. "Bloody hell."

"Yeah, I don't advise jumping," I said as I joined her. "You could probably survive as it's not a sheer drop, but you'd know about it once you hit the bottom."

"How do you know about this place?"

"I used to come here, a long time ago. When the only way to get up here was to climb that slope, or walk the ten miles to get around it."

"You climbed that?"

"A few times; it was good exercise." I made my way back to the truck. "I picked here as we're unlikely to be disturbed. You can ask whatever you want. I won't dodge anything, I promise. No subject is off limits. You got into a fight today. How are you feeling about it?"

Sara continued to stare down into the forest below, her back facing me. She rubbed her neck and turned, then walked back to where I was sitting. "I wanted to hurt him," she said. "He threatened to...well, you know. When I hit him, I just lost it."

"You handled yourself well. I'm proud of you; you should be too. But next time, maintain composure. Losing your temper will get you in trouble one day. Trust me on this."

"You were so calm. You could have killed them all, couldn't you?"

"And a day not so long ago, I would have. But that's not me anymore. I try not to kill those too stupid to know better."

"Why doesn't that scare me?"

"Because I'm awesome," I said with a laugh, which Sara quickly joined.

"I want to know what happened today," she said. "Who murdered that woman? Why did you have blood on your hands when you came out of the farmhouse? What did you do to scare that agent, and who the hell are the LOA?"

They were all fair questions, but I thought starting at the beginning was the best idea. "To explain about the LOA, I need to start with Avalon. Do you know what they are?"

Sara shrugged. "Sort of. I know about people who aren't human. My neighbor when I was little was an elemental. She could move the earth around. I thought it was fantastic."

I grabbed a blanket from under the rear seat behind the driver and unrolled it, laying it on the soft ground. I took a seat, and Sara came and sat next to me a second later, eager to hear what she wanted to know.

"Avalon is a small island off the northern coast of Cornwall. There's only one massive city there, Camelot. And apart from being the island's name, Avalon is also like the nonhuman version of the United Nations. Or it would be if the UN had any real power. Avalon consists of the most powerful members of every nonhuman species in the world. You know those gods and goddesses that you read about at school—Zeus, Hades, and the like? They're all real, and each one has a say in what happens with regards to the laws of the world. Merlin is in charge of

Avalon, although his ability to control what happens has been on the decline for a long time now."

She shook her head. "You knew Merlin? I find that insane. It doesn't feel real. What's he like?"

I tried various words inside my head, but none of them would have left my mouth without a side-helping of anger. "Merlin and I have a difficult history. He's not the man I thought he was, and he turns a blind eye to far too much." I sighed. "Anyway, we're not here to hear me complain about Merlin. Any other questions?"

She thought for a second. "So who were those LOA people?"

"Avalon has several bodies which help it retain power. The three main ones include the Shield of Avalon, or SOA, which is the internal security force, sort of like America's Homeland Security or the MI5. The Blade of Avalon, or BOA, are the armed forces. They deal with external threats. The last is the LOA, the Law of Avalon, a police force, which is similar to Interpol. They investigate crimes perpetrated by humans against Avalon members, or by Avalon members on humans."

"So those agents were there because either the killer or victim wasn't human? Tommy said that most of the people in charge just do whatever they like."

"True enough. The big members of Avalon—Hades, the vampire lords, werewolf alphas, and the like—all have their own security forces or internal investigation people. They'd never allow the LOA to investigate them without a fight and a whole lot of evidence. It's a bit like a huge corporation not wanting the police to snoop around unless necessary."

"But whatever happened today was within LOA jurisdiction?"

"For now, yeah. Neil isn't under anyone's protection, no one too powerful anyway—otherwise Olivia wouldn't have been allowed to let Tommy look into him. That might change depending on who the murderer or victim was. There's a lot of political bullshit that goes into every investigation when the higher ranked members of Avalon are involved."

"And you used to work for them? Avalon, I mean?"

"For a long time, yes. I quit over a century ago."

"I can't believe you're that old."

"I'm much, much older. Sixteen hundred, give or take a few decades."

Sara stared at me for several seconds, her mouth agape, before asking anything else, "What's it like? Living that long?"

I wasn't really sure how to answer that. "I just do," was the best I could come up with.

Sara was silent for a few seconds, and I could tell that she wanted to ask more, but she thankfully changed the subject. "The blood on your hands."

"How much do you know about magic?"

"Tommy told me that there were two types, Elemental and Omega. All sorcerers start with Elemental—fire, water, earth, or air—and you can only learn two from that set. That about right?"

"Close enough," I said. "You can never learn a magic that is the opposite of the one you know." I raised my hand, palm up, and a small ball of flame appeared. It was about the size of a marble and hovered just above my palm. "The orange glyphs on my hands and arms show that I'm using fire magic."

I extinguished the flame and the orange glyphs were replaced with white ones as a small, whirling ball of air appeared where the fire once was. "And this is air magic. So I can never learn earth or water, no matter how hard I might try. Omega magic is the same—four different schools and you can only learn two. Mind, matter, light, and shadow. But there's a third type of magic—Blood magic. My hands were covered in blood because I can use Blood magic to learn from whom the blood came. I now know that the blood down there belonged to the dead girl and four human men."

"Can you tell how they died?"

"I can tell if magic was involved, like it was with the woman. Other than that, just rudimentary details—age, sex, that sort of thing. But if I come across their blood again, I'll know it's the same. So if we find those men, I'll know they're the same ones who were chained in that basement."

"So, how does your magic work? Can you just keep using it forever?"

"No, too much use and I start thinking that magic is the solution to all my problems. And if I don't stop...well, it wouldn't end well. Magic wants to be used, and if a sorcerer isn't careful, it'll change him, turn him into something...*wrong*. We call them nightmares."

"Can you ever get rid of the nightmare?"

"Learning magic is sort of like training for a marathon. You train by running until you can't run anymore, and then next time you push yourself past that point. You keep doing it until you reach your goal, moving little by little. Magic is the same. When you feel the magic inside trying to take over, you stop. And then next time you push it a little further. You do it again and again as you gain power and experience."

"So the magic stops trying to control you?"

I shook my head. "Nope. It never stops; it just gets pushed down deeper and deeper inside you. But it's always there, waiting until you use too much to turn back."

A breeze swept through the clearing and Sara hugged herself, rubbing her arms despite the coat she wore. "I can't stop seeing her," she said. "All that blood. How do you deal with it?"

I thought about telling her a lie to make her feel better, but if she stuck with Tommy, it was likely that she'd be seeing more dead bodies, though hopefully they'd be in picture form instead of tied up and tortured in a basement. "As unpleasant as it seems, seeing the dead really does get easier the more you do it."

"Have you seen a lot of dead bodies?"

"I've seen quite a few, yes." *And been responsible for more than my fair share*, but I didn't say that out loud.

"I don't know if I can do this," Sara said, with a shake of her head. "Work for Tommy, I mean. I love it there, but…your world is so…"

"Violent? Terrifying?" I smiled. I'd given Sara a lot of information to take in, and it felt like it was beginning to overwhelm her a little. "Pretty much both of those are right. There are a lot of nonhumans who'd like to think they can do whatever they like, including killing. But there are also a lot of men and women out there who stop those people. Or try to. Tommy is one of them. He'd move heaven and earth to make sure his people stay safe."

"If I stayed, would you keep training me? And not just in fighting. But to use weapons too."

"Do you want me to?"

"I think I need you to."

"Good. But today was special. You won't be out on assignment. Hell, Tommy only took you today so you could get a feel for what his people do. It was meant to be an easy trip." I stood up and stretched.

"Do you miss it?"

I stopped what I was doing and glanced down at the still seated Sara. "What?"

"I saw your face when we were searching that farmhouse and after the fight. You were in your element."

I leaned against the car's bonnet and half sat on the front bumper. "Sometimes."

"Tommy said that you were some sort of Special Forces guy."

"I was whatever I needed to be—soldier, thief, spy, or... well, whatever I needed to be to get the job done. I did that for over a millennium. Using that knowledge and training, like I did today, feels good. But I'd never go back to what I used to do."

Sara stood and brushed her trousers, removing any stray grass. "I think Tommy told me about you to make me stay away from you."

"He's a wise man," I said. "You should stay away from me."

Sara looked me in the eyes. "Is that because you're dangerous?"

I nodded.

She stepped toward me and placed a hand on my chest. I could feel her warmth through my t-shirt. And I suddenly realized just how alone we both were, and how incredibly bad that was.

"You're a good man," she whispered and kissed me on the cheek. "Don't let anyone say otherwise."

Our closeness lingered for a moment longer than necessary, until our lips touched. Gently at first, but then I had her in my arms as our mouths explored one another with hunger and need. Her hands ran across the back of my neck as one of mine ran up her back into her hair.

My ringing mobile brought me back to my senses and I pulled away, removing the phone from my pocket and answering.

"Where the hell are you, Nate?"

"On my way, Tommy," I said. "Be about forty-five minutes."

I returned my mobile to my jeans pocket. "We need to go," I told Sara, who was staring at the ground, seemingly lost in thought.

I picked up the blanket and shook off the grass. "I'm sorry about the kiss," I said after the silence between us grew almost unbearable. "Shouldn't have happened."

"No. No, that can't happen again." Sara closed her eyes and sighed. I watched her, my eyes traveling from her beautiful face, down her body, taking in every detail. It was beginning to get dark, and the lack of streetlights meant part of her face was cast in shadow. Yet still she shone. The words tumbled into my brain and I felt foolish for thinking them. Women do not shine, they do not glow; the trite idea that any lust or love could somehow illuminate the darkness was just that, trite. A stupid notion held by romance writers and teenagers. But damn it if she didn't glow all the same.

I was sixteen hundred years old and felt like I was sixteen. That's not normal, I was pretty sure of that. And for someone with the kind of enemies I had, it was downright destructive.

"You already have someone, and I'm not good for you, Sara. I can't risk people getting to me through you. From now on, if we can't resist temptation, I'll have to ask Tommy to get someone else to teach you. And I don't want that."

"Neither do I," Sara said softly. She smiled briefly and then climbed back into the car. I hoped we *could* put the intense attraction between us aside, because if someone went through her to get to me, the wrath that would fall upon them would be biblical.

It was almost an hour later by the time I'd taken Sara home and made my way back to Tommy's office. I rolled up to the front entrance of his building and found him waiting outside. "Took your damn time," he said as I got out of his truck.

"I've had a crap day. Murder and explaining about our world will do that to a person." I figured what had happened between Sara and me could wait for a more private setting, considering Tommy would probably start yelling.

Tommy caught his truck keys in one hand and in turn he threw me my bike keys. "Before you go," Tommy said, "come back to my place. I've got some things I need to explain to you."

That didn't sound like something I was going to enjoy. "How angry am I going to be?"

Tommy shrugged. "Pretty angry to begin with, then probably not so much."

My bike was exactly where I'd left it, just in front of the main entrance of Tommy's building. I straddled the black 2009 Suzuki Hayabusa and placed the key in the ignition. "You drive, I'll follow," I said and pulled a black full-face motorcycle helmet on. The skull motif on the front ensured most drivers gave me a wide berth on the roads. No one wanted a skeletal face riding behind them.

The bike's engine roared to life and I was soon following Tommy, struggling not to open the throttle and overtake him. Instead, I waited patiently as he drove at just below the speed limit. I could almost imagine the grin on his face, too. The evil bastard.

Eventually we arrived at his...*home* wasn't quite the right word; mansion was probably closer to the truth. I hadn't been to Tommy's place in over ten years, but the last time I had, he'd been living in a two-bedroom house, near London.

The electric gates opened slowly, allowing us to enter. Tommy parked the truck near the front door, where the floodlights illuminated everything around us. I parked the bike next to the truck and switched off the ignition. Tommy had already exited the car and made his way to the door when a girl opened it and walked out, her arms crossed over her chest. She wore a purple top and dark blue leggings and was barefoot, but that didn't seem to bother her as she walked across the brick driveway. Tommy swept her up and planted a big kiss on her cheek.

"You're late," she said, after squirming out of Tommy's grip and rubbing her cheek as if he'd slobbered over it.

Tommy retaliated by grabbing her in a bear hug, which she quickly gave into.

I removed my helmet and hung it from the handlebars as Tommy released the girl and brought her over to me. She was no older than twelve, with long dark hair and several freckles on her nose. "Hi," I said, slightly confused.

"Nate," Tommy said. "This is Kasey. My daughter."

CHAPTER 7

After the introduction, Kasey and Tommy went upstairs so that he could check her homework and catch up on her day. The nanny, or babysitter, or whatever she was—a cute twentysomething with tattoos all up her arms—said her good-byes, leaving me alone in an expansive living room, where I selected the most comfortable looking couch and took a seat.

Tommy reappeared a short time later and opened a walnut-colored cabinet, which contained bottles of various spirits. He selected two glasses and a bottle of scotch, filling them both and then passing one of the tumblers to me before sitting on the couch beside me.

"So, there are probably a few things we should talk about."

"A few," I admitted. "The first one is…and *I guess* it's the most important…"

"I have a child."

"That would be it."

"She's eleven. Twelve next week, Thursday to be exact."

I quickly did the math and realized something. "I may have had my memories wiped eleven years ago, but I saw you only a few weeks before that happened. You must have forgotten to mention that you had a baby. I can see how *having a child* would be easy to forget."

Tommy took a drink of scotch. "I guess I should explain. When you disappeared, I spent a long time trying to find you. A lot of people thought you were dead, and not all of them were unhappy with that situation. But after about nine months, I needed something else to work on. Looking for you was a dead end, no pun intended, but with no body, I was certain you'd turn up at some point.

"A very wealthy man came to me and asked for help in finding his daughter. She was the latest in a series of missing teenagers. The previous girls had all been found a few weeks after their disappearances, or at least their heads had. I took the case and it brought me into contact with the LOA."

"Olivia," I said. "Are you about to tell me that the director of the LOA is your daughter's mum?"

"We got close, and after a few years together Olivia found out she was pregnant. It's hard enough for an elemental or a werewolf to have a baby, so any option that didn't include keeping the baby were rejected. Kasey was born seven years ago."

I had an idea as to where this was going, but didn't want to interrupt.

"Kasey aged her first five years in under a year. When she reached five, she started to age as if a human child."

"Which is why I'd never met her, or heard of her until today." Werewolf children, like a lot of those born in the supernatural community, aged incredibly fast—both physically and mentally. It took some getting used to when you've only had a baby for three months and they can already walk, talk, and were toilet trained.

"So, Kasey is really only seven? Why tell me she's eleven?"

"Ah, force of habit on my part. Once that first year passed, Olivia and I started to tell people she was five. As she aged normally from that point on, and due to her exposure to humans at her school, it was easier to tell a slight lie. Physically and emotionally, she's eleven years old. Attitude-wise, she's about nineteen."

"I'm guessing you have no idea what she might become?"

"Neither elementals nor werewolves show any signs of their abilities until they reach puberty. She could be an amalgamation of the two."

"An elemental werewolf. That would be unusual."

"But if that happens, would she be accepted as either?"

"You didn't need a pack; it never bothered you. Why would she care? Sounds like you're worrying about something you don't need to."

Tommy poured himself a second glass and took a drink. "Maybe, but I don't want her to miss out on something because she didn't get the chance."

"It'll be fine. Does Kasey live with you?"

"Olivia and I decided it after a few months. She works all sorts of crazy hours, and since my business took off, I can basically decide when I work. I always make sure I get back home in time to say goodnight."

I finished my scotch and poured a second glass. It tasted good, but, then, a twenty-five-year-old bottle tends to. "And Olivia's okay with that?"

"It was her idea. She takes Kasey fairly regularly and comes around to eat with us at least once a week."

"So you and Olivia are still...?"

Tommy shook his head. "We were working on a case together and got attacked. Olivia got injured and the suspect got away, but instead of going after him, I waited with her. I just couldn't bring myself to leave, and she told me afterwards that she had needed me to stay. We both decided that we cared too much to work together and be together. Personally, I think she freaked out, and then the director's job came up and she dove into it."

"But there's still something there, I assume."

A sly smile spread across Tommy's lips. "When she comes over, she tends to stay the night. We tell Kasey she sleeps in the spare room. Technically, that's true. Well, apart from the sleep bit."

I poured myself a third glass. "So, what's it like having a child again?"

Tommy was thoughtful for a moment. "You know, I resented you for telling me I had to leave my family. I never got to see my wife or son again, never got to watch him grow up."

"I'm sorry." I remembered how heartbroken he'd been when he'd realized he could never go home. Never hold his family again.

"Not your fault. And you were right. If I'd gone home a werewolf, I would have been killed or gotten someone I cared about killed. I had to let them think I was dead. And the fact that you provided them a good life went some way to help."

It had been a hard decision for him to make, although I made sure he received regular updates on how they were doing. His wife had been given enough money to buy a home and start a small farm, and his son ended up fighting the French. He managed to ransom off a wealthy French aristocrat and made enough money to increase his mother's land tenfold. I made sure that a member of Avalon shadowed him wherever he went. Nothing bad befell him that could have been prevented. Tommy's son died as an old man, surrounded by wealth and people who cared deeply for him.

"I never realized how much I missed having children," Tommy said. "It makes me feel whole. Like there was always a part missing that I knew nothing about. It's hard to explain. Sorry."

I waved away his apologies. I'd never had children, not any that I was aware of anyway. Sixteen hundred years without a child isn't unheard of. Sorcerers weren't exactly the most fertile of creatures, a side effect of the magic we wielded.

"Anything else you want to tell me? A secret family perhaps, or maybe you're the king of a small country?"

Tommy's laugh was deep and full of joy and alcohol. We'd managed to polish off the bottle of scotch within a very short period of time. "No, I think I've told you everything. You'll have to come to Kasey's party, though. It'll be nice to have people there to talk to who are neither parents nor twelve."

That caused me to laugh. "I'll be honored. What do twelve-year-old girls want as gifts?"

"What all women want," he said opening a second bottle of scotch and polishing off his fifth or sixth triple measure. "Money."

That made us both laugh.

"So where did all this come from?" I asked with a wave of my hand.

"The father looking for his missing daughter was very wealthy, and when I found his daughter safe and sound he paid me a lot of money. More importantly, he put out a good word to a few people who were interested in having some security work. It all sort of snowballed from there. Now I don't even need to do anything. Most days I just make sure everything's ticking along. Although, once in a while I still like to get involved."

"Like today?"

"Yeah, that fucking sucked, didn't it?"

"You said it was going to get worse. How?"

Tommy sighed and refilled his glass. "I was hoping to leave this until it was confirmed tomorrow."

A glare told him to get on with it.

"I recognized the girl in the basement. Or at least she looked like someone I'd met before. I don't remember the name, but I think she was the girlfriend of an LOA agent."

I knocked back the rest of my scotch and hastily refilled it. "Shit."

"You see why I said it was going to get worse?"

"Does Olivia know?"

"I told her my thoughts, yes. We'll see if I was right, but I really hope I'm not."

Neither of us needed to say why the train of thought could only end badly. The murder of an agent's family member was almost as bad as killing an agent himself. The LOA would stop at nothing to find the culprit, no matter the cost. And Avalon would give them their full backing. Depending on who the killer was, and where they were, it could cause all sorts of problems, because I truly doubted that Neil was the only one involved in what happened in that basement. The best that could be hoped for was, if Tommy was right, that the murderer had picked the victim at random.

We both sat in silence for some time, neither one of us willing to add fuel to the fire of what we were thinking. Eventually the scotch overrode sense, and I told Tommy about what had happened between Sara and me at the clearing.

His response wasn't exactly unexpected.

"You're an idiot," he said calmly.

"No argument from me."

"She better not quit, or you owe me a competent assistant."

"If Sara quits, I'll do the damn job myself. She loves working for you; she won't leave without a fight."

"You're still a fucking idiot."

I shrugged. "Why did you keep Kasey from me? I've been back for a few months now, and this is the first I've heard of it."

"I hadn't seen you in ten years, and I wanted to be sure that you were still the person I knew. I wasn't about to put my daughter in any danger, so I had to wait until I knew I could still trust you."

I wasn't about to argue with a man who just wanted to protect his daughter.

After that, we settled into the comfortable conversation of two old friends, reminiscing about the past and discussing drink-induced topics.

I woke up on one of Tommy's couches. Tiny slivers of sunshine made their way through the thick curtains and onto my face, causing me to blink and try to bat them away in my half-asleep stupor.

I glanced at my watch, which said it was nearly eight a.m. I had no idea what time I'd actually gotten to sleep, but the bottles of scotch, beer, and vodka on the coffee table told their own story. I was very grateful that being a sorcerer meant having my magic heal me a lot quicker than a human ever could. It had removed the alcohol from my body and ensured I didn't have a hangover, so all I had to contend with was the horrible aftertaste and a desire to go back to sleep for a few hours.

Instead, I forced myself up and dragged myself into the kitchen. I had no idea where Tommy was. If he'd had any sense, probably back to his own bed. I rubbed my neck and rolled my head to unknot the muscles. The couch had been a comfortable seat, but not exactly the sleeping apparatus of choice.

I was still searching through the various cupboards when someone cleared their throat behind me. "Hi," I said, turning around to find Kasey standing in the doorway. She wore a blue school uniform and carried a green rucksack. She was the spitting image of Olivia.

"What are you looking for?" she asked.

"Tea," I said. "I know your dad drinks it, but I'm stuffed if I can find it anywhere."

She walked into the kitchen and over to the counter, where she opened the lid on a small ceramic pot. "Tea," she said with a flourish.

I smiled and grabbed one of the fragrant bags. White tea—he'd learned well from all the times I'd served it to him. I filled the kettle and put it on to boil as Kasey studied me. "Is there something you want to ask?" I wondered if maybe she was shy.

"You're here to stop more women from getting hurt, aren't you?"

"What do you mean?" I asked. "Where does your dad keep the honey?"

Kasey opened a nearby cupboard and passed me a jar of the orange nectar, which I placed beside the cup I'd taken from a wooden tree-like structure and dropped the tea bag inside. I'd have preferred leaves, but I've been told I'm a fussy bastard when it comes to my tea.

"So?" Kasey asked with more than a little impatience as I filled the cup with freshly boiled water.

"Yes," I said. "I'm here to help your dad, and apparently your mum, too. We'll find anyone responsible, hopefully before anyone else gets hurt."

Kasey considered this for a second before nodding. "They don't think I know what's going on, but I watch the news and read the Internet. They think I'm too young to understand."

I removed the bag from the tea and threw it into the bin. "They just want to protect you."

"From the truth?" Kasey raised her eyebrow in confusion.

I took a drink of my tea. "It's what adults do. If we told you about everything bad that happens, it might scare you. And whether that annoys you or not, they'd rather you had some ignorance about how cruel the world can be sometimes."

"I understand that," she said firmly. "I just want them to be honest with me."

"I'll tell you what, you ask me what you want to know, and I'll answer as honestly as I can."

"I don't have anything right now," she said. "Can I come ask if I think of something?"

"Sure, not a problem."

Kasey walked to the doorway and turned back to me. "It's nice to meet you."

"You too."

She paused for a heartbeat. "Dad says you're the scariest person he's ever met. But that you're a good guy. You don't look scary."

Her words caused me to laugh, but I had to think how best to answer. "I'm only scary to people who deserve it."

Apparently that was the answer she wanted to hear, as her attention was soon on the opening front door.

"Mum," she shouted and darted off toward the front door.

"Olivia," I said with a slight nod as she embraced her daughter.

"Nathan," she said, not exactly sounding happy about seeing me. "I assume you and Tommy spent the night getting drunk."

"Better than therapy," I pointed out, as Tommy made his way down the stairs wearing a clean green shirt and faded jeans.

"Morning, all," he said far too cheerful for the amount of alcohol he'd consumed, which dwarfed my own intake. A werewolf's healing ability made even mine look stagnant by comparison.

"Morning, Dad," Kasey said with a slight glare. "I heard you both singing last night."

Tommy grinned. "Sorry, we were in sort of a groove."

Kasey rolled her eyes as only an eleven-year-old can, which caused Tommy to laugh. "Are you taking me to school today?" she asked her father.

"I am," Olivia said. "I don't know if I'll get a chance to come over tonight, so I thought it'd be nice for me to take you."

Kasey beamed and went to hug her dad.

"See you tonight, Terror," he said as she pulled away.

Kasey stopped beside me on her way back to Olivia. "Please keep them safe," she whispered before running out of the door.

"I'll see you both soon," Olivia said with a scowl.

"I'm going to my place first," I said. "I need a shower and change of clothes."

Olivia passed me a notepad and pen, which had been kept on a table near the front door. "Write the address down; I'll meet you both there."

I did as I was asked and Olivia took the paper, leaving without a word. "She's not happy," I said as the door closed.

Tommy shrugged. "I don't think she was expecting you to be here. She doesn't like showing a soft side in front of people who are working for her."

"I didn't realize I was working for her." I finished the rest of my tea and went to put the cup next to the sink. "Kasey asked me about the attacks."

"I figured she might. Olivia and I haven't really spoken about them with her. I've been actively trying to avoid it."

"I hope you don't mind. I wasn't really sure how to deal with it."

"It's fine, probably better coming from you than some friends at school. Besides, I'd mentioned you to her."

"Yeah, the *scariest man I've ever met* bit. Thanks for that, nice way to terrify your child."

Tommy laughed. "She's always afraid I'm going to get hurt. I figured telling her I was working with you, and that you can be scary might alleviate her fear a little."

"I'm not really that scary, am I?"

He laughed again. "I've seen you lose your temper. Remember Istanbul?"

"Ah, yeah. Well that was a special case."

"You burnt a mansion to the ground and killed a dozen very unpleasant men."

"They butchered women and children for profit. They deserved it."

Tommy raised his hands. "No argument from me. But that's only one of many occasions I can think of when I've been really glad you're on my side."

I wanted a change of subject. "So, can we leave so that I can get a shower? I stink of booze and salt-and-vinegar crisps."

Tommy threw me my jacket and grabbed his keys from a bowl near the front door. "You're right, we'd better go before Olivia gets to your place first and breaks in thinking you're ignoring her."

I would have laughed if I didn't think he was being completely serious.

CHAPTER 8

I used to have a lovely penthouse in Winchester. Unfortunately, a complete psychopath forced me to blow it up as I escaped from his attempt to kill me and a girl I'd been asked to protect. Buying a new home had been high on my to-do list, and I'd decided on purchasing something in a slightly quieter area. Preferably with less distance to fall if I had to jump out of the top floor. Hence, my current residence, which was a large two-story house in a secluded area inside the New Forest.

The thatch-roofed building had been built sometime in the late eighteenth century and then modified through the years to deal with a more modern lifestyle. The previous owners had built a two-story addition on the side of the property, creating several extra rooms. They'd even tried to keep it in style with the rest of the house, although the lack of thatch on the newer portion was a bit of a giveaway.

The house came with a few dozen acres of land, most of which were littered with trees and, once I'd finished with it, an early warning system for anyone who might want to creep up on me. Minute cameras and sensors gave plenty of warning of visitors.

I rode my bike to the front gate and got off, pushing it open.

"Still in the dark ages," Tommy called from the truck with a laugh when I sat back on the bike.

I pushed up the face guard allowing me to speak clearly. "I'm just not lazy," I replied and returned his smile with one of my own. He parked his truck in front of my double garage and turned off the engine, while I left my bike near the front door and removed my helmet.

"Looks like we beat Olivia here," Tommy said, glancing around.

"Probably a good thing," I said and unlocked the door, pushing it open as my alarm started to beep. I dashed over and entered the code, switching it off.

"You own a normal burglar alarm?" Tommy asked.

"You have twenty seconds to enter the code before all the doors and windows lock and gas is pumped into the building. It'll knock out a rhino in about half a minute. "

"Bloody hell, Nate."

When you've made as many enemies as I've managed to over the centuries, it pays to have a little security in place. "I got it from a friend—cost me a small fortune, but it's probably worth it. I'd rather not come home to any unpleasant surprises."

I told Tommy to make himself comfortable, which probably meant I'd find him eating his way through the contents of my fridge, and went for a shower. One of the reasons I'd bought the place was because of the large bathroom that the previous owners had installed in the extension. When I'd first read the words "wet room," I had no idea what to expect, so I was pleasantly surprised to find that it meant a bathroom with an open shower in the middle and drain in the floor. It was quite liberating to use, instead of standing in a little cubicle just so I could wake up and get clean.

Once I'd finished washing and put on a clean pair of dark blue jeans and an orange t-shirt, I made my way back to Tommy, expecting to find him gorging himself on the various pieces of meat that were in my fridge, cooked or otherwise. A werewolf's diet is a scary thing.

Instead, I heard the raised voices before I'd entered the kitchen.

"What should I have done, Olivia?" Tommy asked. "Stopped her from looking at the Internet? Or maybe I should have rounded up all of her friends and forced them to never discuss the murders? They're all over the damn news. Kasey was going to find out about them somehow."

"But she shouldn't be exposed to this shit," Olivia retorted as I walked into the room. "You." She pointed at me and stormed over. "You told my little girl about these murders."

I shook my head. "First of all, Kasey asked me about someone hurting women. Secondly, Kasey already knew. She just wanted someone to be honest with her."

I walked past Olivia and grabbed one of the many slices of toast on a plate on my dining room table, which Tommy had probably made as a snack. The table sat near a pair of patio doors, which overlooked an expansive back garden. The garden was nice to look at, but of no interest to me in terms of actual gardening. Mowing the lawn every now and again, and picking the fruit off the apple and plum trees, was the extent of my green fingers.

"See," Tommy said, chewing absentmindedly on a piece of toast. He must have used an entire loaf of bread. "Now will you calm down? Kasey's a smart girl, and she's old enough to be aware of what's going on."

"Anyone feel like telling me what's happening with the investigation?" I asked.

Olivia took point as I assumed she would. "As you know, I asked Tommy to look into Neil's accommodation. I was hoping to find something to at least warrant a further investigation. I don't like having felons like him walking free on my streets. But considering how he managed to get out of the Hole after such a short period of time, not to mention his sudden wealth, it's clear he has some serious backing.

"In the past three weeks we've found four dead girls, five as of yesterday. They were human girls, with no discernible connection to anything that was supernatural. Thus, the human police took control of the investigation. That changed after the third murder. Agents Greaves and Reid were contacted directly by someone who gave them directions to the third victim.

"As you may not know, Agent Greaves is a werewolf. He found that there was no traceable scent at the third crime scene. As of that time, however, the LOA have taken over the case, while allowing the human police to remain as the public face of the investigation for the duration. The detective chief inspector works for Avalon, and he was happy to take the press off our hands."

Avalon slotted their personnel into important positions in human affairs. They did it all the time, in all levels of government, both local and national, as well as the emergency services, press, and anywhere else where humans might come into contact with Avalon on a regular basis. The personnel were nearly always humans, and rarely got discovered. Avalon had been doing it for thousands of years.

"Those photos in Neil's bedroom," I said. "They're of the victims."

"They're pictures of the girls in here." She removed a sizeable file from a large handbag on the floor and passed it to me. "Every detail we have so far, on both the dead girls and Neil Hatchell."

I placed the file on the table next to me without opening it. "You must have suspected that Neil was the killer."

"Of course, but his old methods and the ones currently being used in these crimes are very different, apart from the level of violence. We concluded, as you did, that he's not working alone."

"Any connection between the victims?"

"We've got the human police talking to the victims' families. Hopefully, they'll pick something up. Our murderer likes to call and let us know when he's finished. So far, four calls. I guess with the call about the farm that makes five."

"What can your agents tell you about the caller?"

"His voice is deep, no background noise, always sounds pleased with himself. One of the empaths back at the HQ thinks he's masking some serious anger."

"No shit, really? Serial killer is angry, that's something different." Empaths were pretty scary. They could not only read but amplify emotions in others. I considered myself quite open when it comes to the races of my world, but empaths weren't people I liked spending a lot of time with.

"Don't be an ass," she snapped, drawing a smile from Tommy.

"So somehow Neil is involved, but he's not the one doing the killing. That just leaves one question. How can there be no useable scent at the crime scene? Is there anything that doesn't leave a normal scent?"

"It's not that the killer doesn't leave a scent," Tommy chimed in after finishing his tenth piece of toast. "I went to the third crime scene a week ago, and there were dozens of scents all working together. It was overwhelming. So what can mix scents up like that?"

"Magic, elementals, probably a few other things I'd really rather not face," I said and grabbed a second slice of toast, gaining a slight growl from Tommy in the process. "Do that again and I'll hit you on your nose with a rolled up newspaper," I told him.

Olivia tried to hide a smirk as Tommy grabbed another slice of toast and stuffed as much of it into his waiting maw as possible.

"So, what does this have to do with me?" I asked, wanting to get back onto the topic at hand.

"With so many murders in such a short period of time, it's looking like whoever's committing them isn't planning on stopping. And I'm beginning to get heat from those above me, asking if I need help."

I suddenly grasped why she needed Tommy's and my assistance. "If you ask for help, you're worried they'll just remove you from duty and replace you with someone who will get the job done. Someone who may not have the best interests of the victims at heart."

"You worked for Avalon," Olivia said. "You know that they'll bulldoze straight through this investigation until they find someone to fit the role of murderer, and then they'll call it quits. It's becoming high profile, and Avalon doesn't like high-profile cases."

"There's more though, isn't there?"

"I'm the first female director in LOA history who isn't in charge of some little shithole in the ass end of nowhere. Asking for help will be admitting that they chose wrong, and that I picked the wrong team to work with me. I'll be assigned somewhere out of the way and my team will be broken up, but they'll always have my stink against them. They're good people and I can't let that happen to them."

I admired Olivia's desire to keep those who worked with her from suffering whatever fate befell her. And it would definitely fall on her. At the moment, Damocles' sword was suspended over her head. If she didn't catch the killer, then Avalon would happily use her as a scapegoat and drop the sword with impunity.

"Okay, let's say I want to help. What do you need?"

"Ha, don't make it sound like you weren't going to help anyway," Tommy said. "The second you saw that girl in the basement, you knew you'd involve yourself."

"You're wrong," I said. "It was the second I saw those photos in Neil's hidden room."

Tommy's laugh was cut short by a glance from Olivia. "From what Tommy has told me, you were never a cop, or an LOA agent, so you probably look at things differently. I need you to read through the file—it's the details of the murders so far. I'd like your input."

I took the file, grabbed another piece of toast, and took a bite, drawing a glare from Tommy. I opened the patio door and took a seat on a comfortable bench as Tommy and Olivia's conversation returned to their daughter. I ignored most of it—it had nothing to do with me—and started to flick through the file.

It contained information on the various murders, just a brief overview and some photographs, but enough to come to grips with what had been happening. I dropped the half-eaten piece of toast into a bin beside me. I'm not squeamish, but eating whilst looking at photos of murdered women struck me as being ghoulish.

The four murders contained within the file showed that the women were all found in exactly the same way: tied to a tree with their throats cut, along with their stomachs cut open and their livers and kidneys missing. No other wounds were mentioned that could have been the killing stroke. I studied the first victim's details carefully—the first is often the key to future murders. Her name was Emily Boucher, twenty-two, lived alone but had a steady boyfriend. She worked for the local council as a personal assistant. There was nothing in her file that stood out. Her toxicology suggested she had no drugs in her system, recreational or otherwise. She'd last been spotted in a bar with some friends, but she was the designated driver. The statement from one of her friends said that it was her turn and that she wouldn't drink and drive.

There was a sheet of paper on her boyfriend. He was on maneuvers with the army, which was a pretty decent alibi as they went, so he was ruled out.

I flicked through some photos of her body and eventually came to one of her when she was alive. She was a beautiful woman; her smile looked effortless, and she was clearly enjoying herself as she stood alongside her friends, drinks in hand. I turned the photo over and saw the name Vicki on the back of it in pen.

"Who's Vicki?" I asked loud enough to have them hear me inside.

Tommy and Olivia stopped talking and left the kitchen to join me outside. "Victoria Penbury," Olivia said. "She worked for me as an agent."

"She knew the victim?"

"They lived on the same street, but that's as much as I know. Vicki had a lot of human friends. It's one of the benefits of having an enchanter on the team."

That was more than a little surprise—I hadn't expected an enchanter to be working with the LOA.

Although anyone could use a rune, you had to use the right rune in the right place for it to have any effect. Sorcerers infused runes with magic to make them more powerful, but as enchanters have no magic to use, at least not in the way sorcerers do, they manipulate the rune itself. Despite having only a human-level lifespan, they're incredibly powerful. They tend to fall into one of two categories, those who keep to themselves and want nothing to do with anyone, or those who sell their services to the highest bidder. To discover that one worked for Avalon was unusual to say the least, and said a lot about Vicki's integrity.

"So where's Vicki?" I asked.

"We don't know. That's one of the other problems." Olivia turned to Tommy. "You were right about the victim in the basement. The body we found was Amber Moore. Vicki's girlfriend."

"So two of the victims knew your agent, and now she's missing." Olivia nodded.

"And that's another reason why you haven't contacted Avalon—you're worried they'll just blame her for the murders."

"Pretty much; it's the easiest solution."

"Are you sure she doesn't know the other victims?" I asked.

"No," Olivia admitted.

"But you don't think she did it?" Tommy asked.

"I've known Vicki for six years. There's no way she killed any of those women. Besides, she was besotted with Amber; she would never hurt her."

"Besotted people do stupid things," I said. "I need to see Amber's body."

"Why?"

"How many enchanters do you know who wouldn't enchant those they love with protection runes?"

"None," Tommy said immediately.

"Then how in the hell did someone get through them to kill Amber?"

Olivia looked pained at the realization of my words. To get past any protection runes on a person meant removing those runes, unless the attacker wanted a very unpleasant surprise. And the only person who could remove them was the enchanter who put them there. That raised some very awkward questions.

"How long have Amber and Vicki been missing?" I asked.

"Vicki was assigned to another department to help with a case. She was supposed to report in twenty days ago. No idea about Amber. Could have been days or weeks, but I'm sure that Vicki would have said something if she'd been missing for weeks."

"Unless she was involved," Tommy said.

"I won't believe she is." Olivia's voice was hard and cold. "Not without evidence."

"Then we'd better go get some," I said. "Because I don't think Amber was the last victim."

"Why?" Olivia asked.

"Because," I said as I re-entered my home, "I think she was the first."

CHAPTER 9

Territory of Montana, America. 1878.

"**W**ho are you?" Sam demanded, brandishing a revolver that wobbled slightly in his grip.

I tore another piece of fish from the stick I'd used to cook it and popped it into my mouth. "Want some?" I asked, ignoring the boy's question.

He looked hungrily at the three fish remaining above the small fire before shaking his head and refixing his gaze on me. "I asked for your name," he said.

"I heard," I told him and ate some more fish. "But as I already told you what it was, when I saved your life, I figured I'd wait for a few minutes, until that gun becomes too heavy for you to hold. Then I'll take it off you and answer your questions in a more civilized manner."

"Where am I?" he shouted, waving the gun around. His confusion was easy to read, especially since the wallop he'd taken had probably done a good job of shaking his head up.

"You're in a cave I found that was big enough for both of us and not already occupied. I've had my fill of Montana's wildlife," I said, tossing the now-empty stick onto the fire. "If that thing goes off and you shoot me, I'm going to be really angry."

"Answer my question, goddamn you."

I picked up another stick and ripped off a piece of fish. "I was just travelling through," I said. "Then you sort of fell out of the sky, and I found myself protecting you from two rather unpleasant deputies who wanted to kill you. Now, considering that I mean you no harm, can you lower that pistol?"

The boy was clearly exhausted, and I wondered when he'd last had a good night's sleep before being knocked out. But he was also distrustful, a trait I could hardly blame him for, given his position. "Eat some fish and get some rest," I said. "Sleep with the gun if it makes you feel better."

"You might kill me," he said.

"What would be the point in saving your life, watching over you for a day, and going out to catch enough fish for both of us to eat, if I only mean to kill you? Besides, if you don't sit down, exhaustion will claim that particular prize."

He glanced at the fish again and lowered the gun, replacing it in a holster far too large to sit properly on his hips.

"Take some food," I said. "There's plenty."

The boy moved to the fire, his hand darting to one of the remaining fish and hungrily devouring it in the corner of the cave. His eyes were always focused on me, flitting back and forth whenever I moved to get more fish or stretched out on the thin mat I'd placed on the ground.

"Do you remember anything of what happened?" I asked after a few minutes.

"Running," he said with a full mouth. "And then nothing."

"Why were you running?"

Sam shrugged.

"The deputies told me that you were a murderer and thief."

That got his attention, and for a moment I assumed he was going to deny everything. "That's right," he said slowly. "I'm a murderer, so don't mess with me."

"Wouldn't dream of it," I said and polished off the fish I was eating. "I'll let you finish whatever's left on the fire. I'm going to see to my horse." I left the cave, pushing aside the ferns I'd placed at the entrance to avoid too much of the wind creeping in. I wasn't worried about predators finding the cave. Valor standing outside would give me enough warning to get rid of them. Besides, I learned long ago to sleep lightly when I was somewhere I considered unsafe.

I'd tied Valor's reins to a fallen tree near the cave, giving her plenty of shelter from the elements. She looked up from eating the grass as I got near and nudged my arm with her nose, a sign that she wanted to have her head stroked.

"What are you going to do with me?" Sam asked from the mouth of the cave.

"Wasn't planning on doing anything with you," I said without turning around. "You're alive, and without any lasting damage. I figure my part is done."

I moved to look at him. "Except that you're a murderer, and a thief. And I can hardly leave you to wander alone, what if you came across some little old lady and shot her?"

Sam's expression was one of outrage. "I'd never—"

"There's a ranch about four hours east of here," I interrupted. "I'm heading there in the morning. If you want to join me you're welcome to."

"And then what?"

"And then you tell me why two deputies wanted to kill you, and what it is you're meant to have done."

Sam didn't even take a second to think about it. "And what do I get?"

That depends on your answer, I thought. "What do you want?"

"Revenge," he said, but re-entered the cave before I could reply.

"He's an odd boy," I said to Valor. "But odder still is why he was being chased. If he's the murderer of anything bigger than a rabbit, I'd be amazed."

Valor stopped eating, nudged my hand again, and resumed her meal.

"Thanks for the chat," I said, scratching her neck.

After a few hours spent outside, collecting some berries for the morning, I headed back into the cave, where I found Sam fast asleep. The fire had long since extinguished itself, and I didn't bother to relight it. The meager light offered from outside stayed with me as I ate some of the fruit before wrapping the rest in a bit of cloth and stashing it near Sam in case he woke hungry. I'd filled my canteen of water and now took a long drink, the liquid still cool from the nearby stream, before settling down to a night's sleep. Hopefully I wasn't wrong about Sam, and I'd wake up with all of my bodily possessions still intact.

My sleep was light, and more than once I woke with the remnants of unpleasant dreams lingering in my mind. I glanced over at a still-sleeping Sam, half expecting to have a gun pointed at me. I wasn't used to sleeping in close proximity to someone who had been threatening to shoot me. Although I wasn't in Montana to sort out someone else's mess, I didn't like leaving people to a horrible fate if I didn't think they deserved it. And without help, Sam would die. I was certain of that.

With newly born sunrays breaking into the cave, I rolled to my feet and ate some more of the fruit. Sam was lying there, staring up at the ceiling, and for a moment I thought that maybe his head had been badly injured in the fall and it had taken its toll.

Sam sat up and took a handful of the fresh fruit. "Will you help me?" he asked after a moment.

"Why do you need my help?"

"I want to find out who killed my dad, and why."

"I'll tell you what," I said, as I stood and stretched. "We get to this ranch, you answer my questions honestly, and I'll discuss helping you out. Sound fair?"

Sam thought for a moment before nodding.

"I'll be back in a few minutes," I told him. "Meet me outside and we'll get started. It's a long walk."

I went to fetch some more water and came back to find Sam stroking Valor's neck. "Ready?" I asked.

He nodded, and after checking that I'd left nothing behind, we set off.

By the time we'd reached the outskirts of the ranch, the sky had turned cloudy and was threatening rain. Sam and I walked together. I hoped the journey would let him open up, but he was still weak and in pain, and spoke rarely. We'd stopped every hour at first, to let him rest, but when it became too much for him to walk, he rode Valor.

The journey still took a few hours longer than I'd expected, and I was looking forward to good food and some sleep in an actual bed. Sam had told me that he'd been to the ranch before. The owner was a widow of about forty who had often let him sleep there throughout the six months he'd been looking into his father's murder.

"Let me do the talking," Sam said. "She'll want us to work in return for a bed and meal."

"Hopefully that work will wait until the morning, when my belly is full and my eyes no longer heavy," I said. "Hell, if I can get a bath into the deal, then I'd happily do any job that needs doing."

"Don't let her hear you say that," Sam said. "She'll hold you to it."

I smiled. "Sam, if there's one thing I've learned, it's that no matter how hard the work, a bath, food, and a good bed make those memories fade pretty damn fast."

The conversation came to an abrupt end when we reached the entrance to the ranch. Ranches were normally abuzz with activity, people working hard at all hours of the day and night. And the sun was still high in the sky. The ranch should have been full of people going about their daily work, but it was barren of any kind of life. I suddenly had a very unpleasant feeling in my stomach.

"Get down," I said to Sam.

He dismounted and then led Valor behind me as we walked onto the ranch. I considered carrying the Winchester rifle outright, but if anyone *was* watching I didn't want to show them any weapons. Just in case they had itchy trigger fingers.

I scanned all around, taking in the large barn to my right, and another to my far left. Several small buildings sat together near the barn farthest from me. They were probably houses for the full-time workers. A somewhat larger building sat nearby them, the door open and a bar clearly visible inside. The owners certainly took care of their employees.

"How many people work here?" I asked.

Sam shrugged. "Thirty or so," he said. "A lot of people seem to come and go."

"What was the owner's name again?"

"Victoria Warren," Sam said. "What do you think happened here?"

I took the reins from Sam and tied Valor to the nearest hitching post, leaving her to drink from the trough that sat under it. "The cattle are still here," I said pointing to the cows in the distant fields at one end of the ranch. "A rancher wouldn't leave their livelihood behind."

I removed the Winchester rifle from the holster on Valor's side and made sure it was loaded, then turned to Sam. "Is that revolver working?"

"Loaded, too."

"Good. Come with me, stay close." The weight of the two silver daggers on the small of my back was suddenly noticeable to me as Sam and I walked toward the main house.

The building was huge, and it would have hundreds of places for people to hide. "How many lived in here?" I asked as I ascended the steps to the porch and peered through the frosted windows of the wood-framed, white front door.

"Just Missus Warren and her servants," he said. "There was a cook, two maids, and a butler. She said it took a lot of people to make the house run. She let the workers eat Sunday dinner in there."

I tried the brass door handle and turned it with a soft creak before pushing open the door. Silence stayed with me as I stepped into the mansion, followed by a hasty Sam.

Nothing appeared to have been disturbed. Paintings were still on the walls, the ornaments—a mixture of vases and brass figurines—were scattered around the room, all immaculate. "See anything missing?" I asked.

Sam looked around. "No," he said with a shake of his head. "But then I rarely spent time in this room."

"How many rooms on this floor?"

"Four. There's this parlor, a dining room, along with a kitchen and study."

"You sure?"

"On occasion, I helped the house staff with their work. It was mostly just cleaning, or doing little jobs around the house, but I enjoyed it. Missus Warren had asked me if I'd be interested in staying on."

I opened the only door from the living room and entered a hallway. The wooden floor was polished to a near-mirror shine, and tables sat along one wall, all with more ornaments on them. Whoever Missus Warren was, she certainly took pride in displaying the many baubles and junk she'd accumulated.

Sam and I made our way down the hallway, opening every door and checking each room as we reached it. It took a while, but I'd soon come to the conclusion that nothing was to be found on the ground floor. "How many rooms upstairs?" I asked.

"Six," Sam said after another moment's thought. "All but one are bedrooms; the last is a large bathroom."

"Okay, same as before. I'll go in front, we go room to room. You keep that revolver at the floor."

"What do you think happened to everyone?" Sam asked, fear encasing every word he spoke, as we were about to make our way up the stairs.

"Nothing good," I said, since there was little point in lying to him. Whole ranches full of people don't just get up and leave without taking anything with them.

We ascended the stairs and searched each of the rooms in turn, all without finding anything to suggest something untoward had happened. The only evidence of anything, beyond the missing people, was a broken vase in the master bedroom and the fact that the bed covers had been strung around the room, as if thrown aside with some force.

We were about to make our way back downstairs when I noticed something weird on the outside of one of the master bedroom's windows. Five little smudges of darkness were pressed against the glass.

I walked over and opened the window, reaching around to the outside to touch the dark substance that stained the glass.

"What is it?" Sam asked.

"Dirt," I said, rubbing it between my thumb and forefinger. I glanced up at the window again and realized what the pattern was. "It's a footprint. Someone had their bare foot up against the window."

I moved back to the window and stuck my head out, looking down at the porch roof beneath me, and then up at the overhanging roof above my head, where a small portion of beam was visible. Just enough for a hand hold. "Someone was out here," I said. "Recently, too. There's no way a woman who keeps her house this tidy would leave dirt marks on a window this easy to clean."

I pushed the window open as far it could go, then climbed up onto the window sill.

"I'll meet you by the front door," I said to Sam before lowering myself onto the porch roof. It was as sturdy as it looked, made by someone who knew what they were doing.

There was more dirt on the wooden roof here and there as it had fallen from someone's feet. I continued to search for anything to tell us where the inhabitants were until Sam appeared in the yard below.

"Where would people go if there was trouble?" I asked as I looked down on him.

Sam pointed to one of the two barns, the one that had been to our right as we entered the ranch. "That's where the horses are kept. If there was trouble, they'd either use them to get away or lock themselves inside. There are huge wooden bars, which slot across the front and back doors."

"Okay, let's go," I said, and the second Sam turned to head toward the barn, I stepped off the porch roof and used a small measure of air magic to ensure I landed softly on the ground. The pale white glyphs vanished before Sam turned back, a quizzical look on his face, probably wondering how it was that I made no sound on landing.

I ran past him to the barn, readying my Winchester for whatever we might find inside. "You ready?" I asked Sam once he caught me up.

Sam gripped the gun tightly in his hand and nodded.

A smaller, man-size door was built into one of the two massive barn doors, and as I moved to push it open, I noticed bloody marks on it. The hands of whoever had closed it had been covered in blood. I kicked the door open and stepped inside, and the stench almost knocked me back.

Sam followed me and gagged at the smell of death and blood hanging heavy in the air. I removed the wooden beam that kept the barn doors closed and pushed them both wide open, hoping the fresh air would help make searching the barn a little more palatable.

"Good God," Sam whispered, taking in a deep lungful of air.

"Stay here," I told him and walked back into the barn, trying my best to ignore the overpowering smell.

The dirt-covered floor had absorbed a lot of the blood that had been spilt, making the ground wet, as if a heavy rainstorm had been localized inside the barn itself.

I opened the stall farthest from the entrance and stepped inside. The number of bones accounted for a whole skeleton's worth, and it was easy to spot the skull and determine what had happened to the horse that had been kept inside the stall, and by extension what had happened to all of the horses in the barn.

I avoided a small lake of blood and picked up a mostly clean bone. It was thick and large, probably something from the one of the horse's legs. I turned it over, and my horror at what I'd seen so far increased. There were teeth marks. Something had eaten the horse, and judging by the spray of blood, it had been alive when attacked.

I carefully made my way back outside, avoiding the worst of the gore, to inspect the bone further under the midday sun. Sam saw me, and his already-green complexion appeared to worsen. "What is that?" he asked.

"I think it's the femur of a horse," I said inspecting the bone. "There are bite marks on it. Small sharp teeth, lots of them, a bit like a piranha."

"A what?" Sam asked.

"It's a small fish found far south of here. They hunt in groups and can strip an animal down to the bone in a few minutes."

"And whatever did this is like that?" The horror on Sam's face told me that the idea of small killer fish was up there with the worst things he'd ever heard of.

"I'm not sure what did this. I've got a few ideas, but nothing I can be certain about."

"What about the other barn?" Sam turned and pointed to the large building on the other side of the ranch.

"I'll check; you go get Valor." I threw the bone back into the barn; it made a squelching noise as it landed. "I want to be out of here as soon as possible."

Sam immediately ran toward Valor. I walked toward the smaller barn with considerable trepidation as what I might discover there, stopping only at a trough full of water to wash the blood from my hands before continuing.

I paused outside the barn and glanced over at Sam, who was untying Valor. I really hoped I wouldn't find what I was expecting inside the building. I pushed open the heavy wooden door and immediately wished I hadn't.

What was inside the barn wasn't what I expected. It was much, much worse.

It was one person's private hell.

CHAPTER 10

The word torture was not enough to describe what had gone on inside the barn. Horrors had been inflicted upon the dead woman, and I couldn't begin to imagine how she'd lived for more than a few moments once they'd started.

I stepped inside and pushed down the part of me that screamed to leave, detaching myself from seeing what used to be alive. It was now just meat, in a human form maybe, but meat nonetheless. No different than any dead animal or human I'd seen in the past.

The woman had been brought into the barn and hoisted into the air by straps on her ankles. She swayed gently, her head roughly four feet above the ground. She would have had to have been already in the air when they started. The blood trails all went down, toward the slick floor beneath her swinging arms. Swinging, skinless arms.

I closed my eyes and let the sickened feeling that had built up subside quietly before continuing my inspection of the body.

After being strung up, they'd removed the skin from her arms, fingers to shoulders, along with her legs, toes to thighs. A sharp knife and patience would have been required to do it, and she was probably dead before they started, so as to cut down on her moving around. God, I hoped she'd been dead. The killer had cut from her navel down to her sternum, in what appeared to be a clean cut with one sweep. They had then forced open the cut, allowing her internal organs to fall out. Her stomach and intestine remained on the floor by her hand, along with her lungs. The lack of blood on the floor, along with the scuff marks of something being dragged, meant that it had been caught and collected.

I searched the spacious barn. It was full of tools and supplies, everything needed to run a ranch. A trough sat in one corner, the inside coated with thick, black blood.

At some point during her ordeal, they'd scalped her, although I couldn't locate the scalp or the weapon used. I'd have to do a more extensive search of the barn's interior in case it had been discarded before the killers left.

A scream from the entrance brought me back to my senses.

I rushed over as Sam darted to the side of the building and vomited repeatedly. When all that was left was dry heaving, he started crying. Big, deep sobs of someone fearful and panicking.

"Sam, how old are you?"

"Wha?"

"Age, Sam. How old?"

"Four…fourteen," he said between haggard breaths.

"Your surname?"

"W…Ward."

"Tell me about your mum and dad."

Sam found it hard to catch his breath, but he forced himself to speak. "Mum was the daughter of a bank robber, Dad was a U.S. Marshal."

"Bet that made for an interesting upbringing."

Sam sighed and took another deep breath. "Mum died when I was four. Smallpox."

"I'm sorry," I said. "How's your breathing?"

Sam looked surprised. "Better. I thought I was going to die."

"You just needed something to focus on until your breathing calmed. You stay here and concentrate on your breathing, okay? I'll be back in a few minutes."

"Stay a minute." Sam's voice was barely above a whisper.

I sat down on the soft ground beside him.

"That is...was...Victoria...Missus Warren," Sam said and spat onto the ground. "Bad taste."

I'd already assumed that the person in the barn was the owner of the ranch, so I kept quiet and let Sam continue.

"Why did they do that? What was the point?"

"I don't know, but I plan on finding out." I let a silence fall between us for a short time. "So, not much of a murderer then?"

Sam shook his head and tears fell in a steady stream.

"You want to talk about it?"

"No," he said firmly.

"If you ever change your mind, let me know." I stood up. "I need to finish checking inside. You going to be okay?"

"Is that the worst thing you've ever seen?"

I didn't know if lying would make him feel better or worse, but the truth was all that wanted to come out of my mouth. "No," I said. "What happened in there is horrific, and disturbing and wrong. But it's not even close to the worst things I've ever seen."

"How do you push them out of your mind?"

"You don't," I answered. "You just learn to deal with them. The brain is great at doing things like that. Eventually, what you saw will be a foggy memory. It'll take time, but it will happen."

I left Sam to ponder my words and re-entered hell. At the rear of the barn, above several closed barrels, was a tomahawk axe imbedded in one of the barn's wooden posts. Blue feathers hung from the bottom of the deep-brown wooden handle, brown hair stuck to the blood-slick blade. I pulled the axe free and found more remains inside the cut on the wood.

I moved the barrels and found Missus Warren's scalp on the floor. It had probably slipped off the axe and fallen onto the floor. I left it where it was and sighed.

"What the hell are you doing?" someone shouted from the front of the barn.

I turned to discover a young woman stepping into the barn, a rifle aimed directly at me. Her features suggested that she was a native, although I wasn't familiar with the tribes in the area, so couldn't be more precise.

"I asked you a question." She glanced at the dead body, and her eyes focused on me once more. They were hard and cold, a dark brown that matched her long hair, which cascaded over slender shoulders.

"You're also pointing a gun at me," I said. "I just got here, too. So how about you lower the rifle? Or we at least go have this conversation somewhere that doesn't smell like blood and shit."

The woman stepped away and waved for me to come out of the barn. I did as she asked and walked around to the side of the large building where Sam was still sitting.

"Sit," the woman ordered.

"No," I replied.

"Mapiya?" Sam asked, getting back to his feet. "What's happening?"

"You know her?" I asked.

"She was staying here the same time as me." He glanced over at Mapiya. "Where is everyone? What happened to Missus Warren?"

"I was going to ask you the same thing," she said.

"Lower the gun and we'll talk," I told her once again.

"You should," Sam told her, agreeing. "I tried pointing a gun at him and I didn't get anywhere."

"You're a child," Mapiya said, and I noticed Sam flinch at her words. "I would have no qualms about killing this *outlaw*."

"My name is Nathan," I said, introducing myself. "Though you're free to call me outlaw, if it makes you feel better. Anyway, you're what, a dozen feet away? I'm pretty certain that you'll only get to fire one bullet. Better make sure it counts."

Mapiya steeled her gaze. "It will."

"Or we could talk." I tossed the tomahawk at her feet. "That was used on Missus Warren."

She stared at the axe with obvious hatred, but the gun stayed pointed at me, "None of the tribes did this."

"Of course they didn't," I said. "There's almost no evidence at the house that anything even happened here. And then they leave a bloody axe next to a dead body? No killer who takes the time to be so meticulous would be stupid enough to leave such an obvious piece of evidence behind."

The rifle wavered for a moment, and then lowered, "I heard something in the woods last night. But it got the jump on me and knocked me out. I ran back here after waking up. Are you a marshal or Pinkerton? You sound like one."

"If I say no, are you going to shoot me?"

Mapiya stared at me for a heartbeat, but she shook her head and winced slightly from the movement. "Still stiff," she said and rubbed her neck.

"No, I'm not the law. Just happened to be in the wrong place and all that. You sure you're okay?"

She nodded. "I never even saw them coming. They were fast, and they could have killed me."

"So why didn't they?"

There was a pause before Mapiya spoke. "I've been wondering the same thing. Any idea what did all of this?"

I shook my head. "From what you've told me, it happened at night. It would have been a concerted effort to get everyone at once. Otherwise, there'd be evidence of at least *some* resistance. And the only blood is either from horses or Missus Warren. She was a message. But that leaves the question, where are all of the other dead bodies?"

"And the horses?" Mapiya asked.

I glanced down at Sam and hoped the memories of the horses wouldn't make him sick again, "They were the celebratory meal."

"There's a fort about three hours ride north of here," Mapiya said. "They're friendly with the local Crow tribe. If we can get there before it's too late, they should let us stay."

"So, you trust us now?"

Mapiya shook her head. "Not really, but you didn't kill anyone here. And I know Sam. If he trusts you, I'm willing to extend the same courtesy. For the moment, anyway. We both seem to want the same thing, so let's at least travel to the fort together. If whatever took these people hasn't quite finished yet, I'd rather have the extra eyes and weapons."

We rode in silence, me and Sam on Valor, and Mapiya on her own dark brown horse. I couldn't help but watch Mapiya riding with confidence. She was a natural.

"She's beautiful," Sam said from behind me.

"Yes, she is," I said and looked down at the hilt of the knife that was sticking out of the top of her boot. I smiled.

After a long ride, Mapiya stopped her horse at the top of a slight hill. She pointed toward a large fort in the distance. "Fort Pennywise," she said. "Named after some general, although can't say I ever learned why."

"There are no lights," I said. "And no one on the walls."

She didn't wait a heartbeat, just went from standing to galloping toward the open front gates. "Hold on," I said to Sam and set off after Mapiya, reaching the gates only a few lengths behind her.

She practically jumped down off her horse, removing a Winchester rifle from its holster before tentatively entering the dark fort.

"Wait a few minutes. If you hear shooting, get on Valor and get out of here," I said to Sam as he dropped down to the ground. I followed suit and grabbed my own rifle, ensuring it was loaded before following Mapiya once again.

"See anything?" I asked when I caught her up.

She shook her head. "Can't see a damn thing."

There was movement from up ahead, past two cannons that lay dormant at the far end of the yard. I raised my rifle. Light flickered on inside the huge main building, and several large men walked out to join us. "We're armed so you should probably identify yourself," I said.

The men didn't answer as they lit several torches around the yard, illuminating everything. One man hadn't moved. He was a head taller than me, with a bare chest and long dark hair that was tied back and hung down to his waist. He wore a feathered headdress, although the light didn't allow me to tell the color.

"I am Chief Blacktail of the Crows," he said; his voice was a low rumble that commanded respect.

"Nathan Garrett," I said.

"You're not from around here."

"I'm from all over the place," I said. "The accent is English, if you're trying to place it."

"Do you not find that an English accent tends to make you stand out?"

"I don't find it much of a problem. And I've always been terrible at putting on accents. Would it make you feel better if I tried?"

"And you are?" Chief Blacktail asked Mapiya, ignoring my remark.

"My name is Mapiya."

Chief Blacktail smiled. "A Sioux name."

"My father was chief of the Sioux."

I pushed my surprise at Mapiya's revelation aside. "Why are you all here? What happened to the soldiers who should be here?"

The chief turned his gaze from Mapiya to me. "I don't think you're in any position to ask questions."

I walked toward him and handed over the bloody toma-hawk. "Someone tried to frame one of the tribes for the murder of a ranch owner not far from here. I think we need to have a talk before anyone else dies."

Chief Blacktail glared at the tomahawk. "I'm afraid it might be too late for that."

CHAPTER 11

New Forest, England. Now.

I hadn't been sitting long, maybe a minute at most. Enough to recline the black leather chair before Olivia had almost thrown the living room door open in her haste to find me.

"Are you going to explain why you think Amber Moore was the killer's first victim?" Olivia demanded. She would have probably questioned me earlier, but her phone had gone off, giving me time to leave the patio.

"I will, but I need to see the body first," I said.

"If you have information—"

"He's not hiding anything from you," Tommy interrupted. "Are you?"

I shook my head. "I don't want to tell you something if I'm wrong, thus wasting your time *and mine.*"

Olivia set her jaw. "Tommy, give us a minute, will you?"

Tommy left the room, presumably to find more food of mine to pilfer.

Olivia closed the dark wooden door behind Tommy and sat at the end of the leather couch closest to my chair. I swung my legs down, bringing myself upright and waited for her question.

"Would you consider working for the LOA to bring whoever is committing these crimes to justice?"

That was basically what I'd expected to be asked, and I already knew my answer. "No."

"Thanks for your help," Olivia said and got back to her feet.

"I'll work for *you*," I clarified. "Only you, not Avalon."

She turned back to me with a quizzical expression on her face. "Why?"

"Don't trust Avalon," I said. "This is an agreement between you and me."

"I can't pay you without putting your name on something."

"I never asked for money," I said.

Olivia sat back down. "What?"

"I've accumulated a tidy sum over the years—I don't need money. But I do want something from you."

"No," she snapped. "I'm not about to jeopardize my career for anyone."

I laughed; I couldn't help it. "Bloody hell, Olivia, nothing like that. What do you know about what happened to me a decade ago?"

"Tommy said that after you left the Faceless, you had an altercation with Mordred. That he grabbed you while you were helping children escape his experiments. That he had your memory wiped. Is that why you left the Faceless? To stop Mordred?"

"That about sums it up. But Mordred was getting help from someone, and I'm certain Avalon was involved. So, all I want you to do is call Avalon and ask them to send you all the information they have on Mordred."

"Why?"

"Because they'll either comply, which means they have nothing to hide, or the merest mention of his name will have someone calling you to tell you to stay away from it. In which case, we'll know something's going on."

"Mordred's fingers were in a lot of pies, that was well known within Avalon circles. He had a lot of friends before he decided to cut ties and go it alone."

"Mordred never 'went it alone.' He just gave Avalon plausible deniability."

"Did you know that he's dead?" Olivia asked.

I'd been the one looking down on him through a sniper scope in New York several months earlier, the one who pulled the trigger and blew the back of his head off. But I wasn't going to tell Olivia that. "I'd heard, yes."

"But you're still hoping to jog loose anyone who was helping him."

I nodded, but didn't say what I was thinking…*and then I'm going to point out to them how stupid it was to let me live. Preferably over the course of many hours in private.*

"That could get me fired, or killed," Olivia said.

"Be quick then."

She raised an eyebrow.

"They're not going to just kill you. You'll get a warning to stay away from anything to do with Mordred long before they go that far. And if you do get a warning, it probably means someone of power is behind the idea of making sure Mordred's secrets stay that way."

"Tommy told me that you saved a lot of kids from Mordred's filthy hands. That they caught you when you went back to save more. Why'd you do it? You didn't work for Avalon anymore. You haven't worked there for about a century."

"I did it because no one else would," I said. "Because it *needed* doing. And because I was no longer required to sit by and watch horrific things happen for the greater good of Avalon. They're not always the good guys."

Olivia dialed a number on her mobile. "This is Director Olivia Green of the LOA."

There was a pause whilst someone on the other end replied.

"I need access to Mordred's file."

Another pause.

"Yes, that Mordred."

A third pause.

"You don't need to know why, just that I want it. How long will it take?"

Another pause.

"Excellent, get back to me." Olivia hung up.

"It'll be a few hours," she said to me. "Most of his file isn't computerized."

"Thank you," I said. "I expect you'll get a call before then telling you to mind your business."

"What do I say when they ask why I want it?"

I shrugged. "Make something up. Just make it sound believable."

"So, do we have a deal?" She held out her hand.

I sighed and shook it. "I'll need full access to the investigation."

"Deal. You're not what I expected from an ex-member of the Faceless," Olivia said as we left the room together. "Every member I've met before was very cold, almost clinical, only interested in their master's needs."

"That's part of the job."

"So, why aren't you like that? Why the altruism of trying to save kids?"

"Because at some point the need to follow one person was overwritten by the need to do the right thing. It's probably why I'm an ex-member."

Olivia's phone rang and she walked away to answer it.

"You two sort out what we need to do?" Tommy asked as he came in from the kitchen, apple in hand.

"Did you leave me any food at all?"

Tommy bit into the apple and shrugged, "Hungry."

Olivia returned and removed her coat from the back of a nearby chair. "Well, you might not be in a minute," she told Tommy. "That was one of the morgue attendants. Apparently there's something we need to see."

Olivia and Tommy took his truck and, as the weather was nice, I decided to use my bike again. Not only did I enjoy riding it, but it also allowed me some time to think.

I'd left Avalon in 1890, under what couldn't exactly be considered the best conditions. I cut all ties and spent the next hundred years doing jobs for friends and traveling the world. It had been a good life, and now I'd almost come full circle, although I hoped this agreement with Olivia would be short term, letting me slip back once again into blissful obscurity.

I resisted the urge to overtake Tommy, now driving at a reasonable speed, so that I didn't arrive at the LOA headquarters in Winchester by myself and have to explain who I was and why I was there. Much easier to arrive with their boss and have people leave me alone.

I'd never actually been to the Winchester office before. It had been built four years ago, when I was in the middle of my memory-wiped years. But as I pulled up to the huge steel entrance gates, it certainly made an impression.

Anyone coming over the fifteen-foot-high, barbed wire–topped brick walls would have to contend with a few hundred yards of open field before reaching the main building. There were two guard posts, one on either side of the front gate, and both appeared to be manned. Further inside the compound, on either side of the main building, were two smaller buildings. Each of these had a sniper nest towering at least sixty feet off the ground. Those inside would have complete view of anything coming in from any side of the compound.

Tommy had told me that the rear of the building was used as a training facility, and often full of highly trained, not to mention heavily armed, Avalon personnel. The only way someone was getting to the main building was if they were allowed in, or had an army.

I pulled up behind Tommy's truck as Olivia spoke to one of the guards, who signaled for the gates to be opened. Moments later I parked my bike and looked up at the structure of the main building.

Thirty stories high, and a mass of steel and glass, it dominated the landscape. The edges of the building were curved slightly, giving it the unusual appearance of twisting as it rose, but it was impressive nonetheless. The front entrance reminded me of Tommy's business. Completely circular, it sat in front of the main building. Although it only had one floor, it was topped with a huge dome of stained glass, giving it the height of a four-story building. From the top of the larger building to the ground that we were standing on, it had to be over three hundred and fifty feet.

I removed my helmet and placed it on the bike's seat. "You work in there?" I asked Olivia as she left the truck.

She looked up toward the top of the building. "Floor twenty-nine," she said. "It has one hell of a view."

"How many people work inside?" I asked as we entered the building.

"Over three hundred during the day, maybe fifty at night," Olivia replied as she nodded to several armed guards who watched us enter.

A woman with dark, curly hair reminiscent of Medusa sat behind the receptionist desk and waved at Tommy and Olivia, reserving a scowl for me as I passed and waved.

The stained-glass dome above looked even better from inside the building. It depicted the removal of the Sword from the Stone by Arthur, and beautiful as it was, I wondered how many people here knew exactly what Merlin had done to ensure that Arthur became king. How many lives had been sacrificed. I swallowed my anger. Damn him to hell.

"You okay?"

Sara sat on one of the many leather chairs in the lobby, reading a magazine, which she placed on the glass coffee table in front of her. "You okay?" she asked again as she walked toward me.

"Miles away," I answered with a genuine smile.

"I called Sara and asked if she'd meet us here," Tommy said.

"At the morgue," I pointed out.

"We're not going to dissect anyone, Nate," he said, exasperated. "But if there is anything that you're uncomfortable with,

Sara, just walk out. After yesterday, I certainly wouldn't be here if I didn't have to be."

"I'll be fine," Sara said as the lift doors opened and we all got inside.

Olivia removed a long, thin key from her pocket and inserted it into a panel under the buttons of the above floors. The panel popped open revealing several hidden buttons, L1 to L6. She pressed L5 and the doors closed.

"Are all six levels the morgue?" I asked as the lift began to move down.

Olivia shook her head. "1 through 3 are all rune work and security; 4 to 6 is where the morgue is. Sometimes you want as much distance between the dead and the living as possible."

Unsurprisingly, the rest of the journey was completed in silence.

The lift reached its destination with a slight shudder before the doors slowly opened, revealing a corridor straight out of any hospital in the world. The only remarkable thing about it was that the signs on the walls had arrows that pointed to "magical dissection" and "rune removal."

Olivia led us past several men and women, all of whom were either reading from clipboards or talking to someone else about what was on a clipboard.

We made our way to the far end of a corridor, and Olivia went through the double doors without knocking. It led to a wash area with one long metal sink, taps above, and liquid soap dispensers fastened to the wall. The opposite wall had a glass window that allowed us to look into the adjoining room. A bald man sat beside a desk, writing—probably something to go onto another clipboard. I smiled. It wasn't funny, but when surrounded by death, I'll take levity where I can get it.

Behind the bald man were several dozen closed silver hatches. On a table lay one body, thankfully covered in a dark-blue sheet with red symbols etched into it. Sometimes the dead *really don't* want to stay that way.

Olivia passed each of us some green scrubs and waited until we'd put them on before she opened the door next to the window.

"Doctor Grayson," she said.

The doctor stood and shook Olivia's hand, smiling the whole time. "It's good to see you, Director. Well, sort of...You understand."

"Of course," she introduced Sara and Tommy, but stopped when it came to me. She obviously wasn't sure if I planned on using my real name or not.

"Nathan Garrett," I said with a shake of his hand. "Nice to meet you."

"An outside contractor, I assume," Doctor Grayson said. "I hope you can help."

"I'll do my best."

The doctor walked past us to the table. He was short, no taller than five foot one or two, with a small white goatee, which did its best to cover a noticeable scar along one cheek. I'd seen scars like that before. Whatever had done it was sharp, and if experience was any indication, it had probably been deliberate.

"So what do you have for us, Grayson?" Olivia asked.

Doctor Grayson picked up a file and started to read from it. "Female, Caucasian human. She was twenty-four, her name—"

"Amber Moore," I said.

The doctor glanced up at me. "That's right." He grabbed the side of the sheet and hesitated. "Are you all okay?"

Everyone glanced at Sara. "I've already seen her dead—not going to get a lot worse than that."

"That's probably not a theory you'll want to stick with if you stay around here," Doctor Grayson said and pulled the sheet down to Amber's waist, exposing her naked and brutalized torso.

"Fucking hell," Tommy whispered when the mass of purple that used to be Amber's ribcage was exposed.

"Yes, this is quite bad," Doctor Grayson said in the same tone as you would ask someone if they wanted milk in their coffee. "The throat was slit from ear to ear—that was the killing stroke, so to speak, but she had a multitude of injuries sustained before that."

"We'll start from the head." Doctor Grayson reached into his blue lab coat, also adorned with red runes, and removed a small metallic pointer, which he extended. He rested the tip of the pointer against the ear closest to us. "The skull was fractured, just above the ear, and her ear drum was burst. Not done at the same time; in fact, the ear drum rupture was probably two months old."

He moved the pointer. "She had a broken nose. It had been broken twice, once several months ago, and again a few weeks ago. Three teeth knocked out, and a broken jaw that was several months old."

"What about recent injuries?" Olivia asked, a slight nervous edge to her voice.

"Okay," Doctor Grayson said without any hint of irritation at being hurried along. "Within the last month, her sternum was broken, along with eight ribs, and her collarbone. The last time I saw an injury like this, the victim had been hit by a truck. The pain must have been immense." The doctor pulled back the sheet completely, exposing all of Amber's naked body. "Her left femur was snapped, as was her left ankle. She was also raped. Repeatedly."

Sara darted from the room.

"I'm sorry, should I stop?"

Olivia shook her head as Tommy left the room to check on Sara.

"Anyway, that's the last of the injuries. Any questions?"

"I have one," I said. "Any evidence of runes either applied or removed from her body?"

Doctor Grayson appeared taken aback. "How did—"

"Educated guess."

"You probably want to see this for yourself." The doctor switched off the room's lights and ignited a black light.

I couldn't help but gasp. "Fuck," I said softly.

Amber's body was covered, from her neck to her knees, in runes, only visible under UV light. To be able to create the same rune over and over again, covering as much of the body as those on Amber, and make them invisible to the naked eye, would have taken an immense amount of power. It explained why I'd felt so much magic back at the farmhouse.

"What do they do?" Olivia asked.

The doctor shrugged. "No idea, we've never seen anything like it before."

"Any idea how old they are?" I asked.

"Four weeks, almost to the day," Doctor Grayson said. "We have an enchanter on staff who did the time measurements."

"Did the enchanter know what these runes meant?" Olivia asked.

"It's an old Celtic word. It means *safe*," I said before Grayson could speak, to Olivia's obvious shock. "Amber wasn't in any pain during all of this, because Vicki etched runes into her girlfriend's skin with enough power to ensure she would feel nothing of the horrific things that were happening to her."

"How do you know that?" Doctor Grayson asked.

"When I was young, the Celts were the enemy for a long time. I was taught their language in case I needed it. Vicki had to listen to Amber scream in pain or whimper in some drug-crazed stupor until the runes could be finished. This took more effort and work than I've ever seen from an enchanter."

"You still think Amber was the first victim?"

"The first taken, yes. She was taken to prove a point, probably to Vicki."

"I still don't think Vicki did this," Olivia told me.

"Doctor, can you give us a minute?" I asked.

Grayson walked away, leaving Olivia and me alone. "The truth," I said. "You know about those old injuries. Where did they come from?"

"No idea what—"

I slammed my hand onto the metal table, causing Olivia to look down at Amber's body. "If you want my help, then you'd better be damn honest with me."

"Vicki had a temper. About five months ago, she punched Amber in the mouth, busting her jaw and breaking her nose. I forced Vicki to take counseling and they seemed to be back on track."

"So Amber's girlfriend, Vicki, was violent and she's nowhere to be found. Not exactly the best impression. But I agree with you, I don't think she did this. There's no reason why she'd take the time and effort to do the enchantments if she wanted to inflict pain on her. And if someone else had put the runes there, Vicki would have known."

"Which means Vicki is still out there, somewhere."

"Were the subsequent victims raped?"

Olivia shook her head. "No sexual injuries, nor did they have the level of torture used here."

I was silent for a moment as thoughts and ideas bubbled away inside me.

"You care to share?" Olivia asked.

"This was personal," I said. "Amber was targeted for a reason, and, as Vicki is still missing, I'm almost certain that it has something to do with her. Did those other victims have a link with Amber?"

"We're looking into that now."

"Okay, I'll leave that to you all. You got anyone at Vicki's place?"

Olivia shook her head. "We've had no need."

"Then that's my next port of call. I'll wait for you upstairs."

I thanked the doctor on my way out, passing Tommy as he re-entered the room. "Sara's waiting upstairs," he said.

"I think it'd be best to keep her out of it from now on."

"I've already told her to go back to the office," Tommy said. "Where you off to?"

"I'll check on Sara, and then I'm going to take a look at Vicki's place."

"Wait for me, I'll join you. I'm certain that some of Olivia's people won't want me hanging around."

I agreed and left to go back to the ground floor. I was glad that Tommy had offered his help. A bad feeling was taking root in my mind, and for the life of me I couldn't dig it free.

CHAPTER 12

"How're you feeling?" I asked Sara, who was stood outside the LOA headquarters drinking a Coke.

"I was fine until he started talking about what had been done to her," Sara said and took a long swig of her drink. "That fucked with my head a little."

"Can't say I blame you," I said and sat on the low wall beside her, staring down the drive to the heavily guarded entrance.

"Your world is amazing," she said after a few heartbeats of silence. "The magic, the wonder and awe I feel just knowing that I'm in the company of a sorcerer and a werewolf. That King Arthur, Merlin, and the Olympians are all real; it's something I don't think my brain has quite managed to process. But alongside all of that, I've seen and heard of violence that I'd never been subjected to before I started working for Tommy."

"It's a violent world," I said. "You get enough species with enough power, a lot of whom consider humans to be little more than a nuisance at best, prey at worst, and bad things are bound to start happening. Power corrupts."

"It hasn't corrupted you."

I couldn't help but laugh, which, from the expression on Sara's face, wasn't what she'd expected. "Power corrupts everyone who wields it. Those who realize this are the ones who try to use it to help. The trick is realizing before it's too late."

"So it corrupted you?"

"It corrupts everyone," I repeated, with no wish to elaborate.

Sara took the hint and changed the conversation, "What was it like when you saw your first dead body?"

"I was eight," I said, my voice soft as I remembered the day. Sorcerers were blessed, and cursed, with fantastic recall. I could pick out events with ease, but sometimes names and faces didn't come so easily. So, even though the day was over sixteen hundred years earlier, I pulled the memory back to the present. It was as if I'd selected a book from a huge library in my mind, each one containing a different year, and found the correct page. My memories started at the age of eight when I found myself waking up in a field in the southwest of England. Before that...nothing but an empty void.

"Eight! Seriously?"

"Yeah. And to answer your question, I'd been in Camelot for about six months and used to sneak out of the castle and into the town itself." I smiled at the memory. I'd loved the bustle of the streets, the fact that I could become anonymous and not just Merlin's protégé, as many in the castle saw me.

"One time there was an argument between two men, something to do with one sleeping with the other man's wife." My memory might be perfect, but it was only in the context of what my eight-year-old self had understood. "A guard decided the best way to deal with it was to let the two of them fight. The man whose wife had cheated defeated his opponent quite easily, but as he turned to celebrate, the first man stabbed him in the heart with a blade snatched from the crowd.

"I remember the man staring at his chest as the blade was removed. He fell backwards, dying before he hit the ground. There were cheers from some in the crowd, and silence from others. The guards rounded up the killer and his friends, and Arthur had them executed a few days later." I stopped there, not willing to talk about how I'd felt at the time. I wasn't angry with the killer for cheating—one look at him and I'd known that he would. I was angry with the dead man for allowing himself to be killed by such a deceitful bastard.

Later that day, Merlin had spoken to me about what had happened and asked how I'd have handled it differently if it had been my wife. *At night, sneak into the house of the man who had cheated with my wife, and kill him in his sleep.* If my answer had upset Merlin, he'd showed no outward signs of it, and within the week I was learning the ways of silent death.

"I thought Arthur was a benevolent man," Sara said, after hearing that he had people put to death.

"To people who deserved it, he *was* benevolent. But not to cowards who thought they could flaunt the rules as they liked. If the man had decided on armed combat, the end result would have probably been the same, but it would have been just. Arthur saw things in black and white. You were either right or wrong."

"You don't sound like you agreed with him."

"No, I saw things differently, more pragmatic. Still do, for the most part. But Arthur was stubborn and inflexible when it came to honor. It caused a few arguments between the knights."

"The knights?" Sara asked, eyes wide. "As in, 'of the round table'?"

"I don't remember a round table. Merlin made that up to make Arthur seem more impressive. But they were still knights, and all of equal rank, so in that regard the stories are correct. Not the knights you think of today, though, with their suits of armor. This was a few centuries before plate armor. They were elite warriors. And not all of them got on with Arthur. In fact, most argued on a regular basis."

"Were you a knight?"

"No, I was never afforded that privilege."

"Why?"

Because I had to be kept separate to ensure that whatever Merlin had me do would never tarnish Arthur's name or legend. But more than anything, because I was never knight material and never wished to be. But I kept that to myself, instead going with, "Many reasons."

Sara seemed to accept my answer and finished her drink, throwing the can into a nearby bin, before sitting next to me, her fingers brushing against mine. "Why did that girl have so many horrible things done to her? What did the killer gain from it?"

I'd been wondering when she was going to get around to asking me about what she'd witnessed and heard in the morgue. "No idea," I said. "But her death was different from the other victims. Everything done to her was to make a point, probably to Vicki, since they were a couple."

"It must have been horrific." Sara's voice was soft, barely above a whisper; she was evidently distressed.

"We'll find him and stop him."

"Do you think you can?"

Before I could answer, Olivia and Tommy emerged from out of the building, almost running in their haste. "Olivia had a call. There's been another body found," Tommy said as they hurried past.

I sighed. "This is where your involvement ends," I told Sara.
"I know," she said, with a nod. "Just go stop him. Don't let
anyone else suffer as Amber did."

The journey took nearly half an hour. Tommy stopped beside
two LOA agents, who directed us onto a dirt track that took us
deep into the New Forest.

It was pitch black under the trees. I didn't have time to stop
and use magic to allow me to see in the dark, so I turned on the
headlights and continued to follow Tommy at a low speed—my
bike was not made for off-road use, and the vibrations felt like
they were crushing the bottom of my spine.

A few hundred yards into the forest and the dirt path opened
into a large clearing with a dozen more agents milling around.
Huge floodlights had been erected at one side, bathing the entire
area in an almost daylight level of illumination.

I stopped the bike next to Tommy's truck, switched off the
engine, and removed my helmet as a man I recognized as the one
who'd pointed a gun at me back at the farmhouse walked toward
us. His name popped into my head, Agent Greaves.

"Oh good, the P.I.," he said when he saw Tommy get out of
the truck. Without a gun pointed at me, I got a proper look at
the agent. Greaves was a tall, thin man with a nasty scar along his
chin. His hair was long and flowed freely over his shoulders, and
there was mud splattered against the trousers of his expensive
suit. He didn't look happy to be searching the woods, and even
less so to see Tommy and me.

"We're here to help," Tommy said.

"Here to get in the fucking way," Greaves snarled. "You're only here because—"

"Because what?" Olivia called, accompanied by the sound of a car door slamming shut. No one spoke as she made her way toward the agent. "Please, Agent Greaves, feel free to enlighten us with your in-depth knowledge of LOA recruitment priorities."

If Agent Greaves were wise, he'd have said sorry and then shut up. Unfortunately, Agent Greaves was an idiot. "All I meant, ma'am, was that Tommy—"

"Agent, if you don't shut up and do your job, I will personally have you shipped somewhere very unpleasant for the next century. Are we clear?"

Agent Greaves darted from view like a deer escaping a hunter's wayward bullet.

"I want your opinion on this crime scene," Olivia said to me.

"Okay, so where's the body?"

Another agent, this one about my height, but without my stocky build, pointed toward the woods behind him and went back to talking to someone in blue scrubs with blood on his sleeves.

I grabbed some latex gloves and Tommy joined me in my trek. It had rained heavily in the area for a few hours, turning the ground to mud. Drenched ferns brushed against my jeans, and I wished I'd had some waterproofs with me. "You sure Sara will be okay?" I asked.

Tommy stopped and looked at me. We were alone; no one could hear us unless they really wanted to. "If she was anyone else, would you ask me that?"

I didn't need to say anything for Tommy to know the answer. "She reminds you of *her*, doesn't she?"

"Okay, moving on," I said and walked farther into the forest.

"Nate," Tommy said as he caught me up.

I spun around, unwilling to have the conversation go any further. "No, drop it. Now."

Tommy sighed, continuing the walk in silence. As we got farther from the clearing, I noticed that someone was sitting against a tree, her bare legs all that showed. The rest of the body was masked in darkness.

I breathed out and continued to the body, unsure of exactly what we would find.

At one point the girl had been beautiful. But as I looked down on her blood-soaked form, I saw that her beauty had been distorted with pain and fear. The back of her head rested against the tree's trunk. Her bare arms were tied behind the trunk with black plastic ties. Her skin was scratched and torn as she'd tried to fight her way free. There were no marks on her face, but her clothes were soaked through with blood. Leaves had stuck to her as the wind picked up.

"Untie her," I said softly.

"We can't until the LOA have finished."

I knelt in front of her and moved her blouse, which had once been light blue and was now a dark red, up from her stomach. The ragged wound it had hidden looked like her abdomen had been ripped open. I took a deep breath and lifted the blouse higher, exposing the entirety of what had been done to her.

The gash in her stomach stretched from one side to the other. Some intestine fell out with a wet noise and landed on the ground. I allowed the blouse to drop once more and got back to my feet. "I'm going to put money on her liver and kidneys being missing," I said.

"Like the others," Tommy replied.

"Let's go."

Tommy stared at the young woman a moment, then mimicked my nod before we walked away in silence, neither of us wishing to say anything until we reached Olivia.

We found her talking to the agent who had pointed us in the direction of the body. He saw me and smiled, offering his hand. "Martin Reid," he said.

"Nate," I said. "Nice to meet you." I removed the latex gloves and shook his hand. "Shame it had to be tonight."

He nodded his agreement as Olivia gathered more agents, including Greaves, around her. "So, Mister Garrett, please tell us what you found."

"Trial by fire," I said and looked around the dozen agents, most of whom certainly weren't that interested in knowing what I'd found, "Fair enough, but are you sure you want the audience?"

"I've explained to my agents that you will be helping with the investigation. And I'd rather you ask questions here than trying to find people at a later time."

"I do have a few questions, first," I said, and Olivia motioned for me to continue. "The woman's car."

"It's the blue piece of shit in the corner," Greaves said.

I turned to follow his directions and spotted the small blue Chevrolet something-or-other, their version of the Mini. I ignored Greaves' glare that followed me as I walked over to the car and examined it, checking the interior and doors. The keys were still in the ignition, and the driver's side door was open and her purse visible under the seat. "Well, it wasn't a robbery," I said as I rejoined the group.

"Good one," Greaves said. "How long do we have to listen to this idiot?"

Olivia shot him a glare and he shut up, but maintained his unhappy expression.

"She drove here herself," I said.

"Fucking idiot," Greaves whispered loud enough for everyone to hear.

My patience was wearing thin. "She was murdered where you found her, and once she was finally caught, she fought like crazy."

Greaves slow clapped.

"Look at the footprints in the soil here—the toe indentation is deeper than the heel. She was running. But the footprints from the passenger side are flat, normal. He stepped out of the car and then stalked after her. He was in no hurry. He knew she'd never get away."

"Anything else?" Olivia asked.

"He wasn't alone. As I said before, there are at least two people doing this. One is bringing the victim here, and one is killing them. That's probably why he was in no hurry to chase after her—he knew someone was waiting inside the woods. All the other victims were the same, apart from Amber. Her heart wasn't torn out.

"Also, it would have taken two people to tie her to that tree. She was fighting as they did it—the arm wounds show that. It's far too much hard work to do it alone; you might as well knock her out and do it then, but there's no head wound that I saw. You're looking for at least two men, not including Neil, who are working together. Amber is the only victim not eviscerated, and she didn't have any organs removed. This all goes back to Vicki."

"That's nothing we couldn't have gotten for ourselves," Greaves grumbled. "We're not fuck-ups."

"Well that's great," I snapped. "Because you have five dead women and a missing agent. Most people in your position would want every bit of help they could get, and right now you're more interested in point scoring. I'd say fuck-up sums you up quite nicely, wouldn't you?"

CHAPTER 13

While Agent Greaves shouted at Olivia about wanting to punch me, I'd taken the few moments alone to read more of the files that Olivia had presented me with back at my house. Each murder scene had the same details. The victims had driven themselves to the crime scene in their car, and any footprints around the scene showed one person running and another walking slowly.

"Don't care," I said as Olivia came toward me. "Greaves is a fucking idiot."

"He's also a good agent and you pissed him off."

We had more important things to discuss. "We're dealing with some highly dangerous people here. Stroking egos can wait."

Olivia sat on the bonnet of a Ford Focus RS, a bright orange car owned by one of the agents, and motioned for me to continue.

"People don't like you sitting on their cars like that," I said.

"It's Agent Greaves' car; he deserves it for being a dick."

I sat next to her.

"And you're right," Olivia said. "We need to stop these people before they kill again."

"We know that Neil is involved. He took the photos of those women, but like I said, he's not killing them. They're too different from his frenzy of violence. These are well planned and executed."

"We got an ID on this latest victim," Olivia said.

"That was fast."

She passed me a tatty passport. "We found it in her glove box."

The name on the drivers' license said Hilary Bingham. Her picture was one of smiles and beauty, and it was a face I recognized. "Fuck," I said softly and passed the license back. "She's in the photos on Neil's wall. He's taking pictures of these women for someone else to kill."

"It certainly appears that way, yes. But why go to the trouble of freeing Neil, giving him the money to buy a penthouse, and letting him live like a king, just so he can take a few photos for serial killers? And another thing. Why call the human authorities for the first few murders, before changing over to calling Agent Greaves? They must have been aware of our involvement, so why not start with the LOA?"

"They might have wanted more time before they had to deal with Avalon searching for them. The longer they only had the human police to contend with, the better for them."

A dark-blue Honda pulled up beside us, and Doctor Grayson stepped out. He appeared tired and haggard, weariness etched into every line of his face.

"Good evening," he said with as much enthusiasm as one could muster when having to examine murdered women.

"You two need to talk," Olivia said, pushing herself away from the car. "Tell him what's missing from the report, Doctor."

"Now, what could she be talking about, Doc?" I asked. Olivia had joined Tommy in whatever discussion was taking place out of earshot. I didn't have the time or effort to use magic in order to listen in. If it was anything important, Tommy would tell me later.

"Come with me," he said, putting on a pair of medical gloves. "You're going to want to see this."

There were a huge number of things I'd rather be doing then trudging back across an increasingly muddy pathway to watch a doctor examine a corpse, but I did it without complaining. No one wanted to be here. No one ever *wanted* to be at a murder scene.

Thankfully, since Tommy and I had examined Hilary, her body had been untied from the tree and placed inside a body bag and left on a gurney. Grayson unzipped the bag and began his examination with methodical, but solemn, professionalism.

Her arms were covered in deep scratches, and Grayson spotted me looking at one of them. "She was standing when she died," he said. "Those scratches are from the tree bark cutting into her as she slid to the ground with her arms still tied around the trunk."

"I noticed. I assume the cut across her abdomen was the killing strike."

Grayson shook his head. "With any other case, yes. It certainly would have killed her. But in this instance, she was already dead when it happened."

"What makes you say that?"

"All four previous victims were the same, one slice across the stomach, the liver and kidneys removed. But each of them had another wound, something I kept out of the reports at Director Green's request."

He gestured for me to examine five small puncture marks, just below Hilary's breast. "Needles?" I suggested.

Grayson removed a marker pen from his lab pocket and drew a ring around each mark, joining them together with an image of a hand.

"Someone's hand did this?" I asked.

"I've not looked at Amber yet, but the other victims had five marks like these. Each one stretched up slightly toward the heart, which also showed five puncture marks. The inside of the heart was black, decaying, as if infested with something. It didn't touch any of the other organs, except for the brain."

"So, why take the liver and kidneys?"

"Sustenance, I imagine. They're both good for you, full of vitamins and the like. Whoever did this probably needed the energy."

"So, we're looking for someone who can kill in that way, *and who then eats* parts of the victim to regain energy?"

"You understand why Director Green wanted this kept silent. Better that people think we have a crazy cannibal on our hands than someone who can kill in such a way."

I studied the puncture marks as my brain tried to figure out what could possibly have caused them. And why. It was a hard way to commit murder. It certainly wasn't a quick or quiet way to end someone's life.

"Anything else, Doc?" I asked.

"It's hard to give an exact time of death, but I would say about four to five hours ago."

I thanked him and, with a head full of information, went off to find Tommy. Instead, I found one of the agents who had been the contact for the killer. "Agent Reid," I said.

"Are you taking over the investigation?" he asked.

"Just a fresh set of eyes; I'm not trying to step on anyone's toes."

He raised an eyebrow. "You pissed some people off earlier. That would be akin to jumping up and down on peoples' toes."

"I get that a lot," I assured him. "Do you mind if I ask you a few things?"

"Go nuts."

"The killer, Olivia says he calls you."

"He calls Greaves," he corrected. "Usually a few hours after he's killed them. Greaves got the call just over an hour ago. We came here first, and then contacted Director Green."

"Greaves is a werewolf, yes?"

"Yes, I am," a rough voice snapped from behind me. "Is there a problem with that?"

I turned toward the surly man with a smile on my face. "No problems. I just wanted to know if you caught any scent."

"And I should tell you, why?" He jabbed a finger at me. I glanced down at the digit and wondered if I should break it.

"Agent," Olivia said, ending my pondering. "Tell us what you found."

Greaves stared a hole through me but did as he was asked. "I searched the woods in a few hundred yards circumference, and for the most part it's the same as always, a mixture of dozens of scents. It's impossible to distinguish between them."

"But?" Olivia asked.

"But, there's a stand-out scent from the north. It's faint, but definitely there."

"Can you tell what made it?" I asked.

"Usually no," he said. "I can pick out if something is human or rotting or some such, but not the exactly details of what carried out the crime. This time was different."

"In what way?" Olivia asked.

Greaves glanced at a newly arrived Tommy.

"Werewolf," Tommy whispered.

"It's faint," Greaves said, "but a wolf was here."

"Neil," I said. "Someone's getting sloppy."

"Any idea on where a werewolf running from the LOA might go to hide?" Olivia asked.

"The local pack," Tommy said. "And if he hasn't already gone to them for help, they'll have more information on where he's likely to hide."

"Then Greaves and Reid, head over to the local wolf pack, see what you can find out."

"That could be an issue," Greaves said.

"Why?" Olivia asked, in no mood for any stupidity.

"It's personal," Greaves said.

"Make it public," Olivia said, very near the end of her patience.

Greaves sighed deeply. "Their alpha has made it clear that I'm not welcome in the pack. If I go it would jeopardize the investigation, and in a worst-case scenario he might have me killed."

"I'm failing to see what the problem is," Olivia snapped. "Fine, you finish here, and then you'll go tell this poor girl's family that their daughter is dead. After that, you and Agent Reid will look into her past. I want anything linking her to any other victims. I don't care if it's only that they went to the same pub for a drink one time. I want to know about it, clear?"

"'Ma'am," the two agents said in unison before walking away.

"He really is a good agent," Olivia said to no one in particular. "He's just an arrogant ass."

"That leaves us with the werewolf pack, I assume?" I asked.

"I can't risk one of my agents turning up there and creating a war zone," Olivia said. "And anyone else with contacts within the pack is busy. Besides, Tommy knows the alpha well, so he should be cooperative."

"We'll get going, then," Tommy said. "You need a lift back?" he asked Olivia.

"I'm going to help out here and then go back to your place to see Kasey. Have you called her yet?"

He checked his watch. "It's a little after eight; I'll do it from the truck."

"Good. Now go, all of you. And please do your best to get something from this lead."

I sat on my bike and started the engine as Tommy waited idly next to me. "Is there something on your mind?" I asked.

"Olivia was right. The alpha and I are on good terms."

"But?"

"But, that might not be enough. This might get to be a really complicated evening for all of us."

I sighed and put my helmet on, lifting up the visor so I could speak. "Well, if I wanted an easy life, I'd have said no. Is the alpha likely to try and kill us?"

Tommy shook his head.

"Then we're good?"

Tommy's expression did not fill me with confidence.

After a few minutes on the road, the Bluetooth headset inside my helmet beeped with an incoming call, which I answered by pushing the button on my bike's handlebars. "Tommy," I said.

"How'd you know it was me?" he asked.

"Good guess. So, what's wrong?"

"Nothing. Kasey wanted me to tell you she's thought of some questions for the next time you meet."

I chuckled. "Excellent, I look forward to my inquisition. I haven't had one of those for a few hundred years."

There was silence for longer than I would have expected. I was about to ask if everything was alright when Tommy came back on the phone. "Nate, I have a bad feeling about this."

"Me, too," I said, as I switched lanes to overtake a caravan and catch up with Tommy, who had managed to get through some red lights before me, leaving me behind. "I saw Hilary's body. Whatever is doing this has a reason for picking the women he's killing. No one goes to that much trouble for random murders. But I'm suspicious that suddenly there's a distinct scent at a crime scene when all of the kill sites before were completely muddled. It shows sloppiness where none previously existed."

"An overconfident killer makes mistakes," Tommy pointed out.

"This guy has always been confident. He calls the LOA, for crying out loud! No one does that unless he's certain he's going to get away with it. And he has no reason to think he's going to get caught."

There's no blood or DNA register in Avalon. *A lot* of very bad things can be done with a person's blood and DNA, and no one would ever willingly give such samples. Anyone found keeping such samples from an Avalon member would be executed on the spot. So even if we found blood or DNA at the scenes, it would be more than useless.

Tommy was quiet for a few heartbeats as I narrowly avoided an idiot who had pulled out without watching where he was going. *Moron.*

"So what's the plan?" Tommy asked, distracting me from the anger I felt at the idiot, who was now behind me.

"You know the alpha best, what type of man is he?"

"He's honorable, usually fair and just. But don't piss him off, or underestimate him, he's more than capable of taking care of himself."

"What's his name?"

"Matthew Sheppard. He's somewhere around seven hundred years old, although no one knows much of his past. He's not exactly forthcoming with the details."

"Will he help us?"

Tommy pulled up to the front gate of a sizeable field. Two large men stood guard at the entrance, and Tommy spoke to one of them before the other pulled the gate open and we entered, their stares boring into my back as I went by.

Tommy drove toward the dozens of cars that sat in the field, and parked. I stopped the bike next to him and noticed that the two guards were still following our movements. I picked up a third and fourth walking around the rows of cars. Every now and then they glanced over in a nonchalant way, making them appear anything other than nonchalant.

"We need to make our way to those trees over there," Tommy said. "It's a few minutes' walk through them into a large clearing. That's where everyone will be."

From the number of cars littering the field, I figured there were nearly a hundred people waiting in that clearing. And I was suddenly very aware of how exposed the two of us were, standing in the middle of a field. "So?" I asked again. "Will Matthew help us?"

We walked away from the cars, and Tommy remained silent until we reached the woods. "If he thinks that someone in his pack is responsible," he said, "he'll kill them himself."

CHAPTER 14

"**W**e're here to see Matthew," Tommy said to the big man who barred our way.

"The *alpha* is busy," the man said, holding out his hand palm first to ensure that we moved no further.

Behind him dozens of people milled about, drinking, eating, and talking to one another. Everyone was still in human form, and, unlike the last pack meet I'd been to, no one appeared to have been murdered and left on the floor. Yet. In the center of the clearing a huge fire roared as it roasted two large hogs. Two other hogs had already been cooked and were being picked clean by the hungry revelers. More food was placed on a long table that was at least twenty feet long. It reminded me of the old banquets we'd had in Camelot many centuries previous.

"It's Avalon business," Tommy tried.

The man laughed. "Fuck your Avalon, and fuck you, too."

"Your alpha would want to see us," Tommy said again, his tone hard as stone.

Violence was coming, and the three large men sitting nearby knew it; they stood as one and walked toward us. My body tensed to put them down as hard and fast as possible.

"Enough of this foolishness," a man's voice boomed from somewhere behind the three goons, and they turned and bowed their head in unison, parting to allow a slender man through. He was no taller than me, and a good ten inches shorter than the monster who had tried to bar our entry, but he was lean with muscle and had a quiet power that rolled over him in waves.

He brushed his long dark hair from his shoulders, never even glancing at the three men who had parted for him, and they all made sure they were doing something else as fast as possible. Despite the cool weather and moist ground, he was barefoot and topless, and showed no signs of either bothering him.

"Go back to your kennel, Randal. I can hear your master calling you," the newcomer said.

The meat mountain known as Randal flinched as if slapped. "You are my alpha; I obey you in all things."

Matthew turned to stare at Randal. "Do not insult my intelligence. Now, leave my sight."

Randal skulked away and the alpha, Matthew, turned to face Tommy. There was a slight tension between them for a few seconds, and then they both burst into smiles and embraced one another.

"My brother," Matthew said, slapping Tommy on the shoulder. "You don't come here often enough."

Tommy looked upset, but the smile returned a moment later. "This isn't a social visit."

"I understand, but still, it's good to see you. Although, I'm not exactly dressed to greet new friends." Matthew motioned to his bare torso, which could have been used to break rocks. His gaze settled on me. "You must be Nate. I heard what you did in Canada."

"They were slaughtering people for fun," I said. "I did what needed to be done."

Matthew continued to stare at me and I tensed for a fight.

"No smile or warm hug?" I asked. "How about you flex those pecks for me, I bet it just melts hearts."

"You mock me?" he asked me with a raised eyebrow.

"I mock everyone else, why would you be special?"

Instead of throwing a punch or telling me to fuck off, he laughed and grabbed me in a hug. "Tommy said you weren't one to let stupid shit pass. I'm sorry for winding you up. You are welcome here as if you were one of my pack."

I was genuinely surprised. Alphas don't usually allow anyone from outside the pack to enter when a meet is on. It's considered a secret, and in some cases, a sacred thing. But I got the impression that he wasn't the gambling type, and a quick glance around confirmed that at least four wolves were watching me intently.

"Nice security," I said, breaking up a conversation between Tommy and Matthew.

"How many did you see?" Matthew asked.

"Four," I said.

Matthew raised his eyebrows in surprise. "Most don't manage more than two."

"I'm not like most people," I pointed out.

"That may be true, but you still missed one."

I followed his pointing finger, turned around and noticed the tiny glint of moonlight touching a lens high up in a tree nearly three hundred yards to my side. Sniper rifle. "Impressive."

"Not for anyone who crosses me."

The warning was there for all to hear, but before I could retort he strolled off, waving Tommy and me to join him. "Try not to get into a pissing contest," Tommy said. "He's not a push over."

"I have no intention of getting into any sort of contest with him. I can't help it, but I like the guy."

"He has that effect on people."

"On you, too?"

"It's why I'm not the current alpha. I don't want to have to kill him."

Matthew led us past the clearing and through some more woods, the whole time flanked by two werewolves who did their best to maintain a respectful distance, despite their obvious unease at having newcomers around.

After a few hundred yards of woods, we exited into a second clearing that contained a massive bungalow, which I assumed was Matthew's home, and a short distance away from it was...part of a castle. An actual castle. Admittedly, it was only a twelve-foot-high portion of a rampart, but the tower behind it rivaled the trees for height, and it was still a damn castle. And unless you were standing in front of it, you'd never even know it existed.

"Come, this way," Matthew beckoned and we continued toward the bungalow. The interior lights were ablaze, and a few more people, both men and women, were clearly visible inside, with armed guards, male and female, stationed around the property.

"You don't take any chances," I said.

"I have to protect my entire pack," he replied. "And it wasn't that long ago my kind was at war."

"That war ended centuries ago," I said.

Matthew nodded to the guards and opened his front door. The warmth from inside was a welcome addition as we all stepped inside and removed our coats, hanging them on pegs beside the front door.

"Our kind fought werelions for millennia," he said. "Far too many died, and there are people on both sides who would like to gain retribution for those they lost."

"It was a needless war, fought by idiots," a man said from the end of the hallway. He appeared to be about forty years old and wore a dark blue suit. He also leaned on a walking stick, an unusual sight for a werewolf. "Matthew gives too much gravitas to what happened. There was no honor or justice in that war, and now it's over. May peace remain always."

"Not everyone thinks as you do," Matthew said. "Hence the protection."

The man scoffed at him. "No one with a brain would attack you. You run one of the largest packs in Europe and are a member of the Avalon council."

"It's those with only half a brain that I fear most," Matthew said before turning back to Tommy and me. "Anyway, welcome to my home."

"Thank you," Tommy said. "It's very impressive."

And indeed it was. The hallway was very tasteful, with no dead animals or weaponry displayed proudly—unlike the last alpha's home I'd set foot in. Instead, there were photographs, dozens of them, taken from what appeared to be all over the world. Each one of a different and magnificent view.

"Did you take these photos yourself?"

"I spent many years walking the world," Matthew said. "I only came back to England a few years ago."

He took us through the door at the far end of the hallway and into an expansive, open-planned room. It contained a huge circular coffee table surrounded by red couches. Bay windows looked out over the front of the property.

"I guess I should introduce *myself*," the man with the walking stick said.

"Forgive me," Matthew said. "This is Gordon Summers, my pack aide."

I shook hands with Gordon, and then he embraced Tommy, much like Matthew had. "You should not have come, Thomas."

"Tommy," he corrected. "And I didn't have a choice."

"Still, Elijah will discover that you were here, and he will not be happy."

"Who's Elijah?" I asked.

"An asshole," Gordon and Tommy said in unison before laughing.

"We'd best be quick then, hadn't we," Matthew said.

We all took seats on the couches and Gordon left the room, returning with three bottles of beer and a can of Coke, which he gave to Matthew. "I don't drink," the alpha said as if he needed to explain his lack of alcohol to us.

I opened my beer and savored the coolness as it ran down my throat while Tommy explained the situation to Gordon and Matthew. Once he'd finished, Matthew sighed and rubbed his neck with one hand, a pained expression on his face. "Well, that's going to cause a problem," he said.

"I'm sorry for asking," Tommy said. "But we need to find Neil Hatchell, and you're the only pack for a hundred miles."

"*That man* is not a member of my pack," Matthew said. He stood, walked over to the bay window, and closed the blinds.

"I understand your coming here, but I can't let you just walk around my pack until you get a smell that fits."

"You know him, don't you?" I asked Matthew.

"He's a violent little prick who would have been skinned alive if I'd have gotten my way. And there's no way on earth I would have allowed him to use my pack to keep him safe."

"Maybe he's under another's protection?" I suggested. "Someone within the pack who wants to undermine you?"

Matthew thought for about ten seconds before a flash of anger came over him. "Elijah, you fucking idiot," he snapped to himself. "I will not have rapists and murderers in my pack."

"So Elijah took him under his protection," Tommy ventured.

"You must be sure of this, Matthew," Gordon said. "Accusing Elijah without evidence would only cause more problems."

"Why don't you just kill Elijah if he's that much of an affront?" I asked.

"Politics," Matthew almost spat.

Each alpha normally takes a selection of people as his council, elder wolves who have experience and power but who couldn't be an alpha by themselves. He also takes a female alpha, someone who takes charge in his absence and deals with a lot of the day-to-day issues. The fact that I hadn't seen a female alpha was a little odd.

"When I ascended to the position of alpha, I removed several of the wolves chosen by my predecessor, as they were more interested in their own power than that of the pack. I assume you saw those men and women through the windows as we walked up to the house?"

I nodded. "So, who are they?"

"They're my council. Gordon did not know that I was planning on bringing you both back here. Once he found out, he had them retire to the rear of the property to await my instructions. I'm sure that Gordon will voice his disapproval of my actions once you've left.

"But my point is that those men and women are utterly loyal to both me and the pack. Elijah is not. He is loyal only to himself. And he has aligned himself with those others whom I removed from my council, the same wolves who were upset that I appointed a two-hundred-year-old werewolf as my aide."

As one, Tommy and I all turned to Gordon.

"Two-hundred-and-three," he said with a smile. "I was forty-four when I was turned."

"Why do you need a cane then?" I asked.

"Silver bullet in the hip, but I got the bastard."

Tommy laughed, but the expression on Gordon's face told me that the memory was not a pleasant one.

"Gordon, can you bring Ellie in? I think she's going to want to hear about this."

Gordon immediately left the room.

"Elijah wants the pack, doesn't he?" I asked, after getting back on subject.

Matthew shook his head. "Elijah is no alpha, and he could never hold the pack. But his son has the makings of becoming a strong warrior, possibly even alpha material. Elijah hopes to maintain the pack's strength and position himself in a useful role until such a time as his son can challenge me and win."

"So if you order him to hand over Neil, it could cause problems," Tommy said.

"Unfortunately, yes. I can't allow him to split my pack. Those men who were blocking you from entering earlier, Randal and his friends, they would gladly take the opportunity to hurt people."

"Is there anything you *can* do?" I asked.

"There's always something," Matthew assured me as the door re-opened and Gordon stepped inside, accompanied by a striking young woman. She wore dark fatigues and a gray hoodie with a pink skull and crossbones on the front. Her long dark-blue hair tumbled over her slender shoulders.

"Ellie," Matthew said, motioning to the chair nearby.

She sat without a word, but constantly glanced past her alpha to Tommy and me, probably wondering what the hell was going on.

"There's something I need to tell you," Matthew said and wasted no time in explaining who Tommy and I were and why we were there. The mention of Neil's name caused Ellie to ball her hands into tight fists and her eyes to harden, but she remained seated and continued to listen to Matthew without interruption.

When he'd finished, she took a deep breath. "What do you need?" she asked.

"I can't order Elijah to hand Neil over to Tommy and Nate without a fight. But you have a claim on Neil's life. One I intend to use if it comes to it. When I give the word, I want you to claim Neil's life as forfeit."

"Does that mean I get Neil?" Ellie asked with a wicked glint in her eye.

Matthew shook his head. "I'm afraid not. I know I can't make you give him to Tommy, and you more than deserve your retribution, but Tommy needs Neil."

"I promise you, he'll get what he deserves," Tommy said.

"I've heard that before," she said bitterly.

"We have one more problem," Gordon said.

I sighed; werewolf politics was making my head hurt. "Yes?"

"Elijah will be most displeased to see Tommy; it will not end well I'm sure."

"Why?" I asked Tommy.

He didn't appear to be happy to have to answer the question. "I've not been entirely honest," he eventually told me. "I'm not a pack member, because if I was, I would have to challenge for alpha. I'm too powerful for Matthew and I to coexist in the same pack. Pack members already come to me for help, and Matthew allows it because I have no desire to replace him."

"But..." I said.

"But, there are people here, mostly the same ones who want Matthew gone, who believe that my involvement undermines the alpha. They want me to either go and never return, or fight for the leadership." He turned to Gordon. "Neither of which is going to happen."

Gordon bowed his head slightly.

"So let me get this straight," I started. "Elijah is probably hiding the man we're looking for, and Ellie can demand that he hand Neil over, but in exchange for this, he and his supporters will try to force Tommy to challenge for the leadership."

"In a nutshell, yes," Matthew said. "He considers Tommy less of a threat. No offence."

"None taken," Tommy said. He downed the rest of his beer and stood. "Well, let's get this over with. Where's Elijah?"

A smile tugged at the sides of Gordon's lips. "He's been confined to his tent. He has one specially prepared and puts it away from the festivities, but close enough to Matthew's home that he can know all who come and go."

"The tent outside?" Tommy said. "He's a little brazen."

"He's pushing his boundaries," Matthew said with a slight growl. "And I'm close to pushing back."

"Matthew," Gordon said. "Do not allow him to do that."

Matthew calmed in an instant. "I was just voicing my displeasure." He stood and sighed. "Let's go fetch the little turd." He walked out of the room, his aide closing the door as he left after him.

"So, Tommy, what's likely to happen?"

"I will not fight Matthew," Tommy flatly replied.

"Leaving the options as…?"

"Elijah will want something. He's a snake, and he'll have a dozen scenarios in his head by the time he gets here. We just have to ensure he gets what he wants without crossing any lines."

"You don't think he'll hand Neil over to you even if he has to obey my right to justice?" Ellie asked. "That…evil…*cunt* of a man raped and beat me for fun. He turned me into a werewolf, not as some great gift bestowed upon me, but because he knew it would cause me pain and suffering. Elijah will hand Neil over, even if I have to tear him from his grubby little paws."

"Oh, he'll hand Neil over," Tommy said. "But he'll want something in return."

"How many of Neil's victims are in this pack?" I asked Ellie.

"Two," she said. "Melody had a harder time accepting what she'd become; she tends to stay away from the larger pack meets. I want you to promise me something. Promise me that he'll get what he deserves, that he'll never see the light of day again. I want him to spend the rest of his life rotting in a pit somewhere. Can you do that?"

"We'll do our best," Tommy said.

"I guess that will have to do," Ellie said, although she didn't look happy about it.

"Is there anything we need to know about Elijah?" I asked.

"Don't threaten him," Tommy said. "He'll see it as a sign of weakness and refuse to help. He responds to sickly sweet compliments, money, and power. The man would spend all day in wolf form licking his own cock if he could do it unnoticed."

"Maybe he just needs some time alone," I joked.

Before we could talk more, the door opened and Matthew strode back in, exuding yet more power than he had before. Gordon was directly behind him, and he held the door open as a thin man walked into the room and draped his coat over Gordon's shoulder, much to the aide's irritation.

"Put that somewhere, will you?" the man said. I wondered how he and his ego could occupy the same point in space and time without creating a black hole of arrogance.

"Elijah, please take a seat," Matthew said. "Drink?"

"No, thank you, I brought my own," he clicked his fingers, and Randal stepped into the room holding a glass of champagne.

"Would you like some?" Elijah asked Matthew, clearly aware that his alpha would turn him down.

"Some other time," Matthew said with no hint of annoyance. He had incredible self-control; I'd only known Elijah for a few seconds, and I already wanted to tear his head off by his short brown hair.

"Tommy," Elijah said.

"You can call me Thomas, or Mister Carpenter," Tommy said.

"My apologies, I assumed you had people call you Tommy."

"My friends do, yes," he said.

If Elijah had been a bird, he would have ruffled his feathers in annoyance, but he soon regained his composure. "And I see you have one of your council members here," he said, going to Ellie and extending his hand. "Nice to see you, my dear. I assume your friend is too busy being terrified of herself to make the effort of coming tonight. I'll send her some flowers to tell her how much she was missed."

Ellie smiled, but neither stood nor took Elijah's hand. "I'm sure she would love them very much."

Elijah smiled as if he hadn't been rebuffed. "And you?" he asked me.

About a million fake names flashed through my mind, as did a few dozen ways in which I could tell him to fuck off. "Nate," I said not wishing to antagonize the situation.

"A human," Elijah said to Matthew with disdain. "Are you slumming it, or is he the new pet?"

"Mind your tongue," Matthew said, his tone ever so slightly hardening.

"My apologies," Elijah bowed his head slightly. "I am only here to discover why you summoned me."

"Tommy is here from the LOA on business. I wish for you to help them in any way you can."

"You work for Avalon now?" Elijah asked Tommy. "I thought that was the duty of your lady friend."

"She asked me to come here on her behalf, as I have history with the pack," Tommy said.

"Ah, an understandable decision for a lady in her position to take."

Tommy opened his mouth to snap something, but wisely thought better of it. "We're looking for Neil Hatchell in relation to a murder case. Do you know where he is?"

"Of course, poor Neil came to me after being attacked in his own home. He was alone and afraid. Worried that some pack thug would take his past into account and kill him."

"We need to find him."

"No."

"I'm sorry?" Tommy said.

"Did you not hear me? Are you deaf or a moron?" Elijah snapped. "I said no. I will not help you find an innocent were-wolf so that Avalon can pin crimes on him."

"Like the rapes and murders that he went to the Hole for?" I asked.

"I don't speak to lesser creatures," he said to me. "The adults are talking."

I suddenly didn't care about the rules, or what we needed—I was going to kill him. But Gordon's vice-like grip on my arm reminded me of the more important reasons for us being there, and I calmed.

"I order you to help," Matthew said.

"Order! You order me, when you can't even keep Tommy here from coming back to the pack whenever he feels like it." Elijah leapt to his feet. "If he wants to be here, he needs to challenge for leadership. And until you can make him bow to you, I see no reason to do anything you say."

Matthew didn't say anything, but one second he was standing by the window, the next he had Elijah by the throat and had slammed him onto the coffee table. "You come into my home and tell me of the law. I'm within my rights to tear out your throat."

"And start a civil war," Elijah managed to croak.

Matthew released the taller man and moved away, giving the barest nod to Ellie, and allowing Elijah to stand and readjust his suit. His face betrayed none of the anger or shame I was certain he felt at being put in his place in front of those he considered beneath him.

Ellie stood and stared at Elijah. "I claim Neil in the name of retribution."

Elijah blinked in what I assumed was surprise. "You're the other woman that Neil…my, that is a surprise. Matthew kept that little piece of information quiet."

"You cannot keep him from *me*," Ellie said. "You've already admitted you have him. And by the rights of werewolf law, I can claim his life as forfeit."

Elijah's smirk wasn't the response I'd expected. "Oh, Matthew, is this your plan? Have the girl claim him?" Elijah tutted, as if scolding a child. "You're right, I have to hand Neil over to *her*, but there's nothing that says when I have to do it."

"What do you want, Elijah?"

"I want to bring you down a peg or two, and I want Tommy to finally decide where he stands. Did he even bring a gift?"

"I'm here on Avalon business," Tommy said.

"No matter," Elijah snapped. "Tommy has disrespected you, and you allow this to stand."

"What gift should he have brought?" Gordon asked.

"It's too late now, but there is a way to save the situation."

"Make your point," Matthew demanded.

"If you want Neil so badly, you will fight for him, champion against champion, and I will consider this matter settled. No matter the outcome, Neil is yours afterward." He walked over to Randal and tapped him on the arm. "My boy here will be a match for Tommy."

"I won't fight for you, just to get one over on Matthew," Tommy said. "That's not going to happen."

"Then Tommy will be banished from entering this pack for any reason," Elijah said with a smirk.

"Avalon's rules state that I can nominate someone to fight in my place," Tommy told him.

Elijah followed Tommy's gaze. "The human?" He asked, laughing hard. "Oh, this *will* be a quick fight."

It took me a moment to realize that he meant me.

"And, since you're so keen on playing by Avalon's rules, Matthew," Elijah said. "I invoke the Accords." And with that he stormed from the room with Randal in tow.

CHAPTER 15

"**W**ould anyone like to tell me what the hell is going on?" Ellie asked.

Elijah's challenge had created an avalanche of activity as people came and went, all giving Matthew advice on the best course of action to take. Several of the council elders had just left when Ellie asked her question.

"Elijah has challenged me to a fight," Tommy said. "If I'd accepted and won, I would have risen in the ranks of the pack and been too close to threatening Matthew for alpha. If I lost, I'd be banished. My only option was to pick Nate to fight in my stead."

"Yeah, he's going to fight Randal. Which is insane, by the way," Ellie said with a sigh. "But I meant the Accords. I've been a werewolf for a while now, but this is the first I've heard of them."

"About three thousand years ago there was a war," I said. "It was fought between a number of different species, but the end result was the same—tens of thousands, probably hundreds of thousands, died. Merlin and those who held the most influence said 'never again' and created the Accords.

"The Accords allow anyone who lives under Avalon rule to challenge any other to a one-on-one fight. The person challenged picks the type of fight and the rules. Entire wars, from that moment on, were settled with one fight. Something even humans decided to take up on occasion. It didn't always work, but it stopped various species from trying to wipe each other out on a regular basis."

"Why hasn't anyone ever mentioned it to me?" Ellie asked Matthew.

"Because it's unprecedented that the Accords be invoked at a pack meet. I've certainly never heard of it happening, and since your involvement with Avalon is limited, it wasn't something that came up. It's usually only used when war is about to be declared. I certainly didn't expect it tonight."

"I'm still foggy on, A, why I was picked, and B, how I'm meant to fight a werewolf without my magic," I interjected.

"Sorry, Nate," Tommy said. "I was sort of put in a corner. I couldn't pick another pack member, and we can't really wait for someone outside of the pack to turn up. If Randal beats you, his stock won't rise by much as you're not a werewolf; by extension, that means that Elijah doesn't gain much either. But *when* you win, the same is true of you and me."

"If Elijah gains so little from my defeat, why bother?"

"He expected *me* to fight. He certainly didn't expect that I'd choose you, Nate. Elijah probably thought he could be rid of either me or Matthew depending on how the fight ended."

"Fighting werewolves without magic isn't exactly my idea of a good time, though."

"You're a sorcerer?" Ellie asked, shocked. "Why can't I smell any magic on you?"

"I haven't used any for a while, so you can't smell it. I'm hoping I can use that to an advantage, somehow."

"So, you get to pick the rules?" Ellie asked me.

I nodded. "No weapons, powers, or abilities of any kind are the only constant rule among all fights. That includes Randal's wolf or beast forms. But it doesn't really matter, as he can still use his natural strength and speed. And I'm not in the same league as a werewolf on those terms."

"Randal is especially brutal, too," Gordon said, offering me no help whatsoever.

"There is another problem," Matthew said. "You will have to lose the fight."

"I'm sorry, what?" I asked.

"If you win, it will increase Tommy's standing. A loss will not hurt Tommy, and while it will give Elijah a small elevation in stature, it will not harm the pack long term."

"Losing shouldn't be too hard," I said. "He only has to hit me once with his full strength and I'm not going to want to get back up."

Matthew shook his head. "You will have to make it look good or there will be cries of a fix."

"You *are* trying to fix it," I pointed out, but no one wanted to listen to logic.

"So what are your stipulations?" Gordon asked me.

I hadn't even thought about it. Fighting a werewolf without magic was not something I wished to do, even if he was only allowed to stay in human form. "First one who quits or is unable to answer a five count."

"That will require a referee," Matthew said.

"Good, I choose Gordon. He has no love of Elijah, and when he raises Randal's hand no one will think it was rigged. Besides, I want someone in there to make sure Randal doesn't *accidentally* kill me."

"I'll take care of that," Matthew said. "But your request is accepted. Gordon will referee the contest."

As more details of where the fight would be, and what time, were hashed out, I decided to use the time to leave the room and find my way to the kitchen. Gordon had given me directions and told me to have a drink, so it didn't take too long to locate the spacious and bright kitchen at the rear of the property.

I found a bottle of juice in the fridge, grabbed a glass from a stack nearby, and sat down to drink.

"You worried?" Ellie asked from the doorway.

"Concerned. Part of me just wants to use magic and get it done, but the storm of shit Tommy and Matthew would have to go through afterward would tear your pack apart."

"Randal's a mean son of a bitch; he's going to go out there to hurt you any way he can."

"I know," I said and finished my apple juice. "I'll be fine. It's not exactly my first fight in the Accords. First against a werewolf, though."

"Yeah, well, Elijah wants to use you as an example. I don't know you, but Tommy and Matthew both seem to like you, so be careful."

"I will, I promise."

"And if you get the chance to hurt Randal, please feel free to take it. Just because you have to throw the fight doesn't mean you have to make it easy for him."

I chuckled. I was beginning to like this woman.

Within the hour, I was taken from the comfort of the bungalow, back into the woods surrounding the property, and into the clearing we'd passed through when first entering the camp.

A few more minutes' walk and we reached a third clearing, this one with a pit dug deep into the ground.

Most of the pack stood around talking as Randal, still wearing his jeans and a t-shirt, kicked and shadow punched at the wooden posts that lined one side of the massive pit. Occasionally, he looked back at his supporters and raised his hand in mock victory. He didn't appear to be taking me seriously.

"Remember," Tommy said, as I removed my coat and hooded top and passed them to him, "make it look real."

"I don't think that's going to be a fucking problem," I said, and dropped down into the arena.

From above, the pit was imposing. From inside, staring up at the dozens of wolf-beast forms all baying for action as they stood fifteen feet above me, it was nerve wracking.

I took a moment to scan my surroundings. The pit was about the same size as two boxing rings put next to one another, with a rope ladder at one end so that people could climb out. The sides were concreted to stop the pit from collapsing under the weight of the people atop it, and the floor was covered in wooden planks.

"I'm going to fucking crush you," Randal said, and punched the concrete wall to emphasize his point.

"Wolves," Matthew bellowed. "Tonight Elijah has invoked the Accords to challenge Tommy, naming Randal as his champion. Tommy has chosen his friend, Nate, to fight for him."

There were a few sniggers at that. The idea of a human fighting a werewolf was laughable, but Matthew continued as if they were silent. "This fight will be until either competitor taps out or cannot answer a five count. My own aide, Gordon, will officiate."

"Fix," someone shouted from the back.

"The next person who questions my aide's integrity will answer *my* challenge."

Silence dropped like a rock.

"There will be no deaths in this fight," he stared at Randal as he spoke. "Anyone breaking that rule will find his own life forfeit. However, if either combatant cheats, his opponent may deal whatever retribution he sees fit."

I saw Randal's face pale; he wasn't happy about that.

"And now the spoils," Elijah shouted. "If you win, I will give you Neil, alive and well, within the hour. If you lose, you will get Neil at a time and place of my choosing."

"And what do you want?" Matthew asked.

Elijah pointed at Ellie. "Her."

"Fuck that," Ellie snapped, and Elijah laughed.

"That's the plan, little one," he sneered. "Repeatedly."

A lot of the murmurs above me, from both the men and women, and they did not sound happy with Elijah's demands.

I glanced behind me and saw Ellie and Tommy drop down into the pit. Ellie waved me over, "We can't say no," she whispered. "He'll tell us there's no chance of him helping anytime soon. He's only asked for me as his price to humiliate Matthew further. I'm a member of his council, and after what Neil did, Matthew is sworn to protect me."

"Can you beat that piece of shit over there?" Tommy asked.

"He's a big bag of rage—if I can get him angry, he'll fuck up. Then he's mine."

"I agree," Ellie shouted, to the surprise of everyone, especially Matthew, who seethed with anger from the moment Elijah had demanded Ellie as his prize.

"Nate, slight change of plan," Tommy said quietly. "Kick the shit out of him."

I looked over at Randal, who was arguing with Gordon about something, and then turned back to Tommy. "Good, because after what Elijah just said, that was pretty much the plan anyway."

CHAPTER 16

While Ellie and Tommy left the pit, there was some more posturing from a few of the wolves above who were unimpressed with one rule or another. I used the time to prepare for what, I was sure, would be a hard fight. With magic it would have been over in less than ten seconds; without magic…well, that was a harder proposition. Eventually, Matthew silenced them with a raised hand.

Randal took that as a cue to walk toward me, cracking his knuckles in anticipation. "I'm going to break you, little man."

"Good luck with that," I told him with a smile.

"When you're ready," Matthew said, and Randal struck immediately, kicking out at me with all of his substantial weight.

It was sloppy and easily dodged by stepping back and to the side, ensuring that all Randal struck was fresh air.

He didn't give up easily and threw a punch, but once again I was already gone by the time he reached me. I moved around him and kept my distance, and Randal quickly got angry at his lack of immediate success.

Out the corner of my eye, I saw Gordon maintaining his distance. He didn't want to get in the middle of a fight, and I doubted Randal would willingly tell the difference between combatant and referee if he got the chance.

"You can't run forever," Randal said as he stalked toward me. I winked at him.

He roared and charged me, his arms open, ready to engulf and crush. I quickly rolled aside, but Randal was faster than I'd anticipated, and he grabbed my leg just below the knee, twisting it and pulling me off the ground with ease. He launched me across the pit, and I slammed into the concrete wall on the far side.

All the air left my body in one rush, as my ribs and back screamed in pain. I fell to the ground, causing my ribs to yell once more. For the briefest of moments a voice inside my head said, *you can't win this.* I shook my head again and got back to my feet, but an instant later Randal was beside me, raining down kicks and punches as I dropped to my knees and tried to avoid or block what I could.

When one punch sailed past my nose, I grabbed his wrist, using his momentum against him and slammed his face into the concrete wall.

I smashed my elbow into his knee, and he cried out in muffled anguish. Another shot, to his stomach, caused the air to rush from his lungs and he dropped to the ground in pain as I got back to my feet.

Randal wasn't finished. He shoved me away with enough force to lift me from the ground and dump me a few feet back. I rolled with the impact and came back on my feet in time to watch Randal get back to his. Blood trickled from his nose and he wiped it with one hand, leaving a bloody smear across his face.

And he charged me again.

I didn't roll. I barely moved until the very last second, when I stepped aside and caught Randal by the elbow, bending the arm up and back until it was past his head. Gravity did the rest, taking him off his feet and slamming him head first into the wooden floorboards, which cracked from the impact.

"Give up," I said, locking Randal's elbow behind him. When he didn't reply, I placed one foot on his shoulder and wrenched until it popped. Only then did I let go.

Randal screamed in pain, his left arm totally useless. But still, he wouldn't give up. Instead, he rolled to his good side and forced himself back to a standing position.

"I was worried this would be hard," I said with a smile, which faded as Randal grabbed his arm and forced it back into the socket with a grin.

He sprinted toward me and caught me with a punch.

It wasn't that I didn't defend myself. I'd put myself in the position to block the punch, but the power behind it lifted me from my feet and almost spun me in the air before dropping me back onto the ground with a thud that took my breath away.

As I tried to get back to my feet, Randal kicked out at my elbow, and it buckled from the blow. A kick to my head put spots in my vision, and I moved as fast as possible to get away, but it wasn't fast enough to avoid a second kick, which glanced against my shoulder.

Randal grabbed the back of my shirt and hoisted me to my feet, pushing me up against the concrete wall and punching me in the jaw. My vision was too fucked up to defend myself properly.

Randal's punch to my solar plexus dropped me to my knees as I fought for breath. I desperately wanted to tear him in half with my magic.

"You're going to die in here," he whispered into my ear as the crowd directly above us roared its approval. "You won't be the first. I've taken people in here before to teach them lessons. Sometimes they don't make it out, but if they do, they always remember. You're going to be one of the unfortunate ones."

The pain in my stomach had subsided enough for me to speak, "You're a fucking idiot." I head butted him on the bridge of the nose with everything I had.

Randal staggered back, holding his face, which streamed with blood, allowing me to get back to my feet.

"Don't ever taunt someone you have at your mercy," I said and slammed my fingers into his exposed throat.

He immediately dropped to his knees and struggled to breathe.

The thought of those Randal had murdered in the very place where I stood sent a cold anger flowing through me.

Randal spat on the floor and pulled himself upright, his breathing still labored. And I caught him on the jaw as he rose to his full height.

I'm pretty strong, certainly stronger than any human, but there was no way I should have been able to knock down a werewolf with one punch to the jaw without the help of magic. Randal crashed to the ground like a sack of bricks, and the shouts from above died immediately.

I stalked over to my opponent as he shook his head free of the cobwebs, and I pulled him back to his feet by his collar, slamming him into the concrete behind us, much like he'd done to me only moments ago. Unlike him, I wouldn't give him time.

I kicked his knee out, dislocating it, and immediately smashed my own knee into his stomach, and then into his face as he dropped. His jaw broke, but he refused to go down. Another punch to his eye ended his fight, and probably his ability to see anything.

He tried to shove me away once more, but I kicked his arm aside, rolling him onto his back. And then I started punching him, over and over again, starting on his stomach and working my way up his torso. The punches came with inhuman speed, each one breaking bones and tearing ligaments until I reached his face, where I destroyed what remained. And when I was finally finished, I stepped back and looked up at Elijah.

"Is that what you wanted?" I shouted at him as the rage inside of me screamed for me to kill Randal, to send a message.

I turned back to my prone opponent, to find him darting toward me. I dodged too late and he slid a knife between my ribs, before he crashed back to the floor.

Someone above me screamed. I had no idea who—the wound took all of my attention. The knife had been silver and the pain inside me was like a fire. I dropped to the ground, and the black marks on my chest came to life. Not too long ago there had been six of them, each one a Blood magic curse designed to do things long since hidden to me. Two of them had vanished, and the use of one was still unknown to me, but the other had uncovered a hidden depth of power that I'd been unwilling to tap into. Until now.

Blood magic glyphs flared, the dark marks covering my arms and chest. More screams sounded from above and then all I felt was calm as my magic went to work healing my wound.

The pain subsided in seconds, the wound closing soon after. I had no idea how I'd managed it, or how it was even possible to heal a silver wound that quickly, but I didn't care. The blood glyphs left me, and glyphs of pure white crossed up my arms, taking their place. I got back to my feet, and glanced over at Gordon who was screaming at Elijah about Randal being a cheat.

Randal was getting back to his feet, his face a mess of ground meat.

I created a sphere in my palm, using my fingers to make it spin rapidly as I placed more and more air magic inside it. When it contained enough, I ran at Randal and drove the sphere into his chest with everything I had. And then I released it.

The devastation was total. The magic that engulfed Randal whirled and roared, swallowing whatever screams might have escaped Randal's mouth. And by the time the magic had dissipated, there was nothing left to suggest he'd ever been standing there. The unleashed magic had destroyed everything behind him, including both the concrete wall and solid earth for twenty feet, leaving a five-foot-wide trench between two groups of spectators above.

No one moved, or spoke. I'm pretty certain there wasn't even any blinking, as every single pair of eyes was aimed right at me.

Elijah broke the silence, "Cheat," he shouted, "A sorcerer."

Noise exploded above me once more, only ending when I did something stupid. I removed my t-shirt and unleashed my magic. Orange glyphs replaced the white as two whips of fire were created, one from each of my hands. I walked the length of the pit, the noise and smell of burning wood tailing behind me as the whips dragged along the floor, until I stood beneath Elijah. "If you think you'd like to continue where your boy failed, you're more than welcome."

Elijah looked pale. "You are no human," he eventually seethed.

"You never asked," I told him. "That's no one's fault but yours." I walked back to the center of the pit. "Anyone who wants to step in here with me, I created an easy access for you." I pointed to the crater and the wolves' eyes followed my hand, either transfixed or wondering if they really could take me.

A thud from behind me took my attention, and I turned ready to strike, but found only Tommy walking toward me.

"Could you stop me from falling over?" I whispered. "I think I may have overdone myself."

Tommy embraced me, just as I fell forward.

Gordon was first beside me. "I guess you win," he said with a slight grin. "I've never seen anything like that."

"It'd be awesome if you could get me out of here without dropping me," I said to no one in particular before passing out.

CHAPTER 17

I woke to the smell of bacon. Nothing bad could come from that. I opened one eye gingerly and found myself on Matthew's sofa. I weighed the pros and cons of sitting up and decided it was worth the risk.

"How're you feeling?" Tommy asked in between mouthfuls of a sandwich.

"Is there more bacon?"

Tommy laughed and handed me a plate full of bacon sandwiches. I ate my fill and instantly felt better.

"So, do you plan on telling me what the fuck happened out there?"

"What in particular would you like me to explain?" I asked, drinking a bottle of water that Tommy had left for me.

"Let's start with the stabbing. I've never known you to let your guard down like that."

"I don't know what happened. I wanted to kill him; it was all I thought about—to end his miserable existence. It was only for a second, but I guess that was long enough."

"That doesn't explain how you healed from a stab with a silver knife." Tommy produced the knife from the pit and placed it on the coffee table between us. Someone had cleaned my blood from it.

"I really do have no idea whatsoever. I just accessed as much magic as I could."

Tommy didn't appear too impressed with my answer, but he left it alone. "And that sphere? What the hell was that?"

"Since I learned that my power has increased, I've been trying to see just what I can do. What I can push. I've managed to create a sphere that contains the power of a hurricane. It's somewhat spectacular when released."

"No fucking shit. They found Randal. Sorry, they found most of Randal. He's alive, but he lost one arm when it vaporized, or whatever the fuck happens when the power of hurricane is contained in something that's eight inches in diameter and then unleashed on one person."

"I've never used it on a person before—lost my temper a bit when he stabbed me."

"Well, it works," Gordon said as he entered the room. "Would you really have fought Elijah?"

"No, I'd have killed him fast. I didn't have it in me to fight. Using the magic in the sphere, *and* being stabbed, sort of takes it out of you."

"You're up," Ellie said as she entered the room. "That was pretty damn impressive."

"I try," I said to her. "Did Elijah tell you about Neil?"

"Within about two seconds of Matthew asking. I called Olivia, who's put together a task force to go get him." Tommy stood and stretched. "I'm going to go talk to my daughter."

"I'd like some clean clothes," I said. My trousers were covered in blood and my t-shirt was probably still in half on the floor of the pit.

Gordon left the room, returning a few minutes later with a pair of dark blue jeans and a green t-shirt. "We have clothes of all shapes and sizes on standby here. You'd be amazed how often werewolves don't think about keeping their clothing safe when they go hunting."

I thanked him, and he left to attend to his duties. Tommy took the cue and left too, leaving Ellie and me alone.

"I'm glad you're okay," she said.

"Me, too."

"I haven't met many sorcerers who I'd say I trusted. You just made the top of a very short list, Nate."

"Honored. Sorcerers have a tendency to think only in terms of magic and how it can be applied in life; it makes some of us appear cold towards others."

"Especially werewolves."

"Oh, not just werewolves, all weres, vampires, trolls— basically anything that isn't a sorcerer. We're not picky; we're just better than everyone else." I grinned, ensuring that Ellie knew I was only teasing.

Ellie laughed. "Humble, too."

"Yeah, sorcerers are basically perfect."

Ellie glanced down at my still naked chest and stomach and gave me a sly smile. "Yes. Yes, you are."

I chuckled and stood up, putting on my clothes. The t-shirt was a little snug, but at least the jeans wouldn't fall down, although the feeling of clean clothes against my skin reminded me that I really needed a shower.

"Maybe we'll see each other again sometime, Ellie," I said. "Hopefully under better circumstances."

Ellie offered me her hand, which I shook. She pulled me toward her with considerable strength and kissed me on the cheek. "I look forward to it," she said and stared at me with her beautiful blue eyes.

I watched Ellie leave the room, or rather, I watched her ass move seductively as she left the room, to be replaced by an entering Tommy.

"Ellie's impressed with you. And she's not easily impressed," Tommy said. "She's turned down half the men in the pack who have been sniffing around her."

"I think my dating life is on hold for the moment," I told him. "How's Kasey?"

"Waiting for me to come home. Apparently I'm out after my bedtime. You want to come to mine for a drink?" my old friend asked.

I shook my head. "I'm going to take a look at Vicki's place."

"You don't need to do that, Nate."

"I know, but I'd feel better taking a look myself. Her disappearance is wrapped up with these murders."

"You want some help?"

I slapped Tommy on the shoulder. "Go see your daughter, have a nice night. I'm only going to look around, and then I'm off home."

"Take care," he said and then shook my hand. "Thanks for your help," he said to Matthew before leaving the house.

"You're not done with this, are you?" Matthew asked. "And I don't mean about just going to search some girl's house."

A smile crept onto my lips. "Something isn't right here. The women are being killed in a ritualistic manner. It's just that I don't know what the ritual is meant to do. I think Neil's involvement is meant to keep us away from whoever is actually doing the killing."

"You're certain the killer isn't Neil?"

I nodded my head. "Whatever the killer is, it isn't some werewolf with impulse control issues. These women are taken somewhere secluded, stalked, and then butchered. If Neil's past crimes are any indication, he would have killed them before they'd even reached their destination.

"I'll leave Neil for the LOA to figure out," I continued. "They've still got an agent missing, so I may as well look into her. Just in case we can't ask Neil questions after his arrest." What I didn't say out loud was that the LOA were not known for their restraint when dealing with the murderer of an agent's family.

Matthew got it anyway. He chuckled. "You make a good point." He held out his hand, which I shook. "I hope this is not the last time, Nate. And maybe in future we can do each other a favor once again."

"You knew that Randal would cheat, didn't you?"

Matthew gave no sign that he agreed with me. "I knew that you'd be able to take care of yourself, although I didn't imagine a knife being involved."

"You could have warned me."

"I *could* have just killed Elijah and be done with the whole stupid mess. As it is, Randal cheating in full view of everyone does nothing to aid Elijah or his cause. Everyone wins. Warning you would have meant you waiting for him to cheat. I now appear to have an incredibly powerful sorcerer in my corner, one who will destroy those who cross him."

I punched him in the jaw, wrapping my hand in dense air, just hard enough to knock him to the floor.

"Feel better?" he asked, rubbing his face.

"Next time, ask." He took my hand and I helped him back to his feet, but I didn't release my grip. "Don't put me in that situation again."

Matthew's eyes hardened. "I did what I needed to do for my pack."

"That's why I didn't take your head off."

"Have you tamed over the years?" Matthew said with a laugh. "I know all about you, Hel—"

"Excellent," I interrupted, hiding my shock at hearing that name almost spoken after so many years. "Then remember this. *That* man is dead. And I can assure you, you don't want him back."

CHAPTER 18

I left Matthew's house abruptly and didn't calm down until I reached my bike. I wasn't really angry that he'd known that Randal would cheat, or that he'd assumed I'd deal with it accordingly. In his situation, I would have done the same thing. But the fact that he nearly called me...I turned and punched a nearby tree, my fist wrapped in fire.

Bark snapped and crackled from the heat and a small fire started, but it was quickly removed from the tree as I absorbed it into my magic.

That name was behind me now, part of a past I no longer needed. The only person who should have known was Tommy, and I would need to have words with him sooner rather than later about who he told my secrets to.

I thanked the guards for keeping an eye on the bike, but they both shrugged as if they only did it because it was next to them.

There were no streetlights around, and only the glow from the nearly extinguished torches lit the road outside of the field. I removed my phone from my pocket and tapped in Vicki's address, something I'd memorized from the file on Amber Moore. Apparently, it would take nearly an hour to get there, meaning I'd arrive just after three in the morning. That would give me a while to look around whilst it was still dark outside and the majority of neighbors likely still in bed and not watching the comings and goings on their street.

I used the bike's lights on the journey to Vicki's, not wanting to try and outrun any police or explain why I was riding in complete darkness. I doubt they'd accept the "I can use magic to see in the dark" excuse all that easily.

The journey took a little over forty minutes. I stopped the bike further down the street and switched off the engine, walking the remaining few hundred feet to Vicki's home. It was a fairly modest detached house, with an immaculate front garden, complete with lawn gnome who had been placed next to a small pond so that he appeared to be fishing. I wondered when, or if, lawn gnomes were ever considered funny or interesting.

"Do you plan on breaking in?" a woman asked as she stepped onto the driveway behind me.

"Hi, Olivia." I turned toward her and smiled. She wore dark fatigues and a white top. I could see the butt of her gun in the holster beneath her dark jacket. "I thought you'd be trying to arrest your werewolf," I added.

"Agent Reid is in charge of that. I got a call from Avalon about my request to get Mordred's file and thought I'd relay the info."

"I assume from your tone that it didn't go well."

"If I ever call with that request again, I'll be lucky to remain in Avalon, let alone in the LOA. You know what that means, don't you? They really don't want anything about him getting out. They're circling the wagons where he's concerned."

"It confirms that someone there was involved. And that they were worried enough about it to wait a while to get back to you, so they could make sure there was nothing you could find for yourself. Thanks for doing that."

"What are you going to do about it?"

"Nothing at the moment; it's just nice to know that I was right."

"Well, while I'm here we may as well search the house together."

She strolled past me and walked up the three steps to the front door, where she unlocked it with a key from her pocket. Despite the alarm box proudly displayed on the front of the house, there were no telltale signs of any alarm needing to be switched off as I stepped into the house.

Apart from a shoe rack next to the door, a rug on the floor, and a small table with a bowl to drop keys in, the hallway was empty—set of stairs led up, and three doors, one a few steps inside the house, one at the far end of the hallway, and another under the stairs. Olivia walked to the doorway at the far end of the hall.

"Kitchen," she said, as she clicked on a torch and opened the door under the staircase.

I took a moment to adjust my eyes with magic and could soon see, even in the almost total darkness inside. "Why don't you just turn a light on?" I asked as Olivia disappeared from view.

Her head popped out a few seconds later. "You want to see this. And I don't want anyone watching the place to know some- one's here. Just in case you're right and Vicki is involved."

"You're coming around to my way of thinking?" I asked.

"Just follow me." And she disappeared from view again.

I did as was asked and ducked my head as I stepped through the door. A set of steep stairs led down into a sizeable basement. "She has an office in the basement," I said, looking down.

"The house is only two bedrooms. I guess Vicki used the basement to get her work done."

And she would have spent a lot of time doing it. One long desk sat adjacent to the staircase. A computer monitor and laptop both had a thin film of dust on them. Two filing cabinets sat at the end of the room.

I took a step toward the cabinet, but Olivia stopped me. "You're not the only one who can get into a locked cabinet." She flicked her finger toward her target and a stream of ice smashed into the lock, pushing it into the cabinet with a shriek, where it ricocheted around the top drawer.

There were no glyphs or marks that lit up under Olivia's use of her element. If I'd been standing in front of her, I'd have seen her irises turn a pure light blue, but that would have been it. Whereas sorcerers manipulated elements using magic, elementals were one with the element itself.

Olivia pulled open the top cabinet drawer and removed a thick file from inside. She passed it to me, then removed a second of equal size and began going through it.

I took mine over to the desk and opened the cover, immediately understanding why it was locked up. The front page had a picture of a man in full police uniform. According to the information written beneath it, he was over six feet tall and weighed twenty stone. His name was Peter Jarvis, thirty-six, and a serial killer responsible for sixteen murders in two years. The victims were the same as those that had been in the files on Vicki's desk.

"So, why was she reading through the victims' files?" I asked.

"Because of this." Olivia passed me the file she'd been reading, which contained a picture of Peter with a young woman. They were standing in front of a large oak tree somewhere in a forest. They both appeared young and in love, the smiles genuine as they held one another. "This is Vicki."

"Your agent was dating a serial killer?"

"Yeah. It led to her drinking problem," Olivia said. "Like I told you, she had some anger issues."

"Anyone else know this about her?"

Olivia shook her head. "Just me. Peter used to beat her pretty badly. He nearly killed her once, just before she left him. She said she drank to forget what had happened. Sometimes she would wake up in a cold sweat at the thought of him coming after her."

"According to his file, he died in prison two years ago."

"His cellmate slit his throat. Vicki took a week off and drank herself silly. I remember because Amber called me, worried that she was going to kill herself."

I bit my tongue, stopping myself from saying what I was thinking, but Olivia pretty much said it for me. "What the fuck have you got yourself into, Vicks?"

I grabbed one of the files inside the cabinet and started reading. It related to a series of murders committed between five and seven years previously. Each of the victims had been young, pretty, and murdered in brutal fashion. Their cars had been discovered on the major motorways around the New Forest, and their bodies found tied to trees with their hearts cut out.

"Fucking hell," I whispered. "Why wasn't this house searched before? Hell, why didn't you mention that Vicki's ex was killing people in the same way as the current murders?"

Olivia snatched the file from me and started reading it. "Fuck. I swear I didn't know the details of the murders. It was a human crime; I was far too busy to take notice. Even with it involving

Vicki, I still didn't find out much about what happened. She wasn't exactly chatty about it, and I was swamped with work."

"And the house?"

"Reid told me some human cops did it on our orders, just a cursory check....Damn it, I fucked up."

"We'll ask Reid why he didn't find anything."

I opened the drawers on the desk, found a rucksack inside one, and used it to place the files inside. "They might come in handy," I pointed out.

We had one last look around the basement, but after finding nothing, decided it was best to head back upstairs.

Olivia's phone rang and she walked off to answer it, leaving me alone to search the large living area of the house. Paintings were hung on walls, and a near empty bottle of vodka sat alone on the coffee table. Apparently, Vicki still had issues.

On a sideboard against the far wall sat rows of photos, all in elegant frames. Most of them were pictures of Vicki and Amber smiling, but one was a picture of seven women, including Amber and Vicki, all dressed up for a party. I picked up the photo and stared at it, until the realization of where I'd seen them before clicked in my mind. They were the other victims. I turned it over in my hands and removed the photo from the frame. A date of four years previously was written on the back in pen.

I raced back to Olivia, who'd finished on her call. "We got the bastard," she said with a smile.

I passed her the photo, fully aware that it would deflate her happiness. "I think we have a really big fucking problem."

Olivia's enthusiasm was quickly dampened when I showed her the photo, and the realization that Vicki knew not only

Amber, but all five of the remaining victims. And that every single person in the photo was now dead or missing.

"You searched the victims' houses. Did any of them have the same photo?" I asked as Olivia placed the frame back where it had come from.

She shook her head, appearing slightly dazed, as if the photo had literally knocked the sense out of her. "Damn it, Vicks. Where are you?"

"We'll find her," I said.

"I hope so. Neil should be waiting for us by now. Maybe he has some answers."

CHAPTER 19

"Why are we at a human police station and not LOA headquarters?" I asked when we arrived at the police station.

"I might be able to answer that," Agent Reid said as he stepped out from between a pair of parked cars. He dropped a cigarette onto the floor and put it out with his foot. "Had to find a nice dark place to hide for a smoke," he said. "I'm meant to go to the designated smoking area, but I don't have the time to hunt for it."

"I have to admit, I was wondering about the locale myself, Agent Reid," Olivia said.

"As the humans are the ones taking the glory for the arrest, we might as well bring the prisoner here for questioning. There are runes on his manacles that stop him from changing. He's not going anywhere, and it gets the humans a little good publicity before he vanishes into a deep dark pit somewhere."

Olivia wasn't buying it. "The real reason, agent."

Reid glanced at me before answering. "I wasn't sure that he would last the night at LOA headquarters. I'm pretty certain he would have had an accident."

"How many non-Avalon are there inside this station?"

"About ten," Reid replied. "There's up to a hundred and fifty during the day, normally about thirty or forty cops at night, but most of them are out working."

Reid opened the door for Olivia, and the three of us walked into the fluorescent-lit reception. "This way," Reid said. He entered a four-digit code on a keypad and pushed the door open.

There were no human police on the way to the rear of the building where the interview rooms were, but when we arrived it was easy to figure out which room Neil was being held in. The two huge guards standing at rigid attention outside the door sort of gave it away.

We walked past the guards and into a small room, which contained two metal chairs, a recording device, and a small table. One wall was made of one-way glass, allowing us to stare at Neil Hatchell, who sat in the next room on one side of a bare table. His wrists were bound with thick steel manacles, which were then chained to the floor. The manacles and chain were both inscribed with runes.

His long black hair had been joined by the beginnings of a beard. His clothes—a pair of beige fatigues and a black hooded top—appeared to be old. The fatigues were frayed just above his shoeless feet. His fingers were dirty, and he had a smudge of redness on his cheek, along with red and puffy eyes. He kept twitching, scanning the room for whatever he expected to pounce out on him. He couldn't have been a more perfect suspect for a murder if he'd actually brought the body to the police himself.

He was ignoring Agent Greaves, who seemed to take the "yelling at the prisoner" approach to interviews. On a person like Neil, who didn't even seem to be taking notice, Greaves might as well have been talking to himself.

After a lot more shouting, Greaves told Neil he was going to die alone and left the room, arriving in ours moments later.

"He'll crack," Greaves said. "Everyone does."

"He's not going anywhere," I said. "He's ignoring you."

Greaves stepped up to me. "You got a better idea?"

"Give me five minutes with him," I said to Olivia.

"You overstep your boundaries, and I'll have you out of there."

"Fair enough." I held out my hand as Olivia silenced Greaves' objections with a wave of her hand. "The manacles key, please."

"Not a fucking chance," Greaves said.

"Give it to him," Olivia ordered, giving me an expression that told me to watch my step.

Greaves all but slammed the key into my hand, and I walked out of the room and into the interview room. Neil stared at the ground, his eyes flicking toward me as I sat down.

"Hey, Neil," I said. "How's things?"

Neil looked up at me and then started the twitching thing again.

"Ah, the marks of a madman: twitching, unable to look at anyone else, slightly unkempt. You're probably going to mumble something in a minute aren't you? You've probably already got something in mind. Well, don't let me stop you."

Neil stopped his movements and stared directly at me.

"I'm going to take a guess here. You were coached. Someone told you that, as the humans were interested in this case, if you made yourself appear to be batshit crazy, they would try you in a human court and put you in a mental institution. As a werewolf, you could break out of it anytime. And even if they put runes on you to stop your transformation, you're still better than any human. You could take care of yourself until you escape. That sound about right?"

Neil continued to stare.

"Well, it's not going to happen. You see, it only appears that those murders are being investigated as a human crime. The LOA is letting the humans take the glory. So, you will go back to the Hole for this, or Tartarus. Whichever they feel you deserve more."

That got his attention. Fear flickered behind his eyes, and I knew which one of the two he feared the most.

Neil had been placed on the third floor of the Hole during his last visit. If he was found guilty of these new murders, he would probably be placed a lot further down. No amount of backing is going to help a murderer of humans get away lightly twice, and people like Neil were cut loose the second they stopped being useful.

But as awful as the Hole was, Tartarus was a whole other league of scary. Every single person there was classed as an enemy of Avalon. And once you were imprisoned there, you never came back. Ever. I'd been there a few times, and the reality and the legend were vastly different. But that didn't stop people from believing the worst. Or stop me from playing on that fear.

"Tartarus scares you?" I asked. "Probably should. I don't think you'll like it there. A werewolf rapist like you, who likes to murder young girls? You'd last about ten minutes before one of the Titans tears you in half. And I mean that literally."

"You're right," he said. "I don't want to go to either of those. So what have you got?"

I placed the manacles key in front of him. "Take them off."

He hungrily picked up the key and removed the restraints, rubbing his wrists once they were off.

"If you try anything, I'll rip you in half myself," I said, and Neil nodded in agreement.

"Why did you get released from jail?"

Neil shrugged. "I didn't want to go. I was told I had to leave, and no questions. I wanted to stay. The beast in me had hurt those women, and I wasn't sure I could control it."

"Bullshit."

Neil had the audacity to smile.

"The beast wants to kill and taste blood," I said. "It doesn't rape. The man does. And if you lie to me again, I'll remove one of your hands."

The smile melted away. "You're not LOA," Neil said after a moment's silence.

"Never said I was, but you're still going to tell me two things. One, why Elijah was protecting you so furiously? And two, who's really murdering these women?"

Neil mimed locking his lips with a key and throwing it over his shoulder.

"So whoever this is scares you more than the LOA."

"I'm not going to help you put me in jail for the rest of my life."

"You want to know what confuses me? You're a predator, and you're free. So why aren't you doing what you've wanted to for so long?"

Neil smirked. "Who said I wasn't?"

"I saw your photos, lots of them, but you never touched any of those women. I think you were castrated, figuratively speaking anyway. I think you had to stay locked away until they needed you, because they couldn't trust you not to fuck it all up. Is that it? Did you have to ask permission to do anything?"

"Fuck you," he spat and slammed a fist onto the table, which groaned from the impact. "I'm not some fucking pussy who wasn't allowed to have fun. They brought me hookers. Fucking served them up to me. I got mine every night." And then he realized that he'd opened his dumb mouth.

I smiled. "Who gave you those girls, and where are they now?"

He shook his head frantically. "No, fuck you. I'm not saying anything."

I stood. "Then we'll take you back to LOA headquarters and see how you fare."

"Look, I can't say anything. They'll kill me. And I don't mean in the way some fucking idiot from LOA will do it. These people do bad things. Each of the hookers was given to me for a few days, but after I was finished they were given to...damn, I don't even fucking know what they were. But I heard the screams."

"They killed more people?"

"Those in the woods are a statement. The others they're just...food."

"Did you see any of them?"

"They took to me a big house near the forest every day, but I only saw the security guys up close. But the others, the ones in charge, there were six of them, all wearing hoods and hanging around together. They scared me. Especially the big guy. He's fucking messed up. I only spoke to him once, but it felt like something was crawling around in my head."

"Anything else?"

Neil shook his head.

"Avalon will protect you." I said.

"Are you dense? Avalon is fucking involved."

I tried to get more out of Neil, but he clammed up, and it was clear nothing short of torture was going to get him to reveal more information. And I doubted that Olivia would be too grateful if I started down that route, especially considering where we were. If there's one thing I've learned about human cops over the years, it's that most of them don't want prisoners dying in their custody. The smart ones, anyway.

Besides, after spending so long in a small room with a slimy piece of shit like Neil, I needed some air. Agent Greaves resumed his shouting as he entered the interview room, but he nodded an acknowledgement at me before he went in. It was probably about as close to congratulations as I was ever likely to get from him.

When I opened the police station's front doors, I almost walked directly into Agent Reid, Eric, who was on his mobile phone. He quickly hung up and put it back into his pocket, with a nervous smile. "Girlfriend," he said. "She's not too keen about me being out all hours when I said I'd be home."

"It's difficult keeping a relationship going, especially with *your* job."

"Tell me about it. She's human, too, so it's hard keeping some stuff from her."

"That I understand," I said honestly.

"You think he was lying about someone involved working for Avalon? You really think he didn't help kill those girls?"

I shook my head. "He's a predator and a psychopath, but he's nowhere near the level of our killer, and he's not our killer's helper either. And as for lying? I doubt it. I've seen a lot of liars in my life, and that would make him one of the best."

Eric glanced over his shoulder as a car pulled up somewhere in the distance. "This case is making me jumpy."

"How long have you been an agent?"

"Four years, served here for two. This is the first really big case I've dealt with. Well, the first with a serial killer. It's all fucking nuts. Those girls murdered like that, sends a chill up my spine." He glanced behind him again and shivered. "Fucking hell, I'm a grown man, shouldn't be spooked at nothing. I'm gonna go help Agent Greaves. He'll probably still be yelling."

"He's very good at it."

Eric smiled. "He's a good agent. He's a prick, but a good agent." Apparently that was the general consensus when it came to Agent Greaves. Eric made his way back inside, leaving me alone in the car park.

I walked further away from the building and stretched my neck. It was freezing cold outside, and I was tempted to use my magic to keep myself warm, but the temperature kept me awake and alert for the moment, so I tolerated it.

"You were impressive in there," Olivia said as she exited the police station and made her way toward me.

"Tartarus scares people."

"None of the LOA would have used that. Why do I get the feeling that you could have called some people and had your threat become a reality?"

I smiled. "It helps having some friends in high places. Or low ones, depending on your point of view."

"I thought you were all cold, heartless bastards, or rather you are until you need to pretend otherwise."

"Maybe my demeanor was the reason I left."

"I'm amazed they let you. I thought the only way out was death."

Olivia was fishing. Damn Tommy for coming up with the idea of me being Faceless, but I wasn't about to break down and tell her the truth.

"A story for another time," I said as a noise in the distance caught my attention. It was a crunching sound, like something walking over a car roof and bending the metal. I searched the area, trying to figure out where the sound had come from, when a second noise came from the opposite side of the car park.

"What was that?" Olivia asked, a hand instinctively resting on her holstered sidearm.

A tall, heavy-set man walked steadily toward us, the darkness obscuring most of his features until he stopped under a street light and the horror of what he was hit me like a nuclear explosion. He wore a long dark coat over a dark suit. Long, gangly fingers, that couldn't have possibly belonged to a human anymore, flexed as he stared at Olivia intently.

The man's face was gray and scarred, and the skin was pulled tightly over the skull. The only color was his bright-red eyes. I'd seen those eyes before, seen them bore into me as they bathed in my destruction, and the memory caused fear to jolt inside me. The face of evil reanimated.

Three creatures revealed themselves all at once, crouched on the roofs of three different cars.

"Hello, Olivia," he said, and I noticed her staring at one of the creatures. "Do you remember me?"

"Peter Jarvis," Olivia said softly. "You're supposed to be dead."

"Ah, death is but a step. You ruined my life, do you know that? Destroyed everything I'd worked so hard to achieve, turned the woman I loved against me. And now I'm going to do the exact same to you. I'm going to burn your life to the ground and make you watch as the embers are finally extinguished one at a time, until all that's left is ashes. And then you'll die. Slowly. I'm very much looking forward to it."

"I'm going to make sure you stay dead this time," Olivia shouted, shaking with rage.

"I'm so glad you remember me," Peter said. "I came back because of you. My hatred of you brought me back here, the need to feel your skin burst open as I carve into it. The need to feel your hot blood down my throat was all that kept me going."

"And those women, the friends of Vicki and Amber, why kill them?" I asked, hoping to get his attention off Olivia.

Unfortunately, it didn't work, and Peter continued to stare at Olivia. "Before I go, Olivia, I have someone you should meet." One of the creatures got down from the roof of the nearest car and half walked, half padded over to Peter, who rested his hand on her head.

"Do you recognize her?" he asked.

"Vicki," Olivia said. "You son of a bitch, what did you do to her?"

"She's my pet. Turning Vicki was the most fun I'd ever had," Peter said. "And now she'll serve me for all eternity. Her pain and suffering is nothing compared to what I'm going to do to you, Olivia."

"Lich," I whispered.

The man's head snapped toward me. "And we have a winner. You must be the outsider. I thought I'd come to deliver you a message. Olivia is going to die at my hand, when the time is right. You, however, hold nothing I require. You can walk away without harm if you allow me to take Neil and do not interfere in my plans."

"I think I can speak for everyone when I tell you to go fuck yourself," I said.

"That's a real shame," Peter said. "In that case, allow me to introduce you to two more of my pets."

He waved his hand toward us, and the two creatures moved faster than any human ever could, springing from the darkness, too quick for Olivia to remove her gun, let alone fire it. The first one ran for Olivia, who dodged aside and used her elemental water powers to take the legs from out under her attacker.

I turned as a second creature dove toward me. A blast of air magic knocked it backward. I solidified the air, just enough to entangle the creature, and then flipped it up, over my head and released the magic as the two attackers neared one another. They both went down hard, eerie shrieks leaving inhuman mouths as they scrambled to get back to their feet.

"What the fuck are they?" Olivia gasped.

"Ghouls," I said, but before I could finish, Olivia emptied a clip into the nearest bald-headed bastard. It dropped back to the floor, and its comrade performed something akin to a smile, its jaw dislocating and dropping open to show rows of razor-sharp teeth as Peter, the lich, laughed.

A second later shots rang out from behind us and Agent Reid ran past, shooting the whole time with his Glock. Each bullet hit the lich in the chest, but he didn't go down. He turned on his heel and ran into the darkness of the streets beyond, the ghoul who used to be Vicki right behind him. I tried to call out to stop Reid, but he didn't hear me and sprinted after the lich, following him around a corner and out of sight.

I hoped he'd be able to hold his own, but I knew from experience that a lich could carve through most people like they were made of paper.

The ghoul on the floor stayed still for a moment and then laughed, regaining my attention to it. The sound was horrible, nowhere near the laugh of the human it used to be. It got back to its feet and spat onto the floor, and the sound of the bullets and blood hitting the concrete floor turned Olivia's face pale.

"What the hell," she whispered and reloaded her gun.

"Only way to kill them is to cut their heads off," I said. "Magic won't work either, so I need you to go get some silver daggers or swords or something. Because right now the best we can do is knock them down."

"I can't leave you out here," she said.

The first ghoul dove toward me and met a torrent of fire, keeping both it and its brethren away. "Magic will hurt them, but not kill them. I'll be fine, but unless we get something to cut them, we're both screwed."

Olivia watched in horror as one of the ghouls jumped through the fire. "Go already," I shouted and slammed another jet of fire into the ghoul, which drove it back.

Olivia turned and sprinted into the police station, and I killed the flames. I couldn't have kept it up all night, and, if I was honest, I had no idea how much magic I had left in me after the fight a few hours earlier, or how long before what was inside of me tried to come out, and then…well, and then things would get a hell of a lot worse.

The first of the two ghouls was allowing its flesh to knit back together; the bullets had all been center mass and had made quite a mess. It would be out of the fight for a few minutes, but the second showed no signs of damage from the fire I'd slammed into it.

The ghoul stood up to its full six-foot height, its powerful muscles taut under dark, leathery skin, and shrieked into the night. At one point it had been human, but dark, evil magic had changed all of that. The proportions were all nearly human, except for the stomach, which was sunken under the ribcage, and the arms, which were long enough that the creature could easily walk on all fours. The fingernails were razor sharp, and its mouth contained venom that would paralyze with one bite. Once paralyzed, the ghoul would eat its victim alive. If the victim wasn't human, and was lucky enough to avoid the ghoul after being bitten, the venom would wear off with no lasting effects. Humans didn't have that luxury; you were either eaten, or you turned into a monster. Either way it was a death sentence.   Even after their death and rebirth as monsters, they retain their human level intelligence, and although their blood lust takes over when given the opportunity, they're more than capable of calculated thought. It makes them incredibly dangerous opponents.

"Let's get to it then."

The ghoul charged, and I dodged the swipe from its claws with ease, but the ghoul backed me up against a car. I planted my hands on the car and vaulted back and up onto the roof as the ghoul embedded its hands in the car's bonnet. He tried to pull himself free, but couldn't. He was stuck up to his elbows, his hands jammed somewhere in the engine itself.

I rolled off the car and sprinted at the first ghoul, which had managed to knit its chest back together. I slammed a fist of air into its temple, dropping it back to the floor. It kicked out at me and caught my knee, almost sending me down too, but I rolled with the blow and came up near another car.

It wasted no time and swiped at me. I ducked, then punched my fist into its chest before unleashing a ball of fire, which picked the ghoul up off its feet and dumped it several yards away from me.

It gave me a moment to rub my sore knee until the ghoul got back to its feet and shrieked at its still-stuck friend. "You guys ready?" I asked.

The free ghoul came at me once more, but this time it feinted with a swipe and caught me with a kick to the stomach. I staggered back and tried to roll out of its reach, but it was instantly upon me. It grabbed my throat and squeezed before slamming my head into the car's headlight, which shattered from the impact.

I drove a blade of air through its chest, and the ghoul released me long enough to allow me to punch it in the face with another air-wrapped fist. I used the time to roll back to my feet, but the ghoul I'd last seen stuck inside a car engine barreled into me and tossed me back onto the car bonnet. My head and elbow struck the glass windscreen and the ghoul jumped on my chest, its mouth and dozens of tiny shark-sharp teeth inching ever closer until I tapped further into my magic and a small tornado smashed into its chest, flinging it off me.

Fighting one on one with a ghoul was hard enough, especially without a weapon, but now that they were both free I was in all kinds of trouble.

I slid off the car's bonnet and was almost skewered by the claws of the second ghoul, but I dodged and caught it in the throat with a vicious elbow, following up with a kick to the knee and punch to the face, which took it to the concrete.

I moved away to catch my breath and readied myself for another round of the unwinnable. As much as I was doing okay, it wouldn't last. They were already dead and didn't need to refill their energy. They just kept going until they couldn't go any further, unlike me who had a finite amount of magic to use before I became exhausted. Or worse.

"Nate," Olivia shouted. She ran past me wielding a large machete.

"Where'd that come from?" I asked.

"Greaves had it in his car."

"Did you bring backup?"

"The guards are keeping Neil company. Greaves is changing."

On cue, a werewolf in beast form, large and gray, charged past Olivia and dove onto the nearest ghoul, the one I'd used a tornado on. He tore into it with vigor, ripping huge chunks out of its chest. The second ghoul glanced back at his comrade's predicament and decided that Olivia and I were an easier bet. He shrieked and ran at Olivia. She swung the machete, but the ghoul ducked under it, bending himself into a position that would have been impossible for anyone alive.

I was too far away and couldn't get to them in time, couldn't stop the ghoul from planting one hand on the ground and spinning up behind Olivia. It landed on her back and sank its teeth into her shoulder.

I was still moving toward them when the ghoul released Olivia and threw her at me, the machete clattering to the ground as I caught her and took her momentum, rolling us both between two parked cars. The ghoul didn't attack me, didn't take the advantage; instead, he went after Greaves.

Olivia convulsed beside me as the venom started its job of paralyzing her. Blood soaked her shirt, and I glanced over at Greaves expecting to see the agent fighting both ghouls. But Greaves hadn't reacted in time to fight them both. The creature that had bitten Olivia had his hands deep inside the agent's back as the ghoul beneath Greaves tore into his stomach, exposing intestine as blood poured over both of his attackers.

The machete was thirty feet away, the silver gleaming in the moonlight. I went for it, but one of the ghouls got there first and flung it into the night before rejoining his comrade, who was still tearing into Greaves.

A crescendo of white-hot hatred coursed through me as orange glyphs burned brightly across my arms.

The ghouls both stopped their fun and turned toward me. And laughed.

I lost my temper.

A stream of white-hot fire caught the first ghoul in the chest and punched a hole through him as if he were made of butter. The ghoul screamed, which made his comrade edge away, fear on his twisted face for the first time.

I removed the stream of fire and a black tar-like substance leaked from the ghoul's wound as he crashed to the ground, placing his hand out in front of him to steady his fall. The stream of fire morphed into a whip, one flick of which removed the ghoul's hand. He fell face first onto the concrete with another scream.

The second ghoul turned to me, looked down at his fallen friend, and ran like his life depended on it.

I walked steadily toward the downed ghoul and noticed that Greaves' injuries were already healing; he'd live.

I grabbed the back of the injured ghoul's head, holding it still as I incinerated it until there was nothing left above its neck.

My brain said: *It shouldn't have worked, I shouldn't have been able to kill it.* Magic won't kill a ghoul, just like it shouldn't have let me heal from my silver wound so quickly during my fight with Randal. I turned and saw the trail of flame footsteps I'd made on the concrete floor. I walked over to Olivia and checked for her vitals, relieved to find a strong pulse. She was paralyzed and needed medical attention, but she would live. I glanced over at the dead ghoul and for the second time that night one thought bounced around in my head.

What the hell was happening to me?

CHAPTER 20

Montana Territory, America. 1878.

Mapiya, Sam, and Chief Blacktail all walked into the fort to talk, leaving me outside surrounded by a dozen very tense Crow tribe warriors. I got the feeling they were all looking for a reason to try and put me down, so I found a nice spot in the yard next to one of the cannons, rested up against a wooden beam, and tried to get some sleep. They weren't about to kill a sleeping man, and I wasn't about to let them think I was nervous about them being there.

I didn't manage to doze off, but I did manage to get a few minutes to myself to try and figure out what the hell was going on.

A few years earlier Merlin had sent me to Mexico to find a book, telling me it would be an easy assignment. Turns out he'd been wrong. The journey from Spain to Mexico had been an easy one, which alone should have told me that things were going to get bad. The fact that the book hadn't been in Mexico at all wasn't the most auspicious beginning, and since then I'd followed its trail all the way north.

Merlin had told me that the book contained some pretty powerful magic, but as far as I was concerned, it had better reveal the secrets of life. Anything less than that and I was not going to be happy.

There hadn't been much weird stuff happening on my journey, right up until I reached Montana. Then, it was as if all the weird shit happened at once. Deputies chasing a boy through the woods at night, an empty ranch, horses that had been ripped apart and eaten, a ranch owner butchered, and now, after all of that, an abandoned U.S. army fort. The bad feeling in the pit of my gut was getting worse with every passing hour. I needed to finish my job and get out of this damn place.

Fuck you, Merlin. It was a thought that was coming more and more easily to me over the centuries. Whatever vision he and I had shared when I first joined him had been steadily eroding. But that was a problem for another time.

Then there was Sam. Someone had murdered his dad and then tried to kill him. There had to be a reckoning for that, and if I didn't help, Sam would get himself killed. Merlin always said that my conscience got me into trouble, and he had a fair point. Didn't mean I planned on changing anytime soon.

"Who are you?" The voice belonged to Mapiya. I opened my eyes and spent a few seconds drinking in her beauty under the guise of waking up.

"I told you who I am," I said.

"Why are you here? In Montana? The real reason."

"Followed an artifact from Mexico, and it seems to have passed through quite a few hands on the way here. Everyone who handled it is dead. The exception to that rule being whoever has it now."

"It's a book, about so thick." Mapiya moved her thumb and forefinger about an inch apart. "It contains bad things. Really bad things."

I stared at the woman next to me for a moment. She carried herself with confidence that was due to more than just her beauty and intelligence, it was also down to her power. "There's no way anyone human should know about the book, so what are you?"

"Necromancer," she said after a moment's hesitation.

I've known several necromancers during my life, and while some of them are nicer then others, there is one rule of thumb that can be said about all of them: they contain an incredible amount of power that can easily rival that of any sorcerer. Mapiya was almost definitely someone I wanted on my side of a fight. "Can I assume that whatever is in that book relates to your abilities?"

Another hesitation. "What do you know about ghouls?"

"They are men or women who were corrupted by dark, Blood magic. They have a venomous bite that paralyzes and turns a human into the barren. They're fast, strong, and very dangerous."

"They're rare. And they're behind the attack on the people of this fort and the ranch."

That shocked me more than I showed. I'd heard of maybe a dozen instances of ghouls attacking people in my entire life. "You sure, Mapiya?"

"Sky," she said.

I tried my best not to look confused.

"It's my name," she continued. "Mapiya is a Sioux name; it means Sky."

I smiled. "So, Sky, how many of these ghouls are there?"

"Up to six."

I got the impression there was more to it than she was willing to share, but I didn't want to push too soon.

"And your employer would be?"

Sky smiled—it was sly and somehow made her more attractive. "You first."

I shook my head. "Can't, sorry."

"Then you have your answer."

"Secrets aside, it's beginning to appear as if you and I have the same agenda. To find out what's happening here, and stop it."

"I thought you wanted the book?" she said with that same sly grin.

"Yeah, well, if there's ghouls involved, they need stopping. I've never encountered them before, but something weird is definitely going on here. When that happens, I usually like to find out what it is. One question though, why kill the ranch owner? And why so violently? You only kill like that either to send a message or because you hate the person."

Sky pondered my words for a few moments before responding. "Someone at the nearest town, Kilnhurst, might know. Although I don't trust anyone in that damned place, so I wouldn't expect the information to come easily."

"I need to talk to Sam, and then I'll make my way there. Alone."

"And what if I say no?"

"You won't. There's another fort west of here; take Sam and go check it out. I'm hoping the fort there hasn't been attacked. If everyone is still in once piece there, they might know more about what the hell is going on."

"Sounds like as good a plan as any."

"What can you tell me about this Kilnhurst?"

"About a thousand people live there, but there are many more who are just passing through. The sheriff is a vicious killer, and his deputies are not much better. Something about the place makes my skin crawl. I think it's safe to say that they hate me. Even more than the usual shit I get when I go into a town, though a young woman with my heritage always raises whispers and stolen glances."

"Maybe they're jealous," I pointed out. "Or they find you irresistible and can barely contain their desire for you."

"Or they hate and fear me because they're a bunch of small-minded idiots."

"Or that." I said and we both laughed. "The chief doesn't trust me."

"You're an outsider in a time when his people are being killed and abused, while justice is in short supply. He doesn't trust anyone he doesn't know."

"He trusts you."

"The Crow tribe and I go a long way back."

I digested the information as Sam raced around the corner, almost running into one of the cannons before skidding to a halt in front of Sky and me. "Chief Blacktail wants to talk to you," he said to me.

I stood and brushed loose dirt from my trousers. "We need to have a talk of our own," I said to Sam and walked off to find the chief.

Blacktail had set himself up in the fort's large dining room. Lamps burned brightly on the walls, but the six Crow warriors still did their best to appear inconspicuous. They stayed far enough from their chief to appear unthreatening, but close enough that they could get to an attacker in a heartbeat. One of the men casually held a bow, an arrow already nocked. The chief sat at one of two long tables eating an apple. He gestured for me to sit opposite him, which I did with a nod of gratitude.

"We found this," Chief Blacktail said as he signaled to one of the warriors, who brought forward a cavalry saber stained red with blood. "It was in the barracks, which appear to have been the center of a large fight."

"Any other traces of the soldiers?"

Chief Blacktail shook his head. "Some blood, though not enough to cause a man to die. They were all taken by monsters of the night, I already know this. They're dead now, there's little chance of any other result. I requested your presence so that we can discuss this." A second warrior placed a tomahawk on the table in front of me. It was identical to the one I'd found in the barn, except it lacked any blood on the blade or feathers.

"Was this found in the fort?" I asked.

"Embedded in the timber outside this room. Someone is trying to make stupid people believe we are involved in these massacres."

"I suspect you weren't meant to find the weapon, nor was I. Someone will probably visit the fort tomorrow morning. The same will be true of the ranch. My guess is this visitor will be involved with the killers. They were meant to discover the tomahawks as proof of the crimes committed in these places to draw attention away from themselves, and put it on people who are still subject to suspicion."

"That sounds true enough. Bring him out," he added with a glance over his shoulder. One of the chief's guards exited through a set of double doors, returning a moment later pushing a hand-cuffed man in front of him. The newcomer was a head taller than the warrior, but the fear in his eyes was easy to see. Or rather, eye. The left one was swollen shut, and blood stained his blue shirt from a cut on his lip. Bruises adorned both sides of his face, and he walked with an obviously painful limp.

A deputy badge shone proudly on his lapel. We were heading into very dangerous waters and I hesitated to voice my concern. "You beat up a deputy," I said. "That's got all kinds of trouble in it for you."

"Tell him," Chief Blacktail said to the now seated man.

"Fuck you, Chief kiss-my-ass." The man's attempt at mockery gained him a punch to the jaw from one of the warriors, knocking him to the floor.

"Would you like to be clever again?" the chief asked as the man was dragged back into a seated position.

The deputy started talking immediately. "I was told to wait until morning when some wagons will be going past on their way to town. I was supposed to ride from the fort, telling everyone that it had been attacked. The people from the wagons would come inside, find the tomahawk, and these assholes would get the blame. But they turned up first."

"You can't kill him," I said.

"He should die for his treachery," the young warrior said.

"Enough," the chief commanded. "Nathan is right; killing the deputy would be disastrous for us in the long run. If we were ever linked to his death, the government would attack us."

"But—" the young warrior started.

"But nothing!" The Chief slammed his open palm onto the table. "This man will not die at our hands. It is my place to ensure the Crow remain strong. Killing him will do the opposite."

"Why show him to me?" I asked, breaking the staring contest that had ensued between the chief and warrior.

"His master is the sheriff. I assumed you would want to question him yourself."

I glanced at the beaten man who spat on the floor by my feet. "Traitor," he said. "You should be helping us, not fighting your own kind."

Air slammed into the chest of the man, ripping him from his chair and throwing him up against the wall, pinning him and holding him still as I walked toward him. "My *kind*," I snarled, "could crush you like the fucking insect you are. If you ever refer to anyone in my company in a derogatory fashion again, I shall strip the flesh from your bones." I clenched my fist and the air wrapped around the man increased in pressure until he was moments away from having his bones crushed.

"Clear?" I asked as tears flowed from the deputy's eyes.

He nodded furiously, so I released the magic and he fell awkwardly to the floor.

I waited for a few seconds and returned to my seat as the deputy dragged in ragged breaths deeply. "Answer my questions truthfully and you live," I said, when he'd finished coughing. "And rest assured that, unlike your current captors, I have no issues with making you disappear."

The man nodded once more.

"Who sent you here?"

"Sheriff Bourne, he runs Kilnhurst."

"A corrupt sheriff," I rubbed my temples. "What a damn shock."

The deputy shook his head. "He's not corrupt. He doesn't take bribes or hurt the inhabitants of the town. He protects us from those who would do us harm. Like them." He motioned toward the nearest warrior.

"So he protects you all, and you just ignore when he has people murdered. Is he human?"

"Yes."

"I assume you've seen the ghouls."

"They protect us too. They help the sheriff in his work, but he doesn't control them. I don't know who does."

I needed to go to the town even more now, if only to check the sheriff out for myself. And hopefully to figure out if the deputy was lying or if there really was someone else out there controlling the ghouls.

"Take him back to his cell," I said to the chief, who motioned for one of the warriors to take the deputy away.

The warrior who had argued with the chief earlier drew a knife and stepped forward.

I intercepted the attack before it even happened, knocking the knife aside and pushing the young warrior back. "Deputy, you will not be harmed," I said, my back toward him, as I watched the warrior glare at me.

Behind me, the deputy calmed and I heard him being led away toward his cell. "One thing, before you go," I said, and the deputy stopped again. "If anyone goes against my word, I will kill them." I did not take my eyes off the young warrior as I spoke.

"Thank you, sir," the deputy said from behind me.

I hadn't finished. "But if you lied to me about anything," I told him, "or if you try to escape from this place, your life is forfeit. And I will let these men do whatever they wish to ensure their anger is sated."

The prisoner was led away in silence, and the second I turned my eyes away from the young warrior, he pounced on me, exactly as I'd known he would. A second knife was in his hand and he swiped it up toward me. I dodged aside, kicked out his knee, and smashed his face into the wooden table before locking his elbow at the joint until he released the blade.

"Are you satisfied now?" the chief asked the young man. "Your behavior was rash and stupid. A superior warrior handled you as if you were a baby. You will apologize, and then you will leave my sight until I summon you for whatever punishment I deem necessary."

Chief Blacktail looked up at me. "You may release my son."

Well, that was a shock, but I did as I was asked and moved away just enough to ensure that any further ideas of retribution would require him to step toward me. I really hoped he wasn't that foolish. Was I that stupid when I was young? Probably.

The warrior nodded slightly to his father before turning to me. "I'm sorry," he said and quickly left the room.

"He is rash and impulsive," Chief Blacktail said. "Like me at his age. Hopefully, he will grow out of it."

"I understand his need for vengeance. You're being set up to take the blame for what would be described as a massacre. I suggest you leave this place at first light and take your son with you."

"I agree. Have you told Sam you will not be taking him with you to Kilnhurst?"

I shook my head. "It's on my list of things to do before I go."

The chief stood. "I wish you luck, Nathan Garrett. I see a rage in your eyes, and I'm not sure I would wish to be around when it is unleashed."

"You're not surprised about my magic?"

"You are not the first sorcerer I've met," he said with a slight grin. "We will take Sam and Sky as far as our camp; they will be protected. Although I doubt Sky needs it, she is a capable woman. You should beware."

"I'm always wary of beautiful women who carry knives."

The chief laughed. "The wise words of someone who has experienced the wrath of one such lady and has a story I would like to hear."

"I promise when this is over, the story is all yours." So long as I wasn't dead first.

As much as I wanted to leave immediately and make it to the town of Kilnhurst before dark the following day, I had to speak to Sam first. I'd grown to like him during the past few days together, and didn't want him to think that I was going to take away whatever justice or vengeance he thought he deserved.

I found him sitting on top of the wall, shrouded in the darkness from the watchtower above. "Someone mentioned you're off to Kilnhurst," he said, his voice hard but composed. As if waiting to spring from zero to anger in a second.

"I need to go and check out this sheriff; he's involved in all of this."

Sam moved forward and the torchlight touched his face. "My dad was a U.S. Marshall. The sheriff of Kilnhurst murdered him."

There were only two reasons why a U.S. Marshall would have been killed by sheriff in a town in the middle of nowhere. Either Sam's dad was working with the sheriff to break the law, or he was trying to stop him. Judging from Sam's disposition, I was betting the latter. "What was your dad investigating?"

"Dad and I lived in North Dakota; we moved there after Mum died. But he would take jobs to track people down. He was still a U.S. Marshall, and that held sway with many. Then some government people turned up about six months ago asking for his help."

He paused for a moment. I got the feeling that Sam hadn't told any of this to a soul since it happened and I didn't want to interrupt.

"He never came home. It took me a few months to track down where he'd gone, but I eventually discovered that he went into that town, Kilnhurst, and never left." Tears began to fall steadily, but he didn't stop to wipe them away.

"I asked the sheriff for help, but instead he got his thugs to give me a beating to keep me away. That was three weeks ago. I healed up and went back, determined to find out what happened to my dad. I waited until dusk and broke into one of the abandoned shops on the main street. I watched the sheriff walk to the cathouse every night at the same time and stay for exactly the same amount of time.

"I did that for three nights until one night when a boy about my age broke into the same shop. His name was Lee and he was on the run from the law. He told me that he'd stolen some food and had then assaulted the army captain who had tried to capture him. He'd been following the sheriff, too, and wanted to break into his house at the edge of town to steal some of the things he'd seen there." Sam removed the silver revolver from his holster and cradled it in his hands. "Lee told me that he'd seen my dad's guns, that the sheriff normally wore them during the day but removed them at night. He said if I helped, the guns were mine, but he wanted anything else we found. I agreed and we started to plan.

"It took us a few days more of planning and going out during the night to scout the house. It was a big property with plenty of places to hide and watch without drawing any undue attention. And then after nearly a week, we watched as the sheriff left to see his whores, and put the plan in motion."

Sam had stopped crying and just looked angry. "We broke into the house and searched it as we'd planned, but we couldn't find the guns. Lee was irate when I wouldn't stop looking, and he refused to help me search further. Instead, he went room to room looking for anything of value. I went to leave the house, but heard the shouts when they found him and panicked. I hid in a wardrobe and was forced to listen to them torture him. He told them everything, but didn't give me up. And then *he* arrived. I heard *his* voice. It was deep and filled with amusement as Lee screamed. Lee told them everything. About me, where I was, and what was happening. I bolted, but they caught me and dragged me to a large living room where Lee was tied to a chair. His face was just blood. Nothing else. I can remember seeing fingers on the floor. They'd cut off his fingers, Nathan."

Sam took a deep breath before continuing. "They tied me up and made me watch as this...*thing* started working on Lee. He was still alive, and they made me watch as they hurt him. Sometimes, that monster didn't even touch Lee with more than a hand, but it made him scream in pain. All night they continued, until all that was left of Lee was a whimpering mess. But by then the sun had risen and the monster who had tortured Lee had to leave.

"They left me tied to a chair for the day, alone to watch the final moments of Lee's life ebb away. I didn't even understand how he was still alive. I knew that would be me the next night, and I knew I had to get away. The deputies who grabbed me, the same ones you met in the woods, hadn't searched me, and I managed to get a knife out of my back pocket and started cutting through the ropes. It was awkward and painful, but it was the only hope I had.

"The sheriff arrived that night, with a deputy, and told me he'd killed my dad. That he'd taken his time and tortured him until my dad had given up the information they needed, and then he killed him with his own gun. He showed me the gun, right under my nose, and pulled back the hammer. I snapped the rest of the rope and plunged the small dagger into the side of his face. He fell back, but the gun went off and caught the deputy in the head. The sheriff cracked his skull on the floor hard enough that he remained still. I took my dad's revolver, the other was still in the holster the sheriff wore, and I wanted to kill him."

Tears fell again, this time in great big sobs. "I couldn't do it," Sam cried. "He was right there. I pressed the barrel against his temple, but I couldn't kill him. I saw the body of the deputy, saw the hole in his head, and felt sick. The sheriff murdered my dad, had tortured Lee right in front of me. But I couldn't kill him. Why couldn't I do that?"

"You're not that person," I said softly. "Don't ever be that person."

"Why? You are." He flinched at his own words. "I'm sorry, I didn't mean—"

"Yes, you did. And you're right. I would have put two in his head and called it a day. The part of my soul that would have stopped me doing that is long gone. I'm not the passive guy who lets things go; I came to terms with what I am a long time ago."

"There's more," Sam said. "Lee was whimpering. They'd cut out his tongue and removed his lips, but I could still hear his words...*Kill me.* It took me...I don't know how long, but eventually I placed the barrel against his head. I couldn't pull the trigger, couldn't kill him. He reached up, his hand was missing three fingers, but he placed his bloody hand against mine and I positioned his finger to pull the trigger. He said thank you and then he killed himself."

Sam wept for a long time—for himself, his dad, and his friend. I sat beside him and he buried his face in my shoulder. I didn't know what to say—sorry wasn't enough—so I just sat there stoic and unyielding as Sam's emotions ran out of him.

"I couldn't get the second gun of my dad's," he said eventually. "The deputies came back and I was forced to flee. I grabbed the nearest horse and rode toward the forest, but they shot the horse and I had to abandon it and go on foot. Then you met me."

"Thank you for telling me that, and I don't want to do this to you, but I have some questions, is that okay?"

Sam nodded.

"Why didn't you tell me that the sheriff was the killer? You asked me to help you find your dad's killer."

"I wasn't sure if I could trust you. And even if you weren't involved, who would want to help me kill a sheriff?"

He had a point. "What can you tell me about the man who tortured Lee?"

"He was tall, but he wore a hood, so I couldn't see his face. I could see his eyes though. They were bright red. And he was in charge. Even the sheriff was wary of him."

"Did you see any other...*things* around? Any kind of odd creatures, for example."

Sam shook his head. "Just the sheriff, his deputies, and that monster."

"Sky knows what your monster is," I said. "I think that's why she's really here."

"Are you going to kill him, the monster I mean?"

"I get the feeling that's Sky's job."

"She's scary."

We both watched as Sky walked around the yard below avoiding any of the Crow tribe warriors, who in turn wanted little to do with her. "She's something," I agreed. "You're going with her to a fort close to here."

"You going to be okay down in that town alone?"

I stood. "I think I can take care of myself."

"I want to kill the sheriff. I need to do it."

"You sure? You can't undo something like that."

Sam stared off into the distance. "I feel like it's something I have to do."

"Then I'm sure you'll get your chance," I said, but my thoughts continued. *And then we'll see if you're the kind of man who can walk away from that. Or if you're more like me than you ever want to be.*

CHAPTER 21

The conversation with Sam had not been an easy one...for either of us. Hopefully, he realized that running into a town, guns blazing, where there were a thousand people, many of them armed, would be a very short mission of vengeance.

There was also the fact that Sam had never killed anyone; I doubted he'd ever hurt anyone in anger before. If it were up to me, that wouldn't change, but he would have to decide his own path. At some point, I was certain that he would get his chance for retribution.

I wished everyone a safe journey and spent the rest of the day riding toward Kilnhurst, with only Valor for company. It started raining after a few hours, and I was grateful for the long coat that at least allowed me to stay mostly dry. The occasional use of fire magic kept me warm as a cold wind swept in.

The weather didn't appear to bother Valor, who kept a steady pace the entire journey, only stopping for five minutes every hour to rest and have a drink of water.

By the time I'd reached the outskirts of the town of Kilnhurst, darkness was once again closing in for the night and the inhabitants were few and far between, with many making their way into houses and shops with a slam of the door as I rode past.

I stopped Valor outside what was easily the largest building in town, a three-story monstrosity that loomed over me as I hitched Valor to the post and left her to drink her fill of the full trough.

The raucous atmosphere inside the establishment hit me well before I'd stepped inside the entrance, from whence emanated a cacophony of noise as dozens of men watched several attractive women dance on a stage at the end of the huge room. They wore bright, billowy dresses that showed off their bodies perfectly, driving the men who watched them crazy with need.

The stage was next to a set of stairs, which led to the floor above. A few women walked up or down the stairs, some with men in tow—either having conducted or about to conduct their business. They wore even less clothing than the dancers and were all very attractive, a rarity that I was sure men paid extra for.

I ignored the crowd of baying, drunken men and walked to the bar, tapping my knuckles on the deeply varnished and sticky wooden counter. A middle-aged man noticed me and made his way over.

"Can I help you?" he asked and stroked his long dark beard, which was the only hair on his entire head. His southern drawl was well hidden in his voice, but I still managed to pick up on it.

"Whiskey," I said and placed ten dollars on the counter.

He eyed it nervously for only the briefest of moments before it vanished, snatched up and stuffed into his trouser pocket. The bartender fetched a clean whiskey glass, something I was actually a little shocked about, filling it to the top.

I knocked back the burning liquid. I've had very good whiskey in my life; what I'd just thrown down my throat was not even close. Hell, it could barely be considered a whiskey. "You got anything even slightly nice to drink?"

The bartender grabbed a hidden bottle from under the bar and placed it in front of me. I stared at the deep amber liquid it contained. "Scotch," he said. "Got it from a traveler who traded it for a night's sleep."

He uncorked it and poured me a glass.

Unlike the horse piss I'd just drunk, this stuff went down smoothly. It was the real deal. I fished out three tens and placed them on the counter. "Leave the bottle," I said and he did as he was bid.

I placed another ten on the bar. Once more it vanished. "I want a hot bath and a comfortable bed for the night. Will that be enough?"

"I reckon it will, yes. Will you want any company?" he asked.

"Not right now, but I'll let you know if I change my mind. I've got another ten for you, after you answer some questions."

That made him nervous, but the idea of keeping ten dollars for a few questions wasn't one to be passed up. That much money was probably more than he made in a week. I put enough tens on the counter to make it a hundred dollars that he'd earned in under five minutes. "Feel better about answering now?"

The money went the same way as all the others had, but he nodded acquiescence and I followed him to the empty end of the bar. "I won't even ask your name," I told him. "See, you have complete deniability."

"Who are you?"

"Not important, just a man passing through who needs a good night. You may want to arrange that bed and bath now."

He walked away and waved one of the girls over, a stunning blonde who stared at me as he told her what I wanted. A little air magic, the glyphs barely visible, carried the words invisibly toward my waiting ears. "Hot bath and comfortable bed," the bartender said. "Get them both ready, soon."

The girl glanced at me. "Will he want one of the girls?" she smiled slyly.

"No idea, but make sure they're ready. Hopefully, we can get him out of here before anyone shows up."

The girl's expression flickered over to fear. "I will." She moved off toward the stairs. I watched her ascend them, her half-bare ass wiggling as she made her way up to the floor above.

"Everything will be ready soon," the bartender said to me, regaining my attention. "So, what do you need to ask?"

"Just a few things. Have you had any recent trouble around here? Any bad blood with the tribes?"

He shook his head. "Can't say we do. I don't trust them, don't trust anyone who isn't—"

"White," I finished for him. "That's the word you're looking for, I assume."

"I won't apologize. Never said I hated them, and I don't wish them harm, unlike those lynching madmen back home. But it don't mean I have to trust them."

I changed topics quickly. "You seem to do well here, even though your town is in the middle of nowhere."

"The sheriff looks out for us; he has powerful friends. And there was gems found in the hills to the north of here a few years back. Means money flows through town fairly regular."

"Gems?"

"Stones, expensive ones, so the sheriff says. Diamonds and the like. Don't know much about it, don't want to neither. I just take their money when they want a fuck, sleep, or drink. Sometimes all three."

"One last question: You heard of a young boy who the sheriff was after? Few days ago now?"

"The murderer? Way I hear it, he tried to rob the big mansion up on the hill just outside town. Killed his own partner. The sheriff has two hundred bucks on him. Hope someone catches the little bastard soon. This is a safe town. We have fights, but no murders. It's unheard of."

"What about the ranch east of here?"

"I know the place. The owner don't care for us, although she'll bring in money to buy goods just like anyone else. Always left quick though. The sheriff doesn't like her, an argument between them or some such. Way I hear it—"

"Maybe you should mind your own business," a voice said from behind me.

The entire place went silent. The girls stopped dancing; those playing cards froze almost in place, their bets still in their hands ready to be thrown onto the pot between them. I turned to inspect the newcomer.

"You must be the sheriff," I said, his shiny badge evident for anyone to see. Hell, I could have probably seen it from Texas.

"And you are the man who interfered in my deputies' duties to bring in a dangerous fugitive. A murderer, I might add."

"The young boy," I said with a smile. "Do you try to kill a lot of people who are running away in the night?"

"That's none of your concern; he's a danger, and you will hand him over to me. Now." The sheriff moved his jacket slightly, giving him better access to the silver revolver on his hip—the twin of Sam's. The urge to take it from him was overwhelming, but I restrained myself. His time would come.

"I handed him over to the U.S. army at a fort nearby. He's going to remain there until *they* decide how to proceed."

Anger flashed on the sheriff's face like an oil fire. "What right—"

"My right," I interrupted. "You tried to kill a fleeing boy in the dead of night. Your deputies are lucky they still have the ability to walk."

One of the four men with the sheriff stepped toward me and placed a gun barrel against my head. I recognized him as one of the deputies from the forest. "You think you can make me leave now, you son of a bitch?"

I turned and stared at the average-size, average-looking man. If it wasn't for the fact that I'd pointed a gun at him, I'd have never remembered him in a million years. "Would you like to remove the gun yourself, or have me remove it for you? The second option is not a pleasant one."

"Enough, Douglas," the sheriff said, and the deputy grudgingly removed the gun. "You will answer two questions, or my companion here will repeat his actions, with far greater consequences for you."

I motioned for him to continue.

"Why are you here?"

"Just passing through. Was only staying the night and I'll be gone first thing in the morning."

"Never to return?"

"I hope not."

"Sort of out of the way, up here I mean? It's not the type of place you just come across by accident."

"I was passing by the ranch near here, but there didn't seem to be anyone home. Figured the fort was my next stop, but once more, there was no one there. Pure chance that I ended up here, if either of those places had been inhabited, I'd be long gone by now."

There was an expression of concern on the sheriff's face that melted into one of ambivalence and then finally innocence. "I'll send someone out in the morning to take a look, but you better be gone by then."

"Oh, I'll be long gone."

The sheriff turned to leave and I stopped him. "Nice gun," I said, making the sheriff turn back toward me. His deputies were nervous; apparently it was the topic that no one wanted to talk about, even more so than what had happened at the ranch or fort.

The sheriff removed the silver army Colt from its holster and turned it left and right, allowing me to get a good look. "It should be a pair, but that little bastard you helped stole the other one. He didn't mention it at all, did he?" he asked in a very nonchalant manner.

I shook my head. "He never said anything; he was unconscious when I left him at the fort. If I'd known he'd stolen from you, I'd have taken it back. Maybe you should contact the fort, ask them if they can take a look for you."

The sheriff went back to being concerned. I guessed that the fort and the sheriff didn't have the best relationship, but I didn't want to press further. I wanted to take a bath and leave his presence as quickly as possible. Hell, I wanted to leave the whole damn town, but I needed to do something before I left.

"Well, maybe I will. I want that gun back." He glanced back at his deputies. "I'd best leave you to it, but don't let me hear you've caused trouble. I won't be having that in my town."

"Of course. I promise to behave." I gave him my best smile of pure innocence and watched the sheriff and his cronies walk back out into the night. The music and rowdy behavior started slowly, like a tiny flake of snow turning into an avalanche by the time it hits the bottom of the mountain. Within moments the room was back to its previous noise level, with only the occasional glances my way.

"I thought you were going to push him too far," the bartender said.

I grabbed the bottle of scotch. "Are my bath and room ready?"

The bartender nodded and pointed toward the women at the bottom of the stairs. "Feel free to pick any of the girls there. They're all more than capable of giving you the evening of your life."

I doubted he'd have said the same thing if he'd been aware of how old I was, but instead I thanked him and told him maybe later. As I reached to the stairs, the blonde girl who had been talking to the bartender approached me with a smile on her lips and a wiggle in her hips.

"I'll show you the way," she said with a sly grin. "Follow me, darlin'."

I did as I was told, and she led me up the stairs and down a long, winding corridor with over half a dozen doors. Occasionally, I caught the sound of a moan or grunt, but we'd moved past before it felt like I was being too much of a voyeur.

The young woman led me up another set of stairs and onto a second landing with even more doors. She opened the one farthest from the staircase and allowed me to walk inside. "If you need anything, just shout." She winked and closed the door, leaving me alone in the spacious room.

The first thing I noticed was that the decor was actually tasteful. Someone had spent a lot of money on a large bed, and there were lots of paintings on the walls, some of which were of a risqué nature. They'd certainly decorated for the clientele.

I walked over to the large steel tub in the corner of the room that was full of water. Grooves had been carved into the floor to allow any water to run out onto some guttering outside. The tub was certainly big enough for two, and steam lifted off the water's surface. I didn't bother resisting the temptation to place my hand inside to feel the heat.

I shook the water off my hand and grabbed two towels off a chest of drawers, placing them beside the bathtub. After another drink of the excellent scotch, I placed the bottle on the table next to me.

I removed my coat, laying it over a clotheshorse, and un-clipped the knife belt that I wore around my waist, placing it over the coat. The six small silver throwing blades that it held were a last-resort weapon. Something I only really kept wearing for the comfort of knowing that they were available to me.

When I'd finished removing my clothes, placing them on the bed, I lowered myself into the steaming hot water with an au-dible sigh. "It's been far too long," I said as the water ate at the knots on my shoulders.

I let the water go to work and reveled in the relaxation that washed over me, even if I knew it wouldn't last. I'd give it an hour from the second I stepped into the room. Maybe less, depending on how nervous they were at my unannounced appearance.

I reached into the nearest coat pocket, removed a small pocket watch, and opened the front to check the time. I'd been in the bath for nearly twenty minutes. I had a little longer. I replaced the watch and orange glyphs lit up along my arms, my fire magic heating the water to near scalding temperature.

It was only a few minutes later when the door knocked. Apparently they were very nervous.

The girl on the other side didn't wait to be invited and just opened the door, stepping into the room with purpose. Long dark-red hair flowed freely over her bare, pale shoulders. She was petite, but curvy, and she removed her purple corset, exposing large, firm breasts before allowing the clothing to fall to the floor with a flourish. "Would you like some company?" Her voice was warm and inviting.

I smiled, mostly because it's always nice to have a stunning, and naked, woman asking if you want company, but also because she was almost my perfect woman. Red hair, short, and curvy.

"Feel free," I said with a wave of my hand.

She removed her tiny knickers and dropped them at her feet before stepping into the tub and making herself comfortable.

"So, can I ask for your name?" I requested.

"Stephanie," she said and rubbed her foot up against my groin, which sprang to life in an instant.

I forced myself to move her foot. Shooting myself would have been easier. "Do you mind if we just relax first?"

"Not at all," she said with a smile. "Turn around and I'll rub your shoulders."

I did as I was told and moved until my back was facing her. She grabbed me and moved me until her breasts were pressed up against my back. The feeling of her erect nipples against my back stirred me back to action and I had to remind myself that fun probably wasn't going to be on the menu.

Stephanie began working the knots out of my shoulder as she spoke. "I saw you talking to the sheriff."

"He was just checking out the newcomer," I said. "Probably understandable."

The movements stopped slightly. "So you're staying?"

"Wasn't planning on it. I plan on having a sleep and then leaving in the morning."

"It can be dangerous walking around these parts at night. I didn't even see you wearing a pistol."

And it begins. "Don't like pistols. They're inaccurate at any meaningful distance, and up close I can do just as much damage with a dagger."

Stephanie pushed me forward. "Let me get out of the bath so I can get your neck properly. I'll get back in after."

I moved forward, and, true to her word, Stephanie stepped out of the bath without bothering to dry herself with a towel. I had to force myself not to watch her dripping-wet body as she walked behind me and started rubbing my neck. "Are you enjoying the scotch?"

"It's excellent." The bottle was nearly half empty, and had absolutely no effect on me.

The neck rub lasted for a few seconds until I felt something cold and sharp against my neck.

"Well, this took longer than expected."

"What?"

I looked up at her and smiled. She pressed the blade of the knife against my throat further. "What are you so happy about?"

"You're naked, holding a knife against me. It's sort of silly. You could have just come in shooting, or, indeed, waited until

I was asleep and then did it. I assume whoever sent you here is really fucking nervous."

"You don't know anything. It's people like you who have to be removed to protect us all."

I tried to nod, but the blade made it uncomfortable. "The sheriff tell you that?"

"You will answer my question, and then you'll either go to the house outside of town, or die here."

"The house...? Ah, the one where the monster lives."

"The what?" Stephanie appeared to be genuinely confused.

"No matter. How about this? You remove the blade and answer my questions, or...well, you won't like the alternative."

"I'm in charge here," she protested.

"That you are." I moved faster than she could comprehend, pushing her arm away, grabbing hold of her, and pulling her head first into the bath with enough force that a large portion of the bathtub's contents shot over the side, drenching the entire surrounding area.

As Stephanie thrashed around, I stepped out of the bath and used my fire magic to instantly dry myself. I watched with amusement as Stephanie continued to make sitting up the most complicated action of her life, although it probably didn't help that each of her legs was draped over opposite sides of the tub. I pulled on my clothes and took a seat on the bed to wait for Stephanie to compose herself.

I'd removed the knife from her hand as I'd thrown her into the bath. It was a nice piece—ivory handle with a four-inch steel blade. It was about as useful against a sorcerer as bad language, but if she had stabbed me, it would have hurt. And besides, then I would have killed her and wouldn't have been able to ask what I needed to know.

Eventually, a seething Stephanie managed to right herself. "If you're going to kill me, get on with it."

I threw the knife behind me. "I want answers."

"Go to hell."

"Now, I know you don't care if I kill you, but if I walk out the front door they're going to know you didn't complete your job. And then I'm guessing you'll end up talking to the sheriff and his friends. Do you really want that?"

Stephanie glared at me, but shook her head. "No," she almost whispered. "What do you want?"

"What are you all doing here? I'm certain everyone is in on it. I just can't figure out what *it* is."

"The hills have diamonds in them. We don't want anyone from outside to find them."

"And that's why you're killing people? To get rich?"

"We're going to make our town separate from the rest of this godforsaken country. The sheriff told us that once we have the diamonds and our protector has his soldiers, we can start to take back what's ours."

"Protector? It wants to take over America?"

She shook her head. "Only Montana. To make sure it never becomes part of the Union. And anyone in our way dies."

"The ranch holder was in your way?"

"She found out what we were doing, what we'd planned. She had to die."

A thought occurred to me and I took a hunch. "You were there, weren't you?"

Stephanie glanced down briefly, but when she spoke she maintained eye contact. "I have no idea what you're talking about."

I knew a liar when I saw one. "You watched her murdered. Did you stab her yourself? Did you enjoy it?"

"I only watched," she snapped before she could stop herself. She immediately realized her mistake. "The sheriff and his men got half a dozen of the town occupants to help kill her. They opened the barn doors so that everyone else could watch."

I stalked toward her and placed my hands on the edge of the tub. "You watched her scream for mercy, watched as people started to cut on her. What the fuck is wrong with you?"

"She went against the town. She had to be silenced."

"Are there any children in town?"

She shook her head. "It's a town rule. Kids can come later when we have things straightened out. The sheriff doesn't want any of them to see what needs to be done."

"What needs to be done," I said absentmindedly. "Goddamn it. Get out of the tub."

"What?" she asked, but I was in no mood to ask again. I grabbed her arm and dragged her from the tub with one pull, dropping her onto the floor with a splat as her wet flesh hit the wooden floorboards.

"Get your ass in that chair," I snapped.

She dragged herself into the wooden rocking chair. Her arm was red where I'd grabbed it, but as far as I was concerned she was lucky to still *have* both her arms.

I removed the tiebacks from the window and tied Stephanie's arms behind the chair, making sure that she couldn't get up. I took the second tieback and attached it to the first, using the other end to tie it to the handles on the chest of drawers. If she started yanking at the rope, she'd get out, but it would take a while.

"You want me still so you can kill me," she said and spat at me, missing by a few feet.

I stood in front of her and rolled up the sleeves on my shirt, letting her watch the orange glyphs light up on my arms. "If I wanted to kill you..." A small sphere of flame appeared in the palm of my hand, and Stephanie's eyes opened as wide as possible. "...you'd already be cinders."

The flame vanished and I put on my coat. "You're going to give your friends in this town a message. They have forty-eight hours to leave. To run as far away as they can. Because in two days I'm going to come back, burn this entire fucking town to the ground, and piss on the ashes."

CHAPTER 22

New Forest, England. Now.

After the fight with the ghouls, I waited around long enough for the LOA emergency paramedics to turn up and check that everyone would be okay before leaving and heading home.

Agent Greaves was almost back on his feet by the time I left, and Olivia was nursing a sore, but healing, wound on her shoulder. Everyone got away with minimal injuries, a lucky break when it came to dealing with ghouls.

I took the time to head home, get a shower, and wash off the grime from the incredibly long day. Dealing with ghouls, finding another murdered girl, searching Vicki's house, and interviewing Neil had left me feeling emotionally, if not physically, exhausted.

Even so, after making an important call, I managed a few hours' sleep, only to be woken by someone banging continuously on my front door until I made my way from the bed to open it.

"Hey, Tommy," I said, with all the joy that I could muster after just being woken. "Could you possibly be a little louder? I think there are some rivets in the house that you haven't worked loose."

"Nice to see you, too," he said stepping inside and closing the door behind him.

"I don't think my kitchen can take another fridge raid," I told him as we made our way to the kitchen, where I made both of us a cup of white tea.

"I'm not hungry," he said.

"Okay, what's wrong? You're always hungry. Are Olivia and Kasey okay?"

He nodded firmly. "Yes, thanks for that. You saved Olivia's life. And Kasey is...concerned for her mum. She'll be okay, though."

I waved his thanks away. "Glad to hear it. We were all in the wrong place at the wrong time."

"They've taken Olivia to the medical clinic at my office building. We've got some of the best-trained people in the world. They want to keep her in for a few days to make sure that the neurotoxin has worked its way out of her system. Olivia's pissed off and wants to hurt something, but she'll live."

"And Agents Greaves and Reid?" Agent Reid had been found unconscious and covered in blood a few streets away from the police station. He'd been incredibly lucky.

"Greaves is less than happy that he's under my people's watchful attention, but he's healing well. Reid was bitten by the ghoul who used to be Vicki. He's going to be in the infirmary for a day or so like Olivia."

"How did you come to have such a good medical team?"

"We did some work for a medical center whose staff were getting harassed by a pissed off ex-employee and his friend; apparently, trolls hold grudges. Who knew? I offered them a place to work without worry whilst we dealt with it, and they ended up staying. So they work for me, but they are pretty much their own little section of the business."

"And I guess it helps having the people who are there for treatment being right next to the people who might look into such things without notifying Avalon."

"The thought never crossed my mind."

"Why are you here? I assume it's not just to give me an update on Olivia and the rest, as good as it is to know they're all okay."

Tommy's expression changed to one of seriousness in an instant. "Ghouls, Nate. There are goddamn ghouls and a lich in my city."

"I know, Tommy," I assured him. "I made a few calls earlier today. I'm expected at the airfield in about two hours."

Tommy chuckled. "Off to Canada?"

I didn't need to answer. Tommy knew full well that the answer was yes.

"Right, well, I'll go get ready and meet you there."

I opened my mouth to argue, but thought better of it. If I'd said no, he'd only have been at the airfield waiting for me anyway. "Fine. Meet me there in two hours exactly."

"Done," Tommy said, dashing up and out of my home seconds later.

The old airfield had been officially abandoned years ago, leaving the twelve-foot-high chain-link fence to guard nothing more than the grass that broke through the tarmac and the vines growing over an old hangar, threatening to consume it like a slow-moving predator.

The fence kept away anyone who might get too interested, or kids thinking that breaking in would be a good for a laugh. But it was just window dressing. Anyone getting past the fence would notice that the runway further into the compound was oddly free of any grass and that the tarmac was smooth and well maintained. And a close look at the front of the hangar would make it obvious that the vines had been allowed to grow in a very specific way, never obstructing the entrance.

Military signs, bright yellow and black, each the size of a manhole cover, adorned the fence at regular intervals. They extolled the notion that anyone caught trespassing would be arrested and charged without fail. Some of them suggested armed guards were still patrolling the area.

The airstrip was in fact fully functional all year long and served as a very private landing spot in the south of England. It was staffed all year, too, although most of the workers stayed in an underground complex, only coming up to deal with those landing and taking off.

Whenever someone landed, the place buzzed with activity. Whoever was arriving usually supplied their own security staff to maintain the area, which was made evident by the armed guards who stood at the entrance and waved me through.

I took the bike into the open hangar and switched off the engine.

"You took your damn time," Tommy said from a nearby chair, his feet up on the table beside him.

I took notice of the sandwich in his hand. The wonderful smell of bacon wafted toward me and my mouth watered. "Yes, you look incredibly pained," I said.

I turned and took in the jet that sat idly on one side of the huge hangar and was surprised to see a young girl exit the plane. "This is awesome," she squealed and almost jumped down the stairs connecting the jet to the hangar floor ten feet below.

"Kasey," I said with surprise and turned to Tommy. "You decided it was a good idea to bring your daughter."

Before he could answer, Kasey raced over to us. "What's the plane called?" she asked with obvious excitement.

"It's called a Pegasus, or a Pegasus 1488, to give it the full name."

"It's amazing," she said. "I've never seen a plane like it."

The Pegasus was an incredible feat of engineering. Its owner, like most of the truly powerful members of Avalon, was probably four or five generations of technology ahead of anything humans had access to. The jet was a sort of amalgamation of a Concorde at the front and an SR-71 Blackbird at the rear. I'd been inside it several times on long journeys and was fully aware of the luxury it contained.

"It has beds in there, Dad."

"I know, Kase," he said with a smile. "She's a bit excited," he told me.

"Never would have guessed. I thought eleven-year-olds were meant to be on their way to being permanently surly."

"She likes flying." Tommy grinned. "Kase, why don't you go on board and pick yourself out a chair."

She didn't need to be told twice and was off like a shot, taking the steps two at a time until vanishing back inside the fuselage.

"What the hell?" I asked.

"I couldn't leave her with Olivia. It's too dangerous."

"Does Olivia know who we're going to see?"

Tommy nodded.

"Does Kasey?"

He shook his head. "If I told her, she'd ask a million questions. And as it's a four-hour flight, I'd rather not have to go the whole way sitting with the Spanish inquisition."

"She has a bunch of questions for me, doesn't she," I said with sudden realization.

"A whole notebook full," Tommy confirmed. "It's in her backpack. She's looking forward to it."

"You could have stopped her, you know."

"Could have, didn't want to."

Before I could call Tommy a very rude name, a female flight attendant came over and informed us that we'd be leaving shortly. I thanked her and she smiled, flicking her long red hair off her shoulder before walking back to the jet.

"How do you do that?" Tommy asked.

"Do what?"

"Have beautiful women want to drop their pants after talking to you?"

I shrugged. "Didn't know they did. Must be my inherent charm."

Tommy laughed all the way over to the jet. "Yeah, that must be it, the charm."

The flight attendant was waiting for us inside the jet with another winning smile. She motioned for me to take a seat, and I selected one of the dozen black leather chairs that I knew to be as comfortable as they appeared.

The door slowly closed, and the jet began to taxi to the runway as Tommy sat opposite his daughter, across the aisle from me.

"You're Nathan Garrett," the flight attendant said, drawing my attention after I'd found myself looking out of the window.

"Umm, yeah, that's me," I said.

She bent down and hugged me tightly, her hair falling across my face and tickling my ear until she pulled away. "I just wanted to say thank you," she said.

"No, thank you," I managed.

"You don't know who I am, do you?"

"Sorry," I said.

"Nineteen forty-two, Berlin. You saved my life."

I studied the woman's face, which I suddenly realized hadn't changed in over seventy years, as an image flashed in my head. A woman being held by the throat by a man. A knife was in his hand, a Nazi insignia on his arm. The memory came flooding back to me in a rush. "I remember Berlin," I whispered.

"You saved a lot of people that night. I've always wanted to thank you for it."

"You're welcome," I managed, and she walked off behind a curtain at the rear of the fuselage.

"Charm, my ass," Tommy said with a laugh. "I didn't know you were in Berlin during the war."

"I get around," I said and noticed Kasey scribbling something in her notebook.

She glanced up and caught the frown on my face. "I had a question about the Second World War," she said and went back to writing notes, causing Tommy to laugh.

CHAPTER 23

I am not a good flier. I don't panic or run around screaming, but I do get very tense and drink far too much alcohol. So it was probably for the best that the flight attendant who had hugged me earlier placed an eighteen-year-old bottle of Japanese goodness in front of me with a crystal tumbler. I knew it was crystal simply because anyone who owns a jet as expensive as this one supplies only the best in tableware.

So, as we banked left and I caught a glimpse of the ground, several thousand feet below me, I knocked back my third glass and poured another.

"Flying is the safest form of travel, you know," Kasey said as she stared out the window.

"So people tell me," I replied. "It doesn't make me any less thrilled about having to be up here."

"Who are we going to see?" she asked with a smile on her face that I was certain was meant to melt my heart.

"Does that work on your parents?"

"Daddy," she said in a needy voice.

"Yes, it works," Tommy said. "I'm going to sleep, so you're on your own, Kase." He glanced at me. "Good luck."

Kasey made a humph-like noise and crossed the aisle, taking a seat opposite me. She placed her notebook and pen on the table between us, opening it to the first page. "You said you would," she reminded me when she saw the trepidation on my face.

"Okay, hit me with your best shot."

"What attacked my mum?"

"A ghoul," I said.

"Is that what murdered those women?"

I shook my head. "No, ghouls are...primal. But they're also intelligent and maintain their human brainpower. It's just that now, they're more interested in causing pain and suffering."

"Is my mum safe?"

"She's surrounded by her agents; she's safer than we are up here."

Kasey chuckled. "So, what's the difference between ghouls and zombies?"

"Have you ever seen a zombie movie? The zombies either run or shamble slowly, but the main part is that they eat people, and those who have been bitten turn into zombies themselves."

Kasey glanced over to Tommy, checking that he was asleep. "Yeah," she whispered.

"Well, those movie zombies are a combination of two different species. Firstly, you've got zombies themselves. They're created when someone who has died forcefully has their soul shoved back inside them. Zombies do shamble, because their bodies don't work properly, but they couldn't eat anyone if they tried. They basically have the ability to move very slowly and talk. That's it."

"They're not dangerous?"

"Only to themselves. The process of raising a zombie is painful for the soul of the person being reanimated. It's frowned upon because it's a bit too close to torture for many in Avalon's liking.

And in truth, very few people even bother, unless they're truly desperate for answers, because once you've forced a soul back into its body, the only way to send it back is to kill the person again."

"And the second species?"

"The second are called the barren. They used to be humans, before they were bitten by a ghoul."

"Does that mean my mum...?"

"No," I assured her quickly. "They only turn humans. In your mum's case the venom simply acted as a powerful paralyzing agent. But in a human, it kills within a few minutes. And they come back...empty." I tried to think of the right way to explain it. "Humans who are turned this way only want to kill. That's it. In that respect, they're a lot like the zombies in the movies, the ones that can run. All they do is kill and feed. A bite won't turn you into a barren, but it will draw blood, which will let every single barren within a mile know that you're alive and bleeding."

"And how are ghouls created?" Kasey asked, without looking up from her furious note taking.

"Two ways. Either through very powerful Blood magic, where you kill someone and then *force* the soul to stay inside the corpse, corrupting it until it changes into something malignant."

"Or?"

"Or you get a lich to do it."

She looked up at that. "What's a...*lich*?"

For a second, I thought about brushing the question off, or lying to her, but I knew neither of those things would help. "They're monsters. Sorcerers who had themselves killed in a violent way so that they could come back as something twisted and wrong."

"Why would they do that?"

"Some people use Blood magic too much—the really vile stuff, sacrifices and really horrific curses. Dark magic that strong corrupts them, makes them paranoid. It drives them mad with anger against a perceived threat. These are people who are already insane before the magic does its work. Once that sort of power gets into your head, it's difficult to shake free. Someone with *a lot* of hatred and some power at their disposal comes across the ability to turn into a near unkillable monster. Some of them jump at the opportunity."

Kasey didn't reply for a while. The flight attendant brought out a cheeseburger and fries for her, which allowed me to doze before I was woken by a jab in the arm.

"I thought we'd finished," I said with a glance at my phone to check the time. We had a few hours left before landing in Toronto. I got the impression that Kasey knew exactly how to fill that time.

"There are other things I want to know."

I glanced at Tommy, who was still asleep. *The bastard.*

"If you're going to work with my dad, I need to know more about you," she continued.

"Okay, go nuts."

"Have you ever met anyone famous?"

I raised an eyebrow. "You mean like actors and actresses? Because I have no idea."

"No, I mean famous people in history. Have you met any?"

"A few kings and queens of various countries, alongside a few popes, emperors, and people of varying levels of influence. I've met Leonardo da Vinci a few times—nice guy, if a little skittish."

"Skittish?"

"His brain is always working three or four sentences ahead of everyone else. It makes him difficult to talk to for any length of time, as he'll often say something and then run off to get some paper and a pencil to draw or write."

"Was he human?"

"Leonardo? No, not human. He was, sorry is, an alchemist."

"He's alive?"

"Was last time I saw him a few years ago."

Kasey wrote something in her book. "Anyone else?"

"I've met most of the Olympians. A few Titans, too."

"What happened to Zeus?"

The question surprised me, not least because it wasn't a conversation I'd had with too many people. "Don't know," I said. "No one has seen him for about three hundred years. Most assume he's dead, but no one is really sure. Why do you ask?"

"Someone at school said that he was murdered by Hera so that she could let Ares take over his businesses."

"That might be true, but tell your friend never to say such things in public. People who have voiced their discontent with the official version of Zeus's disappearance have sometimes vanished themselves."

"You think those responsible would go after children?" Kasey asked, clearly shocked.

"I think at least a few of the parents at your school probably work for Hera or her cronies. These things have a way of getting back to them, and eventually to Hera, too."

"The mythology shows Hera as a jealous, but mostly fair, matriarch."

"Mythology and truth are far apart in most cases. You'll learn that for yourself soon enough."

Kasey flipped through a few more pages of her notebook, but closed it without asking another question. "What's wrong?" I asked.

"Nothing," she said too quickly.

"Kasey, you're as bad a liar as your dad. Is that what all of these questions were about? Because you have something you really *do* want to talk about, and you were easing me into it?"

The barest of smiles crossed Kasey's lips. "My dad taught me to do that. Ease people into a conversation with easy questions before asking the hard ones."

"Smart girl."

"Can I hire you?"

I didn't even try to hide my shock. "What? Why?"

"My mum got hurt. I know that she can take care of herself, but before I left I saw her. She was crying. I've never seen her cry. Not once. Agent Greaves told me that she's getting no backup from Avalon. That someone has refused to send help. They told her that if she was unable to do it herself, that they would remove her. She's in danger. And dad will try to help her, and he'll get hurt. I can't have them hurt. I...I don't want—"

"They will be fine," I said as Kasey wiped tears from her cheeks.

"You don't know that," she whispered with a lot of anger. "I need you to take care of them. I want to hire you to look after them. To make sure they don't get hurt."

Tommy was up from his seat and across the aisle to his daughter in a second, holding her against him as she burst into tears. "Kase, mum's fine," Tommy said softly, as he stroked his daughter's hair. "And I'll be fine, too."

"No," she snapped, pushing away from him. "You don't know that. But you told me that Nate helps people, that he's good at it. I need him to keep you two safe. Jess lost her stepdad a few months back. Her mum's fallen to pieces, and Jess is a mess. I...I can't lose you, Daddy. I can't."

I stood and went to the rear of the jet, leaving father and daughter to have some alone time. I walked down a short aisle and opened a door to reveal a small bedroom. The double bed looked inviting. I lay down and discovered that the dark red duvet was as comfortable as it appeared. I figured I'd wait until Tommy or Kasey came and found me, or until we stopped moving. I discovered a selection of books in a bedside cabinet and selected the one that sounded the most interesting. It was about assassins, and I settled down to read, trying not to think about how upset my best friend and his daughter were.

I must have dozed off, because the next time I opened my eyes was in response to a soft knock on the bedroom's door. The redheaded flight attendant opened the door and told me that we were landing and that I needed to get back into my seat and fasten my seatbelt.

I thanked her and pushed myself up to a sitting position, stretching my arms before making my way back to Tommy and Kasey, who were still deep in conversation.

Ten minutes later, we touched down with a slight bump and came to a stop shortly after.

The two flight attendants opened the jet's door, allowing freezing-cold air to flow into the fuselage uninterrupted. "Your bags will be taken up to the house," the blonde one said with a smile.

"Cheers," I said, returning her smile and using a small measure of fire magic to warm my bare hands. I was grateful that I'd brought a large, thick coat with me as the wind picked up the loose snow littering the airfield and flung it around like a child having a snowball fight.

Kasey, Tommy, and I made our way across the tarmac toward a large building, the only one on the airfield. Just as we'd reached our destination, and the promise of a windless few moments, the door burst open and a man stepped out. He wore a long black coat, but didn't bother to cover his bald head with a hat. He was over six and a half feet tall, and while he was lean in build, he was still broad across the shoulders. Back when he was born, he'd have been considered a giant of a man. He walked toward us with no evidence that the cold was anything more than a slight inconvenience.

"Nathan," he shouted, wrapping his arms around me in a hug before doing the same to Tommy. "And this must be Kasey," he said with enthusiasm. "Come with me; let's get back to the house."

He took us into the building, which contained one large room where armed security checked our bags and made us walk through a metal detector before letting us leave through the door on the opposite side. "Sorry about that," the man said. "If I don't let them do it, they get very whiny about the whole thing."

He led us toward a small motorcade—three black four-wheel-drive Mercedes. We climbed into the middle one; the seats inside had been arranged so that the front passenger could swivel around to talk to those in the rear.

He swiveled around once the car started. "It's good to see you all. I'm glad you called, Nathan. It sounds like we have much to discuss."

Kasey raised a hand.

"You don't need to do that," the man said warmly. "Just ask away."

She lowered her hand, but stared intently at the man in front of us. "Who are you?"

"Nate and Tommy didn't tell you who you were visiting? My manners must seem horrific." He straightened himself in his chair and readjusted his collar, before extending his hand to Kasey. "Hello, Kasey, it's a pleasure to meet you. I've gone by a few names over the years, but you can call me Hades."

CHAPTER 24

"I'm sorry my dear, did that shock you?" Hades asked Kasey as we exited the car. She'd been very quiet since learning of his identity.

"It's just..." she started in a whisper, "you're Hades. We learned about you at school."

"I am he, yes," he said with a large grin in place. "You must tell me what they're teaching these days. Last I heard it was all 'kidnap' this and 'pomegranates' that. Persephone was always entertained with that one. She doesn't even like the blasted things."

We followed Hades up the lengthy path and under a gray stone archway to the front door of dark wood, where he caught Tommy glancing around. "You're wondering about my security, aren't you?" Hades asked.

"Glass windows, gray brick structure, wooden window frames. I assume you have runes etched into everything."

"Every single brick has a rune on it. The wooden frames also have them." He tapped the glass panel in the front door. "Bulletproof glass. It's in every window, pane of glass, and door in the house. I assure you, we are safe here."

Hades opened the door and took us into the foyer—a grand room with a wooden staircase on one side and selection of dark-brown couches on the other. The staircase matched the door and window frames in color.

"The stairs lead to nine bedrooms," Hades said. "Your bags will be taken to the empty bedrooms at the end of the hallway. Each has its own bathroom, so please feel free to make yourself at home."

As if on cue, several women in uniform appeared, taking our bags upstairs without a sound. They were like tiny, luggage-carrying ninjas.

"Why don't you go and get yourselves settled," Hades said to Tommy and Kasey. "I'll be outside with Nate when you're ready."

With anyone else, Tommy would have glanced toward me to check that I would be okay. But there was no need with Hades. We both trusted him with our lives, and although we didn't always agree, he would never attack us. Besides, if he'd wanted me dead, I wouldn't even have made it to the hangar.

"Let's go talk," Hades said to me when we were alone.

I followed him through several rooms until we reached the massive kitchen. A counter ran almost the length of the room, chairs pulled up along one side so that people could cook and serve the food at the same place.

The smell of cinnamon wafted through the room. Someone had been baking.

"Our cook makes apple strudel," Hades said. "I had her make Tommy one all for himself."

"I'm surprised he hasn't caught the scent and run down here like a bulldozer."

Hades laughed as he opened a large glass door and stepped out into the conservatory.

I walked to the glass window and looked out across the fields behind Hades' house. A large building sat several hundred yards to my left. It hadn't been there when I'd last visited. "What's that for?"

"Ah, we built a small house there for guests we don't trust to stay in the main building. There's two more down by the lake. Persephone had wanted another built to house the swimming pool, but I convinced her that moving the entire swimming pool would be best left to Poseidon himself, and I doubted he would be keen on coming over to help my wife redecorate our house."

"How is she?"

"Persephone? Probably on the phone shouting at someone. She's been looking forward to seeing you again. The last twelve hours have been a whirlwind of activity that I'd decided it was best to avoid."

"Sorry for causing you any problems."

"Not me, my friend, but my staff might not be so enthusiastic." He pointed back into the kitchen. "You see those spotlights above the kitchen counter?"

"They look very nice," I said, hoping that was the correct answer.

"Well, one of the bulbs was flickering. Persephone equated this to the end of the world. Apparently, flickering lights are some sort of sign of the apocalypse. Who knew?" Hades walked to a drinks cabinet at one side of the conservatory and removed a bottle of Coke. "Drink?"

"Why not," I said. "Thanks for the bottle on the jet."

"You're a terrible flyer. I saw no reason to burden everyone else with your lunacy."

I laughed as I accepted a bottle and took a seat on a leather armchair. "Thanks for seeing me on such short notice."

Hades sat opposite me and took a drink. "You call, I answer. I owe you too much for it to be any other way. Besides, you said the magic word. Lich. That gets my attention pretty goddamn quickly."

Before I could say anything the door opened and Kasey and Tommy joined us. Kasey had a can of Coke in one hand, and Tommy was eating an apple with the enthusiasm of a man who hadn't eaten in days rather than hours.

"How's your accommodation?" Hades asked.

"Awesome," Kasey said immediately. "My room is massive."

"I'm glad you approve." Hades turned back to me. "Now, let's discuss this lich you're concerned about."

Tommy glanced at his daughter. "Maybe you shouldn't be here for this."

"No," Kasey snapped. "I'm not a little girl, dad. This monster is responsible for Mum being attacked. I need to know what it is."

"I'm not sure," Tommy said.

"Please, Daddy," Kasey pleaded.

"Tommy," I interrupted. "I'd never tell you what to do, but do you remember what we were doing at twelve?"

"Hunting deer," Tommy said. "You?"

"I was learning how to kill people," I said honestly. "If I remember correctly, on my twelfth birthday, Merlin had me doing sword practice in the morning, and herbs in the afternoon. I believe we had cake after."

"Well, I certainly don't want her hunting this thing," Tommy said. "But you're probably right, Kasey; you are old enough to know what's happening."

Kasey beamed as if a huge victory had been won, then stopped the moment her dad glanced her way. "Nate told me that lich are monsters," Kasey said.

"They're more than that," Hades explained. "A lich is created when a sorcerer uses some very dark Blood magic to twist himself. They murder people in a very specific way and absorb their victims' souls as they ebb away. Then, when they've finally taken enough, they kill themselves in as violent a way as possible.

"And there's one more thing they must do. As they die, they must focus on the one person they hate above all others. A lich is created through a combination of the magic, the sacrifices, and the hate. They're known as those born of hatred. And once they've been created, they're capable of such evil as you can't imagine."

"What makes them so powerful?" Kasey asked.

"Each lich can make up to six ghouls. Each ghoul is created by the lich absorbing the spirit of the human and then replacing it with some of his own life energy."

"That's why we smelt so many different scents," Tommy said.

Hades nodded. "Yes, the lich will contain the scents of all the souls it's absorbed, all merged together. But even worse, it means that you can't kill the lich until you've killed all of his ghouls. Otherwise, a part of him still exists out there, and he can come back again and again."

"So, they're unkillable until then?" Kasey asked.

"A lich with six ghouls alive is stronger than your dad is, just as fast, and nearly impossible to hurt in any meaningful way. Magic and weapons will hurt him, but not for long. And once you've killed all of the ghouls, you need a necromancer to kill the lich for good, by removing whatever twisted visage is left of his soul and destroying it. Only then can he be killed."

"So to stop him, we have to destroy all of his ghouls and then remove his soul before killing him?" Tommy asked, before turning to me. "I see why you don't talk about your past lich problem very often."

"It wasn't much fun," I agreed. "I'm here to ask for your help, Hades. Do you have a necromancer you can spare?"

"I'll make a few calls and get someone to the U.K. as soon as possible. Are you certain it's a lich?"

"Yes," I said. "I saw him with my own eyes. His name is Peter Jarvis."

"The trick will be to find this lich before anyone else dies. If you really did kill one ghoul, you have a few days before he will fully recover from his weakened state. He won't risk losing another so soon after."

"Can't he just make more?" Kasey asked.

"Once a lich-created ghoul is dead, that's it. They've lost that portion of their life they placed inside the beast." Hades was about to say more, but the doors opened once again and a woman joined us in the conservatory.

Stunning was the wrong word to describe Persephone. She was one of the most beautiful women I've ever laid eyes on, someone who could give Aphrodite a run for her money in the desirable stakes. Her long dark hair flowed freely over slender shoulders, and a diamond clip in the shape of a butterfly sat just above one ear, which was pierced several times. She wore a simple white t-shirt and a pair of jeans that appeared to have been created especially for her.

She kissed her husband on the cheek before beckoning me to stand and giving me a hug. "It's been far too long, Nathan," she said before releasing me and doing the same to Tommy. "And you must be Kasey," she said and embraced her as if they'd known each other for years.

"Hi," Kasey managed weakly.

"Are you done here?" Persephone asked Hades.

"I need to talk to Nate, but you're welcome to continue with whatever plan you have, my love."

Persephone's smile increased her beauty tenfold. "Good. Nathan you can join us when you're finished. I'm going to take this lovely young lady and her father for a tour of our home." And without another word, Tommy and Kasey were ushered out of the conservatory.

"It's been a long time since we had any kids around," Hades said absentmindedly. "I think Persephone misses it. The house is always full of people, but security, business, and staff are no substitute to the sounds of a child's laughter."

"Are you getting broody, old friend?" I asked with a laugh.

"Maybe. We have five children of our own and adopted six more. Our youngest is twenty-two now. Maybe it's time to extend our family once again." He shook himself, as if clearing the thoughts out of his head. "A discussion for another time. I assume you didn't come all this way to hear me lament."

"Can we go somewhere private?"

Hades stood and opened the door behind him, bathing us both in the freezing cold air of a Canadian winter. Fire glyphs spread across the back of my hands, warming my body, but I was still grateful for the thick hooded top I wore. Hades didn't even seem to notice the cold. He wore only a black shirt and trousers, but he might as well have been wearing a thick fur coat for all the cold outwardly affected him.

"You need to teach me that trick," I said as we walked down a path in his garden, moving past stone statues of mythological beasts—griffins, harpies, and even a stone ogre sat amongst ornate and beautifully tended bushes, their color a deep green, despite the time of year.

"You have an impressive gardener," I said.

"If you hire an earth elemental, your garden tends to stay how you want it." We stopped walking at a statue of Pegasus, and Hades glanced up at the magnificent sculpture. "Have you ever seen Pegasus?"

I shook my head. "Before my time."

"Ah, he was a beautiful steed. Poseidon created him by feeding the blood of Medusa to a normal horse. Not sure when that was twisted to become he was *born* from Medusa's blood, but there you go. I remember the day that Bellerophon captured him. Zeus was furious that anyone would dare steal such a sacred creature."

"Bellerophon I've met a few times. He was always full of anger."

"He started to believe his own press, and eventually he challenged Zeus. Twice. The first time, Zeus beat him with a warning never to cross him again. The second time, Zeus was not so kind. He almost killed Bellerophon, probably would have, too, if not for Poseidon. It left Bellerophon a bitter and twisted man."

"I killed a ghoul today," I said, wanting to get the conversation away from the past and back to events closer to our current time.

Hades fell silent, but didn't turn to look at me. "I know, you've already told me. You've done that before, though."

"With magic, Hades. I killed a ghoul with magic."

That got his attention. "Are you sure?"

"I burnt his head clean off. I'm very sure he was dead."

"They can heal—"

"*He didn't*," I interrupted. "Hades, I killed a ghoul with fire magic. How is that possible?"

"It certainly requires some investigation."

"And I healed from being stabbed by a silver dagger in a matter of *hours*."

Hades raised one eyebrow. "Before it happened, did you feel anything, a surge of strength or light-headedness?"

"I'd been stabbed. I was pretty much focused on the 'not bleeding to death' portion of the day."

"Think, Nate. It's important."

I dredged my mind for anything that might prove useful. "I felt something before I punched out a werewolf with one hit. A sort of cold rage."

"Did you use magic?"

"Nope, so it sort of stuck in my mind."

Hades made a sound that was a cross between being interested and concerned. "I'll look into it. There are a few possibilities that could account for why these things happened."

"Such as?"

"When you first contacted me after recovering your memories, you mentioned that your Blood magic glyphs were vanishing. It's possible that these events could be due to surges of power. Maybe one of the glyphs locked away the abilities of a parent. It sounds like some form of necromancy."

Much like Kasey, it was fairly common for someone to have the abilities of both parents. Although it's largely dependent on the species involved, it's certainly possible that the cursed blood glyphs that had marked me for so long had blocked my access to abilities I'd never even known I'd had.

"Can you look into it for me?" I asked. "I'd rather not have any more surprises."

"I can have you do some tests, but now might not be the best time to do that. We should wait until this lich has been dealt with."

"I have another favor to ask. I need access to the Silver Room."

To his credit, Hades didn't ask if I was sure or if he could help. He just removed his mobile phone, calling someone to inform them that the room would need to be ready. "Is tonight okay with you?" he asked me once he'd finished talking.

"Thanks," I said.

"Have you told your friend what you plan on doing?"

I shook my head, but I knew that when I did tell him, that Tommy was going to start yelling.

The rest of the day flew by as Tommy, Kasey, and I spent time with Hades, Persephone, and various members of their staff and entourage. For a while, I even forgot about what was happening back home, the death and horror that would be waiting for us when we returned. I had no illusions about what needed to be done; the ghouls and lich needed to be hunted and exterminated.

I left the four of them to talk and exited the large room, using a door by some bay windows to step out into the darkness beyond. I needed some air, some time to think.

A few minutes later, the door opened behind me. "A penny for your thoughts," Persephone said.

"It gets so dark here. There're no streetlights for miles. It's quite soothing."

"You sound like Hades."

A smile parted my lips.

"You want to use the Silver Room."

"Hades told you, I assume."

"He's my husband. You don't get to stay married for thousands of years by keeping secrets."

"I wouldn't have thought you could do it by pissing off the mother-in-law either."

Persephone laughed. "My mother is her own worst enemy. She's the one who decided Hades wasn't good enough. She can deal with that loss. Or rather, she doesn't deal with it and still holds a grudge. I heard she had some things to say to you the last time you met."

It was my turn to laugh. "Demeter didn't find it amusing when I didn't do as I was told. Oh, and she hates Hades. That sort of soured any potential friendship."

"She's good at that." Persephone was quiet for a short time as the cold wind silently swept around us. "So, what were you really thinking about?"

"A lich is running around the south of England. I can't think how it's going to end well."

"And going into that accursed room will help?"

"I know you don't approve of it."

"People have died in there, or been driven mad. I understand why my husband keeps it, it's saved lives, too, but that doesn't mean I like it."

"I've had these glyphs on my chest for as long as I can remember. No one could ever tell me what they did. But now they're disappearing one at a time, and the power I can access has increased. I can feel it whenever I use magic, but I need to know what I'm capable of. The Silver Room is the only place I can do that safely."

"For everyone else."

"I can't risk hurting anyone."

"Hades says you'll be fine, that you've used it before. His assurances do little to curb my unhappiness at what you're going to do."

"If it's any consolation, I'm not thrilled about it."

Persephone kissed me softly on the cheek. "No, Nate, it's no consolation at all."

"What's the Silver Room?" Kasey asked as she stepped out of the house.

"You really should make noise when you walk around, has anyone ever told you that?" I replied.

"Dad says he's going to make me wear a bell," she said with a smile. "What's the Silver Room?"

"That's sort of complicated," I said.

"My parents say that when they don't want to tell me something. Guess how well it works for them?"

Persephone laughed.

"You're a big help," I said to her, which caused her to laugh more, drawing Hades and Tommy outside to join us.

"Dad, what's the Silver Room?"

Tommy's expression hardened. "Let me guess, Nate will be using it."

"Is someone going to answer my question?" Kasey demanded.

"It's a large room on the lowest floor of this building," Hades said. "It allows people to use their magic to the fullest extent of their abilities to ascertain what they're capable of."

"It forces people to use magic," Tommy said. "They keep using their magic until they can't use it anymore, and they collapse from exhaustion." Tommy left the words *or worse* hanging between us. "Is this why you called Hades? To use that damn room?"

"No," I said. "But I need to use it. And you know I do."

Tommy's eyes softened slightly. "Doesn't mean I like it."

"I agree with Tommy, Nate," Persephone said. "This is a danger that you don't need to face."

"It's dangerous?" Kasey asked.

"It can be," I said. "If you try to push yourself past your limits, or you allow your magic to consume you. But neither of those things will happen to me."

"You can't say that—" Tommy started.

I cut Tommy off before he could finish. "I am not some child who has no control over his magic, Tommy. I know the risks, and they're worth it. I need to know what I can do, how far I can push myself."

No one spoke for a time, leaving only tension to fill the void. "When are you going to do it?" Tommy asked with a sigh.

"Whenever Nate is ready," Hades said.

"Let's get on with it then," I said. "The sooner we start, the sooner it'll be over."

Tommy, Kasey, and Persephone all went upstairs, although none of them were happy about it. Either because they were annoyed that I was risking my health and sanity, or, in Kasey's case, because they were really interested in what all the fuss was about.

Hades and I used an elevator near the rear of the property to go down the six floors to the very lowest level. We stayed silent the whole time, but I knew that Hades would rather I wasn't doing it. Hell, I'd rather not be doing it myself, but I needed some answers. Sometimes you only get the answers you seek if you risk everything.

The lowest floor consisted of three rooms, all down one long corridor. We walked past the first two. The first was a monitoring station for whoever was using the room, and the second, adjacent to it, was the massive medical suite that took care of any resulting emergencies. I couldn't spot anyone through the glass window.

"Nervous?" Hades asked.

"A little bit, yeah."

"Relax; don't try to stop the magic from coming. When you wake up, you'll be in one of the rooms upstairs."

"Thanks for this, Hades."

We reached the entrance to the room, and I took a deep breath as Hades input a PIN code and then palm print onto an electronic lock next to the door.

A yellow light flashed above the doorway as the door slowly swung open into the darkness beyond. I took a step forward, and Hades stopped me. "If this goes too far, if I think you can't come back on your own, I'm shutting it down."

I nodded.

"I'm serious, Nate."

I knew what he meant. If I couldn't control *it*, if *it* gained control over me, Hades would shut me down. Permanently.

I removed my t-shirt and passed it to Hades, then kicked off my shoes and removed my socks before I stepped inside the dark room, waiting as Hades made his way back to the control room. After a short time, a single light came on above my head, bathing everything in a low-level glow. Not that there was anything to bathe.

The room lived up to its name. It was a four-hundred-square-foot box with polished silver walls, floor, and ceiling. Orange and red runes were etched around the top and bottom of each wall, which ensured no damage could be done to the room itself. The door closed and locked. There was no magic on earth that could be used to force one's way out the Silver Room once the door was locked. And probably everyone who had used the room had tried. I knew I had.

I glanced up at the huge painted rune on the ceiling, a mirror image of the one on the floor. Runes are a difficult thing to learn—each rune does something different. The amount and type of magic, the size and placement of the rune, and a hundred other factors in place during its creation will cause it to have different effects. I don't know what type of magic was used to create the two runes, but the amount of power must have been immense.

I sat cross-legged in the center of the room, and carried out some breathing exercises that let me calm myself. I didn't want to be worked up when the room went active.

"All okay in there, Nate?" asked Hades, his voice coming through the speakers hidden around the room.

"I'm good, thanks," I said. I knew Hades was watching me. The room was fitted with a CCTV system, alongside the microphones and speakers. The cameras were tiny dots in the ceiling. I smiled and waved at where I knew they were concealed.

"Let me know when you're ready."

I took one last deep breath. "Go."

The effect was immediate. Bright white and orange glyphs burned across my skin as my magic was ignited. The effect was similar to trying to push every last drop of water from a dam through a pinhole. It was agony to my muscles as magic flowed freely without pause, without restraint. It was more magic than I'd ever used at once, more than I was capable of before the glyphs had started to vanish. It roared out of my body, smashing into the walls and ceiling of the room, trying to find an exit.

If I'd done it outside, without the runes, the silver, or the support, people would have died. There was no question in my mind. The magic was raw and unfocused. It just wanted to be used, and anyone caught in that maelstrom would be torn to pieces.

As the pain became too much, and my screams turned into something animal, something guttural and raw, I began to feel *it* stirring. The pain subsided the more *it* tried to take control until I could hear *its* voice inside my head; *"Nathan, it's been a while."*

The voice was from pure magic, the magic that tried to take control of a sorcerer's mind and body if they use too much of it. The voice belonged to the nightmare inside me.

I glanced up at the polished silver walls. A darkness was spreading out from my eyes, covering my forehead, and making its way down to my jawline. *"Are you ignoring me, Nathan?"*

I forced a smile.

"It's good that you finally sorted me out. You're getting stronger; those glyphs that stopped me from joining with you are finally vanishing."

"You won't take me," I said as the magic continued to erupt all around me.

The monster sighed. *"You still don't understand what I am, do you? You still think I'm some sort of monster; even after all we've done together. Well, Nathan, we've got some time. Let's talk."*

CHAPTER 25

Montana Territory, America. 1878.

Getting out of the town of Kilnhurst had been relatively easy. I'd left my would-be assassin in the bedroom, naked and cursing my name as I jumped out of the window. A little air magic to slow my descent and I landed without a fuss. A moment later, I'd released Valor from the hitching post and rode out of town at a steady pace.

It took me a few hours to get to the fort that I'd sent Sky and Sam to. It was a small structure, compared to forts in other parts of the country, but placed on top a hill, giving it an excellent view of the land.

Armed soldiers patrolled the walkways above what I was sure would be thick, sturdy walls, scanning the surrounding land as the last vestiges of sunlight died away over the mountains to the west.

One of the guards noticed my arrival as I neared the huge wooden gates and aimed his rifle in my direction. "Stop," he shouted.

I did as I was told.

"Who are you?" he asked. His gun wavered slightly. Probably new at the job.

"My name is Nathan Garrett," I told him. "I sent some people up here earlier, a woman and a boy. Have you seen them?"

The guard left my sight, and for a brief moment I thought I was just being left outside to wait. I was just about to find another way inside the fort when the gates swung open and a man walked toward me. He wore the uniform of an army officer, his revolver still holstered at his hip. But he hardly needed the weapon considering he was flanked by five soldiers, all of whom were holding their rifles in a very nonchalant way, instantly proving how concerned they were.

"And you are?" the officer demanded of me.

"As I told your man, my name is Nathan Garrett."

"You sent some people here, a young boy and an *Indian* woman?" He managed to place a lot of contempt into that one word. Apparently, he was not a fan of the natives.

"They made it here, then," I said.

"Never said that," the officer said with a smug smile.

"Yes, you did. I never mentioned that she was Indian, only that she was a woman."

The smile vanished as if wiped away by the increasing wind that picked up around us. "And who are you to be sending people to my fort?"

I ignored his question. "Where are they?"

"I detained them both pending further inquiries."

"You did *what*?"

"I can't have some Indian spy walking unsupervised around my fort. And when we tried to disarm her, she broke the arm of Lieutenant Burns."

"I don't give a damn what she did or didn't do, get her out of whatever shithole you put her in. Now."

"I am the captain in charge of this fort, and you—"

I reached into my saddlebag and pulled out a piece of paper. "And here is a piece of paper signed by your president that grants me the rank and status of a major of the American army. I outrank you, captain, now get out of my damn way and get me those prisoners."

I ignored the captain's gobsmacked face and rode Valor into the fort.

I counted a dozen buildings inside the fort—barracks, a mess room, the quartermaster's storehouse, even a small medical center were all easily identifiable. But they all paled in significance when compared to the large two-story building at the rear of the fort. It was clearly the officers' quarters.

I dismounted Valor and passed her reins to a young boy who came running up to me. "Take her to the stables."

He took Valor away, just as the captain made his presence known again. "Sir, I'm sorry about what happened back there." He spoke with the displeasure of a man who'd thought of himself as the top rung on a very short ladder and then discovered that the ladder was only half made.

I folded the letter up and put it in my pocket, taking my time to let the silence linger between us. "Just so we understand each other, captain. I'd like the woman and the boy released, and then I'd like to have a chat with you and your officers."

The following few minutes were a hive of activity as people ran around following the orders barked out by the captain. I let myself into the officers' quarters and tried not to scare a young woman who had been cleaning the dining area.

She quickly made her excuses and rushed away up the staircase to the rooms above, leaving me alone to grab an apple from a fruit bowl and take a bite.

It took under three minutes for Sky and Sam to be presented. I knew because I'd watched the time pass on a large black grandfather clock beside me.

"That man is an idiot," Sky said as an army sergeant placed her knives on the table in front of her.

"Yes, ma'am," the sergeant said firmly.

"Was I talking to you?" Sky snapped, snatching up a dagger and placing it in her boot as Sam pounced on the bowl of fruit like a lion.

"No, ma'am," he almost whispered.

"Be nice, Sky," I said. "What's your name, sergeant?"

"Sergeant Roberts," he said and saluted.

"Roberts," I stood and offered him my hand, which he took in a firm, confident handshake. "Nice to meet you. Sky's right though, your captain is an ass."

"Permission to speak freely, sir?"

"Of course," I said.

"He's got a blind spot when it comes to Indians. He hates 'em. They killed some friends of his at Little Big Horn a few years back. Never forgave 'em for that. And he wasn't right pleased about 'em before then. It sort of pushed him over the edge."

"Does he know anything about what happened at the Warren Ranch due east of here?"

"I wouldn't like to say, but we've been ordered not to patrol east for a day or two. No reason why. None that I've heard, anyway. Captain Waltham isn't exactly forthcoming with anyone except Lieutenant Burns when it comes to giving orders."

"Those two close?" Sky asked. The weapons on the table had disappeared back to wherever they were stored on her person.

"Thick as thieves, as my mother would say. I think Burns is the only one the captain trusts. Which is a shame, as Burns is a first-class shit."

"I got that impression before I broke his arm," Sky said.

"I heard about that," I said. "You wouldn't give up your weapons."

"Wouldn't let the shit grope me is more accurate."

"If that's all, sir," an uncomfortable Roberts said and saluted before leaving the room.

Sky waited until she was certain we had no unwanted ears before talking. "How'd you manage to get the captain to let us go?"

I pulled out the paper and passed it to her, watching with interest as she read it.

"Is this real?"

"Probably," I said, taking it back. "It certainly comes in handy when dealing with people like Captain Waltham."

"Why only a major? Why not a higher rank?"

"Too high and people will remember you. The rank of colonel is fairly rare, and the day a soldier meets a general is a big deal to some. Something they remember."

"What if you need to get a colonel or general to do what Captain Waltham just did?"

I thought for a second. "You know, it's never come up. Avalon has enough people scattered in high-ranking positions that I can always find someone to help out. And if I can't, well, then I do things a little more subversively than I did to get into this place."

"You're just full of surprises."

"I like to impress. Did they treat you and Sam okay?"

Sam finished chewing and wiped his mouth. "Not very nice food, but that's about it. That captain yelled at me and Sky a bit, calling us traitors."

"Sounds like you had fun," I said. "Where are the chief and his men?"

"In the woods to the north," Sky said. "Arriving with a full accompaniment of native warriors wouldn't have done us many favors. I told them to wait until morning. I was hoping that you'd have found out more from your trip to Kilnhurst."

"There's something going on there, that's for sure," I said. "Sam told me about the monster that killed his friend. Apparently it's protecting the town, or at least that's how the inhabitants see it."

"It's not protecting them, it's using them," Sky said.

"You want to tell me what *it* is?"

"It's called a lich."

"Is that what the monster's called?" Sam asked, finally having eaten his fill. "I expected the name to be more...horrific."

"Liches are evil in a way I can barely put into words," Sky told Sam. "Hard to kill, too. If you met one of them, Sam, you're lucky to be alive."

"So how do we kill it?" Sam asked.

"*You* don't. That's why I'm here."

"I think you need to explain exactly what's going on here, Sky," I said.

"A lich is roaming the countryside killing people. As a necromancer, it's my job to make sure that stops."

"So, who sent you here?"

"My employer. Don't ask for more, because you won't get it."

"Whom does this lich hate enough to do all of this?"

"No idea. I'll ask it when I tear its soul out. In the meantime, we have a problem. I overheard the asshole in charge of this fort say that he wants some men to ride to the ranch and the other fort tomorrow. I think he's involved in all of this somehow."

As if on cue, the doors slammed open and Captain Waltham marched into the dining room with his pistol drawn. "I can't have you walking around saying things like that," he said and aimed the gun at Sky, but he was far too slow.

Sky's hand moved a fraction of a second before mine and Captain Waltham turned into a statue. He blinked twice in what I took to be shock and then collapsed to the floor.

"What did you do?" I asked

"Moved his soul."

No one spoke; I wasn't even sure I'd heard Sky correctly.

"I didn't tear out his soul," Sky clarified. "I moved it, slightly. Do it just right and you cause a person to freeze. It only lasts a few minutes, though."

"How did you do that?" Sam asked.

"Necromancy," Sky said. "The manipulation of the spirit, soul, or whatever else you wish to call it. Everyone has a soul. No matter if they're evil, angelic, twisted, or otherwise, they still have one. Only the dead don't. If you tamper with the soul of a living person, you can do all kinds of horrible things. Freezing them is one of the more humane. I usually deal with dead spirits or souls just leaving the body, but I'm not without my talents when it comes to the living, either."

"So I can see," I said as I picked up Captain Waltham and carried him to a comfortable chair before depositing him in it. I removed his army Colt and passed it to Sky.

Captain Waltham blinked again.

"You don't have long," Sky said. "And he can still hear you just fine."

"Captain," I said, my voice calm. "You're going to regain the use of your body in a second, but please don't make my companion here angry. She's not too good at holding back the urge to hurt those who have clamped her in irons, stuffed her in a prison, and been generally unpleasant toward her. She's probably tired, too, and that tends to make people a little cranky. So, no shouting, screaming, yelling, or general loudness will leave your lips, or I'm going to find the monster that you've made a pact with and I'm going to feed you to it."

"You won't torture me," the captain said, his words slurred and slow.

"Who said anything about torture?" I asked. "I said I'd feed you to the monster. If he wants to take his time, then so be it. Me, I'm not going to get my hands dirty dealing with a piece of shit like you."

I moved him into a more upright position.

"What's your plan?" I asked him. The captain opened his mouth to answer, but before he could speak, I shushed him to silence once more. "Before you start, we know you're involved, so don't bother denying it. You've been told to ride to both the ranch and the fort east of here, where you will find the various signs of violence left behind—blood at the fort and the ranch owner's body strung up and butchered. You will then cry 'Indians did it' and use the tomahawks as evidence."

"They're savages, goddamn savages. May the Lord burn—"

I punched him in the face with just enough force to shut him up. "Don't bring any Lord of yours into this. You did this for revenge or money. Probably both. So, don't you dare pretend that this was some divine act."

Captain Waltham touched his bloody lip and glanced at his fingertips. "You're going to burn along with them. The righteous will cast your bones into the flames of hell."

I stood back and laughed. It was a full belly laugh, and Captain Waltham's expression slowly evolved from one of anger into one of confusion. "You're an idiot," I said. Fire ignited in my hands. It was only a small sphere, spinning with slow purpose like a planet on its axis.

Captain Waltham scrambled back up and over the chair, ducking behind it.

"As you can see, the fires of hell would have to be *really goddamn hot* to make me concerned."

I stopped my magic as screams sounded from out in the courtyard. The momentary loss of concentration allowed Captain Waltham to sprint away and up a nearby flight of stairs. A door slammed above us.

"Someone's nervous," I said as more screams ripped through the air around us.

"Sam, stay back," Sky told him. To his credit, he didn't argue.

The two of us moved toward the door and opened it slightly. The courtyard was a battleground. Two dead soldiers lay near the barracks, and even from the distance between us I could tell that their throats were torn out.

There were things moving in the darkness around the buildings. Occasionally another scream would sound out, and then those who had finally armed themselves, or found their nerve, would start firing wildly. Sergeant Roberts ran past us as we stepped outside, and I grabbed his arm. "Is there someplace big enough for everyone that can be barred from the inside?"

"There's a room in the basement. The captain had it built. The doors are reinforced with steel plating. It's big enough to hold a hundred people and there's food and water stored there. The entrance is over in the corner." He pointed off past the officer's building to what I'd assumed was just a storage shed when I'd first entered the fort.

"Get everyone down there, now."

"But—"

"But nothing, get your people in that room right now, or you'll have no one left."

He nodded curtly, with more than a little fear in his eyes, but he was soon barking orders and gathering his men. Sam ran with a large group of soldiers as Sky and I covered them. But whatever was hiding in the shadows did nothing to stop their retreat.

"How many men did you lose?" I asked once the massive doors were closed and forced shut.

"I'll do a count," Sergeant Roberts said.

Lieutenant Burns cleared his voice and everyone turned to watch him storm toward us. With his broken arm strapped across his chest, he looked like an even more arrogant Napoleon. "I'm in charge here," he snapped.

"Were you even out there? I didn't see you run in," I said.

Lieutenant Burns glanced around at his men with nervous anticipation. I was certain they weren't about to like his answer. "I was in here already, preparing for my men's retreat."

"Well, and didn't you do a good job, too? If the U.S. had more men like you, you'd still be under English law."

I looked around at our new temporary home. It was mostly a giant open space with a small room at the rear. Through the open door, I could see bags and barrels of food and drink, enough to keep us supplied for some time. There were only twenty-six bunk beds, and most of those were now taken up with the injured. But there was plenty of floor space for the remaining soldiers to take the weight off their feet and try to come to terms with their new circumstance.

Torches on the wall burned brightly, and I could see the holes in the ceiling that supplied the ventilation. There was even a dartboard at the far end of the room. The captain had certainly taken his time to plan out everything he'd need.

A massive pounding sounded against the outside of the door, but stopped soon after. "Someone isn't taking the hint," I said.

"I sensed barrens out there, Nate. A lot of them. Ghouls, too," Sky whispered to me.

"We need to protect the captain," Lieutenant Burns snapped to no one in particular.

"Where is he?" I asked.

"Still in his quarters. He needs to be rescued."

A picture of the maid I'd met earlier flashed to mind. "How many have we left out there?"

"We got everyone we could," Sergeant Roberts said rejoining us. "In terms of army losses, we've lost twenty-two men, thirty are injured, and another six are unaccounted for. But there are still civilians who work in the officer's quarters that we couldn't get to in time. There's probably four or five people still inside. What the hell attacked us out there?"

"I'll answer the 'what' in a second. First we need to get everyone from upstairs in here," I said. "Is there any other way to get out of here besides that door?"

Sergeant Roberts was about to talk when someone shouted him over and he excused himself to go deal with the problem.

Lieutenant Burns was spending his time yelling at anyone who dared to help the injured instead of rallying to find Captain Waltham. Thankfully, everyone appeared to be ignoring him.

"Sam, can you go help any wounded? I know it's not going to be nice, but we can't have people dying in here if we can help it."

"I'll do my best," Sam said with a forced smile.

"You have taken charge very quickly," Sky said. "But if you think I'm going to be nursing people—"

"I need you to find anyone who had been bitten by a ghoul," I interrupted. "We both know what'll happen to them. We can't have people turning in here. I assume a ghoul bite and barren bite can be told apart?"

"It'll be easy enough to find those who were bitten by a ghoul and not by a barren. You want me to use my necromancy to kill them without people knowing?"

"We can't have panic in here. You're the only one who can kill those infected in a peaceful way. My glyphs give it away, and we can't start shooting or stabbing them. I'm sorry to ask this of you."

"Those bitten are already dead, Nate. I'll be doing them a favor. But if you're not back soon, I'm going to find you."

"Deal. But let Roberts know that anyone infected will die. Hopefully, he'll be able to better prepare people for what's going to happen."

I collared Lieutenant Burns as he walked by. "A second exit into the officers' quarters. Where is it?"

Burns shook my hand off. "That's not your concern."

"Do you see anyone else running upstairs? Because if you want that captain of yours back, you'd best point me in the direction of an exit from this place—one that doesn't involve me running a gauntlet through a mob of killing machines."

"In the food pantry, there's a lever beside one of the cupboards; pull it and the cupboard moves. The stairs will take you to the dining room directly above."

"Excellent," I said. "Sergeant Roberts, the men seem to respect and like you, you're in charge until I return."

"You can't do that," Lieutenant Burns whined.

"That slip of paper that says I outrank you tells me otherwise. And lieutenant, if you annoy me once more, I will personally throw you out of that door to fend for yourself, clear?"

Lieutenant Burns nodded furiously.

"Great, now go make yourself useful by helping anyone who needs it." I waited until he was out of earshot. "How the hell did he make lieutenant?"

"Important daddy," Sergeant Roberts said. "I'll make sure he's kept busy."

"I'll be back soon. If he causes you any trouble, shoot him."

"It's not him I'm worried about. What happens if those things get in here?"

"The two slits on the door can be opened to let you see outside, yes?"

Sergeant Roberts nodded.

"Most of what are out there are called barren," Sky told sergeant Roberts. "They can be killed with a shot to the head or heart, just like a human."

"I'm pretty sure what was out there wasn't human."

"That's true, but they die just as quickly once they're reminded of it."

It didn't take long to get through the pantry and up the hidden stairway to the officers' quarters. Finding the civilian help took far longer, mostly out of a desire not to make too much noise. But eventually I found them, four women and a man, all of whom were huddled together in a corner of the large kitchen. The man swiped at me with a butcher's knife, but it was easily avoided and he was disarmed without further incident.

"Please don't kill us," one of the women said with a thick French accent.

"I came up through a secret stairway from an underground room, all of the soldiers are down there," I said. "You'll be safe there."

The woman translated to the other women, who all nodded with enthusiasm.

I stopped by the front entrance and motioned for the others to continue as I glanced into the courtyard beyond. Men shuffled about without purpose. They moved with a slightly unnatural step—it was as if they were unsure they could restart if they stopped moving. They were the barren, and there were dozens and dozens of them. A mixture of army soldiers, still in their uniforms, and ranch hands. These were the missing people from both the other fort and the Warren ranch.

The two bodies I'd noticed dead on the ground earlier were being devoured by several of the barren. They tore apart the flesh and snapped the bones as if they were eating a chicken at a banquet.

I hurried after the group into the dining room and opened the secret door that sat behind a moved cabinet, which I'd pushed away from the wall when I came up earlier.

"Is there anyone else left up here?" I asked. "Apart from the captain?"

Three of the women and the man shook their heads and entered the tunnel, but the fourth woman, the same who had spoken earlier, paused as she stepped past me. "There are two children. The captain keeps them in his room."

"What?" I asked with far too much anger. "Why didn't anyone mention this to me before?"

The woman flinched back as if I were about to strike her. "None of the men know, apart from Lieutenant Burns. I was sworn to secrecy. They threatened to have me executed for treason if I spoke of it. Captain Waltham says they're Indian spies; he's interrogating them. Lieutenant Burns brought them in about a week ago."

I pointed down the path. "Go find Sergeant Roberts and tell him that I'm up here and going to find these kids. If you happen to see Lieutenant Burns, please feel free to shoot him."

The woman's eyebrows rose in shock.

I walked away without telling her if I was joking, mostly because I was pretty certain I wouldn't be able to lie convincingly and say that I was.

Moments later, I was standing to one side of the captain's room banging on the door. "Either you open it, or I will."

A rifle round shot through the wood, exactly where my head would have been, had I been in front of the door.

A quick glance through the hole told me that the captain was alone in the room. I placed a hand on either side of the doorframe and increased the air pressure around it, crushing the wood, until the door buckled and collapsed under its own weight. I immediately grabbed the remains in a bubble of air as they fell inward and flung them into the room beyond, slamming into the captain like a...well, like a door being slammed into a human at near hurricane speeds. I was almost certain it hurt, and from the moaning noise creeping out from under the reshaped wood, I was right.

"You should have opened the door," I said, pushing a heavy trunk that had been used as a barricade aside and stepping into the room, which apart from the trunk was devoid of any other furniture.

The captain moaned and pushed a pile of wood off of himself as he reached for the rifle. I picked up the weapon and emptied it, tossing it through the open doorway. "The children, where are they?"

"Spies."

I kicked him in the ribs and he yelled in pain.

"They were caught running from Kilnhurst." He tried to push the remains of the door off him, so I stepped on it to apply a little more pressure, which caused him to wheeze.

"They found out about the lich," he said breathlessly. I removed the pressure and allowed him to continue. "I had to keep them away from everyone. Couldn't let them go running back to their friends."

"And you couldn't kill them. You couldn't risk their bodies being found. Two dead native children showing up would cause you a few problems."

"Are you going to kill me?"

I kicked the wood aside and dragged him to his feet. "That sort of depends on how much help you give me in finding those children."

"They're behind the wall there." He pointed behind me. "I've been keeping them inside a hidden room to make sure no one discovers them. The door can just be pushed aside."

"Good to know," I said and launched the captain through the wall with a crash that was accompanied by the screams of children. I suddenly felt very bad about using the captain to open the door for me. It probably hadn't helped their nerves. Bits of plaster and wood rained down over the floor, and I waited for the dust to settle before stepping over the prone form of Captain Waltham and into a small room that held two beds, a small table, and two buckets. Two children, a boy and a girl around ten or eleven years old, sat at the end of the room, huddled together in a corner.

"I'm Nathan," I said softly, crouching down to their height.

The boy stared straight ahead, never making eye contact with me. There were marks on his sleeveless arms. Little circles of burnt skin. I pushed down the anger that bubbled inside me. "Can either of you speak English?"

"I can," the girl said.

"Good. I'm here to get you to safety. Some bad people have arrived at the fort. We need to get away before they get inside this building."

"He's bad people," she said, toward the captain, "He hurt my brother when my brother wouldn't tell him what he wanted to know."

"I won't let him hurt you ever again. Will you tell me your names?"

"I'm Tala," she said. "This is Wapi."

"Let's get you both out of here. We'll talk more once you're safe."

She spoke to her brother in a whisper as I stood. I turned to check on the captain and was surprised when he slipped a blade into my stomach. He twisted the weapon and pulled it out as I staggered back.

"You're going to die in here," he said and grabbed a clearly terrified Tala, dragging her through the ruined door and into the hallway.

Wapi stared at the dark glyphs that erupted over my skin as they did their job of healing me, using my own spilled blood to fuel the magic. The knife hadn't been silver, so it didn't take long before I was able to get back to my feet. Captain Waltham had failed to kill or stop me, but he'd succeeded in making me very angry.

"We're gonna go get your sister back, now," I told the young boy, and even though he couldn't understand me, something in my tone must have told him all he needed to know, because he nodded and walked with me out of the room without pause.

The captain's yell from the room at the end of the hallway easily confirmed where he'd taken Tala. They would have a clear view over the courtyard, which meant that anyone trying to follow them into the room could get Tala killed simply by the captain opening the window and throwing her out to the waiting hoard of monsters.

My options weren't great. Take Wapi to safety and leave his sister to the captain's insanity, or keep him with me and risk the barren gaining entry to the house before we could escape.

I'd just decided to get Tala before leaving the house when a single barren reached the top of the stairs at the end of the hallway, next to the room where the captain and Tala were.

The barren, its skin gray and oily, glanced up to where I stood and made a noise more animal than human. Wapi took a few steps back as the monster started slowly toward us. Within seconds it was moving at a full run, barreling toward us at a speed that you'd never have thought possible for something dead.

I raised one hand and a thin jet of flame left my index finger, striking the husk in the forehead. The dead monster stopped moving almost immediately, a black, oil-like substance leaking from its head. It wobbled slightly and then fell to the floor. The fire had incinerated the brain of the barren. They might be dead, but no brain, no motor skills. "It's dead," I said to a still-nervous Wapi. He didn't appear convinced. I kicked the barren as I went by, and when it didn't move, Wapi got the idea, but still hurried to join me.

We reached the end of the hallway without further incident, but two more barren were making their way up the stairs toward us, side by side. I readied a fireball, but they stopped moving and collapsed before they could take another step, revealing Sky in their place. A long dagger, with shimmering blue edges and a translucent center, was in one of her hands, a tomahawk axe in the other. Sky's soul weapons. Soul weapons were a necromancer's abilities in weapon form. It didn't harm the physical body of whomever it hit, but it actually caused injury to their soul, killing them without ever leaving a mark.

"You took too long," she said, stepping over the husks as the weapons dissipated.

I brought Sky up to speed quickly. "We need to get the girl away from that maniac," she said to me after she'd finished talking to Wapi.

"My plan exactly, but you need to keep an eye out for anything coming up those stairs."

The long dagger reappeared in her hand, and, after Wapi pointed at it, she caught me staring. "Haven't you ever seen a soul weapon before?"

"Not often," I admitted.

"You ready?" I asked Sky, who moved Wapi so that he was standing behind her.

As much as turning the door to ash might have given me a sense of satisfaction, it would also get Tala killed.

But any plan I had was forgotten when the window inside the room smashed and someone screamed. I slammed a ram of air into the door's hinges and kicked the door open. Inside the room, a ghoul sat on the windowsill, his long fingers around the throat of Captain Waltham, who was holding onto Tala's arm tightly as she struggled to escape his grasp.

The ghoul glanced over at me, smiled and jumped out of the window, dragging Waltham and Tala out into the cool night air.

I darted to the smashed window and watched in horror as the ghoul, now standing on the roof of the nearest building, threw his captives away with a casual move of his arm.

Captain Waltham crashed into the hard ground and was immediately surrounded by husks, eager to be fed once more. Tala landed awkwardly, rolling toward the center of the courtyard. But at least she was free of Waltham's grip as the barren began to tear into him. The sounds of torn flesh and crunching bone accompanied his screams as they filled the night.

"Two minutes," I said to Sky, as I climbed onto the sill. "You make sure that entrance to the underground room is open in two minutes."

Sky glanced behind her, as glass smashed downstairs. "Looks like I have a few barren of my own to deal with," she said. "You'd better make it ten."

I dropped from the window to the ground outside, using air magic to knock a nearby barren from his feet. I sprinted toward

Tala, who was being surrounded by barren. She'd grabbed a cavalry saber and was waving it toward her advancing attackers. Captain Waltham's screams had gone silent, but the barren around him were still deep in feeding. It hadn't been a good death, but I couldn't bring myself to feel sorrow for his fate. He'd brought it on himself.

Tala kicked out at a nearby barren, driving it back slightly, but they'd smelled a fresh meal and wouldn't be so easily dissuaded. A blast of air magic caused three barren to tumble away, arms and legs flailing; it would have been comical had they not been covered in the blood of their previous victims.

I knelt beside Tala. "Can you get to that door over there?" She followed my hand as I pointed toward the main entrance to the safe room, fifty yards away.

Tala shook her head. "I hurt my foot."

I didn't have time to examine her injuries and deal with the quickly encircling barren. "Ten minutes might be a problem," I said mostly to myself.

"I don't want to die here," Tala said softly.

"Me neither," I assured her. "Tala, I need you to crouch down and close your eyes until I tell you otherwise. Can you do that?"

Tala nodded and quickly assumed the position, her hands tightly over her eyes.

I drew a throwing knife from its home on my belt and waited until one of the barren had gotten just close enough. I sliced through one of my palms, slapped my hands together and then slammed them into the dirty ground. The effect was immediate. The earth cracked open slightly and fire exploded upwards until it had made a complete circle all around Tala and me.

"You can open your eyes now," I said, my hands pressed firmly into the ground. "Try not to touch the fire."

Tala opened her eyes wide, a mixture of wonder and fear flickering through them. "How?" she whispered.

"Magic." The orange fire glyphs and the black glyphs of Blood magic swirled around one another. "But it takes a lot to do this much."

Dozens of barren waited just outside the fire's reach, but something inside them needed to get to us, and no danger was too great. They began walking into the fire one at a time, only to become completely incinerated before they'd taken more than a step. The circle of flame was a yard thick in places, ensuring that nothing could get through unscathed. But every time a barren died in the fire, it took more power from me to maintain the integrity of our only means of surviving until that door was opened.

"Are you okay?" Tala asked after what felt like a lifetime of pouring a huge amount of magic out of me.

I nodded slowly, but daren't speak lest my concentration wavered for even a second, which was all it would take for Tala and me to be overrun. I knew I couldn't keep it up; using such a strong magic for any longer than a few minutes, four or five at the most, took a tremendous toll on a sorcerer. I doubted more than three minutes had passed, and I was already forcing myself not to give up, despite how my body was aching for me to stop. A fifth and sixth barren hurled themselves at the fire, and I felt a cold bead of sweat run down my neck.

"You need me," a voice said from deep inside.

"No," I whispered. "I don't."

"You need to let me free. You need to give yourself over to me. Otherwise, you and the girl will die."

I hated that it spoke the truth. "I will not give myself over to you."

The voice almost seemed to sigh. *"I wonder if all sorcerers are as stupid as you. I am the living embodiment of the magic inside you, and I need you to continue to exist. I wish you no harm. Do we really need to have this conversation again?"*

It had a point. My whole life, I'd been told that giving into the magic would turn a sorcerer into a nightmare, a being of unparalleled power and evil, in equal measure. When I used too much magic for too long, the voice came to me, begging for me to embrace it, to allow us to become one.

"I know what you're thinking, but I can't merge fully with you. Those marks on your chest make it impossible."

"You'll make sure that Tala gets to safety."

"Of course, I'm not a monster. No matter what you may think."

"Deal then." I braced myself and expelled as much magic into the wall of fire as I could manage, until I felt myself slipping, until I could no longer stop myself and it became second nature to allow the magic to flow freely for as long as it wanted. Until I began to feel like I was a passenger in my own body. Until the nightmare inside of me had taken control.

CHAPTER 26

I looked out through eyes that were my own but no longer in my use. It was my turn to be a silent partner as the nightmare took control.

Tala sat next to me, whimpering. The nightmare stared down at her and I felt it wondering why it should help her survive. Why it should use precious resources to help her flee. And then it remembered that I told it to. That it was part of our bargain.

"Child," the nightmare said after a few seconds. The voice was my own, but different—the speech was all wrong, as if the words weren't used to being spoken out loud.

Tala glanced up at me and recoiled slightly when she saw my eyes. I knew what they must look like—blackness spilling out from them, covering my face from my forehead to my mouth, with little patches of pink showing through, the only evidence of my waning influence.

"Child," the nightmare repeated to her. "When I say go, you will run to that door and hammer on it for all you're worth. Tell them Nathan sent you."

"I can't run."

"Then you will die," the nightmare explained. The nightmare placed one of my hands on Tala's leg, and the orange glyphs on that arm turned to black as my Blood magic did its work. "I have healed your foot as much as possible under the circumstances. You can run for now. I suggest that when I tell you to go, you use that ability."

Tala nodded.

The nightmare placed my hand onto the ground once more, and the glyphs returned to orange. It inhaled deeply and the glyphs ignited with a pure brilliance. And then the fire wall exploded outward.

Anything beside the billowing flame died instantly. The force of the explosion was so great that even those who weren't close enough to feel its full force were still taken from their feet and thrown onto the ground a few yards back.

The nightmare stood and stared down at Tala. "Run."

Tala wasted no time and sprinted like her life depended on it, racing to the door and hammering on it while screaming my name. Eventually, it was opened and a nervous Sergeant Roberts emerged, dragging the girl inside. He glanced over at the nightmare and paused before he darted back inside, closing the door behind him.

There was a heartbeat of silence. Nothing moved. The barrens that were still on their feet appeared to be disorientated by the fact that they were no longer faced with an obstacle to their food.

Nightmares were an extension of the sorcerer's true ability. They showed what you were capable of. It was why inviting them into your psyche was so tempting. The one inside me wielded my own magic with an ease and power that was breathtaking. It moved with speed and grace, flinging wind and fire magic at anything that moved. It cleaved barrens as if they were the stalks of flowers. Bodies fell all around it in piles, but no matter what it did, the barrens kept coming, driven by something far more dangerous than a desire to survive—it was the need to feed, to tear into living flesh. It overrode any sense of self-preservation. And the nightmare was more than happy to help them on their way.

The nightmare darted into the stables. Two barrens were already on the floor, their heads pounded to mush as the horses kicked and fought against their would-be attackers. A young boy, pitchfork in hand, stood in front of Valor's stall, holding off the three remaining barrens.

None of them saw the nightmare until it was too late. It slammed my open palm into the back of the nearest one and unleashed a blast of air, which blew out the entire front of its torso. Body parts landed on the straw-covered ground with a splat, but the nightmare had already moved on to the second barren, which was decapitated by a blade of hardened air. The last barren, intent on getting to the stable boy, hadn't even paid attention to what was happening until that same blade punctured through its back and moved upward, exiting through its neck.

The boy, now covered in black barren blood, stared at his savior.

"Take care of the horse," the nightmare said. "You should wash before that blood starts to infect anything."

The boy nodded as the nightmare stepped back out onto the courtyard. A gust of magically enhanced wind picked up one barren and drove it into the fort's wooden entrance. The barren and gate disintegrated upon impact, blood and pieces of wood smeared across the ground and walls.

The nightmare took a step toward the exit and stopped. A noise sounded from out of the darkness beyond the ruined gate.

As one, the remaining barrens stopped fighting and ran through the shattered gate, into the darkness.

In their place stepped a large man. He wore a long, flowing duster that covered everything except for his cowboy boots and hat. His eyes burned red.

This was the monster that had nearly killed Sam.

"Do you know what I am?" the newcomer asked.

"Lich," the nightmare said. "Evil."

The lich laughed, and I was almost certain that if I'd been in control of my body, I would have shivered. "Says the thing everyone is terrified of becoming."

The nightmare remained silent.

"Do you plan on fighting me?" the lich asked.

"No," it said. "I plan on killing you." A torrent of fire and air shot from the palms of the nightmare and engulfed the lich, which didn't even try to defend itself. The outline of the lich was lost somewhere inside the maelstrom of fire and wind, but once it was over and the magic subsided, the lich was still standing where he'd been. The only evidence that anything had happened was that his clothes were burnt and his hat gone, showing a bald head.

"Interesting," the lich said. "Your host has a great deal of power."

"Yes, he does," the nightmare responded. "Allow me to show you more of it." My body went from stationary to sprinting in a heartbeat. It slammed a fire-wrapped fist into the jaw of the lich, which moved slightly. The lich laughed, and I felt cold horror dawn over the nightmare. "*I can't win this.*"

It was the last thing the nightmare thought before the lich punched it in the stomach, lifting it off the ground by several feet, and then grabbed it by the throat before it could fall. "You stupid little sorcerer," the lich said. "You can't defeat me with magic." It brought my body close to it and then headbutted me on the nose before releasing me and following up with a punch that broke my jaw.

The nightmare tried to get off the ground, but the lich was relentless, raining blows that would have killed a human. Every time the nightmare tried to fight back, the lich was faster and stronger. It smashed the nightmare head first into the nearest building and then dragged it back out of the destroyed brickwork by my ankle, only to begin kicking my body in the side. Every blow did damage, and I knew that it could kill me anytime it chose.

"So," the lich said, holding my head up by the hair. "That's a broken nose, jaw, orbital bone, clavicle, and several ribs."

The nightmare tried to see through the damaged eye, which was bloody and swollen, but gave up and settled for just one working eye as sunlight began to stream over the tops of the mountains in the distance.

The lich glanced over at the same mountains. "It appears I have to leave," he said with much disappointment. "We'll have to continue this another time."

The nightmare gurgled something unintelligible and received a punch to the solar plexus, which made me cough up blood, and then I was dropped to the ground as the lich left the fort.

In fifteen minutes, my body, and the nightmare's use of it, had been utterly destroyed by something that couldn't even be hurt, much less killed. For the first time in a long time, I feared for my life. My final feeling as the nightmare retreated back inside me and I slipped back into my own body was of wracking pain. But before I passed out, the nightmare had one last thing to say.

"I'm so sorry."

CHAPTER 27

The nightmare's words sprang to the forefront of my mind as I woke. *I'm so sorry.* Nightmares were meant to be evil, to tempt you into allowing the magic to run free. Sometimes it was hard to remember that.

The thought was quickly replaced by the sight of the tip of a blade close to my throat. "What are you?" Sky asked from the less dangerous end of the dagger.

"You're going to have to be a little more specific," I said. "I still feel somewhat groggy."

"I saw that nightmare take over your body. And I saw it vanish after the lich attacked it. Once a nightmare takes control, it doesn't just stop and allow the host back in." She moved the dagger down to my chest, the tip hovering over my heart. "And I saw the marks on your body. Blood magic curse."

"Can you remove the dagger and let me sit up?"

She held the knife steady for a few seconds, and then grudgingly stepped away.

I sat up and took in my surroundings for the first time. I was in the room that had once belonged to the now-deceased Captain Waltham. The window was still smashed; no one had bothered to board it up, and a pleasant breeze floated past the remaining jagged glass. I swung my legs off the bed and noticed that someone had replaced the door. There was a key in the hole, turned to one side. "You locked us in here," I said.

"Will you answer my question?"

"Okay, what am I?" I mused. "I'm a sorcerer. I'm fifteen-hundred years old and about three hundred years ago I used far too much magic and allowed a nightmare to take hold. Whenever I use too much magic, it rears its head and lets me know that it can help me. On occasion, I've allowed it free rein of my body and mind."

"And it goes back without a fight?" Sky asked, shocked.

"Not exactly," I said. I stood and stretched, causing my shoulder to crack. Sky didn't move an inch. "The marks on my chest? The nightmare can't get past them. It can't ever take me wholly. So, in exchange for its help, I impose a time limit on it. Usually fifteen minutes, sometimes a little longer. After each time, it always obeys and leaves. Usually after telling me it's not evil and only wants to help me become the person I could be."

"You trust it to acquiesce to your bargain?"

"Trust has nothing to do with it. If I had my way, I'd never allow it out at all, but sometimes, there's little choice."

"There's always a choice."

"You're right. The choice last night was allow it freedom or have the barren kill me and Tala in the most horrific way imaginable. How are the two youngsters, by the way?"

"Doing as well as could be expected. Tala is strong. She looks out for her brother. They're mostly staying out of everyone's way, and asking where you are on a regular basis."

"Good," I said. "Do you plan on putting that knife away?"

Sky placed it on the table beside her with care, as if concerned she might need it at a moment's notice.

"How long have I been out?"

"About twelve hours. You're lucky he didn't kill you. Hell, we're all lucky he didn't kill everyone."

"So, what happens now?" I ask. "Do you have any backup?"

"I've sent a telegram. They should be here within the next twelve hours, and then tomorrow we need to go to Kilnhurst and end this. The lich won't be back here tonight. He lost a lot of his forces last night and he'll want to rethink his strategy. But we're working on making the fort more secure for the time being."

"So until the evening, what are we meant to do?"

Sky pushed herself away from the table she'd leaned against and grabbed my shirt, pulling me toward her in a hard kiss.

"What was that for?" I asked once we'd finished.

"We almost died last night, and we might die tonight. I'd rather feel alive for a bit longer, unless you have any objections."

"None spring to mind."

She smiled a wicked smile and pulled my mouth back toward hers once again.

"You could have done this before the whole knife thing," I pointed out as Sky removed her clothes and dropped them to the floor.

"Sex first, discussion after," she said as she unfastened my belt.

I removed my already open shirt and threw it onto the ground before stepping out of my newly freed trousers. I grabbed Sky and picked her off the ground with one arm supporting her body as I licked her nipples, causing her to moan.

I turned us both around and laid us on the bed, tracing my hands down her taut body as we continued to kiss hungrily. She reached down between my legs and pulled me into her, arching her back and letting a deep moan out as I moved.

We moved in time, slowly at first, but were soon lost in the moment of passion until we let out one final cry of pleasure at the same time and collapsed against one another, our passion and our fear of the unknown spent. For the moment.

CHAPTER 28

Ontario, Canada. Now.

"**C**an I assume your little visit to the Silver Room went well?" Tommy asked as he entered the conservatory in Hades' kitchen the next morning.

I glanced up from the huge plate of fresh fruit and meat and threw an apple in Tommy's direction. "All good, Tommy," I said with a smile.

"You were down there for eight hours. Hades said he dragged you unconscious from the room a few hours ago and put you on the sofa to sleep it off. No after effects?"

I knew Tommy was fishing. He was worried that maybe I'd let the nightmare corrupt me on a permanent basis. "I'm not turning into a nightmare," I told him.

"But you did see it, or hear it, or however that works."

I stuffed a strawberry in my mouth. "We had a conversation, yes. Apparently, my increase in power means that I can use more magic before I need to worry about it resurfacing. A lot more."

"It told you that?"

"Yes. It wants me to use magic, to get stronger. The stronger I am, the stronger the nightmare will be. It has no reason to lie or to try and deceive me. I'm not even sure if it can."

Tommy speared several pieces of bacon from my plate and stuffed them between two slices of bread. "It's living magic. I'm pretty sure it can do whatever the hell it wants."

"Maybe you're right, but it won't be taking hold anytime soon." Since it had taken control over a hundred years previously, when a lich had almost beat me to death, I'd begun to think of the nightmare as something more than an evil entity that wants to control me. I had no evidence to support my thoughts, and if I went to anyone with them they'd have me sectioned, but everything I'd always been told about nightmares felt off compared to reality.

"So, did you find out anything else on this trip?"

"Nope, that was pretty much it," I said, pushing the half-full plate away from me.

Tommy grabbed the plate before it was even out of my hands for even a second and started eating a moment later. "Why did you take this trip, Nate?"

"I needed to talk to Hades about getting help. And I wanted to know what my true power level was. I can't go into a fight not knowing what I can do."

"There's more to it than that. What's going on, Nate?"

I told him about how Hades said I may be able to perform some kind of necromancy.

Tommy's reaction was mostly one of indifference, although he did stop eating, so that was something. "A necromancer? That's not something I expected."

"Me neither, and it's not confirmed. But I killed that ghoul with magic, and there's no way I could do that without necromancy. But I still have no way of knowing what type of necromancy or how to use it effectively."

Tommy stared at me. "What aren't you telling me?"

I sighed softly. "The last time I fought a lich, it almost killed me. With ease, Tommy. And when that bastard appeared in front of me in front of the police station in Winchester, I would have gone for him if Reid hadn't charged in. But after, when I was thinking about what could have happened if he'd decided to end me there and then, I just felt afraid. For the first time in a long time, I was scared. Because I know I can't beat him. I know it with the same certainty that I can say the sun is hot and water is wet. And not knowing what I was capable of only added to that fear, which is why I had to come here and find out."

"You've been scared before," Tommy said.

"That's true. But mostly, I'm scared for others. Scared I won't get somewhere in time, or not be able to get everyone out of a situation in one piece. I'm frightened of failing other people. But with a lich, I'm scared for myself, too. I already know that if I go up against it, I'm going to fail."

"But you're still going to try and stop it, right?" I turned to find Kasey standing in the doorway. "I mean, you're going to fight," she said.

"Yeah," I said with a gentle nod. "I'm going to fight. I have to. I can't let fear stop me from doing what I know is right. And I won't let anything keep me from stopping more people getting hurt."

"But if you're afraid, why don't we all just run and hide?"

"Because if we do that, we're leaving something evil to have its way with whatever it wants. And I won't let that happen. And I know your mum and dad won't either. I fight because if I don't, I'm not the man I thought I was. So, yeah, I'm afraid of this thing. But that just means I'm going to try harder to beat it. Because fear should never be a reason for not doing the right thing."

"You promise?"

"I promise I'll fight with everything I have, Kasey. And with Hades' help, we're going to make sure that once we find it, it won't hurt anyone else, ever again."

"Thank you," she said and turned back into the house.

"I guess I should thank you, too," Tommy said, when his daughter was out of earshot.

"What, for that?" I gestured to where Kasey had been standing.

"No, well…yes, but not just that. For what you did on the plane. For allowing Kasey and me some time alone. Thank you for that. She needed to talk to someone."

"You thought it would be me, didn't you? That's why you brought her?"

"I figured that you'd get the ball rolling, yes. You didn't see her face when she saw Olivia in hospital. She crumpled like paper. She stayed so strong for Olivia and me, but I could tell she was breaking apart. She needed to get that out. It would have eaten at her otherwise."

"You're a good dad," I said and poured each of us a glass of orange juice from the large pitcher on the table.

"That I am, my old friend." Tommy laughed. "Although, any future boyfriends are going to learn to fear the werewolf who answers the door."

"You're allowing boyfriends? Wow, that's very progressive of you."

"I've gotta learn to give a little."

"No, don't do it," Hades said, as he sat beside us. "Just tell them she knows me, that we're very close. It's surprising how many boys didn't want to go out with the daughter of Hades."

"You never even had to dissuade them," Persephone said, kissing her husband on his forehead and sitting beside him.

"I had a whole spiel written. There were smoke and mirrors. I was going to raise spirits, actual spirits right in front of them. Maybe even a zombie. I didn't get to use any of it."

"To be fair, Hades," I said. "When most of your children were of a dating age, it was several hundred, if not a thousand years ago. I don't know about you, but I don't recall a whole bunch of school dances in the middle ages. Hell, there weren't even many schools."

"Good point," Hades said with a smile. "But, Tommy, if you want to use my plan, it's all yours."

"Why are you all laughing?" Kasey said as she entered the conservatory.

"Parenthood," Tommy said. "Something you don't have to worry about for a very, very long time."

Kasey gave her father a stare that suggested the conversation had better change and soon, before she was sick.

Tommy's mobile started ringing, and he excused himself from the room to go answer it as Persephone and Kasey arranged their next visit's itinerary with great enthusiasm.

Hades motioned for me to join him outside, so we stepped out into the cold just like we had the night before.

"How are you feeling?" he asked.

I explained what I'd already told Tommy about the nightmare and my time in the Silver Room, leaving out my thoughts about just how evil or not the nightmare might be.

"I assume you'll be going back soon," he said. "A necromancer will meet you at Avalon's Winchester office within the day. I don't know who it'll be yet, but they'll be there. With or without Avalon's clearance."

"Nate," Tommy called from the conservatory door. "We've got a problem."

I jogged back to Tommy, who stood back to let Hades and me into the room. "What's going on?"

"We need to get back to Winchester. That was Olivia. The prison there was attacked a few hours ago, it looks like the lich was involved. Olivia has only just received word from the human police. There are large numbers of prisoners missing or dead. Nate, this sounds like a bad one."

"How long before the jet can fly?" I asked Hades.

He picked up a cordless phone from the table next to him. "Twenty minutes. I'll get everything arranged."

CHAPTER 29

True to Hades' word, we were all back in his jet within twenty minutes. There was no scotch to ease my flight on the return leg; I didn't need any. All I could think about was how the lich had attacked again so soon after trying to have Olivia, Agents Reid and Greaves, and me killed. And it had attacked a prison. What could possibly be so important that it would attack a prison with a huge population like Winchester's?

The four hours in the air went by quickly, and we were soon landing at the same secluded base we'd left the day before. There was a quiet concern that was easy to spot not just on Tommy and Kasey, but the flight staff, too. They knew something was wrong, and even if they didn't know all the facts, I doubted Hades would normally have had them ready the jet so quickly unless it was a dire emergency.

"I'm taking Kasey home," Tommy said. "Will you be okay going by yourself?"

I swung onto my bike, which was still in the hangar where I'd left it. "I'll be fine. I'll get Olivia to call you when I see her."

Kasey waved as she and Tommy got into his car and drove off, leaving me alone with the jet's flight crew and the maintenance team, who were getting the jet ready to fly again.

I placed my helmet on and pulled down the visor, letting the bike roar to life before taking it out into the early morning sun.

My mind wandered during the ride to the prison. I had no idea what I was going to find, but I was glad that Kasey wouldn't be there to see it. I'd been younger than her when I'd seen my first dead body, but that didn't mean it was okay.

The police presence outside the prison was extensive. They'd blocked off the entire road to the front entrance, with the LOA using the human uniformed police to deal with crowd control.

A large group of people were milling around on the road to the prison. They got in my way as I rode toward the barriers that had been placed to stop the curious. The press were out in force, too, trying to take photos, or busy talking into microphones about the developing story.

I stopped the bike near a haggard-looking policeman who didn't appear too happy at having to tell one more person to bugger off. I raised the visor on my helmet. "I'm Nate Garrett. I'm here to see Director Green," I said before he could tell me to leave.

He didn't acknowledge that he'd even heard me speak. Instead, he picked up his radio and spoke into it for a second, then listened to the reply.

"You can go in," he told me after replacing the radio on his belt. "Straight through into the parking area."

He pointed the way and I thanked him. I dropped my visor and passed several more officers until I rode under a huge stone arch that marked the entrance to the parking area.

I'd used my phone to do some research on the prison during the flight back. The prison itself was an imposing structure, consisting of one large building and two smaller ones. Sixty-foot walls topped with razor wire encircled the entire prison grounds. There were only two exits; one was a service entrance for the various vendors and employees to come and go during the day, and the other was the main visitors entrance.

I stopped the bike at the visitors' entrance and switched off the engine, removing my helmet and hanging it from the handlebars as someone shouted from behind me, "You took your damn time."

"Hi, Olivia," I said. "Nice to see you, too. Takes a while to fly from Canada."

Olivia marched over to me and opened her mouth to say something, but instead her shoulders sagged and she leaned against the nearby wall. "Sorry, I'm just tired. How are Kasey and Tommy?"

"Good. Tommy took Kasey home. I told them you'd call."

"So, did you manage to get us any help?"

"A necromancer should be here in a few hours, maybe sooner depending on where he or she is coming from."

"And with your necromancer in tow, we should be able to stop this thing, right?"

"That's the plan. Now, what happened here? Tommy said that a bunch of prisoners are dead or missing."

"I'm at a loss for words." Olivia rubbed her eyes, the past few days had clearly been hard on her. "You need to see this for yourself."

Olivia led me through the prison entrance, which was guarded by another uniformed officer who nodded to us as we walked past. A series of corridors later and we reached a heavy-duty door made of steel and painted blue. It was the last gate to freedom for those locked up inside. Olivia unlocked it with a key, and a buzzer sounded from above us as she pushed it open, ending when the door was closed once more.

We continued on, passing a small break room where several LOA agents were talking with a few of the prison guards.

We went through another two heavy doors, and we were in the prison itself.

"How many wings are there?" I asked.

"The prison is made up of one central hub—that's the smaller building we just walked through. That hub feeds into five spokes, all of which house the prisoners, and a sixth much smaller spoke, where they keep the supplies. Each spoke is capable of keeping about five hundred prisoners, along with the various guard facilities, waiting rooms for visitors, interview rooms, and the like. All of the spokes are independent of each other; to travel between them you need to come through the main hub.

"The wing we're currently in houses those who are considered highly dangerous to themselves or others. There are thirty-four guards working exclusively in this spoke on every shift. Each shift is ten hours long, overlapping so that there's never a complete change of guard all at once."

"It looks quiet here." I glanced around the magnolia walls and blue and white tiled floor, which probably hadn't been changed in decades.

"We've not reached where we need to go yet. There's a large hall at the far end of this building. It was considered a reward for prisoners to be allowed to work in there."

"What did they do?"

"The usual, metal and wood work. There's a library, too. Most of what happened earlier took place in that part of the prison."

We walked along one row of cells and down yet another long corridor with barred windows down one side. A second corridor intersected it, and the lack of lighting down that hallway gave it an eerie quality.

"What's down there?" I asked Olivia.

"There's another security door and after that, a second guard checkpoint. Beyond that are the solitary confinement cells. Not everyone in this place is able to play with others. The most dangerous prisoners were housed down there."

"Were?"

"You'll see in a minute."

We walked on, and before long I noticed blood smears on the walls, continuing through the closed doorway at the far end of the corridor.

"You need to be prepared for what you're about to see." Olivia's words were spoken with such trepidation that I was certain walking the other way would spare me a lot of misery. Unfortunately, my path was set and walking away was no longer an option.

Olivia stopped walking a few feet back from the open door.

"You're not coming?" I asked.

"I have no intention of stepping foot in there again if I can manage it. There's a door on the opposite side. It leads to the cells. I'll meet you there. And here, you're going to need these." She handed me a pair of shoe covers, which I quickly put on.

As Olivia walked away, I wanted to mock her, to say something to break the tension, but I bit my tongue. It didn't feel right.

Instead, I turned and pushed open the door.

The stench of death hit me like a train as I stepped through the doorway. The first thing I saw was the remains of...of a human, although considering how little was left of him, it was hard to be sure. Dozens of bodies littered the large area, their blood and gore soaking the floor and walls.

The machinery the prisoners had worked with was scattered in pieces around the room, deep dents in the wooden walls testifying to the violence of its destruction. Some bodies lay over their workstations; others had clearly tried to get away and were caught before they reached anywhere near freedom.

At one end of the room, in a portion devoid of the blood that covered so much of it, stood Agent Reid.

"I thought you were off healing up?" I said as I got closer.

"One sec," he said and then started counting. He stopped at thirty-two. "Shit."

"Thirty-two bodies?"

"Thirty-two bodies that are identifiable without serious medical knowledge."

"Where are all of the Avalon agents? I thought there'd be dozens of you in here."

"They've got to wait for the docs to finish in here," he said. "Doc Grayson didn't want anyone else going through here until his people had finished. I don't envy their job."

"So why are you here?"

"Waiting for the doc to come back. Director Green wanted a count of the bodies, but there's too much mess in here to give an accurate number."

"What do you know so far?"

"These people were torn apart," Agent Reid said. "Grayson said he thinks ghouls did it. The barren wouldn't have left any flesh for us to find—his words, not mine."

"So let's say forty people died in here. Where are the rest of the prisoners?"

"Forty-seven," Doctor Grayson said as he entered the hall wearing dark-blue coveralls that even covered his shoes.

"And you know that how?" Agent Reid asked.

"I have a very special sense of smell, agent," Doctor Grayson said, tapping the side of his nose. "Nice to see you again, Nathan."

"You, too, Doc, although this isn't exactly how I thought I'd be spending my day."

"On that, we can agree," he said with a forced smile. "Forty-seven dead down here—a further eighteen upstairs in the library; it's quite the display of brutality."

"Were they all killed in the same way?"

"Partially eaten, yes. But that's not all. I believe Director Green has something to show you in the main hall. You may wish to steady yourself for what you'll see there."

"Olivia said the same thing about what happened in here. How much worse can it get?"

"Ah, Nathan, now you know it can always get much, much worse."

More people arrived to help clean up, or tag the bodies, or whatever horrific job they needed to do, and I was happy to leave them to it.

"You never answered my question," I said to Agent Reid, who'd received the information he'd needed and had left the hall with me via the nearest door.

"I can't really sit on my ass all day when there's someone out there doing this," Reid said, removing the shoe coverings from his boots and placing them with his blue latex gloves in a yellow hazard bag that had been left outside the hall.

I removed my own covers and shoved them in the bag, then used fire magic to heat up my hands, burning off any blood that might have remained on my fingertips.

"Nice trick," Agent Reid said.

"It's sort of depressing that I need a trick to get rid of blood on my hands."

"You think what we're about to see really *is* worse than that?" he pointed to the hall behind us.

I didn't answer right away. Instead, we followed the directions of several agents who said Olivia was searching for me until we came to a room that was guarded by two more LOA agents. They moved aside to let us in, and I immediately realized that I was wrong. It could get worse.

The room we entered housed a large TV, a pool table, and a few other games for the inmates to enjoy, including a collapsible table tennis set that had been folded in half with someone still inside it, crushing the man to death. Three massive couches had been upturned and thrown to the sides, exposing a large, empty section of floor. A lone arm, torn off from the shoulder, sat in the very center in a pool of blood.

At the far end of the room, the TV had been torn from the wall and tossed aside. In its place was a body. Or at least the remains of one. Two pool cue ends protruded out of his chest, and blood had sprayed from his torso where his arms should have been, drenching the wall in red on either side of him. Identification would be difficult since the victim's head was missing.

"What the fuck happened here?" I asked, not sure if I wanted to know.

Olivia turned away from talking to one of her agents. "The best Doctor Grayson can determine is that Neil was nailed to the wall by those pool cues after having his arms and his head ripped off and thrown into the nearest bin."

"*That's* Neil Hatchell?"

Olivia nodded.

"So, the lich did this," I said. "But how? Surely Neil would have transformed to at least fight back. He'd have still lost, but there'd be more evidence of a struggle."

Olivia passed me a clear bag containing a bracelet. "This is how."

"A sorcerer's band? You mean he couldn't defend himself?"

"We had to make him wear one. He was in a human prison—we couldn't exactly have him running around turning into a wolf whenever he liked."

"Why was he in a human prison at all?"

"He implicated members of Avalon. We had to put him somewhere anyone involved wouldn't find him. Looks like it didn't work."

"I hate these damn things." Sorcerer bands were narrow bracelets with runes etched into the silver that prevented the wearer from accessing their abilities. Neil would still have been fast and strong, and his innate ability to heal wouldn't have changed, but he wouldn't have been able to access his wolf form at all. I'd worn a sorcerer's bracelet for a while a long time ago, and it had felt like I'd lost a part of myself. They're horrific things, and to compound my dislike, each one has a rune inscribed that sits against the wearer's skin. If the band is removed by the wearer, or by someone else with a band on, the runes ignite with the equivalent of magical napalm. The rune can be changed depending on what will hurt the specific person the most, but the end result is always the same. Death.

"You and me both," Olivia said.

"Wow, this is not what I was expecting."

I turned at the sound of the newcomer's voice, watching as LOA agents darted to the room's entrance, barring her from entering.

"It's okay, she's with me," I said, and the guards parted.

"Nate, it's been a while," she said with a smile, sweeping past the guards without a glance, her high-heeled boots clicking on the linoleum floor.

"And you are?" Olivia asked, taking the bagged bracelet back from me and passing it to a nearby agent.

"Ah, you must be Director Green. I've been sent here to assist you with your lich problem."

"Olivia," I said. "Let me introduce Sky. She's our necromancer."

Olivia's expression softened and she shook Sky's hand. "Good to have you on board. I hope we can figure out how to kill this thing."

"I'll be doing that," Sky said. "The lich killing, I mean. But first bring me up to speed on what happened here, and why that man has no head."

For the next few minutes we did just that, explaining about the ghoul attack on the prison, and everything that came before it. Sky didn't ask questions, but she occasionally glanced at the headless body as it was removed from the wall by some of Doctor Grayson's men.

"This lich is strong," Sky said when we'd finished. "I heard that you killed a ghoul with magic, Nate. The lich will want revenge for what you did. You should be careful."

"Then we'd better hurry up and kill it," I said. "What's the plan?"

"How many prisoners are unaccounted for?" Sky asked Olivia.

"Nearly four hundred."

"Then we've got a few hours before we'll have to deal with four hundred new barren as well as a lich and probably five ghouls. Not great odds."

Another agent called Olivia over, and she quickly ran off to find out what they needed.

"I've been wondering something," I said to Sky. "How did four hundred men disappear at once? Where'd they go? And how did the lich get them there without a fight?"

"You kill a few of those who want to fight back, and everyone else becomes very compliant. Besides, the thought of freedom is a big motivator," Sky suggested.

"How many guards are missing?" I asked one of the agents.

She flicked through several sheets of paper on a clipboard before answering. "Twenty-two; ten are confirmed dead and fifteen were locked in the comm or guard's room. Apparently there was no communication with the outside world for an hour, and all internal alarm systems were shut down. One of the guard's wives got worried that she couldn't get through to her husband on his mobile and called the police. The police notified us two hours later, and we gained entry and secured the building an hour after arriving."

"Why let any of the guards live?" Sky asked.

"They were on a break," the agent said. "They weren't in the wing when the attack commenced. My guess is they locked themselves in to stay alive, and they weren't important enough for the lich to bother with."

I did some quick math in my head. "I need to speak to Olivia. Now."

"What's got you all worked up?" Agent Reid asked, as Sky and I made our way over to him and Olivia.

"They were in here for an hour before anyone was even notified that something was wrong," I said. "What time did you actually gain entry?"

"Half eight this morning," Olivia said.

"It was light then, yes?"

Sky tapped something into her phone. "Dawn was at 06:58. So they would have been gone well before then. But that still means they had the place to themselves for three hours at least. By the time they left, all of the prisoners would have been pretty much on the way to becoming husks."

"How do four hundred prisoners leave without anyone noticing?" I asked. "That's what doesn't make sense."

"I'll be back in a second," Olivia said and marched off toward where I'd seen the guards being interviewed.

"The lich will have a home base. He'll want to go there, although if he has four hundred people about to turn into husks, it must be somewhere big. He'd have known the LOA would be all over this place after his attack, and he wouldn't want to be left vulnerable."

"That still doesn't explain how the hell he got out of here with all of those prisoners in tow."

"Maybe I can be of assistance with that," a middle-aged man in a very nice, immaculate gray suit said as he arrived with Olivia.

He glanced at Agent Reid and me and then extended a hand to Sky; apparently we weren't important enough. "Maxwell Perkins," he said with a smirk.

"Okay, so who are you and how can you help?" I asked as Sky rolled her eyes once Maxwell had decided to stop staring at her.

"He's the assistant warden," Olivia said for him. "You need to listen to what he has to say."

Maxwell straightened his already perfectly straight tie, and I resisted the urge to hang him with it for being a pompous ass. "As I was explaining to your lovely director, there are tunnels under the prison. The whole building was built during the Georgian era, and those tunnels were never permanently sealed up."

"You have a set of open tunnels under a prison?" Sky snapped.

"They're not open, my dear." The smugness oozed out of him like oil. "A very large, thick steel door bars the way. And there's no prisoner in existence that has ever gotten even close to it. And even if they did, the exit is sealed with a three-foot-thick concrete wall."

"How long is the tunnel?" I asked

"Two miles; it ends near a selection of woodland."

"Why would the original architects have built a two-mile tunnel under the prison?" Olivia asked.

"The tunnel was designed to move people in and out of the prison in a discreet manner. There are rooms down there where they used to torture people, and the tunnel made it easier to dispose of the bodies."

"Can you show us the way?" Agent Reid asked.

Maxwell beamed. "Of course, follow me. And ladies, you'd best stay close, don't want you to get spooked by anything."

CHAPTER 30

We followed Maxwell down the corridor to the solitary confinement cells, which had lost none of their creepiness from when Olivia and I had walked past earlier. Some of the gore-splattered cells still had bodies inside where the ghouls had attacked and spared no one.

"These men were helpless," Agent Reid said.

"They were serial murderers and rapists," Maxwell said. "I would feel more pity for their victims. These men lost their lives in as brutal a fashion as their own victims."

No one made any further comment about what we saw as we made our way by the cells and up to a door that had the word "Maintenance" in big red letters. Maxwell entered the code into the keypad next to it, and the door lock clicked open.

"The tunnel is through here," he said. "But it won't do you any good, the end is blocked."

"Still worth a look," I said and opened the door fully to reveal a set of stairs that led down and a row of low-level lights that lit the wall as far as I could see. "Are these lights on all the time?"

Maxwell nodded. "It's easier to leave them on than to turn them off and on every time we go down here."

"What do you come down here for?" Olivia asked as we all descended the steep stairs into the tunnel.

"A lot of the cables and pipes that run through the prison start down here, and occasionally we have a few glitches with the electricity or hot water. And we use the empty rooms to store supplies."

We made our way along the dingy tunnel, with Maxwell and Olivia taking the lead and Agent Reid following behind Sky and me. Occasionally, we passed locked doors with handles rusted through lack of use, or open ones showing stacks of boxes. But there certainly didn't appear to be anything down here except for the five of us. After a half hour of walking at a steady pace, we arrived at the remains of a concrete wall. Something had punched its way through the concrete to get to the old exit beyond, leaving pieces of broken wall all around.

"I think we've found how the lich got everyone out of here," I said.

I stepped over the pile of rubble and pushed open the rusted iron gate with a squeak. The lock had been torn off by someone, ripping part of the gate in the process.

The rest of the group followed me out into the clearing near an area of woodland.

"So, these bastards could be anywhere?" Olivia said as she exited the tunnel.

"And they had maybe three hours to start the transformation before they left here," Sky said. "Tonight, the shit is going to start hitting the fan."

Maxwell laughed. It started as a slight chuckle, but soon made its way into a full-throated roar of laughter. "You have no idea what's happening," he said after everyone had turned to stare at him. Blood trickled from his mouth and nose, dropping onto his shirt.

Agent Reid's Glock was out of its holster in an instant and aimed at the assistant warden, who regarded him with mild indifference. "This bag of meat is already dead," Maxwell said. "He was the first to die when I turned up to claim what was mine."

"You're the lich," Sky said.

"And a brownie point goes to the American, although technically I'm still just a useless human."

"Puppeteer," Sky whispered.

Maxwell clapped his hands and laughed. "That's right, aren't you a smart one? Bet you haven't seen this before."

"You controlled Maxwell all this time."

"From the moment I arrived to kill that snitch, Neil, until just now, Maxwell has been my puppet to control as I wished."

"Where are the rest of the prisoners?" I asked.

"I warned you to stay out of this," he said to me. "I told you to let it happen and nothing would befall you. But you ignored me. You killed my ghoul, and now I find you here trying to help them catch me once more. You can't kill me, sorcerer. You can't even hurt me. For your disobedience and for killing my ghoul, you will feel my full wrath."

His mention of the ghoul I'd killed reminded me that I'd had his blood on my hand. "The men in the farm basement, you turned them to ghouls."

"I look forward to feasting on your heart and having my ghouls tear you limb from limb."

"Well, you're down one ghoul already, so it'll probably take longer."

Maxwell spat bright red blood onto the grass. "You will regret those words, sorcerer."

"You know, it's funny," I said, "but everyone who says I'm going to feel their wrath tends to die a horribly violent death. Guess I can add one more to the list."

"I've heard enough," Agent Reid said and shot Maxwell in the center of his chest, throwing him off his feet and onto the soft grass.

Nobody admonished Agent Reid for the act. Hell, if I'd been holding a gun, I'd have done the same, but even so, no one moved or spoke.

"You stupid fucking idiots," Maxwell said, getting back to his feet. His shirt was drenched in red and clinging to his chest, two large holes where his heart used to be. "You can't even kill my puppet. What chance do you have of killing me?"

"The head," Sky said.

"Going to tear all of your flesh from your bones," Maxwell said. His voice was raspy and no longer resembled anything remotely human.

Olivia walked over to him and raised her gun. "Go fuck yourself," she said and pulled the trigger, destroying Maxwell's brain and a large portion of Maxwell's skull. The corpse fell to the ground, where she put another two in what remained of his head. Just in case.

"What the hell was that?" I asked, as Olivia stepped back from Maxwell's body, rage almost radiating off her.

"A puppet," Sky said, not sounding all that together herself. "Some liches can take control of the bodies of those they've killed." She raised Maxwell's sleeve to show a marking painted on his forearm in blood.

"This is all new to me," I said and noticed Agent Reid checking on Olivia.

"New to me, too, Nate. I've heard of it happening twice. Ever." Sky removed a phone from her pocket. "I need to make a call—this has just gotten a lot worse."

I left Sky to her conversation and walked over to Olivia.

"We didn't have time before. I rushed off to Canada and you were injured, but are you okay?"

"Angry," she said. "Really, really fucking angry. I'm going to tear his fucking head off for this."

"This guy has a real fucking problem with you," Sky said as she returned. "You feel like telling me why?"

"Peter Jarvis would dress as a cop, pull women over, and pretend that they'd done something or that there was a problem with their car. Once he got them into his own car, he took them to a secluded house he owned where he would rape and kill them. He took a week with each one. He murdered sixteen women in a twenty-four month period, until he got caught by Vicki."

I remembered reading the file in Vicki's basement.

"His own girlfriend caught him?" Sky asked.

"After she left him, Vicki had heard rumors that he was involved in some bad stuff. She thought it was drugs or something, so followed him to his little nest and caught him as he was about to murder a young woman."

"So, why does he hate you?"

"Because she called and asked if I'd go with her. She was terrified of him. He fought back when we found him and pretty much got his ass kicked by me while Vicki freed the latest girl he'd taken."

"He changed his MO," I said. "These new girls aren't raped, aren't held for a week. What happened?"

"He did," Sky said as she rejoined us. "Liches can't get it up. So, if he can't have his fun, then why keep them alive?"

"So who raped Vicki's girlfriend, Amber?" I asked.

"Neil confessed on the way to the prison," Reid said.

I was suddenly no longer bothered that he'd died. Horribly. "So, do you have a plan?" I asked Olivia.

"Peter's apartment isn't too far from Winchester city center. We could go look around, see if anything jumps out at us."

"It's been a few years. What if someone else lives there now?" I asked.

"About six weeks ago, Vicki got me to check the place out," Olivia said. "She wanted to make sure no one lived there. I think the anniversary had her spooked."

With good reason, I thought. "Did you find anything?" I asked.

"No one had lived there since Peter was arrested, but it was still paid for on a regular basis."

"Who's paying for it?"

"No idea. Someone opened a bank account and deposits a few grand on the first of January every year. It's used to automatically pay the bills and that's it. I tried tracing the account owner, but that was a dead end. It's under an assumed name with no apparent ties to anyone Peter might have known. Whoever arranged it covered their tracks well."

"Well, let's go find out what the apartment's been used for."

CHAPTER 31

Agent Reid and Sky went to watch over Tommy and Kasey, while I went with Olivia to investigate Peter Jarvis's old building.

The building was an unassuming four-story block of flats. One might have expected it to be dark and creepy, or at the very least have the aura of a place where a serial killer once lived, but instead it looked the same as every other building on the road—red bricked with a small, tidy garden out the front and steps leading up to the front door.

We walked up to the blue front door, which was unlocked. Olivia pulled it open and we stepped into the hallway.

"Not too concerned about security, are they?" I said.

"This is an affluent neighborhood, with little crime. And five years is a long time. Most of the people here wouldn't have been around during the time of Peter and his crimes, and no one who lived in this building back then is still here."

"You really did check up on this asshole, didn't you?"

Olivia and I started up the stairs.

"Apparently not enough."

"You couldn't possibly think he was going to turn himself into a lich."

Olivia stopped walking before we'd reached the landing above. "No. You're right, I couldn't have. But I should have done...something, Nate. Should have anticipated that he'd staged his death."

"You're blaming yourself for nothing. A lich is such a rare event that it would be near the bottom of possibilities for the attacks on those women. I've fought a lich before, and even I didn't consider that one could be behind those murders."

"I know, I just...I feel like I've been five steps behind since Vicki's disappearance. And now she's dead. Turned into a monster by that...*cunt*. After all that, he threatens my family."

"Your family is safe. They have agents and Sky with them, and Tommy isn't exactly a slouch when it comes to taking care of himself. We both know how safe Kasey is with that much security around her; they're safer than we are."

Olivia forced a smile. "You really are not what I'd expected."

"I'm an enigma wrapped inside a riddle, all bundled in something quite wonderful."

"It's nice to see you have a healthy opinion of yourself."

"It's a burden I live with every day."

Olivia's smile was genuine. "You and Tommy are both idiots."

"Says the woman who had his child," I said as we stopped outside Peter Jarvis's door.

"Moment of weakness," she said and stared at the plain brown door intently. "I hope there's something important in there. Or at least useful."

"Only one way to find out."

Olivia stepped back from the door and created a sledgehammer of water in her hands, freezing it solid and then smashing it into the door just above the lock. It took two swings to destroy the lock and knock the door open. The ice instantly evaporated and she walked through the ruined door.

I followed, closing the door as best as I could behind me. It shut out most of the natural light from the window on the landing and encased Olivia and me in darkness. Not the ideal start to invading a serial killer's home.

Olivia soon found the light switch and dull fluorescent light showed us a normal hallway, albeit a dark one, with pictures on the wall and some bookshelves along with several doors.

"You know, this is the second home I've been in that was owned by a psychotic murderer," I said. "And both of them have appeared completely—"

Olivia opened the first door inside the apartment.

"Holy shit," I said as I stared at the madness beyond.

The room itself was fairly normal—a rather hideous green carpet with a small camp bed in the center, one small bedside table, and a lamp. It was what was on the walls that frightened and horrified. There were pictures of Olivia. Someone, probably Neil, had been stalking her, but there were hundreds of photos covering the walls. They were interspersed with photos taken of the bodies of the dead women, creating the most disturbing wallpaper of all time.

"He slept in here," Olivia said, removing a photo of herself from the wall and throwing it on the floor with disgust.

"These photos of the murdered women weren't taken by Neil. Peter must have done them himself. It would be more personal for him."

"I feel sick," Olivia whispered. "Neil was following me around all this time." She tore another picture from the wall and showed it to me. "This is one of Kasey and me. That fucking cunt took a photo of my daughter. If he wasn't already dead, I'd tear his fucking head off myself."

I took the pictures from Olivia's shaking hands and tossed them onto the floor.

"Burn it," she said. "Burn all of it."

"We need to look around more—we can't do that if I set fire to the building."

Olivia grabbed a large bunch of the photos, most of which appeared to be of her and Kasey, and tore them all off the wall, exposing the blue paint beneath.

As I was leaving the room, I noticed one picture that stood out from the rest. It was of Peter and four other men, all of whom were in police uniform. "The four ghouls he created in that basement, they were his friends. And they were cops."

"It was thought that some people in the police tried to conceal evidence during his trial, but nothing was ever proven." Olivia shuddered. "Let's keep searching."

I made sure to shut the door on our way out of the room; I didn't want Olivia getting all pyromaniac on me. There were four more doors along the hallway. The first two led to nothing but empty rooms, and by the time we'd reached the second-to-last door, I was beginning to think there was nothing here worth bothering with.

I opened the door and very quickly realized how wrong I'd been. Although it didn't contain anything quite as crazy as the first room, I did find three leather-bound books on a desk. I picked up the first book and turned it over in my hands.

At first I thought it was just a journal, as there were no markings to set it apart as anything important. But when I opened it, I realized exactly what I was holding. "I don't know how this is possible," I said to myself.

"What's wrong?" Olivia asked, taking the book from my hands and flicking through it. "What is this?"

"It's a copy of a six-hundred-year-old book that details how to become a lich. A book that should be locked away in Avalon."

"What are the other two?" Olivia asked, picking up the second book and handing it to me without opening it as she flicked through the last one.

I read the information contained within the second leather book with haste. "It's his journal," I said. "It details every single murder he's ever committed. Including the ones since he became a lich. He says he wanted to make them all pay. He blames you a lot, Olivia. Mostly for taking away Vicki and getting him caught."

I flicked through a few more pages and came to a photo that had been glued into the back of the journal. It was a copy of the one I'd found in Vicki's house, the picture of her and her friends, the six other victims. I showed it to Olivia.

"He wrote something underneath," I said. "He wrote, and I quote, 'Those fucking bitches need to die. They helped Vicki get away from me. She was never meant to leave. She said she'd love me always. Fucking whores will all pay for what they did. Vicki is paying right now. I can hear her scream when I close my eyes. And when everything is done, when I'm content that all of the wrongs have been righted, I'm going after that LOA bitch.'"

I paused, then said, "And, you know what, Olivia? I think I'll stop there."

"Keep going."

"No. I'm not giving you more ammo to do something stupid. You're already angry and emotions are running high—you don't need to hear any more of his insane ramblings."

"Point taken. You should take a look at this." Olivia passed me the book she'd been reading. "It's a history of insanity."

The last book was a chronology not only of Peter's behavior, but that of several of his ancestors. A mixture of paper cuttings and copies of the crime reports from the police gave a stark and dangerous view into Peter's mind. His father was a drunk and regularly beat both him and his mother, finally getting himself arrested at the age of thirty-six. He was dead a few hours later, found hanging in his own cell. Peter would have been eight years old.

Peter's grandfather was similarly tainted with a seemingly endless rage. He was arrested and convicted of the murder and dismemberment of three prostitutes in Leeds during the 1950s. A fellow prisoner slit his throat six weeks after he started a life sentence. I began to wonder how anyone could be a member of this family and not be a psychotic madman.

It was endless misery and hatred in printed form—Peter's great-grandfather died after a drunken brawl outside a pub in London. Someone shot him to stop him from stabbing a man to death with the end of a table leg.

The very last page was just a photo, taken in the 1860s. Beneath it was written *great, great-grandfather.* The man's evil eyes bore into me. I'd seen those eyes before. When he'd almost killed me. Peter's great, great grandfather was the lich I'd met in Montana.

CHAPTER 32

Montana Territory, America. 1878.

"Your plan appears to settle on the insane side of crazy," Sergeant Roberts said from the opposite side of the long table we were sitting at.

Next to him Chief Blacktail stared intently at the map that was laid out before us. "I have to agree with the sergeant, Nathan. Your plan has some fairly major holes in it."

"Such as?" I asked. It had been a long afternoon. Once Sky and I had finally left Waltham's old bedroom at the fort, everything had almost happened at once. Chief Blacktail had arrived with his warriors, eager to spend a night behind some walls. The lich had everyone on edge, and to Sergeant Roberts' credit, he'd agreed immediately. Chief Blacktail positioned the armed Crow tribe members around the fort to help keep it safe during what, I was almost certain, would be a very long and tense night.

Once the preliminaries of getting the army and the Crow tribesmen to work together were out of the way, Chief Blacktail, Sergeant Roberts, Sky, and I sat down in the officer's quarters to try and ascertain how we were going to take the lich and his men on.

"What about the house that sits apart from the city of Kilnhurst? Your plan doesn't explain how anyone will be taking it," Sergeant Roberts commented.

"I will be dealing with that property and its inhabitants," Sky said.

"Alone, it would seem." Sergeant Roberts didn't sound happy about it. I got the feeling he thought that fighting was a man's job and sending a lone woman into an unknown hornets' nest was a death sentence.

"I am more than capable of taking care of myself," Sky said with a smile. "But I will not be alone, my men will accompany me."

"And these men," Chief Blacktail interjected. "Where are they?"

"They'll be here before sunrise. Trust me; your help would only get your men killed."

Sergeant Roberts and Chief Blacktail clearly wanted to argue more, but instead kept their mouths shut.

"Any other problems?" I asked.

"There are three entrances into the town—north, south, and southwest." Sergeant Roberts pointed to each area on the map as he spoke. "Your plan is that my men and I take the north, Chief Blacktail takes his to the south, and you take the southwest. Alone."

"That's the plan," I said.

"And to do this you plan on using your…magic." The word stuck in his throat; he'd seen the aftermath of my battle and how quickly I'd healed from my wounds, but he was having difficulty believing what Chief Blacktail had accepted so readily.

"Magic isn't a dirty word," I pointed out.

"I know, but it's just…I was raised to believe in certain things, that there's logic to the world. My father was a scientist and my mother his assistant. The possibility of magic flies in the face of that. The idea of men walking around with the power of a…a god—it's a foreign concept."

"I'm not a god, far from it."

"You can create fire and air from your body, what would you call it? I understand that you're a sorcerer, I really do, but it's hard to accept."

"You need to trust that I can do this," I said. "And you all need to be aware of the dangers. Sky spent time describing what both the ghouls and the barren were, and how best to deal with them. I need you to relay that information to your men."

"All-out attack," Chief Blacktail summed up.

"But be careful, these things will kill you quickly. Don't underestimate them."

"I will talk to my men," Chief Blacktail said and stood up, leaving the building. We had purposely decided to sit next to the entrance so we could watch both the tribesmen and soldiers getting ready. I watched through the window as he walked across the yard outside, stopping occasionally to talk to his warriors.

"Some of my men are unhappy at fighting alongside Indians. No matter how dire the circumstances."

"Ask them if they'd be happier dead."

Sergeant Roberts sighed. "Distrust is hard to overcome when it's ingrained."

I looked through the window as Chief Blacktail's son walked past a group of army soldiers, snarling at them as they turned to glance his way.

"On both sides," I added.

"I'll talk to him," Sky said. "Or break his skull, depending on how he reacts to me." She made her way across the yard and slapped the chief's son on the back of the head.

"She was concerned about you," Sergeant Roberts said as I returned my attention to the maps on the table. "She beat the hell out of Lieutenant Brooks, broke his nose and jaw. She blamed him and Captain Waltham for your condition. And as the Captain's remains are now buried, Corporal Brooks was the only one she could explain her...*displeasure* to. She's quite the woman."

"Yes, she is," I said with a smile. "How are Tala and Wapi?"

"I put them together in an upstairs bedroom. Chief Blacktail took a lot of convincing to leave them here until this is over. I wanted to make sure they were uninjured before they traveled back to their tribe. It's too dangerous out there with those monsters running around."

"Thanks for your help. You might want to get some rest. Tomorrow is going to be a very long day."

Sergeant Roberts held out a hand, which I shook. "It's been an honor," he said. "If anything should happen to me tomorrow, I wanted to tell you that."

"You'll be fine," I said. "And the honor is mine. You're a good man, sergeant, and you'll make a fine officer one day."

I stared at the map once Sergeant Roberts had left me alone and wondered if I really believed that everything was going to go well. No, probably not. People were going to die. I just hoped I could limit how many. Hopefully, my going in alone would let any ghouls or barren see me as the weaker prey. And I'd only have to worry about myself.

"So, what's my job?" Sam asked as he walked over to me.

"You're staying here."

"No, I'm not. I've got just as much reason to go back to that damn town. I need justice for my dad, for my friend."

"Sam, I promise you that I'll do my best to keep the sheriff alive for you. But you have to stay here. Tala and Wapi are both staying, as are all of the civilians. You need to stay here because I need people I can trust. I've already spoken to Sergeant Roberts and Chief Blacktail; they've each agreed to leave five men here to protect the fort. Your job is to help them."

"My job is to—"

"No! There are two terrified children upstairs right now. All they've known since they arrived here is fear and pain and suffering. I know you want revenge for what happened to you, to your dad, but it has to wait. If ghouls and barren turn up here with everyone gone, I need someone here that I can trust to protect these children with his life."

Sam's eyes immediately dropped to the floor. "I'm sorry," he said.

"Don't be. You're so close to getting what you've wanted for so long that you can taste it. But I need to ask you something. Will killing the sheriff bring anyone back? Will it help with that knot of rage inside your gut?"

Sam stared at me. "I don't know."

"What matters in situations like this is doing your best to help those who can't help themselves. Those two children need someone they can trust. You're not too much older than they are, and you're not a member of the U.S. Army. They need you more than you need that rage satisfied. When this is over, if you still want to kill him…" I placed my fingertip against his forehead. "You aim here, and you pull the trigger."

Sam nodded slowly, his eyes remaining on my fingers. "It's getting late," he said finally. "I'll check on the two upstairs and get some sleep."

"I'll see you tomorrow, Sam, but be safe, okay?"

He nodded again and ran toward the stairs, taking them two at a time until he reached the floor above.

"You're really trying to stop him from getting revenge," Sky said from behind me.

I turned around. "How long were you listening?"

"Not long after you started looking at my ass when I walked away."

I couldn't help but smile. "And a lovely ass it is, too."

"What happened upstairs," she said. "It wasn't a precursor to some sort of relationship."

"Don't worry, I never assumed otherwise. And to answer your point, I'd rather he didn't start killing people."

"You mean you'd rather he didn't turn into you?"

"He would have had to start a lot earlier to do that. He's a good kid, and not a killer. I can see it in his eyes, in his expression. Killing someone for revenge would do something to him."

"You can't know that."

"Are you saying that you think he'd be fine with it?"

Sky shook her head. "It would break him, but it's still his decision. He has to figure it out for himself or he'll always resent himself."

"When I was growing up, a fourteen-year-old killing someone would have felt almost normal. But now, after such a long time, I'd have hoped things would have improved. Sometimes I don't think we've moved on at all."

"That's a very melancholy attitude."

"I'm going to have to kill people tomorrow morning. I don't want Sam to feel like I do now."

"And what do you feel?"

"Nothing," I said honestly. "I feel nothing. It just has to be done. A bit like killing the wolves that want to eat a farmer's sheep. Merlin always said that I have this ability to turn into a killer—emotionless and cold, like someone turning a lamp on and off. He's right, I can. I can go to a place and kill without concern." *Most of the time,* I added silently.

"Then I'm glad you're on our side," Sky said. "But this is the life we lead. We kill to keep those we care about safe. We trade in our own futures to ensure that others get to have them. How many times have you taken a life to save another? How about a hundred or a thousand others? You're too hard on yourself."

"I'm just tired. It's been a long few weeks. You and your team take care tomorrow, okay?"

Sky hugged me tight. "You, too. Don't go doing anything crazy."

"You need the ghouls dead. I'll make sure that any in that town are gone before you meet the lich."

"I know you will," she said and kissed me on the cheek. "Get some sleep, Nate. Tomorrow will be a long day, too."

I watched Sky walk away and waited as the darkness of night came and the tension rose inside the camp. Sky had been positive that the lich wouldn't launch another attack so soon. That he wouldn't risk losing anyone else. But even so, there was a nagging doubt inside my head that he could do something. That doubt stayed with me as I fell asleep on the comfortable chair next to the large table.

When I woke someone had placed a thick blanket over me, and I shook it off as the crisp morning air woke me fully. There was already a lot of commotion in the courtyard—Crow warriors and army soldiers working side by side to prepare for the coming fight. Tala and Wapi were walking around with Sam, who appeared to have taken the job of protecting them to heart. My Winchester rifle was in his hands. I wasn't going to have much use for it and I was glad he had something important to do that would keep him busy.

Sergeant Roberts appeared holding a cup that he placed in front of me. "Good morning, sir."

"Nathan will do."

"Not today, today you're in charge. Everyone here knows it. I can't call you Nathan in front of the men. It's too familiar. So, I'd best get used to calling you sir, sir."

I smiled and picked up the cup. "Tea?"

"You're British, so I thought it would be nice to have some. No one else here drinks the stuff."

"Uncouth ruffians, the bloody lot of you," I said, which made Sergeant Roberts laugh.

The humor soon faded; Sergeant Roberts and I shook hands. "Good luck today," he said.

"Keep everyone safe," I told him before drinking the rest of my tea and handing him the cup. "I'll see you all in the town after we clear it out."

Sergeant Roberts saluted and left me alone with my thoughts as I got ready. I'd told the woman who had wanted to kill me that I was coming back to burn down their town and piss on the ashes. I aimed to keep that promise.

CHAPTER 33

I leaned forward in the saddle, patting Valor's neck to calm her as the Crows tribe joined me. The town of Kilnhurst was close by— we could see it clearly as we waited on top of the hill to the south.

Sky had taken her men to the big house outside the town. One of them was going to throw a ball of fire into the sky—our signal to begin the assault.

Chief Blacktail sat next to me on his dark-brown horse, his twenty warriors behind him. I hoped it would be enough. It would have to be. "I wanted to talk to you about the deputy we spoke to back at Fort Pennywise. The one my son wanted to kill."

"Is he dead?" I asked.

Chief Blacktail shook his head. "We left him there, tied up in the jail. I felt it best to let him live."

"By now people will have wondered why they haven't heard from him. They're probably out there searching for him. Maybe they found him, maybe they took him back to town."

"Does he still need to live?" Chief Blacktail's son asked as he rode up next to his father.

"If you find anyone in that town who doesn't surrender, make them. They brought this on themselves."

The boy's smile was cruel and evil. Today, he fought side by side with the army to eradicate a mutual threat, however uneasy that made them both feel. But I wondered if one day someone from that same army would be coming back here to end him because he'd become a problem to the local communities.

A flare-like bolt of fire shot into the sky and Chief Blacktail raised his rifle into the air. "To the glory of battle," he cried and urged his horse on, followed immediately by his warriors.

I rode with them for a short time, the anticipation of the battle ahead almost palpable amongst the men. As we reached the town, everyone slowed and I nodded toward Chief Blacktail, who returned the gesture. I rode off alone toward my planned entrance.

A few minutes later, I entered the town itself and got down from Valor, tying her to the nearest hitching post. I hoped she'd be safe this close to the edge of town.

As Valor slaked her thirst at the trough, I removed my *jian* and ensured that my throwing knives were secure on the sides of my belt, three on each side.

I patted Valor on the neck and she stopped drinking. "I'll be back for you." I loosened the reins slightly—one quick tug and she'd be free. I didn't want ghouls or barren getting hold of her.

She nudged me with her head and I rubbed her nose until she went back to drinking. I fished a few apples out of my saddlebag, acquired from the fort's larder, and tossed them into the water. She snatched one immediately and set about crunching it into a fine paste.

The wind whipped up around me as I walked further into the town, tossing around loose grit and earth. It was cold today, even with the sun out, and the building clouds gave the impression that the sun wouldn't be a permanent thing. Darkness was rolling in from the east. It would get here soon, but hopefully not soon enough to cause any problems for the assault.

The town was abandoned. Doors were open and the contents inside were thrown about. I stepped up onto the sidewalk and pushed a door all the way open with the toe of my boot, exposing the mess inside. Blood had been smeared on the walls; there'd been a fight here. A big one.

There was movement inside, and I readied a ball of fire just as something barreled into me from the side, sending me sprawling onto the ground outside. I flung the fireball at my attacker, but it was already dashing aside as doors opened all around me and barren flooded out onto the street.

I rolled back to my feet and caught the first two barren with a blast of fire, which threw them back against the nearest wall. They tried to get up, but the fire quickly spread over them and ended their fighting days.

Three more barren charged at me, dying before they got close as I lashed out with a whip of fire and severed their heads. That left five more, while the ghoul that had hit me initially prowled around behind them, waiting for its moment to strike.

A plume of fire left my hands, engulfing the five barren and incinerating them where they stood. The ghoul dove aside before the flames reached it, sprinting toward me with cruel purpose.

I unsheathed the *jian* in preparation for his attack, but the window nearest to me shattered as a second ghoul flew toward me. It was too fast to avoid, and it slammed into me, knocking us both to the ground as the sword fell from my grip.

The second ghoul sat on my chest, pinning me down, and unhinged its jaw, showing rows of razor sharp teeth as it tried to bite me.

I took hold of the second ghoul's jaw with both hands and forced its head to one side, using air magic to blast it off me. The ghoul flew through the air, straight into the first ghoul.

I didn't wait to watch what happened and dove for the *jian*, grabbing it as another barren came charging out of the nearby house. A blast of air removed its legs from under it, sending it tumbling to the ground, where I finished it with a sword thrust to the back of the skull. I twisted the sword with a sickening crunch, removing it just in time to see the two ghouls get back to their feet.

"Okay then," I said. "Let's see what you both can do."

The first ghoul ran directly at me, its razor-sharp claws looking for purchase in my flesh. I dodged the swipe and smashed an air-covered fist into its temple, sending it to the ground. The second ghoul didn't wait for an invitation; he had been moving from the moment the first had run at me.

I waited until he was close enough and then swiped up toward his neck with the *jian*, but he anticipated my move and launched himself into the air, catching me with a clawed foot in the chest. It cut through my coat and I felt the familiar sensation of blood trickling down toward my stomach.

I reached out with air magic and grabbed hold of the ghoul's foot before it hit the ground, hardening the air in an instant and then using the ghoul's own momentum to spin him into the wall of the nearest building.

Brick and dust exploded from the impact, but I had no time to rest as the first ghoul was back, swiping at my face and neck with his claws. He was too close for me to use the sword effectively—all I managed were superficial cuts. And death by a thousand cuts wasn't something that worked well with ghouls.

I used air magic to push him away, but he'd sprung backward, the gust of wind missing him by inches. We circled one another, watching for any signs of attack. My magic couldn't kill or seriously hurt him, but my sword could, and he knew it. And so could my other blades.

He avoided the first of the small daggers, but the second and third kept him on his toes long enough for me to close the gap between us and stab the sword through his heart.

The ghoul shrieked as I dragged my sword from its chest, black blood oozing out of the wound. The ghoul collapsed to the ground, and I wasted no time in using the *jian* to decapitate it, just before its friend rejoined the fray.

I barely managed to stop the second ghoul from tearing my ribcage apart, its claws glancing off my arm.

Blood dripped down the back of my hand, making the sword's hilt slippery.

The ghoul barely paused before launching another attack, sprinting toward me and swiping continuously with its deadly claws in the hope that something would catch. I dodged or blocked the first few, but I couldn't keep it up forever, and the ghoul only had to get lucky once.

I released an explosion of fire directly between us, which gave me space, but the ghoul merely waited until the flames had died down and then walked toward me.

I waited until the ghoul was close enough and unleashed a fresh inferno. There was nowhere it could dodge in time to avoid the flames, and, while it wouldn't kill the ghoul, the howls of pain told me that it had done enough. The ghoul flailed wildly in my direction, and I dodged aside, plunging my *jian* into its neck and tearing open the jugular. A few seconds later its head joined that of the first, rolling across the ground until it stopped by a set of steps.

I left the ghouls to dissolve into the earth and made my way toward the bar at the end of the street. As I stepped into the shadow of the large building, several windows were smashed and shots were fired at me. I sprinted behind the nearest wall and tried to ascertain exactly where the shots were coming from.

I edged to the far end of the wall and peered around to the bar again. The ground-floor window was smashed and a rifle barrel poked through the broken glass. The same was true of the window directly above it. Both rifles were still aimed at the point where their users had last seen me, before I vanished from sight.

A quick sprint across to the nearest adjacent building, and through the open front door, made sure that I was no longer a target for either of the two rifles, but it also put me in direct contact with another barren—the young red-haired woman who had been sent to kill me in the bath.

She was crouched on the ground, feeding on a small animal of some kind and hadn't noticed me. A small jet of fire left my fingertip and hit her in the temple, ending her suffering. She slumped forward just as a bullet crashed through the broken window beside me. I ran through the building to the rear and blasted the locked wooden door into tiny pieces.

I darted down the narrow opening between the buildings, stopping before it opened back out into the street. More shots were being fired at the front of the building I'd just left, and I wondered if the shooters actually had any idea of what they were doing.

I made my way to the edge of the opening and, still concealed by the shadows of the buildings on either side of me, used air magic to gather as much of the loose dust and grit from the street as possible and set it rotating until I had something that resembled a small sand storm. The shots stopped as the mass of grit and dirt got larger and larger until I flung it at the front of the bar.

Glass shattered as the wind-controlled mass slammed into the bar windows, quickly followed by shouts and screams as that same glass was plucked up and added to the contents of the spinning cyclone.

The entire front of the building was ripped apart and flung inside at whoever was hiding there. I sprinted to the front of the bar as the wind died down and found two men inside who were rubbing their eyes, both of whom I recognized as having worked for the sheriff.

Too disorientated to fight back, they were easily put down with a gust of air, lifting them from their feet and slamming them into the nearest wall. They fell to the floor with a thud as I made my way up the stairs to check for any other holdouts.

Sure enough, they were found without too much trouble. Two more armed men sat by the window at the end of the corridor. Neither of them appeared to be moving, and on closer inspection, I saw the long jagged piece of glass that had been torn from the ruined window and embedded in the throat of one of them. The shock had apparently caused him to spin around and fire his shotgun directly into the chest of his companion—the same man that Chief Blacktail had taken prisoner. A fitting end to a partnership with murderers and monsters.

It took only few minutes more to check the rest of the upstairs and discover it empty, so I made my way back to the ground floor, where I found Sheriff Bourne crawling toward the entrance. A large cut was seeping blood down his face.

"So what hit you?" I asked as I kicked him onto his back and relieved him of the silver revolver still in its holster. The sheriff winced in pain. Apparently, the cut wasn't his only injury. Good.

He pointed behind me at a table leg, which had come loose from its home and apparently struck him in the head.

"Well, you stay right there." I punched him in the face, knocking him out. I wasn't finished with the town yet.

I took Sam's father's revolver with me and stepped out of the bar as the first drops of rain fell. I fastened my coat and walked toward the sounds of battle as Sam ran around the corner of a nearby building, followed by two barren.

"Drop," I shouted, and he dove to the ground as I launched a jet of fire at the two barren, incinerating them where they stood.

"What the hell are you playing at?" I snapped at Sam, dragging him to his feet. "I told you to stay back, to stay away."

"And I told you, I need this," Sam's retort was full of anger, at me or at the sheriff, I wasn't sure which.

I swallowed my reply and I got back to more important things. "What are you doing here?"

Sam pointed behind him. "Sergeant Roberts and Chief Blacktail are fighting barren at a crossroads up the road from here, and they're being overrun. Sergeant Roberts asked me to find you. They need your help."

I was moving before he finished speaking, running in the direction he'd pointed. Sam kept pace for a few steps.

"How many?" I asked.

"Forty, maybe more. I think the whole town was turned into those things."

"Stay here," I commanded Sam and sprinted away without waiting for a reply.

I was almost at the end of the street when two barren burst from a house and ran toward me. I picked them both up with a gust of wind and flung them back at the building. The impact and loud crack suggested it would be the last thing they ever did.

I rounded the corner and saw Chief Blacktail and Sergeant Roberts, fighting side by side with daggers and swords, killing barren that got close, their men following suit. I was a hundred yards from them when Sergeant Roberts was knocked to the ground by a barren, who then leapt onto his back. Chief Blacktail killed the barren with an axe to the head and offered his hand to Sergeant Roberts, who accepted and together they continued fighting.

Despite their camaraderie and superior numbers, they were fighting barren who felt no fear or pain. There were no such things as retreat or surrender. If it wasn't a killing stroke on the first blow, they might not get a second chance.

I readied a huge charge of magical energy, but as I was about to release it, the barren stopped attacking en masse and turned toward the opposite end of the street. The human fighters took the opportunity to dispatch many of their foes, but around a dozen barren had already started to make their way toward whatever it was they were waiting for.

"Get back," I shouted, fearing that Sky had failed her job and the lich was about to make an appearance.

Chief Blacktail and Sergeant Roberts did as I asked and moved all of their men away from the now-stationary barren and back toward me. Some of the men had cuts, and at least one had been rewarded for his efforts with a nasty gouge across the arm.

"How many did you lose?" I asked.

"Nine," Sergeant Roberts said. "Four were too wounded to continue and the other five died fighting."

"Eight," Chief Blacktail replied. "Three of those are wounded."

"Anyone got any bullets?" I asked.

"We're out," Sergeant Roberts said. "We sent the wounded back to the fort to get treated and prepare for the worst. We kept shooting the bastards, but they wouldn't stop coming."

"Is this about to get worse?" Chief Blacktail asked.

I didn't answer. I wasn't sure what the answer was. The barren were milling around, all of them staring at the corner of the adjoining street.

I thought about having everyone attack the barren, but if the lich were to make an appearance the humans would be too close to retreat without suffering heavy casualties. "I think we're about to find out," I finally managed.

A man in a long dark duster emerged from around the street corner, ignoring the barren who suddenly took a great interest in the newcomer.

I breathed a sigh of relief. "Lower your weapons."

Everyone obeyed my order without hesitation.

The wind blew the man's long white hair over his shoulders, and one of the barren decided that was the moment to strike. It howled something and sprinted toward the newcomer, whose response was to raise one hand out in front of him. The barren kept running for a second and then just fell to the ground, twitched twice, and was still.

Several of the remaining barren sought their own opportunity and charged the man. This time he raised both hands, and once more the barren stopped running and fell to the ground.

One barren climbed onto the roof of a nearby building and launched himself toward the stranger. The man didn't even move; he simply raised one hand, like before. But instead of dropping to the ground, the barren just stopped in mid-air, held by some invisible force, until the man clenched his hand in a fist and the barren exploded in a shower of blood.

All of the remaining barren ran at the man, but none of them got within six feet of him. He waved one arm and they fell like downed trees, until only one remained. The man grabbed it by the throat as it ran toward him, lifting it off the ground until its feet were a few inches above the dirt and gravel.

"Vermin," he said. "Your master is dead." He touched the snarling barren on the forehead with one finger, and the body went limp before being dropped back to earth, where it began to dissolve like its kin.

Despite my order to lower weapons, the fear and awe radiating off both the Crow and the soldiers was almost tangible, a measurable fog of thick terror that hung in the air from what they'd just witnessed.

The man walked past them all and embraced me. "It's good to see you," he said.

"Hades," I said with a smile. "I didn't realize you would be here, it's good to see you, too."

"I was in the area; a lich is not something to trifle with." He turned back as Sky and six men followed in what had been his path—one of them helped to walk by another, his leg heavily bandaged.

"The lich had silver knives," he said, almost anticipating any questions I had about what had happened. "But he's no longer an issue."

Sky helped the injured man sit on the ground and then came over, embracing me. "I'm glad you're not hurt," she said.

"I'm fine," I said. "Though both Chief Blacktail and Sergeant Roberts lost men today."

"I'm sorry to hear that," Hades said, turning to the two men. "They were brave to fight against these things. Your men will be honored tonight when we remember our fallen."

"Thank you," Sergeant Roberts said, sounding more than a little confused. "What did you do back there?"

Hades glanced behind him. "Oh," he said as if only just aware that he might have done something out of the ordinary. "I removed their souls."

"Their souls?" Chief Blacktail asked.

"Everything has a soul, even the most evil, deplorable beings on earth. They might not be technically alive, but everything needs a soul to be able to function. A barren's is just twisted and rotten. I removed them."

"But one exploded," Sergeant Roberts said.

"I used the energy I'd taken from absorbing the souls to put them all back into that one barren. The effect is quite spectacular."

I left Hades to talk to the two confused men and found Sky by herself, washing blood from her hands at a nearby water pump.

"Everyone survive?" I asked.

She nodded. "I have something for you." She reached into her coat and removed an old leather-bound book. "I assume this is what you're looking for here in Montana. I spoke to my father, and he agreed that you can have it."

"Thank you," I said, and then realized what the rest of Sky's words had been. "Your father? Hades is your father?"

"I was adopted by him and Persephone a few centuries ago. I'm sorry that didn't come up before." She smiled a wicked, sly grin.

"You do realize that having sex with Hades' daughter might not have been my greatest idea."

"Good thing I didn't mention it at the time then," she laughed and walked off to talk to her father as a single shot rang out across the town.

I darted into the bar and found the sheriff knelt on the floor, his hands tied behind his back and his ankles tied together. Sam stood in front of him; his father's other revolver in his hand, a match to the one I'd taken off the sheriff earlier. A large bullet hole pierced the woodwork close to the sheriff's head.

"Sam, what are you doing?" I asked, taking great care to keep my voice calm and careful.

Sam's eyes were trained firmly on the sheriff. "I'm doing what I need to do—what I have to do to make everything right."

"He should die," I agreed. "He made a pact with an evil monster, and then when everyone else in town was being killed and turned into barren, he got to keep his life."

I turned to the sheriff. "You were useful to him, that's why he let you and your men live."

The sheriff nodded. There appeared to be no fear in him, no concern that anything would happen to him. "He needed someone who wasn't dead to help during the day."

"He chose you, because you had power, and you convinced the rest of the town. You told people that the lich would protect them and make them money, but you always knew he was going to kill them all."

"Yes, I knew. It wasn't meant to happen so quickly, but when he discovered that you'd been here, he knew he had to act. So he started the transformation of the townspeople. But there was no lie. Montana was going to become a haven of the kind of America that we wanted. Free from outsiders. Free from crime."

"You just all had to become monsters to do it."

"You say monster, I say free."

"You murdered Sam's father and took his revolvers. Sam here wants to kill you with one of them."

The sheriff shrugged as best he could. "He doesn't have the balls to kill me."

"Screw you," Sam screamed. "You killed my dad. He was just doing his job. He was here trying to protect people."

"He was in my way." The sheriff spoke in the same way you'd describe trimming a hedge or knocking down a wall, a job that needed to be done to make life easier. "He was looking around. A marshal in my town; I couldn't have that. So we killed him. Or we did after the lich was through with him. Do you want to know how he screamed? How he begged to be allowed to see his son again? How he cried and pissed himself like a fucking coward?" The sheriff stared directly at Sam, his eyes never leaving the boy's face. "He died slowly and painfully screaming your name over and over until I put a bullet in his head just to shut him up."

Sam pulled the hammer of the revolver back as tears fell from his eyes. "You ruined my life. I have nothing now."

"So, kill me. Don't be a fucking pussy, just shoot me and be done with it. Because I'm not spending the rest of my life in some fucking prison, rotting for all to see."

Sam's shoulder tensed, as if he was willing himself to pull the trigger, but he couldn't bring himself to do it.

"Sam," I said. "You have every reason in the world to kill him. Hell, no one out there would turn you over to the authorities if you did. This man deserves justice. Your dad believed in justice—I'm betting that's why he was a marshal. But this isn't justice, this is vengeance. And I know vengeance, Sam. I know it well. I know what it feels like to hold the life of a man who took someone important from you. To be able to decide if they live or die. And I know what it's like to kill him."

"Just let him fucking do—"

I kicked Sheriff Bourne in the head, knocking him to the floor. "Sam, look at him. Look at the man who tortured you and your dad. Look at this pathetic excuse for a human. If you kill him, you're going to lose a part of yourself. His face will stay with you forever, the face of the man you executed. Whenever you think of your dad, that piece of shit on the floor will always be close by. I promise you, it will fester your memories until just thinking about your dad will cause you to remember what you did here. Or you can walk away, right now. Go live your life; do what your dad would have wanted for you. The choice is all yours."

There was no painfully slow wait to decide what he was going to do. He released the hammer and re-holstered the gun.

"Fucking pussy," the sheriff said as he got back to his knees. "I knew you were a gutless coward. Like father, like son."

Sam shook his head. "You had to tie my dad up and torture him to make you feel like a man. You were too scared to face him one on one. He will always be the better man, because you couldn't bring yourself to deal with him like anything but the tiny coward you are." Sam walked out of the bar and back outside.

The sheriff laughed. "I actually thought he might shoot me for a second. So, where are you going to take me to prison? Or do I get a hangman's noose? Because I have a whole lot to talk about to whoever wants to listen. The army's involvement in murdering Indians, monsters roaming the lands killing ranch folk. It will be quite the tale."

I picked up an army Colt that someone had dropped on the floor during the fight and checked to see that it was loaded. Three shots left. It was an old piece and well used. I placed it on the table near me.

"Sam's a good person," I said and glanced outside onto the street in front of the bar, but couldn't find him. "He's going to move on from this, get a nice job, and settle down with someone who cares for him. Or not. His life is utterly open to live how he sees fit."

"Why do I care?"

"Why? Because, although Sam is a good person, I'm not." I picked up the Colt and shot the sheriff through the eye. The bullet exited through the back of his skull and sprayed blood and brain matter over the destroyed room behind him as he toppled to the floor. I emptied the last two bullets into his forehead. I didn't want him coming back as anything, just in case.

I dropped the gun on the ground and poured fire out of my hands all around me. The alcohol-soaked room ignited and was quickly turned into an inferno. I stepped out of the fires of hell back onto the street, where I was greeted by Sky.

"Sam went for a walk with the chief," she said. She passed me the leather book. "You dropped this."

"Thanks, I'll make sure that Merlin gets it."

"And then what?"

I flicked through the old pages and fought the urge to incinerate it. "If it's up to me, it'll never see the light of day again."

"So, do you have any recommendation as to what you want to do with this place?" Hades asked as he joined Sky and me.

The fire from the bar was hot against the back of my neck. "Burn it to the ground. Wipe it off the face of the earth."

Hades' smile contained no humor. "With pleasure."

CHAPTER 34

Winchester, England. Now.

Olivia asked me a question, but for the life of me I couldn't have said what it was. My attention was centered totally on the picture of the lich who had almost killed me over a hundred years ago. The realization that I was unlikely to fare better against his great-great-grandson hit me like a truck. I was grateful I was already sitting down, because I was pretty certain that my legs had gone weak.

"Nate?" Olivia said, crouched before me, concern in her eyes.

I told her about the photo and what it meant.

"So, he's a fifth-generation psychopath."

"Someone gave him these notes on how to become a lich. I'm glad we've got Sky here to help with this. Otherwise, we wouldn't stand a chance."

"Peter Jarvis was a misogynistic coward who couldn't even kill those weaker than him unless they were tied up and powerless."

"He's not going to need to tie us up to kill us anymore," I pointed out and threw the journal onto the desk.

"Yet he still has to tie women to trees in order to kill them. And he's now so physically hideous that he has to enlist someone to bring the women to him. He sounds pathetic. And he will be even more so once Sky gets done with him. You and Sky have history, I assume."

"You could call it that, but we're just friends." I didn't really want to discuss it, but was grateful for the excuse to get off the topic of liches and their psychopathic tendencies.

"Sure, *friends*," Olivia said with a smile. "I'm going to check in on Tommy and get some more agents in this building. I want Peter's home gutted and searched from top to bottom."

She walked out of the room to make the call, leaving me alone with my thoughts, and with the fear of what was out there, waiting. I pushed it aside as I'd learned to do long ago. *"Fear is just a tool to be used like any other emotion,"* Merlin would say. *"You need to control it. Do not let it control you."*

It was a lesson he'd drilled into me, over and over again, making me face my fears until I could control them. But I never stopped feeling fear. No one can do that. No one sane, anyway.

The vibration of my phone shook the memory away.

"Hello, Nathan," Peter's voice, his actual voice, was deep and wispy, the sort of voice you'd imagine a snake would have.

"I figured you might call at some point," I said. "You want to brag about something really impressive? Killed a few more defenseless werewolves or something?"

"Are you really upset over Neil's death? He was a rapist, a murderer, and generally the scum of the earth. I did you a favor."

"Is that why you paid for his nice penthouse?"

"Paid for?" His laugher sent shivers up my spine. "I think you're overestimating the cash flow of a man who recently returned from the dead. You need to look elsewhere for that answer."

"The answer will wait, then, I guess. So, what do you want, Peter?"

He laughed again, a humorless, evil noise that would have made fingernails on a chalkboard sound like a symphony of elegant beauty. "How's Olivia holding up?"

"She wants you dead. Again. Preferably on a more permanent basis."

"We both know she can't do that, but I'll give her the opportunity to try soon enough. But the reason I'm calling is you, Nathan. I warned you to leave this alone. That it didn't involve you. I warned you to run away and never come back, and you not only ignored me, you brought a necromancer with you to end my plans."

"Sorry about her, her father just insisted I bring someone along to kill you."

"Her father?"

"Hades," I said. "Her father is Hades. So even if you do manage to get away from Sky, what do you think Hades will do to you?"

There was silence for a few heartbeats. "You think I fear him?"

"That shake in your voice tells me you do, yes. You're not stupid. You hurt Sky, even by accident, and Hades will rain down such horror on you as you can barely comprehend. He will tear your soul in two and keep the pieces as a plaything for when he gets bored."

Peter chuckled. "He can't come onto English soil. Not without starting a war."

That surprised me. And the shock of his knowledge quickly turned to concern when I realized that someone had to have educated him on matters of Avalon court. I decided to take a gamble. "Your friends in Avalon tell you that?"

"My friends tell me all sorts of things. They tell me that you stumbled into this from loyalty to your friends. That was the only reason I was going to give you an out. But you wronged me, and now it's time to pay the price. I warned you."

"Are you about to blow your old place up?" I asked flippantly as I quickly searched around the room for anything that might suddenly explode.

"I left you a gift, something very important that I think you're going to want to see. I'm looking at it right now. The cliff that lets you look down over the forest. Apparently this place is special for you. Your gift is here. And you might want to hurry. I don't think it's going to keep long." And the phone went dead.

I don't even remember leaving the apartment. The next thing I knew, I was on the stairs, sprinting to the building's front door as Olivia's calls for me to slow down rang out behind me. I jumped onto my bike and started the engine.

"Nate," Olivia tried again as she ran down the outside stairs.

I forced myself to stay and tell her about the call.

"I'll get help; they'll follow my GPS," she said.

I opened the bike's throttle, speeding off toward my destination, weaving between traffic and ignoring both traffic cameras and stoplights alike. It didn't take long to reach the outskirts of the forest I'd taken Sara to.

I pulled into the clearing, my heart pounding a beat in my throat. At first I couldn't see anything out of the ordinary. I stopped my bike and climbed off, ignoring the calls in my head to run and find whatever Peter had left for me. The more rational side of me insisted that the lich could still be around, waiting for me to make a mistake.

But my rational thought lost out the second I saw the woman tied to the tree, a hood pulled over her head so that I couldn't make out who it was. I sprinted toward her and pawed at the hood, tearing at the poppers holding it to her coat, ripping it off and throwing it aside.

Sara's beautiful face was untouched apart from a slight bruise on her cheek. But her eyes were closed and I had no idea if she was dead or alive. I forced myself to calm and searched for a pulse on her neck, finding it to be slow, but steady.

I used a small measure of wind magic to create a hardened blade of air and remove the cable ties that held her arms behind her around the tree trunk. She sagged forward, but I caught her, lowering her to the ground as sirens exploded all around me. I couldn't see any obvious injuries and there were no marks on her bare legs or blood on the blue and white dress.

Olivia's car skidded to a halt near my bike, followed closely by an ambulance. It hadn't been too long ago that I'd had to watch another friend of mine, Holly, be carried away in one of those with life-threatening injuries. It wasn't something I wanted to do again.

The paramedics moved me aside and got to work on Sara. One of them, a young woman, sat with her and asked her questions, tapping her on the shoulders and shouting in her ears in an effort to get a response.

The whole event was a bit like a terrible dream. I watched with horror as nothing the young paramedic did appeared to rouse Sara from whatever stupor she was in. And then, just as my thoughts turned to the darkest corner of my mind, Sara coughed and opened her eyes.

A flood of emotion crashed down over me and I had to lean against the tree until it had eased. Peter, and whoever was supporting him, had taken Sara as a message to me. And for that someone was going to suffer.

Sara's scream from the rear of the ambulance had me sprinting toward it.

"Nate," Sara said, her voice groggy and soft.

I climbed into the ambulance and sat beside her as she forced a smile.

"They didn't do anything to me," she said softly. "You need to know that. You need to know that nothing that happened here was because of you. I know that's what you're thinking. This is not your fault."

I nodded, but daren't say anything.

"They're going after Tommy..." she started to say more, but she passed out again. Olivia retrieved her phone from her pocket and started calling.

"It's okay," I assured her. "Sky and your agents are with them; they're safe."

She nodded but made the call anyway, walking off to talk as I left the ambulance and watched it drive away. Once it was gone, I glanced over to the tree to discover a small black bag beside where Sara had been held.

I picked it up, hoping to find something that might tell me where Peter and his men were hiding. I didn't really expect to find anything, but it was either do something pointless that took my mind away from Sara, or start hurting people to get the answers I needed, and Olivia probably wouldn't have liked that very much.

I glanced up in time to see Olivia's face turn to one of horror as she sprinted toward her car.

CHAPTER 35

Olivia was in the car and off like a rocket before I'd even had time to ask what had happened. I raced over to my bike and followed her. Unfortunately, she had a good thirty-seconds head-start, but that was soon cut down as I sped through the traffic to catch up. Olivia had her lights and siren going, something the LOA rarely use. Clearly whatever she'd been told was enough to spook her into charging off.

I wasn't worried about Tommy or Kasey; they had Sky and Agent Reid with them, along with half a dozen other agents. And no lich is going to willingly attack somewhere a power-ful necromancer happens to be staying. *But Peter wasn't just a lich,* I thought. What he had against Olivia was personal. And personal shit often overrode any sense of self-preservation. I opened the throttle further and the speedometer shot upward, the front wheel of the bike lifting off the road slightly for a moment.

The journey probably didn't take long, but it felt like a life-time as all of the horrific things that could have happened ran through my head. I had to keep telling myself that everything was fine, over and over again like some sort of mantra.

I arrived at Tommy's house soon after Olivia, who was already out of her car and sprinting toward the front door, as I switched off my engine and…noticed the front window was broken. I dropped my helmet onto the ground and ran to join Olivia just as she pushed the unlocked door open and stepped inside.

The house was eerily quiet, and Olivia drew her gun as we walked down the hallway toward the living room, the room where the window had been broken. It looked as if there'd been one hell of a fight; there were huge dents in the walls. The dining room table was in pieces, and I counted three bullet holes in the ceiling. Someone had fired shots as a warning. A note had been stuck to the TV screen…*We left you a DVD.*

I almost had to drag Olivia away, but the rest of the house needed to be searched, in case someone was hiding. Be it friend or foe.

We went to the kitchen first, as it was closest, and found Agent Greaves with his face pulverized. A bullet hole sat right where his heart would be, and blood soaked the front of his body, making a substantial puddle beneath where he'd fallen. In the middle of the puddle sat a pair of silver knuckle-dusters, probably discarded after his killer had finished with them. A second agent was slumped beside him; he'd been decapitated with something sharp. His head had rolled under the counter and blood had sprayed up the wall and ceiling.

We left the kitchen and finished searching downstairs, but found only the bodies of yet more dead agents in the den. There were four of them, and, unlike Greaves, they'd been torn apart. Ghouls had been at work on them. The rest of the search was exhausting, and not because of the size of the house. I could tell from her body language and silence that Olivia was doing everything she could to hold it together. I hoped she could keep that up until we knew what was going on.

The four upstairs bedrooms were all empty and immaculate—no one had been searching for anything. But the bathroom held the body of the babysitter in the bath, a bullet hole in her head and another in her heart. There was blood splatter up the blue tiles. She'd been standing in the bath when the first shot had been fired, and then shot a second time as she collapsed into the tub.

Olivia's phone started to ring and she answered it immediately. I left her to talk and went back downstairs to give the front room a more in-depth search. Claw marks had defaced one of the walls, leaving deep gouges in the brick. It was then that I remembered that Tommy had a shed outside.

I pulled open the patio door and walked through the conservatory. The back garden was as much of a war zone as the front room had been. Two more dead agents lay on the ground, teeth marks in their throats and deep gouges in their chests. More ghoul kills. But someone else had put up a hell of a fight against the intruders. I stepped over destroyed plants and an upturned bench, making my way toward the huge shed at the end of the lengthy garden. Someone had piled up garden furniture in front of the door, but a blast of air sent it spiraling away. I ignited a ball of fire in my hand as I opened the door…and immediately extinguished it as I found a bound and gagged Sky lying unconscious on the cold wooden floor.

Silver cuffs adorned her wrists, and a thick rope had been used as a gag. I unfastened the gag and tossed it aside. I'd need keys for the cuffs, so I had to leave them on for now. That's when I noticed the sorcerer's band on her left wrist. I'd never seen one used on a necromancer outside of a prison before, but it was on the other side of the cuffs and so impossible to remove without magic. And using magic would cause whatever runes were inscribed to ignite, possibly removing Sky's hand along with it.

I felt for a pulse. Like Sara's it was slow, but strong. I needed to get the cuffs and band off of her before she woke. It would be easier and faster to let her healing ability do the work. So I picked her up in my arms and carried her back to the house, as a cold rage swirled inside of me. First Sara and then Sky. Someone was going to pay dearly for that.

The front room was empty, but I heard Olivia talking outside to the agents who had arrived in double-quick time. If your director calls and says her family was attacked, you make it your new mission in life to make sure that it gets dealt with.

I laid Sky on the mostly undamaged sofa and went outside to find someone who might have keys.

Olivia's talking had turned into a full-blown rage as she demanded that her agents find out everything about what had happened and report back to her and her alone. She saw me and sighed.

"Get to work," she told everyone and the agents dispersed without a word.

"Did you find anything?" she asked me with more than a little anger. I doubted it was aimed at me, so I let it drop.

"Sky was in the shed, bound, gagged, and unconscious. Someone put a sorcerer's band on her wrist. I need keys to some cuffs so I can remove it."

Olivia fumbled in her pocket and passed me a set of small silver keys. "A sorcerer's band?" she asked, almost to herself.

"Whoever did this has access to Avalon tech," I pointed out as we walked together back into the living room. I unlocked Sky's cuffs and removed them, almost tearing off the sorcerer's band from her wrist and then throwing it across the room.

"We should watch whatever message they left us," Olivia said, switching on the TV and ripping the paper from the screen. "How long will Sky be out?"

"I don't know," I said, moving her arms so they were no longer behind her. "Probably a few minutes. She's not going to be happy when she wakes up."

"She can join the fucking club then, can't she?" Olivia flicked the TV onto the right channel and started the DVD.

Agent Reid's face came into view. "Hey, boss," he said. There was a cut above his lip and blood trickled down his chin. Another was just below his eye. He'd taken one hell of a punch.

"Actually, I guess it's time to tell the truth. You're not my boss. I don't work for you. I work for someone else, someone considerably more powerful than you, my pretty little director. And they want this lich to have his way. My job was to make sure that happened. And when he decided he was going to take your family, well it was my job to make sure that he got exactly what he wanted there, too."

He motioned off camera as one of the ghouls dragged Kasey into the room, pushing her onto the couch. Reid turned the camera slightly to reveal a semiconscious Tommy on the same couch, his face a bloody mask. A sorcerer's band adorned his wrist. "Your bloke here put up a hell of a fight," Reid continued, touching his swollen lip. "He had to be taught how to be civilized, and it's amazing how quickly one learns with a gun to a child's head."

Kasey started shaking her dad, begging him to get up, to help. To not be dead.

"Will you shut up, you stupid little bitch," Reid snapped, delivering a swift kick to Tommy's chest.

Kasey screamed and positioned herself in front of him, protecting him from further damage. Tommy looked at her through one good eye and I saw tears roll, cleaning some of the blood from his cheeks.

Reid watched all of it with an amused smile on his face. "Brave little fucker, isn't she?" He looked back at the camera. "So, I guess you want to know what's going to happen next. Well, at midnight tomorrow, you're going to come to a place of our choosing—we'll let you know where—and then you're going to hand yourself over to Peter, and he's going to kill you. If you do all of this, he may let your boyfriend and kid go. Probably not, but at least I'll make sure they die quick. You will die very slowly, I'm almost certain of that.

"Oh, and sorry about the mess with Greaves, but he was a useless fucking idiot and I basically did you a favor." He laughed to himself. "Seriously, I couldn't have hoped for a partner who was less observant. Not once did he question why we got the calls when a murder took place. He was just happy to take a lead on the investigation.

"And now onto Nathan Garrett. Nate. Do you want me to tell you something that no one else knows about you? You're not a member of The Faceless. I know that with a hundred percent certainty. And do you want to know, how I know?" Reid brought the camera closer to his face. "Because I'm part of The Faceless," he whispered. "And we know our own."

I felt Olivia's eyes burning into me as the truth was revealed, but Reid wasn't done yet.

"Oh, we didn't kill the necromancer. Hurt her quite a bit—I had to remove her from the issue first as she'd have killed the ghouls. But having Hades after us for killing his daughter would go against our plans. I hope she takes this as a hint to go home, because if she doesn't, and she goes up against Peter, he *will* kill her before she kills him."

I doubted very much that Sky would be going home. In fact, I was pretty certain that she'd be even more eager to go after Peter and dish out some retribution.

"So, Olivia, you dumb fucking idiot. I look forward to seeing you flayed. Maybe they'll put someone with some balls in the position of director now. Maybe someone who doesn't hire unknown cunts like Nathan Garrett to do their work, or fuck werewolves and give birth to some half-breed little bitch. I've been waiting for a long time to see you fall. Ever since I was told about the job I had to do. And Nathan, if I see you again, I'm going to kill you. I don't care who you are; no one lies about being Faceless and gets away with it. Although, to be fair, by the time I'm done with you, I'll make sure that the name of faceless really does fit."

"Who are you?" Olivia snapped, pushing me back against the wall and drawing a dagger, which sat a little too heavily against the skin of my throat.

"A friend," I said. "You don't need to know more."

"Fuck you. A man I trusted turned out to be an evil bastard who has my child. You will answer me, or I will kill you."

"No," Sky said from directly behind Olivia. "You won't."

Olivia spun around to face Sky, but the necromancer was quicker and had her disarmed and thrown onto the couch in one smooth motion.

"Nate is a friend," Sky said. "You can trust him. Maybe he'll tell you the truth, maybe he won't, but if you ever hold a knife to his neck in my presence again, I will gut you."

Sky casually tossed the knife into the wall, burying it a few inches into the plaster. "I assume Reid took your daughter and Tommy," she said to Olivia, who nodded, her eyes narrow and angry.

"He blindsided me," Sky said. "I didn't expect it. Last I saw was Tommy taking a silver knuckle-duster–aided punch to the jaw. Your boyfriend is a tough son of a bitch, isn't he?"

Olivia nodded.

I left the room, hoping very much that Olivia didn't try to go for round two with Sky, and retrieved the knuckle-dusters, which were being bagged up by one of the agents. He didn't question why I wanted them, just handed over the bag and didn't once complain when I washed the blood from them in the kitchen sink.

I took them back to Sky and showed them to her.

"That looks like them. Are they important?"

I shrugged. "No idea." I turned the dusters over in my hand. A wolf head motif adorned the sides. Someone had inscribed *"for the pack"* on the inside. "We need to go see the werewolf pack," I said and tossed them to Olivia, who had remained silent since being disarmed.

"We go there now," she said firmly.

I glanced down at the sorcerer's band that had been on Sky's wrist. "I'm going to need you to get someone to bring something to Matthew's for me," I told Olivia.

She left the room, throwing the knuckle-dusters back toward me without a word.

"You going to tell her the truth?" Sky asked.

"I don't know." It was an honest answer. If I told Olivia exactly who I was, would it make things worse? I wasn't sure how, but if there's one thing I've learned in my life, it's that things can always get much, much worse.

CHAPTER 36

I took my bike once again, not really wanting to spend time in an enclosed space with a pissed-off LOA director, who would have used the opportunity to ask me some very interesting questions. I arrived at the werewolf alpha's house before Olivia and Sky, who had worryingly opted to ride together.

Matthew and Gordon had been informed of my arrival the second I'd been stopped at the main entrance to the land, and they both stood outside of Matthew's house. Gordon wore a dark-blue suit; apparently even when it wasn't a pack function, he still dressed to impress. Matthew, on the other hand, wore jeans and a t-shirt with a picture of Animal from the Muppets on the front.

"What happened?" Matthew asked. "Is Tommy not joining you this time? Did he get lost?" Matthew and Gordon's laughter ended when I didn't smile.

"What's going on?" Matthew asked, instantly concerned.

"We're fighting a lich," I told them. "And it has Tommy and Kasey."

"Sweet Jesus, no," Gordon exclaimed.

"We need your help."

"Anything," Matthew said.

Olivia's car pulled up behind us, and she got out, her eyes tired and heavy. The previous few hours had taken its toll on her. She appeared exhausted and drained, but she would keep fighting until she got Tommy and Kasey back; I was one hundred percent certain of that.

Matthew walked straight past me and enveloped Olivia in his arms. She went to push him away, but couldn't, and eventually let him hold her as he told her it would be all right.

"I know," she said, her voice cool and detached. "Has Nate told you why we're here?"

Matthew didn't even blink as she changed the subject, instead glancing over to me. "Let's go inside, we can talk in private. In case there are any ears that should not be listening to such things."

I didn't imagine that anyone would be listening in. I doubted that Matthew kept any but the most loyal members of his pack around during the day, but he clearly saw Olivia's need to sit down, so I wasn't about to argue.

"She's wound up tighter than Demeter," Sky said as she stood next to me. "I apologized for disarming her and throwing her onto the couch, but she didn't even seem to care, just kept asking about you, and about how I was going to kill the lich."

"You think she can hold it together?" Gordon asked as Matthew led Olivia into the house.

Sky shook her head. "I'm surprised she's not crumpled on the floor crying her eyes out. Hell, that might help. She's terrified for Tommy and Kasey, anyone can see that. But she's angry. Really angry. She's been betrayed by people she trusted, and I think she classes you in that column, Nate. She needs to let some emotion out, or she's going to get herself, or someone else, killed."

"How do we go about doing that?" Gordon asked as we made our way to the house.

Everyone was silent as we walked down the elegant hallway and stepped into the living room. "We find out who helped set this all up," I said.

"Olivia has caught me up to speed," Matthew said. "You have something that leads you to believe a member of my pack was involved?"

I drew the silver knuckle-duster from my pocket and threw it to Matthew's open hand. He barely even glanced at it before his lips drew back in a snarl. "Elijah, what have you done now?"

"You sure this is his?" I asked Matthew.

"He wears a ring that has the same motif. A wolf's head with the same stupid inscription. He's an idiot if he allowed this to be left at the crime scene, and Elijah is no idiot."

"He wasn't the one using them," I pointed out. "Agent R—" I forced myself to stop; Reid was no longer an agent of the LOA, and I doubted Olivia wanted to be reminded about his traitorous status. "Reid used them on Tommy and another wolf, Agent Greaves."

Matthew passed the knuckle-duster to Gordon, who examined it carefully. "This must be met with swift retribution," Matthew said, speaking slowly as he picked his words carefully.

"Where is Elijah?" Olivia asked.

"In his home," Matthew told her. "Probably, anyway. I know how we can find out." He picked up his landline phone and dialed a number, asking for Randal to come to his home and then immediately hanging up.

"There's a small hospital unit about ten minutes from here. We use it for any wolves who get hurt, or when they're first changing. Randal is still there, recovering from his injury at Nate's hands."

"What did you do?" Sky asked with raised eyebrow.

"Tore his arm off," I said. "In my defense, he did try to murder me."

A few minutes later, as everyone was seated on the comfortable couches, the doorbell rang. Gordon went to answer the door, returning a moment later with a pale Randal in tow. He appeared almost healed, although when he saw me, his eyes dropped to the floor. He wasn't afraid, or too proud to meet my gaze, his expression was one of sorrow. For a werewolf, losing an arm meant a long, hard recovery, and a serious question of whether he'd be able to participate in any hunts the pack went on in the future. His stature within the pack had diminished, and he would have to fight for everything he needed to reclaim.

"My alpha," he said and dropped to one knee.

"Get up off the floor, you imbecile," Matthew said. "You owe your life to me, yes?"

"Of course, my lord, you allowed me to be saved after my wound. Even though I'd dishonored myself."

"What game is Elijah playing?"

Randal's expression switched from that of bootlicker to confusion in an instant. "I do not know what you mean."

Matthew tossed the knuckle-duster onto the carpet beside Randal. "This was used in the murder of an LOA agent and the abduction of Tommy and his daughter. It's Elijah's, isn't it?"

Randal picked up the weapon like it was made of radioactive material, holding it gingerly between thumb and forefinger. "This is Elijah's, yes. But he would not be so foolish as to use it on Tommy. No one would wish to incur the wrath of Avalon and yourself, my alpha."

"Would Elijah have given it to someone else to use?"

"I don't know."

"Can I talk to Randal alone?" I asked.

Matthew and Gordon exchanged a glance, but Matthew allowed it and everyone left the room. Although Olivia had to be almost picked up and dragged at first, she eventually allowed herself to be led outside.

The turning of the cogs in Randal's mind was as clear as glass. He knew the answer, but didn't want to give it. "Old allegiances die hard," I said. "I should know. It takes a lot to remove those chains, even when they're not really there anymore."

"Like my arm," Randal said. "It itches."

"You lost your arm because you tried to kill me. You're lucky I didn't return the favor on a more permanent basis."

"I'm a cripple," Randal said, launching himself to his feet, the silver knuckle-duster held tight in his hand until he was forced to drop it to the floor.

"You were a thug, a bully, and a murderer," I said. "If you want redemption—"

"I do, I swear."

"Then you will help us. The truth, all of it, now."

"Elijah is working with someone by the name of Peter. I only met him once, but he's...horrific. He scared me—I mean really scared me. I was charged with getting women for that idiot Neil to have his way with. He liked to fuck prostitutes, to hurt them, too. Sometimes he went too far, and then Peter's ghouls would dispose of the body."

"What does Elijah hope to get out of this?"

Randal shrugged. "I have no idea. He was just helping. He never told me why."

"Where is Elijah now?"

"Tonight he'll be at home. He's always at home during the night; he would never stay anywhere else. It's why he doesn't travel abroad often."

"How many guards?"

"Ten or twelve, depending on their shift."

"Will any stop the alpha from entering the building?"

Randal shook his head. "No, they all know what would happen. They work for Elijah, but none of them want to put their lives on the line for him. He just pays well."

"After tonight, I'm going to bet that it won't be enough."

Randal nodded and sighed. "I'm going to go to prison for what I've done."

"Matthew told you that?"

Another nod. "Matthew...sorry, my alpha, wants me to atone for my behavior under Elijah. There's a werewolf prison in Canada. I'm to be transferred there for the next twenty years. I helped Neil get women that he hurt. I helped dispose of bodies. Human bodies. I...don't know if I can atone. I don't know if I can be a wolf anymore."

"What do you want?" I asked. "Are you looking for absolution? Forgiveness? Because I'm not a priest. And if I was, I'm pretty certain I'd still tell you to go fuck yourself. You committed crimes because you liked it, because you had the power to do it. And now that you've lost that power, you want everyone to believe that you've found your lost soul, that you've decided to turn your life around and be a better person. But that decision isn't one you've taken, it's one you've had forced upon you. You were a piece of shit with two arms, and now you're a piece of shit with one. The only difference is you won't be able to hurt people as easily with only one arm."

"You're wrong," Randal said. "I am going to change."

"Then you go to jail, you serve your time, and you leave a better man. Because until that happens, until you prove to everyone that you've really changed and that it's not just some bullshit 'I feel sorry for myself' nonsense, everyone is going to think the exact same thing I do. That nothing has changed, and you'll go back to your old ways just as soon as you figure out a way to cause people pain. Because let me make this clear to you: you will never hurt people in the way you did before. Never. You will never be allowed to maim and kill for fun, or to help Elijah in his standing with the pack. To intimidate those you deem weaker than yourself. I would bet a huge bag of money that Matthew will make sure of that."

Randal nodded once and left the room, the front door closing with a thud as he exited the house.

"So, what did he tell you?" Matthew asked a short time later as he entered the room with Gordon, Sky, and Olivia in tow.

I explained everything about Elijah's involvement, which only served to anger Matthew even more. "We will go to Elijah's, and he *will* give us the information we require."

I retrieved the knuckle-duster from the floor and placed it in my pocket as a shot rang out from the woods outside of Matthew's home.

Olivia was the first outside, gun drawn, with Matthew and I close behind as chaos erupted around the grounds. People were running toward the fight pit, something I had very little interest in going back to, but I followed Olivia and Matthew anyway, until we reached the crowd that had formed around the still-destroyed edge of the pit.

I knew what I'd find from people's reactions. Some were in-different, some were almost happy. A few looked mournful as their friend, Randal, lay dead in the bottom of the pit. A pistol in his only hand and a bullet hole in his head.

CHAPTER 37

"**W**hat the hell did you say to him?" Matthew asked me as Randal's body was removed from the fighting pit and placed into a body bag.

I didn't ask why a pack of wolves would keep body bags around; I was almost certain it was an answer I didn't want to hear.

"I told him that his days of bullying people and doing what he liked were over. That if he really wanted a chance, he'd have to earn it."

Matthew sighed and rubbed his eyes. "We need to prepare to go to Elijah's. We leave in ten minutes." He turned to Gordon. "I want a full security team ready to go."

Gordon removed his phone from his trouser pocket and walked off to get some privacy.

Matthew glanced back at the blood where Randal had once lain. "What a fucking waste."

"I didn't think he would kill himself," I said.

"No matter. It saves me the trouble of arranging him a lengthy prison stay. No one but that piece of shit Elijah is going to get upset over his death. And even then it'll only be because it's causing him problems." Matthew followed Gordon, and they were soon in deep conversation.

"What's the plan?" Olivia asked.

"We go to Elijah's and ask him where the lich is."

"And if he doesn't cooperate?"

"We ask him less nicely," Sky said with a slight grin.

The following ten minutes saw an explosion of activity as people all around us got ready for what, I was sure, was not going to be an easy task. I hoped the guards at Elijah's house were smart enough to value their paychecks less than their lives. Otherwise, it was going to get very bloody, very quickly.

It was a thought that sat with me the entire way to Elijah's house, which was in an exclusive area of Winchester. No one lived within a mile of him, which certainly eased any fears of a fight getting out of hand, but I needn't have worried in any case. One quick word to the guards from Matthew, and the gates opened, allowing our three-car convoy and my bike into the compound.

Elijah's house wouldn't have looked out of place as a royal holiday home. It was massive, and certainly gave credibility to the idea that he considered himself very much above the level his life had selected for him.

The two SUVs belonging to Matthew's men, and Olivia's own four-by-four stopped outside the ornate front entrance, a huge wooden door with what appeared to be gold leaf inlaid into it. It sat under an arch that wouldn't have looked out of place in ancient Rome.

I stopped the bike and got off as one of Elijah's men made his way toward Matthew, who was exiting the front vehicle, flanked by several very large werewolves in human form.

"Does Mister Bennett know you're coming?" he asked Matthew, stopping the alpha's progress by placing his hand in his way.

"Move," Matthew demanded.

"I'm sorry, but without an appointment, you cannot come into this house."

Matthew's fist moved so fast that it was a blur. The guard fell to the floor, holding his stomach and trying to get air back into his lungs.

Matthew ignored the prone guard and opened the front door, stepping into the house. Gordon, Sky, and Olivia followed soon after, but something stopped me from joining them. Instead, I spoke to the guard. "Which room is Elijah's?"

The guard pointed behind him, into the house. "Top of the stairs," he said between haggard breaths. "Turn left, it's the third door down the hallway."

I thanked him and left him to his pain, ignoring the front door and making my way around to the side of the house and glanced up at the top-level windows.

A few minutes' use of air magic and I'd climbed up the side of the house, using old bricks and windowsills as handholds, until I reached the window I'd been looking at from the ground.

I placed my palm against the cold glass and used more air magic to blast the pane into the room. I'd caught the shards in a bubble of air, which made the noise of breaking the glass much less noticeable.

The room was lavishly furnished, with a large four-poster bed and an expensive collection of artwork adorning the walls. I crept through the room and opened the door to the sounds of Matthew shouting at someone downstairs.

I exited the room and walked down the brightly lit hallway and knocked on the door that the guard had said led to Elijah's room. "Is the coast clear? I don't want to have to deal with that asshole Matthew."

"All done," I said, hoping it sounded at least something like one of his employees. Although, I doubted Elijah even knew their names and faces, let alone what they sounded like.

"Thank fuck for—" he opened the door and I punched him in the nose with a fist wrapped in air. It was akin to being punched with a sledgehammer.

Elijah stumbled back onto the ground, holding his nose, as I stepped into the room and walked toward my prey while he spat blood onto the floor. He got back to his feet and took a swing, which I dodged, and I struck him in the kidney. He dropped back to one knee, placing a hand against a bedpost to steady himself.

When he next looked up at me, Elijah's eyes had changed into wolf yellow, but that soon stopped as I slipped a sorcerer's band over Elijah's wrist and snapped it shut with a click that held promise of horrors to follow.

"Do you recognize it?" I asked, as Elijah's eyes went wide with terror. "It's the one they used on Neil, right before they tore his arms off."

A sly smile settled on Elijah's face. "You're not going to kill me. You need me."

"I know," I told him. "That's why we're going to have a nice long talk. But first..." I grabbed Elijah by the scruff of his shirt and dragged him to his feet. The sorcerer's band still afforded him his strength, but he knew that if he fought he wasn't going to win. Even if he defeated *me*, Matthew would destroy him.

I marched him from the room and out into the hallway as Matthew reached the top of the stairs. "I thought this would be easier," I said and pushed Elijah toward his alpha.

"Hello, Elijah," Matthew said in a friendly tone. "We're going to have a nice long chat about what happens to those who cross me." And then he threw Elijah over the banister and down the stairs.

CHAPTER 38

Two hours passed and I was beginning to get impatient. Olivia had started pacing up and down the room within ten minutes of Elijah being taken into his basement. It turned out that he'd had a soundproof room built some time ago. No one in the house moved to stop Matthew from dragging him down there—no one even spoke. The paid guards had all left within seconds of Elijah's head striking the bottom of the stairs. The toss had dislocated his shoulder, and Gordon had popped it back into the socket without giving warning, an act I was certain the aide had enjoyed.

Gordon had told me that the soundproofed room was equipped with a small adjacent room with a one-way window so that people could watch whatever happened inside. I hated to think about what Elijah had done to people in there, but I hated even more to think that he'd had people watching it happen.

"How do you think it's going?" Sky asked. She'd been calm the entire time we'd been sitting in Elijah's large living room. The couches were uncomfortable, purchased more for show than functionality. Actually, that pretty much described the entirety of the room's furniture. Expensive and uncomfortable.

"He's not going to say anything," I said.

Olivia stopped pacing and stared at me, her eyes hard and cold. "Why would you say that?"

"He hates Matthew," I said. "Really hates him. Did you see the look of rage on his face when Matthew dragged him away? And that had nothing to do with him having been launched down a flight of stairs. He won't say anything to Matthew, or any of his wolves, because doing so will mean he lost, and that's what he can't stand. The idea of losing to Matthew."

As if on cue, Gordon entered the room. He appeared tired and fed up as he carried a glass of water over to a chair and sat down. "He won't say a damn thing," he said after taking a long drink. "Just insults Matthew over and over again."

"I don't know how much longer I can do this," Matthew said from the doorway. He was drying his hands on a tea towel, which was stained pink. "He's not giving anything up."

Sky glanced at me. "Can you break him?" she asked.

I was aware of everyone in the room suddenly staring at me. I wasn't sure of the answer. "Yeah," I said anyway. "But I'm going to need a few things."

"Such as?" Matthew asked.

"Did you find anything in that soundproofed room of his? Like knives, saws, implements of torture."

"A set of knives," Gordon said.

"Get them for me. And I'll need a gun."

"You can't kill him," Olivia said. "There's only six hours before Reid said he'd call. We need to know where Kasey and Tommy are before then. We need to get them out, Nate. I won't leave them with those...*monsters*."

"I don't plan on killing him. I just need to use a gun."

"Anything else?" Matthew asked.

"You mentioned that Elijah wanted his son to be alpha. Where is he?"

"He lives with his mother; word is he hates his father," Gordon said. "Do you need him here?"

I shook my head "No. At the moment he's a future ally; he doesn't need to see his dad being interrogated." I stood and stretched. "Okay, let's go see our guest."

Olivia and Sky followed us as I made a slight detour and filled two glasses with ice-cold water from the fridge. And then we all went down to the basement. Two huge werewolves in well-made dark suits stood outside one of two doors. They moved aside at Matthew's gesture.

"We'll be in here," Matthew said, pointing at the door on the right. "We can hear and see you, so as soon as he gives you what you need, we'll be ready to go."

I spotted a group of folded chairs against the far wall and grabbed one before entering the soundproofed room. I'd expected a dungeon, all dark and grim with chains hanging from the ceiling. But it was actually a large white room, with a sprinkler system in the ceiling and a drain in the middle, which I knew had been installed to remove blood. I dragged the chair across the floor with a noise akin to fingernails on a chalkboard and placed it in front of Elijah.

He was sitting in a sturdy metal chair in the center of the room, above the large drain hole, his wrists bound to the sides of the chair with thick rope. The sorcerer's band I'd put on his wrist was still there. His face was bloody and swollen, but he still managed to grin when he saw me. "Matthew couldn't get it done, so he sends you, that right?"

"Oh, I'm not here to hit you. I don't really feel that punching people does anyone any favors. In the long run, all it does is hurt your hand and make you tired."

"So what are you going to do?" Elijah sneered.

I remained silent, unfolding the chair and placing it in front of him before leaving the room. I returned with Elijah's tray of exquisite knives, each made from silver with a mahogany handle and a golden "E" engraved on the hilt. I also brought in a small table and placed it next to Elijah, who grinned when he saw the knives.

"Those aren't going to help you. You might as well start punching again."

"You do jump to a lot of conclusions," I pointed out as I sat in front of Elijah. "I'm here to tell you a story."

Elijah spat a lump of red blood onto the floor beside me. "You can go fuck yourself."

"It's just a story, so there's no need to get upset about it. If you'd like, I can gag you while I tell it."

Elijah forced a smile. "Feel free to continue."

I nodded my thanks. "It was roughly 440 A.D. when Merlin took me to China for the first time. I was around thirty years old, give or take a few years, and Merlin had described the trip as 'training.' So, I trekked for thousands of miles to a strange land. I learned the language on the way and was left on my own within a year to work with a warlord. I lived and worked there for half a century, and it was good training, but that's not the story. You see, after those fifty years had passed, Merlin re-appeared and told me I had a new assignment, a new task to explore. So I was taken south and introduced to the lord of the area. I assumed at the time that I was going to be working for the new warlord in a fighting capacity. Instead, I was introduced to a baker by the name of Xiao Jing.

"I spent three months living with Jing, his wife, and family—two young girls and an older boy—helping bake bread. That's all I did for three months. Bake bread. I actually got pretty good at it—in fact, I'm still pretty good at it—but after that length of time I began to wonder what Merlin's point had been. Merlin had already left to go who knows where, so I just continued baking and living my life with Jing's family.

"Then one day, Jing was called to the warlord's palace, and I was asked to accompany him. I followed Jing through the palace and down into the basement, where I started to notice that the guards gave us a wide berth. We walked down dark corridors and opened a door at the end. Inside was a man strapped to a chair in the center of a room, much as you are in this one. Like you, his face was bloody. The guards had beaten the shit out of him for hours."

I grabbed my glass of ice water and took a long drink, leaving the second glass full without asking Elijah if he wanted any. "There was no one-way mirror like the one behind me. Instead, there were little slots inside the wall that people could open from a room on the other side and watch what was happening."

"Is there a point to this?"

I slapped Elijah across the face hard enough to snap his head to the side. "Don't be rude, I'm getting there. You see, Jing wasn't just a baker; he was also a very specialized information gatherer. In fact, his skills at torture were used all over the south of the country.

"In this instance, the man in the room was accused of raping and murdering a thirteen-year-old girl, the daughter of a prominent member of the higher class that lived near the palace. At first I thought that Jing would start cutting on him, or breaking bones. But instead, he just sat and talked to him for hours. He explained what was going to happen and asked the man if he was going to tell them who had committed the crime, but the man re-fused to speak. So Jing had the man's son, a fifteen-year-old boy, brought in to sit beside him. And Jing tortured that boy for an hour. He used sharp pins to cause the boy to scream in pain, and the man broke. He told Jing that it was his other son who had raped and murdered the girl. That he was just trying to protect his older son.

"I'll never forget what happened next. The boy got down from the chair he was in, hugged his father and walked out. It had all been a ruse. The boy had gone to the warlord and begged for his father to be released, saying that it was his older brother who had committed the crime and that he'd done it before. Jing had hatched the plan to get the father to try and protect his in-nocent son, by giving up the guilty one. That's why Jing spoke to the man before anything happened; he wanted to know what kind of man he was. You see, Jing had this extraordinary ability to tell when someone was lying."

"So what happened to the older boy?"

"Oh, the man was released and the older son brought in. Jing made him confess to half a dozen similar crimes over the next few hours. Then he had the boy taken outside and beheaded. It was the first time of many that I would work in the palace with Jing. Over the coming years, Jing taught me how to torture some-one. Not always with pain and brute force, but with psychology, knowing what works for what person. The ability to read some-one and know, just know, how to break them. I studied with him for a long time."

"And what kind of man am I?"

"You see, now, there's the problem. I don't have time to sit and chat with you for hours. I can't afford to do that. So here's what's going to happen. You have one chance. Right now. You tell me where Peter took Tommy and his daughter."

Elijah laughed. "Who the fuck do you think you are? When I get out of here, I'm going to have you and everyone you care about flayed."

I sighed. "My name is Nathan Garrett. I worked for Merlin doing the things that needed to be done. You might know me by another name." I leaned toward Elijah. "You can call me Hellequin."

Elijah's eyes never left mine, and I saw the utter fear in them at the mention of my old name. But he soon covered it with bravado. "Bullshit, he's a myth. He never existed. Avalon created him to scare children."

"I figured you might say that." I grabbed a four-inch knife and drove it into Elijah's knee just above the joint until it hit the bone.

I walked over to the glass as Elijah screamed in pain while the silver caused the wound to burn. "Can we get some bandages?"

A few seconds later the door opened, and one of guards brought me a selection of still-wrapped bandages. He gave me an odd glance—he'd probably heard my old name—but I ignored it and took the bandages back over to Elijah.

"This is going to hurt," I said and removed the knife.

Elijah screamed obscenities at me as I opened a bandage and wrapped it around his leg. It took two bandages before the blood no longer seeped through, by which point Elijah was panting as the pain subsided.

I held the last part of the bandage in place. "You plan on telling me now?"

"There's nothing you can do that would make me tell you."

I raised my eyebrows in shock. "Nothing? Nothing at all? Oh, dear Elijah. Everyone breaks. Everyone. It's just a matter of stimulus and time. But I don't have the latter. So, one last chance."

"Go to hell, you fucking prick."

"We don't seem to have any pins for the bandage. It's not much use without one." I turned back to the glass. "Can we get a pin in here?"

"Turns out Hellequin's a pussy," Elijah sneered.

"No pins?" I said to the mirror. "That's okay, I've got one." I grabbed a six-inch but incredibly thin blade from the tray and plunged it through the bandaged knee. "There we go. We can use that."

Elijah commenced screaming once more.

I grabbed the hilt of the blade and pushed it further until the blade came out of the opposite side of the leg, cracking the bone as it moved. "Still think I'm a pussy?" I whispered.

Orange glyphs lit up across my arms as I started to heat the blade. Elijah bucked against the chair, trying to free himself, but within moments the smell of burnt flesh filled the room.

"Do you still consider me a fairytale, you son of a bitch? Where are my friends?" I remained calm as I spoke, never raising my voice.

The bandages ignited, bathing Elijah's leg in fire.

I stood back and let the smell engulf him, allowing his screams to echo around the room before using air magic to put the flames out. Elijah's screams had become a whimper.

"Fuck—" he started.

He never got to finish his sentence; I drew the gun and put two rounds into the good knee and one in his shoulder. The explosion of noise bounced off the walls as the silver bullets shattered bone, ensuring that, even if Matthew allowed Elijah to live, he'd be crippled for the rest of his life. Never able to run with the pack again. Almost a death sentence for a werewolf.

"I didn't want to do it," Elijah mumbled. "But they offered me so much. The pack. They offered me the pack."

"Who did?"

Elijah shook his head weakly. "I don't know. I swear. They're from Avalon. I dealt with…with Reid and Peter. But it was Avalon who arranged for Neil to be broken out of jail. He was meant to take the fall just long enough for Peter to kill that LOA bitch. That's why we had him follow all of those women. Why we let him keep the pictures he took. We needed to make it look like he was back to his old ways. But Neil got caught and Peter started to get crazy. He wanted more barren, wanted to send a message. And Reid just let it happen. He said that Peter would kill Olivia, hurt the LOA, and then go after Matthew. And then I'd be alpha until my boy was old enough to do it."

"Why do you hate Matthew so much?"

"I can't follow a queer."

"What?" I asked genuinely confused.

"He's a fag."

I kicked him in the chest so hard that it flipped him and the chair over onto his back. "You are the single most moronic werewolf I've ever met. What does his sexuality matter?"

Elijah coughed as I pulled the chair back to an upright position. "It's wrong. We should have a strong alpha, not someone who can't even give us a female alpha because he's too busy fucking men."

"I don't care about any of this. I only care about one thing. Where are Tommy and Kasey?"

"You won't get to them in time."

He had the audacity to smile, so I kicked the hilt of the blade where it jutted from his leg, making him cry out.

"LOA office," he whispered.

"What?" I asked, unsure if I'd heard him right.

"The LOA office in Winchester. Peter should be there right now, killing every single fucking agent he can get his hands on."

CHAPTER 39

It took all of thirty seconds to confirm what Elijah had said, but we left him in the room for nearly an hour as Olivia, Sky, Matthew, and I discussed our next move, all of us sitting in the living room of Elijah's grand home.

"What do you need from me?" Matthew asked.

"Your wolves," I said. "Whoever wants to fight, have them here in an hour."

Matthew walked off, phone in hand.

Olivia had stared at me intently since I'd left the basement, a flicker of anger the only emotion she'd even remotely shown.

"I'll leave you two to talk," Sky said. "I'm going to call my father and let him know what's going on. He may be able to convince Avalon to let him send more people to assist."

"Thanks," I said as Sky left Olivia and me alone.

Instead of talking to me, Olivia walked out of the room, leaving the house by the front door and slamming it behind her. I left it for a minute, hoping she would calm down, before going after her. I found her stomping around to the side of the property, a look of thunder on her face.

"He's taken two people I love the most in the world, and now he has the people I'm meant to look out for. The phone lines are cut, and no one is answering their mobiles. There were maybe forty good people in that building and now they're probably dead. If I call Avalon, they'll never even try to save Kasey and Tommy, nor their own people. They'll just flatten the whole place."

"It's going to be okay," I said.

"Fuck you," Olivia snapped, turning on me. "You lied to me. If I'd known that you were a fucking monster, I'd have never let you anywhere near my daughter."

"You're upset."

Olivia shoved me. "Upset? You're the fucking Bogeyman. My mum used to tell me that if I misbehaved the Hellequin would come for me."

I wasn't really sure how to respond to that. "I care about Tommy and Kasey, too."

"What the hell do you know about caring? You're a killer—that's all you ever were. What could you possibly know about loss? About having your soul ripped out at the possibility of losing the people you love the most."

Olivia turned to walk away. "Her name was Jane," I said, and Olivia stopped walking. "We were together for two years, married after a few months. I was happy, genuinely happy. Even though she was human, and I knew I'd outlive her, I just wanted to enjoy the time that we had together.

"It all ended on a damp November morning in seventeen eighty-two. I'd been away working for Avalon for a few months and had been eager to get home. I found her inside the house we'd shared. She'd been butchered. Her blood decorated our bedroom. She was naked and appeared to have been dead for several days. My rage was...terrifying. I buried Jane with my own hands, placing her near a field that we used to love going to. And then I burnt the house to the ground."

Olivia's shoulders sagged, but she didn't turn and face me.

"I hunted her killer for a year. I didn't care who I hurt to get the information I needed. I was so single-minded, so determined to have vengeance. Eventually, I discovered that her murderer had been part of the king's army, which had been going through the area.

"The killer was an officer by the name of Henry. No idea what his last name was. It didn't matter. He liked hurting women, and once he'd finished with them, he kept their hair as a souvenir. The rest of his squad had waited outside while he brutalized and murdered the woman I loved. No one had helped Jane, and no one had tried to stop him.

"I discovered that they'd been on training maneuvers the day of the murder, just their squad of thirty. And after all my searching, I found them and I killed them. They died in one night of blood and rage. All but one. I left Henry until last. I took him away to a secluded place and had my fill of vengeance. It took a week for him to die, and when he finally succumbed, I buried Hellequin with him."

The memory of Henry's blind and bloody form flashed in my mind—his pleas had long since silenced because I'd removed his tongue. I hadn't wanted information from him; I'd just wanted to make him suffer. Before he'd lost his ability to talk, he'd told me that someone had paid him to do it, but he never said who. No matter what I did to him, he took that secret to his grave. And after a few years of searching, I decided he'd been lying. Trying to prolong his life for a short time more, hoping for mercy where there was none to give.

"I no longer had the desire to go by that name," I continued, still talking to Olivia's back, "I no longer wanted to instill fear with a word. I hoped that the legend would die, but it didn't, it grew, became more...fanciful.

"You're right, I'm a killer. I've killed thousands, and very few of them have ever stained my conscience. I can go to a dark place and do whatever I need to. But for those I care about, those I love, I will move fucking mountains to keep them safe. And I care about Tommy and Kasey, whether you grant permission or not."

I turned to walk away.

"I'm sorry," Olivia said and placed a hand on my bicep to turn me around, her tears flowing freely as we stood in silence. "Will you promise me that we'll get Tommy and Kasey back?" she asked.

"I promise." My words were spoken with utter conviction. "And no one will stand in our way."

Olivia stepped toward me. "They have my little girl," she said softly. "They have my princess." Olivia took another step and broke down in my arms. Her sobs continued against my chest and shoulder, quickly drenching my shirt. She collapsed in my arms, and I had to sit us down on the damp grass before we fell. I held her for a long time, until her cries of anguish brought Sky to check on us. She took one look at Olivia and me, and tears fell from her eyes.

Sky helped Olivia back to her feet, with more than a little struggle. "I'll take her to clean up," she told me.

"Thank you," I said as Olivia let go of me.

"I'm so sorry," Olivia choked out. "I had no idea what you'd been through."

"Not many do," I said. "Go get yourself ready; we have a long night ahead of us."

Olivia straightened up. "What do you need?"

"Blueprints of the LOA building," I said. "We need to know what we're dealing with."

"Then you'll get them," Olivia told me. And with that Sky led her away.

I wasn't really sure what to do after that. I felt drained. I rarely talked about Jane. Very few people knew about her, even fewer than those who knew that I used to be Hellequin. But it had been the right thing to tell Olivia. I'd needed to regain her trust, and sometimes you can only do that by revealing the things you most want to keep private.

I started walking through the expansive grounds that belonged to Elijah, although *used to* belong was probably the more accurate phrase. I had no idea what would happen to Elijah or his property after he'd confessed to being a traitor.

"Nathan," Matthew called out.

I turned to find him sitting beneath a tree. The low-hanging branches created shadows to partly obscure him, and I'd have never noticed his presence if he hadn't called for me.

I walked over and Matthew smiled at me; it was an easy expression and one of friendship. I exploded at him.

"This is your fault, you know," I snapped. "All of this shit that we're going through, it can be traced back to you."

Matthew stammered for a second, clearly not having expected me to go off at him.

"You created a situation where that stupid prick down in the basement got enough support to challenge you. If you hadn't done that, he would *never* have even thought about challenging you. Hell, the first time he mentioned it to someone, they would have shopped him straight to you."

Matthew got back to his feet, fire in his eyes. "How dare you insinuate that this is my fault? That this is something I could have avoided by not being gay."

"What the hell are you talking about? I don't give a shit what you are. This is to do with that fact that your sexuality is your weakness, because you're making it one."

"Fuck you," Matthew snapped.

"So, you're telling me it's not your weakness? Okay, where's your female alpha?"

Matthew recoiled like he'd been slapped. "I don't have one."

"Why?"

"Because I'm *gay*."

"What does that have to do with anything?"

"I would think it had everything to do with it. I'm not about to pretend that I'm something I'm not. Not so I can appease a bunch of assholes who would be against me no matter what I did."

"It's not about appeasing anyone; it's about having a strong pack. The female alpha is half of your rule. She deals with the female pack members…she backs you and keeps the pack strong. That's her job."

"I have Gordon to do those things."

"No matter how nice Gordon might look in drag, he's neither an alpha nor a woman."

"Nathan has a point," Gordon said from behind me. "My lack of a vagina does get in the way of dealing with the ladies."

"That's not what I meant," I said, exasperated.

Gordon laid a hand on my shoulder. "I was just joking." He turned to his alpha. "Nathan is right. You're missing a large part of your hierarchy by not having a female alpha. I've told you this several times."

Matthew placed one hand on Gordon's shoulder and Gordon covered it with his own and for the first time I realized something.

"You're together," I said. "That's why Elijah hated Gordon, too."

Matthew nodded. "I love this man, and I will not belittle that by bringing a woman into our house to pretend that we're something we're not."

"Then don't," I said. "Everyone in your pack probably knows you're gay—you're not trying to pretend otherwise. You don't have to fuck her, Matthew. You just have to bring her into your life and allow her to do the job a female alpha is meant to do. Without it, you're going to have more people using that as a way to hit you, making your sexuality your weakness."

"I pretended to be straight for centuries, always knowing I lived a lie. I will not go back to it."

"Then don't," I said. "But don't let your hang-ups cause something like this again. Yes, Peter would have found someone else to use, but probably not in your pack. Elijah would have been an annoying little shit instead of someone who arranged to bring you down so he could put himself into that position. Get a female alpha, someone you trust. You don't have to live with her or marry her, but you do have to have a woman in that position. Otherwise, you might as well step aside and let someone else take over. Because sooner or later, another wolf is going to succeed where Elijah failed, and next time you might not catch it in time to stop it."

Matthew stared at me for several heartbeats. "Are you truly the Hellequin?"

"Change of subject?"

Matthew smiled. "I will think on the female alpha situation. My pack deserves to be strong, and I will ensure that nothing like this happens again. Maybe the centuries of living a lie have caused me to think unclearly when it comes to other people's perception of me."

"And I shall shout at him until he relents," Gordon said.

"So, do you plan on answering my question?" Matthew asked.

"Yes," I told him. "I'm really the Hellequin. Did you expect me to be taller?"

Matthew shook his head. "More intense. I thought you'd be all fire and brimstone. Do you really think we can get Kasey and Tommy back in one piece?"

"Yeah, I do. Peter wants Olivia to suffer, so he's not going to do anything until she arrives. He won't want to jeopardize his revenge."

"Matthew," Gordon said, and pointed over to a young man who was running toward us.

"Yes, Evan?" Matthew said to the newcomer.

Evan stood up straight, clearly proud at being spoken to by the alpha of his pack. He was well over six feet tall; if he'd brought a few more wolves like him, I knew we'd have a greater chance of getting Tommy and Kasey out without injury. "The wolves are here," Evan said, "Everyone who wanted to fight came, more than fifty in all."

"Over fifty werewolves?" I asked, shocked.

Matthew smiled. "Let's go see my army."

I watched Matthew and Gordon walk off with the young werewolf and decided to take Matthew's old spot under the tree and make a quick call to the local hospital. It took me several minutes to find out if Sara had been admitted there, and I was finally put through to the correct department after explaining that I was her colleague and wanted to know how she was doing.

The nurse told me that Sara had a concussion and was groggy, but she was awake. She then took great pains to explain that she was to have no visitors except family for the remainder of the day, which, considering how late it was, didn't surprise me.

I hung up the phone with the knowledge that Sara was okay and sighed. Reid and his cohorts were going to pay for everything they'd done, but knowing that Sara was in no danger took a weight off my mind.

"Sara okay?" Sky asked as she sat on the grass next to me.

"I'm going to make you wear a bell," I told her. "And, yes, they say she'll be okay."

"Good." Sky was silent for a few seconds. "Are you?"

"I'm going to make them pay," I said without emotion.

"My father told me about the necromancy. You don't think you can use it to kill the lich, do you?"

I said nothing.

Sky shifted from next to me and sat in front, taking my hands in hers. "Nate, promise me, you won't try to kill him by yourself. Promise me. You may have some necromancy ability, but there's no way of knowing what you can do and no way of knowing how it will work. You cannot beat this lich by yourself."

"Sky—"

"Promise me, damn it."

"I promise I won't try to kill him alone. I'll leave him for you."

Sky's shoulders slumped in relief and nodded briefly before releasing my hands. "I thought I'd lost you ten years ago, when Mordred erased your memories. We all searched, but couldn't find you. You didn't tell anyone what you were doing, that you were going after Mordred alone. We had no clue where to even start looking. I thought…Nate, I thought you'd died. I don't want to go through that again. I missed you."

I reached out and pulled Sky toward me, embracing her tightly. "I'm not going anywhere," I told her after we pulled apart.

"You're one of my closest friends, so don't do anything stupid," a faint smile crept onto her face.

"Do you remember the last lich we went up against, the one in Montana?"

"I was grateful my father was there. You were shocked."

"Well, you could have mentioned he was your dad."

Sky laughed. "Whatever happened to those kids?"

"Wapi and Tala went to live with their family on a ranch; I stayed around long enough to help clean up and make sure everything was cleared with any authorities who showed up to investigate. We all made a lot of noise that day."

"Burning a whole town to the ground will do that. Did you ever look in on Sam again, I mean after you gave him your horse and everything?"

"He went to live in California, found some gold, made some money, had a nice family. Before he left Montana, I gave him an address in Avalon to contact me in an emergency. He sent me a letter, years later, telling me he would like to say goodbye. He had some disease, I never learned what. I arrived just before he died and said my good-byes. That was 1936."

"You saved him," Sky said. "He was a good kid and you made sure he stayed that way. You helped destroy the lich that day so that people could live on and have families. We'll do the same today."

I kissed Sky on the forehead. "Thank you."

"Just be careful tonight," Sky said as she stood and stretched. "Olivia sent me out here to find you. She's got some blueprints you may be interested in."

I smiled. "I guess this is where I divulge my plan."

"You have a plan?" Sky chuckled. "And I thought you just winged it."

"Not this time. Everything is going to be planned out."

"Care to share?" Sky asked as we walked back to the house.

"I don't have the finer details," I said. "But the basic premise is we kill them. Every single motherfucking one of them."

CHAPTER 40

We found Olivia, Matthew, and Gordon huddled over a table in the dining room. It wasn't until I got closer that I could see the A3-sized printouts of the blueprints Olivia had said she'd find.

"How'd you manage to get copies of these?" I asked as I thumbed through several sheets.

Olivia removed her phone from her jeans pocket and waved it in my direction. "I can access the LOA files for the building wirelessly. I knew we kept blueprints of where everything was. Now do you mind telling us all what you wanted them for?"

I flicked through the pages until I found one that showed one of the subbasements. "Your LOA building is equipped with a similar system to the one Tommy uses. It removes the abilities of everyone who enters, unless you're wearing one of those anti-sorcerer band things," I said, bringing the sheet of paper to the top and pointing at one corner of it.

Everyone stared at where I pointed.

"That's the third-floor security room," Olivia said. "There's nothing there except…" Olivia smiled. "You want to disable the security system allowing everyone to use their abilities inside the building."

"Bingo," I said. "There's no way in hell that Peter is going to come out and face us. That means we need to go in. Actually, it means I need to go in."

The shouting that followed was expected, but even so, we didn't have time to argue. "Listen," I said over the din. "I have to be the person to go into the building."

"Why?" Olivia snapped.

"You promised me, Nate," Sky said. "About half an hour ago, you said you weren't going to fight the lich."

"Okay, let's calm down and let Nate talk," Gordon said.

I thanked Gordon. "Right, Olivia you can't go into that building. For one thing you're the only one who knows the way to get into that security office, you're the only one of us who has been there." I removed another page and pointed to an exit at the side of the building. "You'll need to enter here, as you can't go down by lift. You know the combinations for any numerical locks. And Sky has to go with you, because she's the only one of us who knows how to disable this kind of system. It's not like flicking a switch; you'll need to break specific connections to the runes around the building. And you'll have to do it in a specific order."

"It's similar to the one my father uses," Sky said. "In fact, it looks like yours might be based on his. But that still…"

"Just wait before you start yelling again," I said. "Sky knows how to disable the security and Olivia knows how to get there, and that leaves me to get Tommy and Kasey away from the very dangerous lich before he kills them."

"You think the lich won't be affected?" Matthew asked.

"I doubt it. There's about one lich every few centuries; why would the LOA prepare for such a random eventuality? We have to assume that he has his abilities—otherwise, why bother attacking the LOA building?"

"Nate's right," Olivia said. "There's nothing in the security that I'm aware of which would stop a lich from using his abilities."

"So where will he be?" Gordon asked.

I searched for another blueprint and placed it on the top of the pile. "Olivia's office, on the top floor. This is about you, Olivia; he's going to want you to witness your destruction from where you find the most safety. He'll be there, I guarantee it."

"Why can't we all go in after we get the security cut?" Sky asked.

"Two things," I said. "One—the second the security is disabled he's going to notice something weird is happening when everyone attacks his citadel at once. And two—he's not about to let a necromancer stop him, and he actually wants Olivia to see Tommy and Kasey die in front of her, so the second he sees either of you, they're dead. He thinks of me as a mild annoyance, at best."

"You killed one of his ghouls," Sky pointed out. "That's gonna piss him off."

"Yeah, but I'm no threat to *him*. Even if I can do necromancy, I don't know how, and I doubt even if I did I'd be able to stop him. But I can buy you time, hopefully keep him occupied and try and get Kasey and Tommy away from being in danger."

"So what do we do?" Matthew asked.

"There's going to be several hundred barren inside that building and a few ghouls. We want them outside so we can work unhindered. That's where you and your wolves come in. You're there to get them to come outside and fight you, and then kill as many of them as possible."

"Now that we can do," Matthew said. "How long do you need?"

"Be ready to go in an hour. And make sure they know no biting. Barren and ghouls have poisoned blood; it'll paralyze anyone who ingests it."

"We'll be ready," Matthew said and left the room with Gordon.

"Your plan stinks," Olivia said. "But you're right; if he sees me, he'll think Christmas came early for him. You have to be careful though."

"I will," I said and watched Olivia leave the room.

"You are a pain in my ass," Sky said. "You're going to fight that lich and if you do that, you're going to die. You understand that, yes?"

"I'm not going to fight, but I do need to keep him busy…so, any chance of a few lessons?"

Sky's mouth dropped open in shock. "Learning how to use necromancy takes years, Nate. I can't show you how to use it in an hour. And even if I could, we don't know what type of necromancy you can use."

"That's fair, but when I fought with Randal in that pit I felt some sort of coldness over me. Somehow I absorbed a spirit. I just need to know what I did, just in case."

Sky sighed. "I can show you some techniques to search for a spirit, but there's no guarantee they'll even work."

"It's better than nothing."

"Nate, the better plan would be to get Kasey and Tommy out of there and then run like hell. Once that security is broken, I'll be with you as fast as I can, but until then you'll be basically human."

"Thanks for reminding me," I said with a smile.

"Don't, Nate. Don't make this out to be nothing. Until that security is cracked, you will have nothing to throw back at someone who would tear a werewolf apart with his bare hands."

"And once that security is down, I still won't have anything. That's why I'm asking for you to show me something that might save my life."

"Then let's get started."

Forty-five minutes later and I was no closer to actually reaching out to a spirit. I thought I'd managed it at one point. A coldness had settled inside me like before, but it vanished before I could use the technique that Sky had taught me, to use the energy of the spirit for my own needs.

A quarter of an hour after that I was watching fifty-six werewolves pile into five M35 cargo trucks. I didn't know where Matthew had appropriated them from, and quite frankly I probably didn't want to know, but they were probably slightly less inconspicuous for transporting large numbers of werewolves than having to use a fleet of cars. Only slightly, though.

Of all the werewolves who turned up, maybe half of them had experience fighting outside of a pack environment, but all of them wanted to help rescue Tommy and Kasey. Besides, a werewolf with no battle training is still a giant killing machine, so I figured so long as they took care they should make it through whatever was going to happen with few casualties.

The massive engines of the trucks roared to life, and we were soon driving along the moonlit roads heading toward... hell, I didn't have a clue. War, probably. I sat in the back with Sky, Olivia, Gordon, Matthew, and a couple more werewolves who were all, I hoped, prepared for whatever was going to happen.

In my experience, there are two ways that most people on their way to a conflict prepare. First, there are the talkers; they joke and laugh and chat about anything and everything to keep their minds off whatever is going to happen. The second group are the quiet ones; they tend to find a comfortable spot in the transport and read or sleep, or anything else that allows them to remain calm. I belong to the second group. I like to find a quiet corner and rest my eyes. I learned a long time ago that if you have time in war to get some sleep, use it. The same goes with food and water. You never know when you're going to go a lengthy time without them, so I get them while I can.

I wasn't entirely asleep, though. It's hard to actually fall fully asleep while there are people around you making a lot of noise. Besides, the last thing you want is to be in a deep sleep when someone attacks the transport, so I opened my eyes the moment someone tapped on my leg.

"Hello, Matthew," I said as the werewolf alpha sat opposite me.

"I have something for you."

He passed me a large bundle of cloth, which I unraveled and stared at the contents. A sword that was roughly the length of my old Chinese *jian* and a much smaller dagger that was about the size and shape of a *tanto*, about a third of the size of the longer sword. Both had black hilts with rope wrapped around them, in the style of a samurai sword. They were a combination of two different types of blade put together to create a very dangerous weapon.

"Where did you find these?" I asked.

"They were Elijah's," Matthew told me. "I appropriated them from his collection. They're made of carbon steel, but they have silver in them, too."

I unsheathed the smaller blade and noticed the small trace of blood on the edge of it.

"Let's just say that Elijah has been dealt with," Matthew said when he saw me glance at the blood. "Will they help tonight?"

I tested both in my hand, unsheathing them to get used to the excellent weight distribution before tucking the dagger into the belt of my jeans and placing the sword across my lap.

"Thanks," I said. "Those are *definitely* going to come in handy."

"Just get Tommy and Kasey out of there safely," he said, then stood as the truck came to a halt. "And get yourself back in one piece, too. I'd hate to have to deal with a pissed-off Sky."

I glanced over at Sky, who smiled.

"You and me both," I said as I smiled back.

One of Matthew's wolves poked his head through the rear of the truck. "We're here," he said. "But this doesn't look good."

We all scrambled out of the truck as quickly as possible to witness the utter devastation of what used to be two thick iron gates that barred the entry to the LOA compound beyond. The gates had been torn from their moorings, and the four guards who had been stationed in the two huts to either side of the entrance had been torn to pieces, their weapons still holstered.

"Ghouls did this," Sky said as she glanced into one of the huts. "I'm sorry, Olivia."

"They were good men," Olivia said, her voice hard as steel.

I stepped over the ruined gates and stared up the driveway, which I knew ended at the LOA building. The open field behind the destroyed main gate was completely empty; both of the sniper huts had been destroyed, their remains scattered across the ground beneath where they'd once stood. Several large spotlights were lit up, illuminating everything in front of the massive LOA headquarters building.

"I don't see anything unusually suspicious," I said and checked the time. "We've still got an hour before Reid is due to call."

"Speaking of him, you think he's in there, too?" Sky asked.

"If he isn't, we find him after," Olivia replied as she climbed back into the truck.

"That is one very pissed off lady," Gordon whispered. "You think she'll be okay?"

"She's going to go through anything that gets in her way, so I'd say aiming her at those assholes in there is going to be cathartic for her."

"I almost feel sorry for them," he said absently.

I raised an eyebrow in question.

"I did say *almost*," he said with a smile "The bastards deserve whatever she decides to do with them. And I hope it hurts."

I glanced into the truck and found Olivia staring at the bare floor. She noticed me and wiped her eyes quickly.

I stepped up into the truck and sat beside her. "It won't be long before they're both back in your arms and you can take them home."

"I'm okay," she said softly, but I wondered if that would ever be true again.

CHAPTER 41

The trucks crashed through the ruined gates and only stopped moving once they reached the large open field, where we all piled out into the cool night air. I left Matthew and his werewolves to get ready, going over to talk to Olivia and Sky.

"You think they know we're here yet?" Olivia asked.

I shrugged. "Prepare yourselves either way. This is going to get really ugly, really quickly."

I turned around to find that all of the werewolves, including Gordon and Matthew, had changed into their wolf-beast forms. Fifty-six killing machines, all ready to help save Tommy and Kasey, and end Peter.

I noticed one wolf had dark-blue fur that mixed in with the light grey. She noticed me and nodded in my direction, a gesture I returned. Ellie might not have received Neil's life to take as she pleased, but I hoped that her need for vengeance would be sated after the coming battle.

"I'm going to speak to my wolves," Matthew said, his voice low and gravelly.

"Go do what you need to," I told him. "We'll wait here."

The werewolves lined up shoulder to shoulder as Matthew stalked up and down in front of them. "My wolves," he bellowed. "You know why we are here tonight. Most of you know

Tommy. He's helped you when you needed it; he's stood up for the pack and is considered a friend and ally. Someone has dared to cross our pack and take a wolf we consider to be our brother."

The wolves started to growl at Matthew's words, their violence barely contained.

"But they've not only taken Tommy, they have his daughter, Kasey. She's been at our pack meetings, she's played with your children, and you've watched her grow from a baby to a wonderful young lady. That bright and beautiful girl has been taken by the monster in that building, and *it will not stand.*" Matthew screamed the last few words and the growling grew louder.

"We will not let a child be tainted by evil. And we will not stand by and allow one of our own to spend another second in its grasp. Our enemy will try and stop us. Several hundred barren stand in our way along with a handful of ghouls, but we will tear them all apart. No one will stop us from ensuring that Tommy and Kasey come back to us safe and whole. *We will not fail.*"

The growls were now accompanied by several low barks.

"Some of you might be afraid and that's okay. Feel that fear; use it to make you stronger. But the ones who should be afraid sit inside that building. Because we have someone they never could, someone who will show them true fear. We have Hellequin."

The growls ceased as Matthew motioned toward me and every single set of eyes followed his hand. I wasn't sure how I felt about my secret being laid bare for all to know, but that moment wasn't the time to argue about it.

"Every one of you has heard his name, maybe in whispers, and maybe you didn't believe it. But he's real and he's going to get Tommy and Kasey back. And by the end of tonight, people will know that to cross our pack is to cross Hellequin. Future generations will speak of tonight with reverence. Your children and grandchildren will ask you to tell them about the time you fought by Hellequin's side to save one of our own. Here and now we make our mark, and we will not falter. On this field tonight, we will make sure that everyone remembers that werewolves are to be feared, and that retribution will be swift and deadly."

The wolves growled and barked as one, creating a huge amount of noise as Matthew knelt on the ground and started to pray. The din quickly ceased as his entire pack quickly followed suit, kneeling in silent prayer.

"What is he saying? Olivia asked.

"It's Latin," I told her. "I've heard it before, although not for many centuries."

"Where?"

"The third crusade. It was a prayer uttered by some of the Knights Templar before battle. It basically says that the petitioner would gladly sacrifice his own body if it meant that innocents would be spared. He asks for a swift victory for his men and for the strength to overcome his enemies."

"So, let me get this straight," Sky said. "Matthew is a gay werewolf alpha who used to be a Knight Templar. Nate, you have the most interesting of friends."

"I have not been a Templar for many years," Matthew said as he stood, followed quickly by his pack. "Nor do I subscribe to their philosophy. But some of their teachings are still worthwhile, and offering a prayer to whoever might listen eases me before the inevitable death and brutality that always follows."

I followed Matthew's gaze and looked up at the large building, which loomed in the darkness. Most of the lights were still on inside, but it was eerily quiet, and despite the darkness, none of the current inhabitants had bothered to join us.

Matthew walked back over to his wolves, who immediately gave him all of their attention. "It appears that our enemy is unwilling to come out and face us. Maybe they're afraid and are hiding under desks, or perhaps they know this will be their last day on earth so they've decided to sleep in."

The wolves chuckled, but there was no humor in it. Only menace.

"Maybe we should let them know we're here. Maybe we should wake the dead."

As one, fifty-six werewolves stood as tall as they could and howled. Goosebumps rippled up my arm and the hairs on the back of my neck stood to attention.

It certainly did the trick. Hundreds of barren flooded out of the headquarters. They stood together in front of the massive glass windows of the reception building. It was the most barren I'd ever seen in one place.

"Holy shit," Sky said. "This is gonna be a hell of a battle." She drew a knife and a small axe, twirling the axe's handle between her fingers in what I knew to be a sign of nerves.

"Be careful, you two," I said.

Sky hugged me, and Olivia nodded in my direction, both of them keen to get started. I watched as they jogged off toward the side of the building.

"Ready when you are," Matthew said to me as his wolves growled eagerly behind him.

I controlled my breathing in preparation for what was going to happen. "Let's go show these bastards how to stay dead."

I was at the head of the charge, next to Matthew and Gordon, as the wolves moved as one giant wall of teeth, claws, and snarling rage, ready to tear their enemies to pieces.

The barren rushed forward to meet them, but the end result was never in doubt. The wolves crashed into the barren like a car through a paper wall. Within seconds the wolves were carving their way through the hundreds of barren that had left the confines of the LOA building.

The noise of battle can play havoc with your senses, so it's much better to watch your enemy than try to decide their position based on sound alone. So, even as I watched Olivia and Sky run off to the side entrance, I kept one eye on the rapidly approaching horde of barren. When Olivia and Sky had covered a suitable distance between themselves and the approaching enemy, I unleashed a plume of flame that engulfed the barren. The heat was incredible, and I poured more and more power into the magic, turning a dozen barren to ash in a few seconds and scarring the earth for twenty feet in front of me.

The remaining barren didn't stop, or even slow down, they just continued toward me as if nothing had happened. I drew my swords and ran toward them, slicing and cutting through flesh and muscle with every strike.

I killed six before one got too close and I was forced to pierce it in the throat at an awkward angle before managing to spin it around into a second barren and narrowly missing being raked with its nails. I pushed the sword deeper into the first barren until it sank into the head of the second. I couldn't remove the blade from the two bodies in time to fight a further four barren that had made their way toward me.

I stepped away from the sword and sheathed the *tanto*, placing it in the belt of my jeans. I couldn't afford to lose it. I formed a blade of fire, using it to slice through the throat of one barren, then spinning around and catching a second in the neck, decapitating it.

The barren never stopped attacking, even if they had to scramble over the bodies of their comrades to get at us.

I kicked one barren back and stabbed him in the forehead with the fire blade, extinguishing the weapon and using air magic to fling his corpse back into a group of his kin before they could reach me. They toppled to the ground like bowling pins and were quickly swarmed by wolves before they could get back to their feet.

I killed two more barren with a whip of fire, cleaving them both in two and leaving their remains behind as I noticed that Sky and Olivia were being attacked by a large group of barren.

The two women had used the initial charge as a diversion to run off to one side of the building, but at some point some of the barren had become interested in them, and that had forced Sky and Olivia to pause to fight them off, something they didn't have time for.

I sprinted toward the quickly growing group of barren and launched a wave of hardened air at them, throwing several away from their targets and giving Sky and Olivia some room.

One of the barren closest to me had avoided the wave and now turned to face me, but another harder wave of air removed his head from his shoulders, along with those of two more barren directly behind him.

Although neither of them had any apparent wounds, both Sky and Olivia were panting as a dozen barren lay at their feet.

"There are a lot more of these bastards than when we were in Montana," Sky said.

"There's about to be a lot more," I said as a large group of barren made their way toward us. "Just go, I've got this."

Sky placed a hand on my shoulder. "Be careful."

"I will," I shouted. "Now go!"

A dozen more barren quickly made their way toward my position, and I readied myself to fight once again, but Matthew barreled into them with a mighty crash, tearing the four barren into sodden chunks of meat before my eyes. He fought with such a ferocity and viciousness that I would have been very interested in seeing him fight when he was human.

"You fight like a wolf," Matthew said as he threw aside a barren's arm.

I turned to study at the carnage all around me. The wolves were destroying the barren in spades, but there were so many of them that the dense packs of barren stopped any serious progress toward the front entrance.

"How about your wolves clear a path?" I asked.

Matthew howled and pointed at the barren before us, and within seconds a dozen wolves tore into them, carving a path through them to the entrance.

"Take care," I told Matthew, who ran off to join his pack in their fight.

I ran as quickly as possible, using air magic to make me faster, and headied for the glass front door of the LOA building, dodging pieces of barren as I went. At some point they had been living people, but to think of them now in such a way would do no one any good. The living had been replaced with rot and decay. Ending their torment was the only humane thing to do.

I reached the glass door and kicked it open, taking one last glance at Matthew's pack fighting with everything they had before stepping inside the first building of the headquarters.

I'd prepared myself for what was going to happen, for the complete loss of my abilities, but it was still a massive shock to the system. I made it to a group of leather couches next to the reception area before I finally succumbed to what the security had done and dropped to my knees. I'd worn a sorcerer's band before; Merlin had wanted me to learn how to operate without my magic. But the fighting I'd done outside tonight and then the abrupt removal of my magic forced me to pause and take a moment to get my breath back. You never realize just how much you rely on magic until it's gone and you're just left with nothing but a void inside you. If this was how humans felt every single day, then their lives were not something I wished upon anyone.

After composing myself, I got back to my feet as four loud thuds sounded from outside the building. Four things had struck the ground with massive force, causing one of the large glass panes at the front of the building to crack slightly. Then I saw one of them. The ghouls had arrived to back up the two hundred or so remaining barren.

"Good luck, Matthew," I said softly and turned toward the stairs that would lead me to find Tommy and Kasey.

CHAPTER 42

The four thuds that had sounded as the ghouls had hit the ground outside told me that I didn't have to worry about bumping into any of them as I made my way through the two buildings. With one ghoul dead at my hands, Peter only had four left. And while that did leave the possibility that he'd made a replacement for the ghoul I'd killed, I doubted he'd hold it back to guard him when he had so little to be concerned about.

Even so, I jogged the forty flights of stairs, keeping an eye out for anything that might cause me problems. Blood was smeared along the walls on several flights of stairs, but nothing more concerning than that, until I hit the top floor and found the bodies of two LOA agents—a male and female. The smell hit me before I saw them. Their shirts were drenched in blood, their throats torn open. They'd been murdered in a cold stairwell, yet more victims of the lich and his men needing to be avenged.

I left the two agents where I found them—there was nothing I could do to help them—and opened the door to the top floor of offices.

The blueprints that Olivia had gathered showed three large meeting rooms on this floor, along with two bathrooms and several massive offices. One of those offices was Olivia's, which sat at the far end of the floor toward the front of the building, overlooking the grounds below.

I crept down the corridor, glancing in the windows of two offices adjacent to one another, but found them empty. At the end of the corridor was a wall with the letters LOA spelled out in highly polished chrome. I was about to turn left, toward Olivia's office, when I noticed bloody scuff marks on the otherwise clean carpet. Someone had been dragged along the hallway here.

I followed the trail down the right-hand corridor until it finished by the door to a meeting room. I tried to look through the glass into the room, but the blinds had been pulled down, hiding whatever was inside.

I gripped the door handle and turned it slightly, and I pushed open the door slowly, in case a nasty surprise waited for me. When nothing jumped out to attack me, I opened the door fully and stepped inside the room, closing the door behind me with a soft click. The room itself contained a large meeting table, a dozen chairs, and some bookshelves. A large plasma-screen TV sat on the wall at one end, but someone had knocked it and it hung from only one of its hinges.

The blood trail continued around to the far side of the table. I followed it only to discover Tommy lying on his side, hands tied behind his back. I rushed toward him and noticed his t-shirt was slick with blood and he had gashes on his arms. I wiped away the blood on his neck and found a weak pulse. I exhaled and realized that I hadn't taken a breath since I'd found him.

His hands were bound with a sorcerer's bracelet, probably the same one that had been put on him when Reid had attacked him in his home. I tore it from his wrist and flung it across the room, wanting to put as much distance between him and it as possible.

"Tommy," I whispered. "You hear me?"

Tommy made a sound that might have been a yes, but quite frankly I was just happy he was able to talk at all. He looked like he'd had the shit kicked out of him; his face was swollen and puffy, and his jaw and nose were misshapen where they'd been broken. The burn marks on his face suggested it had been silver knuckles that had done the job.

"You won't have access to your wolf," I said. "Don't try to move."

"Ka...Kasey." His voice was hoarse and croaky; the pain it took for him to talk easy to hear.

"I'm going to find her," I told him. "I'm going to get you both out of here, but I need you to stay in here for now. Okay?"

I didn't get a response as Tommy had slipped into unconsciousness. The security system blocked him from changing, but it didn't take away everything his werewolf nature gave him. The re-emergence of his werewolf healing would hopefully mean he'd be able to escape from the building under his own power.

"You just stay safe," I said. "I'm going to go find Kasey." I didn't know if he could hear me, but on the off chance he could, I wanted to calm him as much as possible.

I left the room as quietly as possible and quickly searched the remaining offices on that side of the floor, but found only a few ransacked rooms.

Once I was certain there was nothing to find there, I made my way to the opposite side of the floor and Olivia's office. The meeting room I reached first was empty, but I could hear the gentle sobs coming from the one directly next to Olivia's office well before I'd reached the door, which was ajar.

I pushed it open and made my way inside the room. The window's blinds were pulled shut and there was paper all over the floor, but other than the fact that it was slightly larger, it was identical to the one where Tommy lay.

I found Kasey huddled between two bookcases, her knees pulled up to her chin and her eyes closed tight.

"Kasey," I whispered, and for a second I wasn't sure if she'd heard me, but then she opened her eyes and almost flung herself at me.

"Whoa," I said as I caught her. "Are you okay?"

Kasey held me tightly. Her eyes were puffy from crying and she had a slight cut on her lip. It took all of my will power not to run directly into Olivia's office and attack Peter.

"Where's my dad? That man kept hitting him."

"He's going to be fine, but I need you to go to the room he's in and sit with him until your mum gets the security back on. Then you two need to get out of here—you may have to help him."

Kasey shook her head. "*He'll* hear me, *he'll* hurt me. *He* said he would if I did anything to annoy him."

"He won't do anything to you, I promise. But I do need you to go to your dad. It'll be safer there."

A realization appeared to dawn on her. "Is my mum really here?"

"She's getting the security shut down, but she's going to be a little while. I'm going to make sure that the lich doesn't hurt anyone else. But I can't have you here. I don't want you to get hurt."

"Okay, I'll—" The next sound out of her mouth was a scream as I was picked up by the back of my neck and flung through the hallway window, crashing to the floor outside.

Covered in bits of broken glass, I felt the blood trickle down the back of my arm. I'd apparently caught myself on a shard. Hopefully it wasn't too deep, but I didn't have time to look as the lich picked me up and threw me back into the meeting room, using a second window as my entry point. I hit the meeting table, skidded over it, and landed roughly on the floor.

I'd managed to get back to my knees when the lich's fist crashed into my jaw, knocking me back to the ground. I spat blood onto the carpet and tried to get back up again, but a kick to the ribs ended that dream. I rolled onto my side and tried to protect myself, but Peter was already walking away, picking up the dagger that had come loose when I'd been thrown through the window.

"Did you really think you could kill me with this?" he asked, unsheathing the *tanto* and throwing the scabbard through the broken window and into the corridor. He ran the blade across his hand, drawing blood, which he licked from his palm with a smile on his face, and then he threw the sword out into the corridor. He showed me the palm, healed within moments of his licking it.

"Stupid little sorcerer."

Kasey began to cry, and Peter smashed his hands onto the table, breaking it in half. Pieces of wood hit the dagger and skirted it across the floor to the far side of the room. "Will you shut the fuck up?"

Kasey tried to stifle her sobs, but they came out anyway.

"Do I need to hurt you and give you something to cry about?" he snapped, pushing one half of the table away and walking toward the upset girl. But before he could reach her, he suddenly doubled up in pain and dropped to his knees, using the remains of the table to steady himself.

I immediately grabbed Kasey and rolled us away from danger, stopping by the far wall.

"Bastards," Peter snapped, getting back to his feet and steadying himself against the wall. "They killed three of my ghouls," he shrieked.

"Good."

Peter launched himself at me, grabbing me by the throat, lifting me off the floor, slamming me into the nearest wall, and holding me there. "*You* killed one of my ghouls. How did you do that?"

"Trade secret," I said as his grip suddenly loosened and he screamed in pain again.

"Looks like you've lost another," I said and pushed his arm away. "With the one I killed, that's all of them."

"Now, now," Peter said with an evil smile. "That's only five, and I get to make six. You didn't think I'd leave my sixth ghoul unmade did you? I was just waiting for the right time to wake her up."

I wondered. The four police officers and Vicky had made up the five I'd known about. And they were all dead now.

"Vicky's slut of a girlfriend," he said. "How do you think we got into the building? She was just lying there on that doctor's slab until I woke her up. She's down there now, just in case anyone thought to disable the security to this place."

The realization I'd been in the room with that young woman's body, talking about her murder, while the whole time she'd been a ticking bomb was a horrific thought. Even worse was the thought that Doctor Grayson might have been down there with her when Peter finally woke her up.

"She'll be dead, too, soon enough," I told him.

Peter punched me in the solar plexus, driving every ounce of air from my lungs and dumping me on the floor as I fought to breathe. He turned his attention back to Kasey, who scampered along the side of the room toward the office door. I took advantage of his distraction to grab the *tanto* and drive it into his leg.

Peter let out a scream of agony as I pulled the dagger out and plunged it up into his stomach. I tried to get away from him, but he grabbed my arm and headbutted me before I took a step, breaking my nose.

Peter grunted with pain as he removed the dagger from his gut. "Someone likes to play with knives," he said and grabbed my hand, forcing it onto the remains of the table and driving the blade through the hand and pinning it to the wood.

I yelled out as the silver burned my hand, both inside and out, and tried to use my free hand to pull it out, but Peter kicked my arm away and then stomped on my hand when it touched the floor. Over and over again he brought all of his force down through his booted foot and onto my hand, breaking bones and snapping tendons until it was a raw, bloody mess. Only then did he remove the knife from my other hand; the burning sensation creating a whole new kind of pain as blood pumped freely from the wound.

I dragged my ruined hands onto my lap and tried not to think about the agony, or about having Kasey watch me die.

Peter kicked me in the head, knocking me to the floor and causing darkness to appear at the edges of my vision. But he hadn't finished. He grabbed me by the front of my shirt and smashed my face into the already broken table before flinging me across the room and into the far wall, where I fell to the floor next to a terrified Kasey.

She stood in front of me. "Stop it," she shouted. "Leave him alone."

Peter watched her with a mixture of amusement and disdain. Kasey was twelve years old, with no powers or weapons and no training, yet she still stood up to one of the most evil and powerful things on earth. She was so much like her father.

I was not about to let a young girl get hurt to protect me, and I forced myself back to a kneeling position.

Kasey glanced down at me and was suddenly trying to help me to my feet, placing one of my arms around her thin shoulders and trying to lift me up.

Peter's laughter filled the room and I tried to warn Kasey, but my jaw was broken and the words wouldn't form properly. Peter rushed across the room and tossed Kasey aside into one of the windows, which splintered from the impact. She fell to the floor, limp and unmoving.

"I guess that solves that problem," he said and started laughing again as I collapsed back to the floor, and he walked off to the far end of the room, opening the blinds to look down on the battlefield far below.

Without warning, Peter clutched his chest and collapsed to his knees, screaming out in pain as somewhere in the bowels of the building, his last ghoul died.

If I could have moved my face, I would have smiled. Instead, I felt the surge of energy, as my magic rushed back into me like a tsunami. My body immediately started to heal itself, but I remained motionless as I searched for a spirit to absorb using the technique that Sky had taught me. It wouldn't be long before Sky and Olivia reached me; I only had to hold Peter off for a few minutes.

I have no idea how long I remained like that, trying to find a spirit. A lot of people had died here today, so I knew they were there. I could almost sense them, but that was all I could do. I tried so hard to absorb one like I had when I'd fought Randal, but I couldn't get it to work.

And then something happened. I'd tried searching further outside the top floor, desperate to find anything that could help, when I felt it. The spirit was angry, hurt, and full of pain and grief. I could feel its emotions as a coldness started inside my stomach and soon filled me entirely. I was just beginning to accept what was happening when I realized that it wasn't one spirit filling me, it was two. The two agents I'd found on the stairway, their names were Margret and Lee. I knew that with one hundred percent clarity, although I had no idea how.

As the coldness traveled through me, I activated my Blood magic, using my own blood as a source, and grunted as the bones in my hand started to heal. I felt my body healing itself at a rate I'd never known before, my face and hands returning to their original state within seconds. Once I'd healed myself and deactivated my Blood magic, I felt part of the coldness leave with it. I stood and rested momentarily against the wall behind me.

"Got your magic back?" Peter asked with a chuckle as he walked toward me. "You heal pretty damn fast, even for a sorcerer. But it won't help."

When I didn't reply, he punched me in the stomach, doubling me over, and slammed the back of my head into the wall. I dropped to the floor in a seated position. Peter grasped me around the throat and picked me off the ground, holding me against the wall as he squeezed my throat.

"No fight left in you?" he asked with a sickening grin.

"Can't fight," I wheezed. "Concentrating."

"On what?"

As Peter had kept his eyes on me, I'd created two spheres of air, much like the one I'd used on Randal, one in the palm of each hand, spinning them faster and faster with my fingers until they were a blur.

"On this." I plunged both spheres into Peter's chest as white-hot rage exploded inside me. At first all I heard was Peter's laughter as the magic touched him and he squeezed tighter on my throat. And then the laughter was abruptly replaced with screams as the spheres tore into the flesh of his chest. He released his grip and staggered back, but I stayed with him as his screams were lost in the maelstrom of sound that the spheres created. Right up until the moment I released the magic.

The magic, needing to go somewhere, rushed into Peter like a tank hitting a wall. Peter was lifted from his feet and thrown across the room, through the wall behind him, and into Olivia's office where he crashed against her desk.

I took a step forward to go after him and immediately saw Kasey. My rage was extinguished and I dropped to Kasey's side. "Hey," I said softly as she stirred.

"My arm hurts," she said, as she opened her eyes.

I called more Blood magic and placed my hand on the arm she had cradled against her.

"That better?" I asked.

"I had to stay still when he threw me. I'm so sorry I didn't fight more."

I helped her back to her feet and made sure she was steady. "You stood up to a lich, Kasey. You are now officially the bravest person I know, but I've got it from here. Your dad is in the room at the end. He's hurt, but should be okay. You need to get him down the stairs and out of this building. No matter how badly he's hurt, you have to get him away from here."

Kasey walked toward the door. "Please stay safe," she said.

"I'll be fine," I told her. "Go see to your dad."

I watched Kasey leave the room and run off in Tommy's direction before I stalked toward the hole in the wall. I climbed through and continued into Olivia's office, which until a few minutes ago had been beautifully decorated. I allowed the cold rage inside me to come back, powered by the energy I'd absorbed from the two dead agents.

Peter was making a whimpering noise as he dragged himself out of the remains of Olivia's once-large desk.

I waved my hand and fire leapt from it, striking Peter's legs and igniting the jeans he wore. Peter started to yell once more as the magic hurt him.

"Apparently, I'm not so helpless anymore," I said and kicked him in the ribs so hard that I felt them buckle under the blow.

Peter sucked in air and rolled onto his back, showing me the two large red holes in his chest. They'd stopped oozing his black, tar-like blood, but still showed raw muscle beneath the tattered remains of his shirt.

I dragged the battered lich to his feet and punched him in the jaw with everything I had. He dropped to one knee and I unleashed a flurry of kicks and punches, my hands and feet wrapped in dense air to do more damage as I drove Peter to the floor. I used the anger, the fear, and the hatred at what Peter and his friends had done to people I cared about to continue my assault until the lich's face was a ruined mess of blood and flesh.

I dragged him to his feet and pushed him up against the desk, continuing the barrage of blows until my hands hurt. Only then did I allow Peter's limp body to drop back to the floor.

He spat blood onto the carpet as he got back to his knees. "Can't kill me."

I drove a blade of flame into his chest and he screamed out in anguish once more. At the same time, he wrapped his hands around my wrist and twisted his body, dragging me sharply to one side. He released his grip just as I lost my footing, and I flew over the ruined table, crashing onto the floor just beyond.

"Looks like you've lost whatever let you hurt me," Peter said as he got back to his feet, his face already healing at a rapid pace.

As much as I wanted to tear the smug grin off Peter's face for a second time, I knew he was right. I had very little left in reserve. Whatever I'd taken from the two dead agents had been all but used, leaving me with a very powerful lich problem to deal with.

My options were limited, and I had no idea how much longer it was going to take Olivia and Sky to reach me, but I certainly didn't have time to spare. I took the only course of action I could. I ran at Peter with a sphere of wind in my right hand, using up whatever necromancy power remained inside me.

I'd hoped to use the sphere to knock Peter back, through the window and down a few hundred feet, through the glass roof of the smaller building below, and then to the ground. Even he wouldn't have been able to shake off a near four-hundred-foot drop before someone got to him.

The sphere was an inch from his chest when he moved, pushing my hand to the side and causing me to lose balance, then punching me in the jaw with enough force to almost spin me around.

Instead of trying to hit Peter again, I let the momentum carry me around until my back was toward him, and then I released the magic. But instead of releasing it in front of me, I released it back toward Peter. The blast of air did no damage to me—you can't be hurt by your own magic—but it whipped around me with fearsome intensity, slamming into Peter, lifting him off his feet, and shoving him toward the window. He grabbed hold of the sword holster on my back and dragged me with him as we were thrown through the glass and into the void beyond with an almighty crash.

It was all I could do to use my air magic to slow my descent as Peter grabbed hold of me, forcing us to spin rapidly toward the glass dome as we closed the four-hundred-foot gap.

Peter snarled against my ear so I snapped my head back, slamming his nose and causing him to release his grip slightly. I used the leeway to blast air at him, but he held onto me and I couldn't get any real distance between us. The blast of air magic had the side effect of spinning me around him so I was against his back. I hooked my arms under his arms and around his neck in a full nelson, pinning his own arms behind him as we crashed through the dome. And my magic vanished.

At first I thought that something had gone wrong with the security system, but then I saw the sorcerer's band on my wrist. Peter must have slipped it on while we fell.

Falling four hundred feet and smashing into a marble floor is not the kind of thing you walk away from, even if you use someone else's body as a giant cushion. The shockwaves rode up through Peter's body and into my own, shattering the bones in my right arm, along my wrist, clavicle, and several ribs. I'd broken enough bones in my life to recognize what those injuries felt like.

I somehow rolled off the squashed form of Peter and onto the floor as pain wracked my body in nauseating waves. My vision darkened and I coughed blood all over the floor—apparently, I'd punctured a lung. The lack of magic meant that it was entirely possible that I was going to die if I didn't get medical attention, and soon.

I rested the back of my head against the cool floor and cradled my broken arm against my chest, taking some of the pain away so long as I remained completely still. I turned my head slightly as a noise caught my attention and saw Peter climbing back onto his feet, his broken bones and lacerations healing themselves before my eyes.

I wanted nothing more than to go to sleep, to just lie on the cool floor and let someone else deal with him. But I couldn't do that. I wouldn't let him hurt anyone else.

"What part of *you can't kill me* do you not understand?" he asked. The bones in his neck cracked when he moved his head. "How's all the broken bones? I'm assuming you're in a lot of pain right now. Once I knew there was a sorcerer after me, I thought that band might come in handy." He glanced up out of the large windows nearby. "I'm going to go help the remains of my barren kill your friends. And there's nothing you can do to stop me." He started walking to the door, his movements stiff and awkward. His body still not completely healed from the impact.

I couldn't let him get away. I had to stop to him. But my pain was so great that I could barely move.

Get up. Something inside of me said.

Get on your damn feet, Nathan.

For a moment I thought it was the nightmare inside me coming back to the fore, but I couldn't be certain.

I forced myself to a kneeling position as the sound of screams filled my ears. My screams. I leaned against the nearest wall and used it to get myself back to my feet.

Peter turned back toward me. "You're a tenacious little fucker, aren't you?"

He took a step in my direction as shots rang out from behind me, each one slamming into Peter, driving him back toward the wall. He wasn't yet recovered enough to withstand the bullets as he normally might have, but he still wasn't going to let bullets stop him.

"Doesn't anyone know that you can't kill me with gravity, or magic, or goddamn bullets? I'll spell it out for you. You. Can't. Kill. Me."

Sky ran in from the side and slammed her spirit dagger into Peter's chest and twisted. "I can," she said.

Peter screamed in agony as Sky pushed her translucent blue dagger deeper into his chest until her hand disappeared into Peter's body. She twisted her arm and snatched it free, holding something in her clenched fist. The thing oozed blackness through her fingers, like tar, as she squeezed it tightly until it vanished.

Sky staggered back and placed one hand against a nearby column. "Now you *can* kill him," she said.

Olivia walked past me and emptied a clip into Peter's chest, one shot for each step she took, closer and closer, until she was inches away from him. And then, she placed one hand against his chest, and a dozen, foot long spikes of ice shot out of her fingers to impale Peter, throwing him back with so much force that it shook the wall when he careered into it, the spikes pinning him in place.

"No one fucks with my family," she snarled and decapitated him with a blade of razor-sharp ice.

I coughed again and crashed back to the floor, the pain overwhelming me. Sky ran over and dropped down next to me. She was shouting, but I couldn't hear her words as the darkness closed in and I succumbed to its gentle comfort.

CHAPTER 43

I opened my eyes to the glare of fluorescent lighting. If by some miracle I'd gone to heaven, it certainly wasn't how the brochure had described it.

"Ouch," I said as I moved my stiff neck, which cracked loudly.

"Ah, I was wondering when you'd rejoin us."

I followed the voice and found Doctor Grayson sitting on the chair next to me, a clipboard in his hand.

"Hey, Doc, glad to see you're okay," I said.

"Ah, I can take care of myself, Nathan, don't you worry about that. I've been around long enough to know what to do."

I studied him for a second. He wasn't a large man and certainly didn't appear to be muscular. "So what are you, Doc? Because you don't use magic."

Doc Grayson smiled. "Another time maybe. I just came down here to check on you."

"We still at the LOA building?"

"No. No one wanted to hang around there for very long after the wolves had finished tearing the barren into small stains on the grass outside. The LOA lost forty-two good men and women to those undead creatures. I had no desire to stay and observe the clean up, so I came here with you. This is Tommy's building, and his facility is quite amazing."

"Yeah, Tommy doesn't believe in doing things halfway. How is he?"

"Tommy is fine. It's been all I could do to stop him sitting next to you around the clock since you arrived. Kasey, too. Along with Olivia, they've been inseparable. They'll be keen to come say hello."

I pushed myself up to a sitting position and felt every muscle in my body groan in response. "How long was I out?"

"First, some context. You suffered a broken clavicle, eight broken ribs, a punctured lung, and damage to the spleen and liver. Your right arm was broken in six places below the elbow and three above it. Your left wrist and three of your fingers were broken so badly that if you'd been human I would simply have amputated the hand. You also suffered a head injury, a broken jaw and nose, and you somehow managed to break three of your toes on your left foot. My point is if you were human you'd be dead. The impact alone would have turned you to paste."

"Thanks for the pep talk, Doc. How long was I out?"

"Twelve hours."

My mouth fell open. "That's it?"

"Well, eleven hours, fifty-one minutes, and several seconds to be exact, but I thought I'd round up to make things easier."

"How is that possible?"

Doc Grayson did something that no doctor should ever do if they want to inspire confidence. He shrugged. "No idea. Your powers of healing are incredible. Certainly up there with some of the best I've seen in a long time. Not quite werewolf or vampire territory, but still very impressive. Especially for a sorcerer."

Apparently, the extra power gained with the loss of one of my Blood magic marks was a lot more than I'd first assumed.

"How long do I have to stay here?" I asked.

"You can leave when you're ready. Your clean clothes are in the wardrobe over there." He pointed to a wooden piece of furniture that had been painted white.

"Where is he?" Sky demanded as she flung the door open and stepped inside.

"And that's my cue to leave," Doc Grayson said, nodding to Sky on his way out.

"If you kill me, the healing I've just done would be a dreadful waste of time," I said as Sky fumed down on me from the end of the bed.

"You promised, you fucking asshole," she snapped. "You sat and promised me you wouldn't try and kill him yourself. Are you aware what a promise is?"

I opened my mouth to say something and then wisely closed it again.

"You could have died, do you know that? Died. You fell four hundred feet while fighting a lich, something you said you weren't going to do."

I kept my mouth shut. It saved time on opening it first.

"You utter fucking asshole."

"He was going to kill Kasey," I said. "I had to stop him."

The fight visibly evaporated from Sky, and she slumped into a chair next to the TV on the far wall.

"Fuck!" she shouted and punched the wall. "I know," she admitted in a far more subdued tone. "I spoke to Kasey. I'm just so damn mad at you."

"If it helps, I don't plan on doing it again." Sometimes, I swear, I just can't help myself.

"Are you being flippant with me, Nathan Garrett?"

"Ma'am, no, ma'am," I said quickly. "Please don't hurt me; I'm still in a hospital gown. I'd look very silly."

Sky smiled, and I knew I'd won her over. For now.

"If you smile, I will kick your ass anyway," she said as she rubbed her eyes.

"No smiling, not a problem."

"You're as bad as my father. He's always being flippant to my mother when she catches him doing something he shouldn't."

"Persephone would terrify anyone," Hades said as he entered the room. "And I learned long ago not to piss off beautiful women who sleep in the same bed as you." He hugged his daughter before turning his attention to me. "Has she threatened to hurt you yet? I believe she was looking forward to it."

I nodded. "It was very well done."

"Ah, good. I'd hate for it to have been a disappointment after she built up to it so well."

"I hate you both," Sky said.

"Do you need time alone to hug it out, or can I interrupt his recovery?"

Sky started to laugh, followed by me. Mine caused me pain. "Serves you right," Sky said with a wicked smile. "You did good, Nate. Stupidity aside. You saved Kasey and Tommy, and you did it using necromancy. You hurt a lich. That's damn impressive. Heal up and I'll let you buy me a beer."

"Deal," I said. Sky gave me a hug and kissed my cheek before leaving me alone with Hades.

"I never understood why you two didn't get together," he said as nonchalantly as a father can when saying such a thing about his daughter, removing his jacket and laying it over the end of the bed.

"When we first met, I worked for Avalon and Sky worked for you. After I left…well, it became a timing issue. Both of us like our independence, and neither wants to risk our friendship on the chance that being a couple wouldn't end in utter disaster."

"That, and she'd have killed you by now. Or I would have if you'd broken her heart," Hades said with far too much enthusiasm.

"And there's that, too."

"So, how are you feeling? Doc Grayson tells me you're a medical marvel."

"Apparently so."

"When you're better, and not before, you will come to me in Toronto, and I will teach you how to use your necromancy. You will not teach yourself, you will not get someone else to teach you. Are we clear on that?"

I nodded.

"As for the why—and yes, I know what you were about to ask—I need to know what you're capable of. You hurt a lich and killed a ghoul with magic. Neither of those things is insignificant. Left to your own devices, who knows what you'd end up doing."

"So what type of necromancy do you think I have?"

Hades shrugged. "Something pretty potent from the sounds of things. But I've no idea exactly what at the moment. That's another reason for me helping you—you're a rare species. You obtained a gift from each of your parents, one a sorcerer and the other a necromancer. Those two together doesn't happen very often. The training may help unlock the rest of those marks. They were put there for a reason."

"And you'd rather I was somewhere safe when they vanish."

"There is that," he admitted. "We don't know what they do. Better safe than sorry. Besides, at some point your Blood magic will vanish now; it can't coexist with necromancy. You're going to have to learn how to use your necromancy to defend yourself."

I sighed. In all the rush of the last few days, the loss of my Blood magic was something I hadn't even thought about. It was also a large blow. No more using it to heal, to increase my power, or even to track someone. It was a lot to take in. "Okay, I'll come out to Toronto and let you teach me about necromancy. I need to learn how to keep myself and those I care about safe."

"Good." Hades stood and picked up his jacket. "Get dressed. You have a lot of people who want to see you. Tommy is in his office. I told him I'd let you know."

"Thanks. How'd you get a pass to visit? Who convinced Avalon?"

"Ah, well, apparently I can be very persuasive when I want to be. That and the fact that Olivia threatened to tear some people in half if anyone mentioned that I was here. It appeared to do the trick. She's quite impressive, isn't she?"

"She's not a shrinking violet, that's for sure."

Hades paused at the door. "Hellequin's back then, is he?"

"I don't know."

"Too late now. You let the name drop. And that werewolf alpha told even more people. It won't take long for the wrong people to hear it. You've painted a bull's-eye on your chest, Nate. Someone inside Avalon arranged for Peter to get the help he did. And those people are going to come after you sooner or later."

"If they come after me, maybe they'll stay away from the people I care about."

"And maybe they'll use them. And if they do, if anyone else comes after your friends, you know what you have to do. Crush them. Make *them* an example that no one will forget. Hellequin's turned into a nursery rhyme to be told to naughty children— you need to make sure it's the adults who start checking under the bed."

"Hades, when I find the people who arranged all of this, I'm going to make sure that everyone remembers *exactly* what it means to cross Hellequin."

"Good. Because you'll only get one chance to make sure people remember what it used to mean to cross *you*." And then he was gone, leaving me to my thoughts.

Being able to don fresh clothing, once you've been in a hospital gown for any length of time is one of life's little pleasures.

During the ten-minute journey to Tommy's office on the top floor, I was helpfully informed of the fact that Tommy was looking for me twenty-something times, along with receiving more than a few cautious or nervous glances. The news that Hellequin was back had traveled much faster than I'd expected.

When I reached Tommy's office, I paused for a moment and took a deep breath, reluctant to intrude on a family moment, especially after what they'd been through. I breathed out as I opened the door and stepped inside.

I'd been in Tommy's office once in the months since regaining my memories, and that was only to say I'd arrived, after which Tommy hastily ushered me out without giving me time to take in any of the details. Now, finally having the chance to look around the massive office, I figured out why. One full side of the room, the one opposite an entire bank of windows, had a dozen shelves on it with photos of Olivia and Kasey, while the wall adjacent to the door I'd walked through held several beautiful works of art, including many from an artist named Kasey, aged six, seven, or eight. Tommy hadn't wanted me to know he had a daughter, because he was concerned exactly which Nate he was getting. If I'd been in his office for more than five seconds, his entire effort of security would have been pointless.

Olivia sat on the desk at the far end, watching me as I scanned the office. She stood and walked toward me, and before I knew what was happening, she'd embraced me in a tight hug as tears wet her cheeks.

"Thank you," she whispered into my ear. "I can never repay what you've done for me…for us." She kissed me on the cheek and moved away, wiping her eyes with the back of her hand.

"You never have to repay a thing," I told her. "Where're Tommy and Kasey?"

"Kasey went for a Coke; Tommy went to deal with his issues."

"He's hitting something, isn't he?"

"In the gym. He's having more trouble dealing with what happened than Kasey is."

"He was almost beaten to death. That's going to screw with anyone's head. Besides that, he's a wolf who in any other life would be the alpha of a powerful pack. It's probably a lot for him to take in that he couldn't help his daughter. I'll talk to him, if you like."

Olivia nodded as Kasey walked in, can of Coke in hand. "Nate," she shrieked as she saw me and ran over, hugging me tightly.

"I like the artwork," I said.

Kasey pulled away and glanced back at the pictures on the wall.

"I'm a big fan of the rocket picture."

"That's an airplane," she corrected.

"Oh, so what's the slug thing underneath it?"

"That's a mountain with eyes."

I raised an eyebrow in question.

"I was six," she said, explaining everything.

"He hurt my dad," she said after a moment's silence. "I couldn't do anything to stop it." The second the tears began to fall, Olivia enveloped Kasey in her arms.

I let them have their moment together until Kasey pulled away and glanced up at me. "I'm sorry I couldn't stop him from hurting you either."

I've seen many things in my life that have pulled at my heart in one way or another, but that? That damn near broke it. "Kasey, you stood up to a monster that most adults would have run from. You have nothing to be sorry for. Neither I nor your dad would ever think any less of you for being unable to stop the lich. We think more of you for trying. It's not your job to fight monsters; it's your job to enjoy being young. Maybe one day you can be the big monster killer, but right now we don't want you to put yourself in danger. Not even to protect us."

Kasey sniffed. "My dad is angry."

"I'll deal with your dad," I told her. "Some people are more stubborn and proud than they should be. I'll go get him for you."

Finding Tommy was easy. I heard the grunts of pain and the sound of the punch bag's reinforced chain straining to take the blows before I'd even reached the gym's entrance.

I stood at the door and watched Tommy go to work on the bag with a combination of savage blows. Two previous bags lay on the floor nearby, their contents spilling out across the floor.

"You know, if you're going to be breaking every single punch bag, it's probably a good idea to start buying ones that are made for a werewolf."

"Go away," he said and continued punching the bag.

"You're not healed," I continued, ignoring him. "You keep that up, and you're going to end up a long-term resident for Doc Grayson to look after. I saw your wounds, Tommy. That silver can't be anywhere near healed yet. You're only doing more damage by being a stubborn pain in the ass."

"I'll be fine."

I walked over to him and placed a hand on his shoulder. "Tommy, stop it."

He shook me off and planted a hand in my chest, shoving me back. "I said, go away."

When I didn't move, Tommy growled and threw a punch at me this time, but he was still injured and the punch lacked power and speed. I deflected it, causing him to lose his footing and fall forward.

"Don't be an ass, Tommy."

He sprang up to throw a second punch, but a quick kick to his injured leg ended that plan before it started.

Unfortunately, it didn't deter Tommy so much as it pissed him off even more. He charged at me, so I stepped into the attack, grabbed his arm, and spun him up and over my shoulder. He landed with a loud thud, crying out with pain as the silver wounds struck the floor.

"Enough," I said one more time. "Don't make me hurt you."

I stepped back to give him some room and he charged again. I tried to avoid him, but he grabbed my t-shirt and tackled me to the floor, where he quickly found himself in a triangle choke-hold. He tried to use his strength to power out of it, but I had it locked in, and he wasn't at full health. So the question became, what would give out first, his remaining strength or his oxygen supply?

As it turned out, it was his strength. He sagged against my legs, his fight gone, and I released the hold, pushing him onto the floor next to me as I panted with exhaustion. Apparently, Tommy wasn't the only one who hadn't fully healed yet.

I sat up. "You feel like telling me why you're being a dick?"

"He forced Kasey to watch as he beat me," Tommy said, clearly upset. "I begged him to stop, to let her go. And he just laughed and kept on hitting and cutting me. He screamed at Kasey to watch, forced her to see me bloodied and helpless on the floor. I couldn't protect myself, let alone my own daughter." He started to cry as the rage and helplessness overwhelmed him, and we stayed like that for several minutes.

"How do I help Kasey get over what she saw?" Tommy asked me finally.

I got back to my feet and offered my hand to Tommy, who took it, allowing me to help him up. "Tommy, your daughter is one of the bravest people I've ever met. I don't mean brav-est girl, or bravest twelve-year-old, I mean bravest person. She stood between me and my quite-probable death, and she stared that son of a bitch down without blinking. And when I got to see her a few minutes ago, she apologized to me for not being able to stop him. I don't think you're going to have much to worry about with her in the long term. She'll have nightmares, she'll be a little short with you and Olivia, maybe a little withdrawn, but she'll see her friends, and so long as you're both there for her, she'll be just fine. I'm more worried about you."

"I've been beaten up before." He waved off my concern. "Several times. I've thought my life was over on occasion, too. But seeing Kasey there, being unable to keep her safe—that's crushed me. My whole job as a dad is to protect my daughter. And I couldn't do it."

"Damn, Tommy, I think you're being a little hard on yourself. You'd been knocked out by Reid, who put a sorcerer's band on you, and then you were attacked by something that you couldn't have hurt even with your full abilities. You did fuck-all wrong. Hell, you should be commended for being too stubborn to die in the first place."

Tommy laughed and some of the tension that he'd kept inside almost visibly left him. "What happened to Reid? I'd quite like to have a few words with him. And by words, I mean tear his arms off and beat him to death with them."

"I'm sure you'll get your chance at some point. Whoever he was working for probably won't be happy that Peter got killed before he could finish his job. For the moment though, Reid has vanished."

We started to walk toward the exit, and I noticed several of Tommy's employees craning their heads around the door to get a look at what was happening. After a few steps, Tommy stopped walking. "Oh, I almost forgot. Matthew said thanks for the help. Apparently having Hellequin as a friend changed the minds of a few people who'd been supporting Elijah."

"I'm glad I could help."

"Are you sure about Hellequin? That's a big step for you. I remember when you buried him, and it was not a good time for you."

"I know, Tommy. But it's been long enough. Hellequin is who I am. I may have different values, different wants from back then, but it's still me. And if dropping the name to get information on you and Kasey means I have to deal with the aftermath, then so be it. It's a deal I'd gladly take again."

"Thanks for everything, Nate. Have I ever told you that you're a damn good friend?"

I stared at Tommy for a heartbeat. "You should mention it more often; maybe create a huge banner to hang at the entrance of your building to tell the story of how great I am. You could write a song about it…"The Ballad of My Great Friend, Nate.'"

"You're an asshole," Tommy said in between laughs. "Be serious."

I smiled and clasped his hand. "You know I've always got your back. You and your family. Anything you ever need me to do, it's done. No thanks are ever needed."

Tommy started walking again as everyone in the doorway made sure they had somewhere else to be before we got there.

"You need to call Sara. She's been discharged from hospital, and she'll probably be at home by now."

"I will. What's going to happen to Olivia?"

"She's going to have some serious questions to answer. She didn't ask for backup and involved a large number of werewolves in reclaiming the headquarters, which she lost in the first place. Avalon will want a full investigation, and she's already been told to stay away from Winchester until the Avalon representative turns up in the morning."

"She did the right thing."

"I know, but she didn't do the Avalon thing. She put people ahead of being detached from the situation. She may lose her position, but more likely she'll be suspended. Which will probably do her some good, although don't tell her I said that. I hear you're off to Toronto."

"In a few weeks, yeah. I need to learn how to control whatever it is I can do now. Hades is a good teacher."

Tommy's grin could have split his face in two. "He's going to kick your ass every single day."

"Yes, yes he is."

"I wonder if he'll film it? I'd quite like a copy."

I chuckled. "Now who's being the asshole?"

"Hey, it'd be educational. And funny. Very, very funny."

"I'm glad my misery will amuse you. Anyway, about that song…," I called after him as he left the gym to go see his family.

I didn't take Tommy's advice to call Sara. I went to see her instead. A personal visit had two benefits. First, it allowed me to actually see Sara, something I felt I needed to do. But it also let me ride my bike, and getting out into the admittedly cold weather felt wonderful. Although by the time I pulled up outside Sara's house my body felt a little sore. Still, it was worth it.

I opened the gate to the small front garden and knocked on the front door. Footsteps, heavy and slow—someone was in no hurry to answer the door—were audible through the wooden door, which opened to reveal a man. He was about thirty-five, maybe forty, with shoulder-length dark hair and a few days of stubble. He appeared tired; the bags under his eyes making him look a little like a raccoon.

"Can I help you?" he glanced at me, and then at the bunch of flowers I'd purchased from a florist on the way to see Sara.

I switched the flowers from my right to left hand, and offered my free one. "Sorry, I'm Nate. I came to see how Sara was doing."

The man took no time before he smiled and took my hand. "Nice to meet you, I'm Will." His handshake wasn't compensating for anything and he maintained eye contact. "Come on in."

I followed Will into the house and along the hallway, walking past a kitchen where some pleasant aromas made my stomach rumble.

Will turned back to me and chuckled. "My rhubarb crumble always has that effect on people." He opened a door, and I stepped into a small study.

Sara was sitting in an old leather armchair reading one of the books from the hundreds that lined the shelves all around us. For a small room, it was quite the library.

"We're quite big fans of reading," Will said. "Can't stop us—it doesn't help that I'm a university professor. I swear, I bring home more stuff to read than it's possible to read in one lifetime."

Sara smiled and got gingerly to her feet, using the desk in front of her to steady herself until Will, moving quickly, was at her side to help. "I'm fine," Sara protested and was soundly ignored.

"You need to be careful," Will told her. "You're still sore from the fall."

"Fall?" I asked.

"Well, yes," Will said, looking a little confused. "The fall down the stairs at work."

"Sorry," I said, "I thought you meant another one. I was worried for a second there."

"There will *be* a second one if she's not careful. She's lucky she only got bruising and a concussion."

"These are for you." I passed the bouquet of flowers to Sara, who took them with a smile as she smelled the mixture of scents. "We were worried about you."

"I'll be okay," she said and then had a short conversation with Will about shopping, which ended with Will saying his good-byes and leaving Sara and me alone.

"I'm sorry," I said. "I never thought they'd go after you."

Sara forced a small smile. "None of this is your fault. Reid lied to us all. And they didn't want to hurt me, not badly. They only used me to get you and Olivia out of the way while they went to get Tommy and Kasey. I'm glad they're all okay, by the way. I spoke to Tommy on the phone this morning. He was trying very hard not to ask me if I'm coming back to work for him."

"Am I allowed to ask?"

Sara's smile came easily the second time. "Yes, I'll be back. If I left now, I'd always feel like I missed out on something important. I got to help you catch someone who'd murdered dozens of people. I got to help you bring justice to those families. Even if all I did was hang around and listen and learn, it's still a hell of a feeling to be a part of something like that."

"I'm glad."

"There's one thing though. When I got hurt, Will was the first person at my side. I love him, Nate. I hate that I've had to lie to him about what happened. But whatever the attraction between you and me, it's not worth throwing away what I have with Will."

I wasn't sure how to respond to that. But when I found my voice there was only one answer that felt right. "I agree." I genuinely meant it. It wouldn't have been fair of me to disrupt Sara's life for something that might never be.

"Tommy tells me you're off to Canada, anyway. When do you leave?"

"A few weeks, I imagine. I'll be gone for a few months, so I'll make sure that Tommy assigns someone else to train you. Which is probably for the best anyway."

"You're right, it would be."

I offered my hand, and Sara ignored it, choosing to kiss me on the cheek. "Thank you for everything," she said as the front door opened behind us.

"Get better soon," I said to her before turning and leaving the house.

EPILOGUE

The movement sensor went off well before the car pulled onto my driveway. I had it positioned at the bottom of the long, winding path that led to my house. If an approaching car was going at a normal speed, it gave me up to sixty seconds to prepare. In this case, the car was moving slowly, the driver obviously in no hurry, and I counted ninety seconds before the headlights appeared. It was daytime, but the sky had been so dark with clouds that it was much darker than it would normally be during the day.

It had been three weeks since Peter's death, since the battle at the LOA office and the return of Hellequin. And it had been mostly quiet. As Tommy had expected, Olivia had been suspended from her position until Avalon decided that leveling several miles of city in order to keep the lich contained wouldn't have been a good idea. Mostly because it wouldn't have worked. But Avalon, like all structures of power, has always liked having boxes to tick and procedures to follow. Even if they're incredibly stupid.

The gates to the driveway were already open; I hadn't bothered closing them from earlier in the day. But the car, a red Mazda of one model or another with almost blacked-out windows, stopped at the start of the driveway and then just sat there. My initial thought was that someone had heard that Hellequin was back and decided to take a shot at me.

I stepped out onto my porch and leaned against one of the wooden posts, wondering how long I was going to be made to wait, but someone was making a point.

A short time later the car stated moving again, eventually parking with the driver's side door facing me. It opened a few seconds later, and Reid stepped out into the cool air.

I suppressed my initial instinct to kill him. He was working for someone, and I wanted to know who.

"Nathan," Reid said with enough smugness that I immediately regretted not blowing his car up. "I'm sorry it took so long to get to you, but I've been very busy dealing with the fact that you stopped Peter. You pissed off a lot of people with that."

"Good, they deserved to be pissed off." I stepped out from under the porch. "You feel like telling me who those people are?"

"It's your lucky day. I'm here to take you to them. I think I'll even get some rewards for bringing you in. Dead or alive, though, I'd prefer the former."

"They can't interrogate a dead person, right?"

"Something like that. Personally, I'd like to kill you. You impersonated one of the Faceless, and that can't go without punishment."

"Your bosses don't know you're here, do they?'

"How perceptive. No, I kept that information to myself. I wanted to surprise them. Besides, if I'd told them what I was going to do, they'd have sent far too many people to get in my way."

"You have a plan, I assume."

Reid stepped forward and shook off his jacket, revealing a white t-shirt beneath. "I invoke the Accords."

"I'm sorry, what?"

"I heard about you and that werewolf. Clearly you're a man of honor and I want to make sure you don't die. If I use my abilities to take you in, it may take too long. A one-on-one fight between the two of us will be short, I assure you."

"No powers, no weapons, just you and me?"

"I win, you'll be unconscious. You win, I'll tell you what you want to know."

"You're very sure of yourself."

"You have to agree, you have no other options."

"Actually, I can think of one," I told him and then shot him in the throat.

Reid crumpled to the ground, holding the wound in his neck as blood pumped through his fingers. I walked toward him and placed the gun on the roof of his car. I'd grabbed the Heckler and Koch from the table near the front door on my way out to greet my guest, just in case.

"You're a fucking idiot. You think you can come to my house and quote the Accords? I don't live by the Accords. The only reason I didn't tear Randal into tiny bite-sized chunks was because following the Accords was better than not at the time." I searched Reid's pockets and found his mobile. "Which number is your boss?"

Reid made a noise that sounded like pleading.

"I shot you with a silver round. You'll die from it without help, but you have a few minutes yet. You answer my question truthfully, and I *may* help you live to see the sunset."

He held up three fingers and I hit speed dial 3. I held the phone to my ear and waited for it to be answered.

"So, can I assume you completed whatever you needed to do?" a male voice asked.

"No, he's currently bleeding to death all over my driveway," I told him.

"Mister Garrett, I assume," the man said without bothering to keep his disdain from his voice.

"And you're the asshole who sent Reid to infiltrate the LOA and then betray them. He got a lot of good people killed and hurt a lot of people I care about. I assume you won't be telling me your name."

"You have no need to know it, but you should know that Mister Reid will tell you nothing."

"I know, he's a member of the Faceless and they're all tough and never betray their master, but he was pretty quick to tell me what number yours was."

"I never said I was his master."

"That's true, and that also means that you can give Reid's master a message for me."

"Are you going to threaten me, Mister Garrett? You have no idea who I am, and certainly no idea whom I work for."

"And you clearly have no idea who I am." I put my hand over the mouthpiece and bent down to whisper into Reid's ear. "I'm Hellequin."

I stood up under the watchful terror of the injured man.

"Your pet Faceless now knows who I am, and I think he just shat himself."

"You're making a grave mist—"

"Shut up and listen to me, you pompous ass. You can come after me as much as you like, you can send assassin after assassin to do your dirty work, and I'll send them back to you in tiny boxes. You can bankroll a serial killer and pull strings to get a psychopath released from prison. Hell, you can even buy him a nice penthouse and let him do whatever he wants. But if you *ever* come after people I care about again, I will hunt *you* down. And

I assure you that by the end of our time together, you will have a very personal view of exactly who I am."

I picked up the gun up and aimed it at Reid. "You tried to get my best friend and his daughter killed. You murdered your own partner and betrayed everyone who counted on you." I put two silver rounds into his forehead, killing him instantly.

"You're going to need a new pet," I told the man on the phone. "And if our paths ever cross, you're going to need a whole lot more than him." I crushed the phone with air magic and tossed the remains over Reid's body before walking off to make a call of my own. I needed a piece of crap removed from my drive.

ACKNOWLEDGEMENTS

2012 has been a bit of a crazy year. The release of my first book, *Crimes Against Magic*, went better than I could have expected, and in any other year it would have been the highlight. But the birth of my third daughter, Harley, in August, has it beat, hands-down. Oh, yeah, and we moved house, probably because I'm insane and like to pile on stress while trying to get a second book finished.

The number of people I have to thank for not only helping me achieve any form of success with my first book but also getting *Born of Hatred* finished and out there is huge. My year would have been much worse without the help of the following people.

Vanessa, my wonderful wife. You are, without doubt, my better half, and I thank you with everything I have for the time and patience you show me when I'm stressing out about anything and everything writing related.

Keira, Faith, and Harley, my beautiful daughters. You have always been, and will always be, the reason I write. Along with your mother, I love you all more than I can possibly put into words.

To my parents, thank you for being so interested and supportive about my writing. Oh, and Mum, just for future reference, Kindles don't come pre-installed with my books. It's a fantastic idea though.

To my friends and family who have been so supportive of my work. To those of you who ran through ideas with me or hosted me on your blogs. To everyone who told people about my book and how much you liked it. I would never have achieved any success without you. You guys are awesome. Every single one of you. And I can't possibly thank you enough.

I have to single out my good friends and crit partners, D.B. Reynolds and Michelle Muto. I can't think of two greater writers or two nicer people. No matter how many times I need your help with something, you are always available to give it. Both of you are incredible.

Special thanks go out to four incredible writers: Terri, TJ, Krista, and Kelly. You took the time and effort to go through my book and correct the errors, and when you'd finished you still told me you enjoyed it.

Once again I have to thank everyone on Kelley Armstrong's forum, especially those in OWG Group 6. Each of you is an amazing writer, and all of you have helped make me the writer I am today.

To my editor, Bea. Thank you for taking the time to go through the book. It was very much appreciated.

And to my superb cover artist, Eamon O'Donoghue. Dude, throughout all the years I've known you, you're still constantly surprising me with just how good you are.

Last, but by no means least, I'd like to take a moment to thank you, the reader. You took a chance on a new author and I thank you for that. I can only hope that I made the time you spent in my world worthwhile.

ABOUT THE AUTHOR

Steve McHugh was born in Mexbrough, South Yorkshire, but grew up in Southampton, Hampshire, where he now lives with his wife and three young daughters. While at school, Steve discovered a love for history and mythology, along with the beginnings of a passion for writing, which in spite of—or maybe because of—numerous sucky jobs, never went away. When he's not writing or spending time with his kids, Steve enjoys watching movies, reading books and comics, and playing video games. He is the author of the Hellequin Chronicles, including *Crimes Against Magic* and *Born of Hatred*.